TAKE ME WITH YOU

FREDRICA PARLETT

LAMPPOST PRESS
Berkeley, CA

ISBN: 978-1-954744-01-1

Library of Congress control number: 2021904241

Book design consultation:
Margery Cantor, Ellen Zaslow & Rue Whittaker

Cover and author photographs: Richard Whittaker

Cover photograph manipulation: Cleo Huggins

Distribution by Epigraph Publishing Service

Lantern logo: Smashicons

To Beresford

1

GRIFFITH PARK ZOO, LOS ANGELES, AUGUST 1945

"It's too damn hot here."

"I know, but you promised us, Dick," Henry's mother said. "The boys have been waiting so long. Every time I brought them here, they said, 'We want to show Daddy our favorite animals.'"

Henry, walking between his parents, looked up toward his father's red, puffy face, which he was wiping with a handkerchief. The sun glared white behind the rim of his black hat, and as he replaced his handkerchief in his trouser pocket, his knuckles pressed against Henry's shoulder. Henry leaned toward his mother, the smooth, sweet-smelling fabric of her dress sleeve brushing against his face. Sam, his older brother, walked on his father's other side.

"Today was going to be my third golf game since I was discharged. I forgot about the zoo. I hope Bill found someone to take my place in the foursome."

"The tiger, Daddy," Henry said. "You've got to see the tiger."

"These animals stink," his father said. "Don't they ever clean up after them?" The family stopped and looked up at a group of screeching monkeys, who stared back at them from their high perches.

"Let's go," Henry pleaded, pulling on his father's arm.

"Your tiger isn't the only animal in this zoo," his father muttered.

Henry broke away and took off running. He heard his father shout,

"Henry, come back here!" But he could not stop. His tiger was waiting for him.

People were standing on a raised stone platform set back from the tiger's cage, way too far back. The last time they had come there, he'd tried to grab hold of the bars, right in front of the tiger, but he could not reach them. And his mom said no, he was not supposed to do that. Now he could reach the bars. They felt cold and rough as he wrapped his fingers around two of them. He pulled himself up onto the low wall below the bars. Standing on top of it, he held the bars and looked through, pressing his face against them. At that moment, the tiger came out of his cave and slowly came down the brown stone stairs, looking at Henry with those glittering eyes.

"Hi, Jake," Henry called. "Remember me?"

Jake stopped and then growled. What a wonderful sound! Henry sang his tiger song:

Jake, Jake, you can be free
Run, run away with me.

The tiger was looking off in the distance away from Henry. But Henry knew Jake really liked the song. He began to sing it again.

Suddenly he felt himself yanked off the bars from behind. It was his father. "The sign says 'Keep off,' you imbecile."

Henry fell down onto the hard concrete, scraping his cheek.

His mother's hands lifted him. "You should have stayed with us," she said. "Why did you run off like that?"

"Don't touch him," his father said. Her hands disappeared. Henry saw his father's black shoes near his head. He dared not move.

"I told him to get off the wall," Sam said. "He wouldn't listen."

"Dick, here comes a guard."

His father yanked him up off the ground by one arm. A group of people stared at them. The guard's keys rattled as he came up, his face red like his father's.

"My son can't read the sign. He can't read anything." The guard stopped, looked at them, then grunted and walked off. The people turned back to watch the tiger devour a huge piece of bloody meat that had just been thrown to him.

"We're going home," his father said. "You have ruined our day. We're not bringing you to this zoo again."

"I told him you aren't supposed to climb up the wall," Sam said, moving close to their father.

Henry looked up at the two round angry faces. "I'm sorry, I'm sorry," he said. "Please don't make us go home. I want to see the tiger. I want to see all the animals. I won't run away again."

"No. You've got to learn."

Henry cried as they walked back to the car. His mother dropped back to walk with him, her hand reaching out to him.

"Edna!" his father yelled. His mother took two steps away. His father looked around again but said nothing more as he strode ahead toward the car. Behind two large yellow reflectors that looked like huge tiger-eyes, the sun reflected off the chrome bars of the radiator of their dark blue Buick,

Henry flattened himself against the door in the back seat, his hand over his mouth to muffle his sobs. His father turned on the radio to a football game. No one spoke.

Once home, his father opened the front door, pulled Henry inside, and started to remove his belt. He was going to get another beating.

"Oh, to hell with you," he said, refastening the buckle of his belt. "Go to your room. No supper for you tonight."

Henry looked at his mother's frightened face. She was not going to help him. As he walked down the long hall, he heard his father say, "He's only eleven, but you can't control him. You must have spoiled him rotten while I was gone."

"He's not bad, Dick. He's always loved that tiger. But he isn't bad."

"And I could have been playing golf right now."

Henry closed the door to his room. On his pillow lay another tiger, his stuffed tiger, dirty, with a torn ear. His mother had given it to him for Christmas before his father came home from the war. She knew he loved Jake at the zoo. This tiger was named Jake, too. Henry pulled off his shoes, climbed under the covers into the darkness, where he cradled Jake in his arms. He started to dream even before he fell asleep. He and Jake, the big Jake at the zoo, were going into the jungle to hide from his father, into a secret place that no one but he and Jake knew about.

2

PASADENA, CALIFORNIA, 1952—SEVEN YEARS LATER

Hearing his mother call him for dinner, Henry removed the headphones of his crystal set, disappointed to miss the end of *The Green Hornet.* And then he opened his door, closing it behind him quickly, so that his stuffed animals couldn't escape. He had to be careful with those animals—they could get vicious. He crossed the hall into the dining room, moving silently, watching. As he slid into his seat, his mother, wearing a bright blue apron with white frills, her blond hair frizzy around her hot face, was placing mats on the sideboard. His father, at the head of the table, had brought the newspaper with him and did not look up.

"I thought the lamb chops were done, but when I just cut into one, it came out too rare, so you'll have to wait a few minutes." She disappeared through the swinging door back into the kitchen. His father lowered the newspaper with a sigh and frowned at Henry.

"What did you do at school today?"

"I learned to do decoupage. We cut up little pieces of tissue paper that come in all kinds of colors, then we brush them with glue and put them on a piece of cardboard to make pretty pictures. I've got one in my room I can show you. I made a picture of the Mojave Desert."

His father shook his head. "I wish I had never asked." He picked up his newspaper again. "God, with Ted Williams on the team you'd think the Red Sox wouldn't be so pathetic."

Henry smiled. "You're right, Dad. The Red Sox lost their last game of the season yesterday. They ended up with seventy-six wins and seventy-eight losses and won .494 percent of their games. But Ted Williams has been gone most of the time, flying airplanes in the Korean War."

"How do you know all that?" his father asked, staring at him.

"I listen to the radio," Henry said. "I have that crystal set Sam put together for me before he went to Harvard."

His father's puffy face showed surprise. "So, you remember all that?"

"The Red Sox are my favorite team. I know a lot about them."

"Too bad you can't read. You would know a lot more." Henry looked down. "But you have a good memory."

"Yes, I do. I remember all kinds of things."

His father's jaw tightened. And then Henry's mother came through the door with a platter of lamb chops, placed it on the sideboard, and returned to the kitchen. She backed through the swinging door with bowls of mashed potatoes and green beans, served their plates and sat down.

"Dick, we're ready for grace." His father folded up the newspaper and reached over to put it on the sideboard. They all bent their heads. His mother whispered, "Bless, O Lord, this food you have provided us, and help us to love and respect each other. Amen."

"Thank you, mom. I liked that."

"You're welcome, honey," his mother replied, smiling at him. As they ate, his father talked about baseball, but Henry did not dare say anything more. Finally, his mother stood up, collected their plates, and disappeared through the swinging door.

Henry lowered his head. His father picked up his newspaper again.

"Peach pie," his mother announced, coming back. "The last of the season." From the sideboard she cut and served three pieces. She returned to the kitchen and brought from the freezer a box of vanilla ice cream. The scoop snapped as she ejected the ice cream onto the men's pies. They ate in silence.

"That was yummy, Mom," Henry said, turning towards her. "Would you teach me how to make that pie?"

"Women do the cooking," his father said.

"What about cowboys in the desert?" Henry asked. "They have to do their own cooking."

"How can you be a cowboy? You don't even know how to ride a horse."

"He could learn," Henry's mother said. "I could teach him. Remember I grew up on a horse."

"That's ridiculous, Edna. Your riding days are over. You haven't been on a horse for years. Don't encourage him."

His mother reached for the empty desert plates, clattering them as she stacked them. Henry winced. She jumped up and disappeared into the kitchen. Henry stood up and threw his napkin on the table.

"Don't be mean to Mom," he shouted. He took a few quick steps toward his father, towering over him, his fists clenched at his sides. His father drew back in his chair.

"What the hell?" his father said, his voice quiet and raspy. "Get out of here before I call the police. You can't come at me like that."

Henry turned and ran for his room. He heard his father shouting, "Edna, I told you this would happen. He was about to hit me. He can't live here any longer." Henry slammed his door and then turned, staring at it. If only he could lock it on his side. He could hear his mother crying and the fast clicking of her heels down the hall to her bedroom.

He moved over to one of his windows, raised it, and took hold of two of the bars his father had installed years before. He shook them, but they did not move. He leaned his head against them, breathing hard. Then he heard his father's footsteps coming toward him. He held his breath. He heard the rasp of the bolt on the outside of his door, locking him in, then his father's receding footsteps down the hall. He exhaled, relieved. He was glad he was locked in.

His mother had begged him to stop running away. Now it might be too late. He fell face down on his bed, pulled the pillow out to cover his head, clasping it with both hands to hold it down tight. Dirty old Jake lay up against his cheek, comforting him. His mind began to drift—he wanted it to take him somewhere, anywhere.

He began to hear a drumbeat that grew louder and louder. A brass band joined in. Behind his closed eyes, he led the band and a troop of soldiers over a green hill into battle, one bass drum booming the first note of each rhythm, an agitated piccolo playing a fast-running tempo to speed up the brave soldiers. His men were dressed in green with peaked caps, just like Robin Hood. In front of them he carried a blue flag with a white river winding down the diagonal and a crescent moon in the upper right corner.

What was on the other side of the hill? Henry shouted, "Halt!" He walked to the crest and peered beyond. Yes, there was his father down below trying to load a cannon with a long black barrel pointed towards Henry. But his father didn't see him—he was bent over, peering into a box, looking for ammunition to load the canon.

Henry's heart beat faster. He gave the command: "Advance!" As the troops rounded the crest, Henry saw his father straighten up and rush behind the cannon.

"Prepare to fire!" Muskets clicked.

"Ready, aim. . . ." Time stopped. No, he could not. "Lower muskets." He heard the men behind him groaning. His father and the cannon became a wobbling image, a reflection in a black pool. He himself was sinking into it, but he did not care any more. Then his breathing slowed and he slept.

Later, he sat up in his bed, holding Jake against his chest. He looked up at the narrow white shelves on the opposite wall, where he had lined up all his stuffed animals. They waited for him: one moth-eaten dark yellow lion, one giraffe, and one elephant with a pink mouth. Even now he imagined them coming alive and smashing down the room, pushing out the bars, crushing the door and its lock. Maybe he would ride out on the back of Jake, who would turn into the real Jake with a tiger's roar, tiger's claws, and tiger's teeth. They would go to the dark forest where the wild tigers lived.

No, he could not go with them. Although he loved his animals more than anything, Henry could not live in the jungle. It was too far away. The desert was just on the other side of the Sierra Madre Mountains, which he could see from the backyard above the high brown fence that had no gate.

He had a plan. There were little towns in the desert. So there had to be gas stations there, too. He could get a job pumping gas, washing windows, checking people's oil, and he would live in a little cabin on the edge of a town in the Mojave Desert. When he wasn't working, he would walk to the Joshua trees. He had a photo of a Joshua tree with its strange hairy arms reaching toward the sky. He would see the purple mountain and the golden light he dreamed of almost every night.

Henry stood, took the jungle animals down and lined them up, noses close to the crack under the door, as if they could indeed spring to life the moment his dad opened it.

At that moment, he heard the sound of the bolt. His heart raced, his breath stopped. But it was his mother who came through the door.

"I'm sorry, Mom."

"Let's sit on the bed," she said. Henry picked up the animals

"You still love your animals, don't you?"

"It's kind of dumb, I know. I'm too old to be playing with stuffed animals, aren't I?"

"Well, maybe . . ." She smiled.

"I can talk to them. They are my only friends."

His mother's smile disappeared. "You are here alone way too much."

Henry sat on his pillow, feeling Jake underneath and his mother sat further down toward the foot of bed, facing him.

"He is frightened of you now. You're bigger and stronger than he is. He wants to send you away."

"Where?"

"Somewhere with other kids who have problems. But I don't want that. I need to tell you, I've written Uncle Ed. He's refused to have anything to do with me since I married your dad. But I've begged him to let you live with him on his ranch. He has two ranches now—the one in Montana where I grew up, and one near Phoenix, which I've never seen. You can be a cowboy, just like you said. I haven't heard back from him yet, but I hope to real soon."

His mother reached out a hand, placing it gently on his leg. "You need to know—your father had a younger brother, Robbie. He looked a lot like you. He was strange and everyone told your father's parents, your grandparents, that he was dangerous. They didn't believe that. Then one day he went out and hurt a little girl. He was taken away to a mental hospital and died there of pneumonia. His parents felt disgraced in that little town in Iowa where they lived. No one came to his father's hardware store anymore. They moved to another town far away, where his father had to work for a farmer. Your dad got into Harvard and when I met him, he said we would move as far away from Iowa as we could. Now he's terrified that you'll be just like Robbie. I tell him you aren't at all like Robbie, but he won't listen to me."

"Would you come to the ranch with me?" Henry asked.

"I wish I could, oh, I would be so happy, if I could. I dream all the time of being back in Montana again, riding up into the mountains, breathing that air."

"What if Uncle Ed says no?"

"I don't think he will. I just have a feeling he'll say yes. While we wait, don't try to run away and don't scare your father. We just need some time."

"I'll try, Mom. I'm sorry."

3

"Looks like you'll have to stand me the first round of drinks, Clive," Dick Hamblen said. "I shot an eighty-two to your... ?"

"Ninety-three. Not a good day for me. I usually do better."

"It was kind of you to fill in when Jim Cochran cancelled on me yesterday. Gives us a chance to get to know each other."

"I'm glad for the opportunity," Clive replied, squinting in the sun.

Clive Wilson's black greasy hair clung to his scalp, but otherwise he looked respectable enough in his tweed plus fours and white V-neck sweater. They moved into the men's lounge, where other golfers were eating sandwiches and drinking. Cigarette smoke filled the room. A big vase of birds of paradise on long stalks caught the sun filtering through a south window. Dick strode past the sunlit orange and brilliant blue, heading for a table off in a dark corner.

They ordered ham and cheese on rye and bourbon on the rocks. Both lit up cigarettes and chatted about their golf round until a young Mexican man placed food and drink before them. Dick pulled his handkerchief from his pants pocket, wiped his face, and replaced it slowly.

"The election is day after tomorrow. Do you think Stevenson might win?" Dick began.

"Not a chance," Clive answered. "Ike will take most states, I bet."

"Stevenson is one of those brainy types," Dick said, grimacing. "He's out of touch with the real world. Despite what he says, I think he's soft on communism."

Clive nodded. "And Ike promises to do something about Korea. "It's getting worse and worse over there. Our men are dying—again. Ike knows what he's doing. We need a military man now more than ever." Clive slapped his hand on the table.

"If we don't blow ourselves up with these super bombs," Dick added.

Clive nodded. "You mean if the Russians don't blow us up. This Cold War is frightening."

"At least we have Senator Joe McCarthy nailing those communist sympathizers in the government and army, and HUAC goes after those damned intellectuals and film guys, who want to turn us into a communist country. Most of them are Jews, too." Clive glanced away, then took a sip of his drink. "We never should have let them into our country," Dick continued. "But McCarthy will stop them."

"We even have communist sympathizers in the hospital where I work," Clive said. "Damned pinko doctors." This was the moment Dick was waiting for. He took a breath.

"Oh, right. I hear you are a psychiatrist. Where did you do your training?"

"I went to New York University Medical School and then did my residency at Beth Israel Hospital."

"But isn't that a Jewish hospital?" Clive blinked.

"Yes, but they take non-Jews. I wanted to work with a well-known doctor there."

"And what brought you to California?"

"My wife. She came from New Hampshire and she hated New York City. She thought living in California would be exciting and different. She has a close friend in Pasadena, so that's where we landed."

"She plays golf here, too?"

"Yes, but it's the social life she loves. She's here playing bridge three times a week, particularly when I'm away working in San Bernadino."

"Let's get another round." Dick caught the eye of a waiter and pointed at their empty glasses. "So why do you work so far away?"

"When we moved here three years ago, the state mental hospitals were looking for more psychiatrists. I was hired by Stanyon State Mental Hospital there in San Bernadino."

"I've heard of it."

"It seemed a good place to start. Since then, I've been slowly building up my private practice at a clinic in Pasadena."

"Where in Pasadena? I live in Pasadena."

"Just off of Colorado Street."

"Does your wife complain—you know—you being gone so much?"

"Barbara doesn't like it at all. But she thinks Pasadena has much more to offer than San Bernadino. In a year or two, I should be able to switch entirely to the Pasadena clinic. In the meantime, I try to keep my weekends free so I can come here. Doesn't always work out, because the head doctor in my ward calls the shots."

The drinks arrived and Dick tapped out a Camel from the pack in front of him. "Someone told me you were hoping to join the Board here?"

Clive put his drink down so hard it banged on the table. "Keep your voice down," he said. "We're not supposed to talk about it. My wife is very friendly with Mrs. Davidson."

"Ah, that explains it. Davidson mentioned you the other day. Did you know I'm on the Board?" Clive pressed his lips together.

"No, I didn't. You weren't on last year's annual report."

"I was elected six months ago when Bill Peters died suddenly. Well, all the better we get to know each other before the Board meets next month."

Clive looked around the room. He leaned toward Dick, his forehead sweaty, and whispered, "Let's change the subject, OK?"

"Fine. So, since you're a psychiatrist, can I ask you a question?" Dick raised his glass and took a deep gulp of bourbon.

"Sure—shoot." Clive leaned back, looking at the smoke curling up from his cigarette.

"I have a friend," Dick began, "who has a seventeen-year-old son who is mentally retarded and very disturbed. He's grown so tall his father can't control him any more. Just a few days ago, he threatened to hit my friend. And he runs away whenever he can. My friend is afraid he's going to attack someone out there."

"Has this young man been given a diagnosis?"

"They say he's mentally retarded, maybe psychotic. How can my friend protect himself?"

"Your friend could bring him to me for an official diagnosis that would allow the young man to be committed, if, of course, such a diagnosis is warranted. He's still a minor so the parents don't need the boy's consent."

"My friend's wife refuses to sign anything. She's completely against putting him away."

"Then he has a problem, doesn't he?" Clive smirked.

A silence followed. Dick saw Clive's eyes dart back and forth—he was thinking, that was clear. Dick signaled to the Mexican for more drinks.

Clive raised an index finger. "I have a proposal that might interest you—I mean your friend. This may be something he has not thought about. There is a wonderful procedure out there now, you may have heard of, called lobotomy. Many families with violent relatives come to me. The two halves of the frontal cortex are separated with a long needle inserted through the eye sockets. It's a simple procedure. Usually we just stun the patient with electroshock and it's over in ten minutes. After that, the patient becomes calm and docile, and no longer needs restraining. It's quite miraculous. Sometimes the patient can return home—or if he goes to an institution, he'll be quiet—and much happier."

Dick grimaced. "Cutting into the brain sounds extreme. Is there no other way?"

"Institutionalization. We do lobotomies there, too, but the red tape can take up to six months at Stanyon except for extreme violence."

"This has to be completely confidential, Clive. I hope I can count on you."

"Of course. I understand how delicate this is." Clive handed him a card. "Here is the address and phone number of the clinic and the days I'm there. Tell your friend to bring his wife—I'm good at convincing the wives that a lobotomy might be the best solution. I've never seen a patient be violent after a lobotomy."

"Thanks for the advice."

"Not at all," Clive said, smiling. "I'm glad I can be of service. And let me pick up the bill."

"No, let's split it right down the middle, fair and square. Except that first round of drinks for your bad golf day."

Clive raised his chin, straightening up to his full height. "Well, next time, then. Maybe we'll have more than one thing to celebrate."

Dick felt his right cheek muscle tighten. "I can recommend a couple of really good golf pros. You want to do something to improve your game. We're serious about golf here, you know. Bud Hollister is the one I used to take lessons from."

"I wish I had started when I was a boy," Clive said, glancing away.

"I began when I was at Harvard."

"Preparing for medical school took all my time," Clive said, standing up.

"Well, better late than never, huh?" Dick said, pushing his chair back. "Let's go—I need to get home."

"Drive carefully," Clive said, squinting his weasel eyes. Dick barely refrained from telling him to go to hell. He had his nerve.

"Don't worry. I can handle my liquor. Look—there's the maître d' over by the cash register." As they walked over to the counter, Dick glanced at Clive's thin face. Of course, the S.O.B. knew he was talking about his own son. It was bad enough pretending to like this man, but the next humiliation would be having to tell him the boy in question was Henry.

In the parking lot, he found his car and pulled the keys out of his pocket. He struggled to get the key in the door lock, but it kept slipping to one side or the other. "This goddamned key. What the hell is wrong with it?"

4

The next day, Sunday, Henry sat at his desk listening to *Dragnet* through the earphones of his crystal set. A knock on the door made him jump, as the bolt slid open and his mother came in.

"We're going to the Staffords—they just invited us over."

"Can't you just leave me here? Lock the door. I'll be OK."

"No. What if the house caught fire? And Betty Stafford says she hasn't seen you for ages. Bring some of your picture books."

Henry sighed as he removed his headphones right at an exciting part where Sergeant Friday was about to get the truth out of a suspect. He grabbed two books of nature photos from a stack on his desk and followed his mother into the hall. Her high heels clicked on the wood floor—*tack, tack, tack.* She wore a green plaid skirt and her frizzy hair was pulled back under a matching green band. He was about to tell her he liked those colors, but then his father appeared, frowning at Henry.

"Don't you dare say anything unless they ask you a question—understood? I assured them you would sit still and not bother anybody. Understood?" Henry nodded, clutching his books against his ribs.

The Staffords lived in the foothills, right against the Sierra Madre Mountains. Henry pressed his nose against the window of the car, staring at the steep slope of the mountain for as long as he could. It was right there, so close.

His father drove past two stone pillars, down a long driveway with lawn and trees on one side and a brushy canyon on the other. Henry rolled down the back window and stuck his head out to try to see the bottom of the canyon. The long driveway widened into a parking area in front of the Staffords' white shingle house.

Mrs. Stafford opened the door. She was short and plump and wore a black skirt with a bright red belt and a white fuzzy sweater. "Henry, you're so tall now," she said, smiling as she looked up at him. "Come in, come in."

Mr. Stafford stood when they came into the living room, folding up a newspaper he had been reading. He had very black hair and was tall and thin. He gave Henry a quick glance, then said, "Can I get us some Manhattans?" He went off to the kitchen while Henry's parents and Mrs. Stafford sat on two loveseats in front of a big window. Through the window Henry saw a deodar tree—Mrs. Stafford had once told him its name and he had even climbed up its horizontal branches with Sam before his mother spotted them and made them come down.

"Sit over there," his father said, pointing to a small alcove lined with books. Mr. Stafford came out with the drinks and a bottle of Coke for Henry, which Mrs. Stafford brought to him, still smiling.

"Thanks," Henry said, smiling back at her. She was always so nice to him, treating him like a normal person, even if he wasn't.

Mr. Stafford came over, waving his cigarette in the air. "Maybe you'd like to listen to a football game? The Pittsburgh Steelers are up against the Cleveland Browns right now."

"Sure." He would have preferred to look at his desert nature books, but he thought it might be rude and his father would punish him later. He laid the books down on the carpet.

"You'll have to sit close and keep the volume down," Mr. Stafford said. Henry threw himself into a black, high-backed leather chair and swiveled it around so that he faced away from the adults. Mr. Stafford tuned the station.

"Thanks," Henry mumbled. The chair was perfect. By scrunching down a little, he could make himself invisible. He hoped his legs didn't show underneath. Sure enough, in a few moments, his mother's anxious voice called out, "Henry?"

"Yeah, mom, I'm here."

"Don't worry, Edna," he heard his father say. "He knows what will happen if he tries anything."

Henry said nothing but reached for the knob on the radio, turning up the volume. He did not want to hear his father's voice anymore.

"Turn it down or else," his father said. "What did Mr. Stafford tell you, you idiot? Can't you for once not ruin everything for us?" Henry lowered the volume. He wasn't listening to the radio anyway. Dimly, far away it seemed, he heard his mom and Mr. Stafford arguing about the presidential election. His mom wanted Stevenson to win. The others sounded angry with her for liking him. He liked Stevenson, too.

He peeked around the edge of the chair and saw his father gesturing with a hand that held a cigarette. Talking louder and louder, they no longer remembered to watch him. He might as well not be there. No one wanted him around. Uncle Ed had not written back and his mother wasn't going to save him from being sent away. If he could just get to the desert, the silent desert . . .

He stood up slowly, hoping the chair would not squeak. He moved silently across the plush beige carpet to the hall at the back of the house, his heart pounding. And yes, the door to the outside was wide open.

Running past the Stafford's swimming pool, he spotted a low wall just beyond that he could jump over and disappear into the canyon below.

But a girl with pigtails, wearing a red plaid shirt, sat on the wall, facing out towards the canyon—the Staffords' daughter, Fannie, a skinny kid, or she used to be.

Henry jumped on the wall but instead of plunging over the other side, he sat down a few feet away from the girl. He knew he did not have long. This was his last chance. Yet he could not move. Fannie scooted a few feet further away from him, her face turned away. Why didn't she say something?

Across the canyon stood a grove of eucalyptus trees with their white, peeling bark. Their leaves rustled and he breathed in their sharp smell. He heard a dog howling on the ridge on the other side.

He glanced to the right. Up above were the mountains, so near, rather bare except for boulders, rocky cliffs, scrub brush, and a few little trees. Small paths crisscrossed their way up. One of those must lead to the top, into the dark forest he felt sure must be at the summit, and then down the other side—to the Mojave Desert!

MO-HAH-VAY—he formed the sounds with his lips. Then he sang the syllables, drawing out the *MO* by repeating it three times at a low pitch: *MO-MO-MO,* then *HAAH-a-VAY,* more quickly, going up to a higher pitch and then down a few notes.

He looked around and saw a pine tree branch lying on the ground up against the wall on the lawn side. He twisted back to pick it up. It was rough and knobby in his hand. He beat it against the edge of the wall in a rhythm to match his song: long, long, short, short, short, short, long. He tried it a few times, glancing at Fannie, who remained immobile as he sang. Across the canyon, the leaves of eucalyptus trees turned in a breeze, dancing to his song. He closed his eyes, rocking back and forth, singing. Then he heard another voice, so faint, he wondered if it were part of his dream. He sang more quietly. Yes, there it was—a higher girl's voice. It felt like an angel answering. It was Fannie. He didn't dare open his eyes or look at her. Finally, he stopped and when he turned his head towards her, there she was, sitting cross-legged on the wall, facing him, not smiling. He lifted his arm as far back as he could and pitched the pine stick off into the canyon. He heard it hit the ground and slide a little further, accompanied by some loose dirt and pebbles.

"Don't do that," she whispered. "There are Indians down there waiting to attack us. You're going to make them mad."

"Well, why didn't you tell me?" he replied. "Do you want those Indians to kill us?"

"They won't kill *me*."

They both returned to silence.

"I think," he said, "I see the tip of a feather sticking up above that big rock down there."

"California Indians do *not* have feathers sticking up," she said. "Those are Plains Indians."

At the same moment, he heard his dad's voice calling from inside the house, "Henry, HENRY! Get back in here right now." Panic. He only had seconds before his father came out and saw him.

"Tell him I went to the left."

"Where are you going?" Fannie asked.

"I'm going to the desert on the other side of the mountain." Fannie smiled for the first time. But why had he told her?

"Take me with you."

"No, no, I can't. You're too young. I have to go by myself."

"I'm fifteen," she said.

"No. Stay here. Don't tell them where I've gone."

He pushed himself off the wall, and half-running, half-sliding down the side of the canyon, he fell toward the bottom.

• • •

Henry walked up a sandy path to the lower part of the mountain where it became a narrow winding trail. So many dreams had informed him about this mountain, how he would cross it, and what he would find on the other side. Sometimes in those dreams he could fly; sometimes, like now, he had to plod along or even drag himself forward on hands and knees, as if some evil force were pulling him back.

The mountain seemed much higher than it had appeared from over the fence in his backyard. Was he ever going to reach the top? Grey lizards scuttled off in front of him. Some blue jays squabbled in the manzanita bushes. The sun felt hot on his head; he had no water.

He walked as fast as he could. His throat felt dry, his breath raspy. He stopped a moment to look back down—the few visible houses looked tiny.

He listened to his feet—*step, step, crunch, crunch.* He started counting to one hundred and then back down again. Each number pulsed like shimmering sunlight, each with its own tint—pale blue, lavender, deep green. The rhythm of walking, the perfect order of the numbers, made Henry feel protected. White rocks, grey and brown bushes, a few scrubby pines with their dusty smell in his nostrils, the sound of the propellers of an airplane—it all fitted in between the numbers, creating a matrix through which he walked.

Henry stopped counting, panting for breath. He had been completely unaware of time. Now he turned and looked down again. The light was fading. When a cold breeze came up, he realized he didn't even have a sweater.

He heard footsteps further down the trail behind him. Someone had found him; he was going to be captured. But his legs were tired after so many hours of walking. Could he run ahead and escape? He turned, ready to try to make a dash, to find a hiding place, but then he heard the sound of someone crying.

In the dim light, he saw a girl coming toward him. It was Fannie —she had followed him! "You should have stayed at home," he called out.

"I know," answered Fannie, coming up to him, limping. Tears ran down her smudgy, scratched face.

"Why did you follow me? Now I'm going to get into real trouble."

"I thought it would be fun, but now I'm scared."

"We'll figure something out."

Fannie stopped crying, wiping her face with a sleeve. "I was already part way down to the bottom of the canyon when I heard your father calling from the wall. I hid behind a bush so he couldn't see me. My mom thought I was over at my friend Jean's house, and maybe she still thinks I'm there. But I've been following you a long time. Then I twisted my ankle and fell into a prickly bush. I couldn't see . . ."

"Yeah, it's almost dark. We're going to have to stick it out here for the night. When the sun comes up, we'll find our way back down."

"OK," Fannie said, wiping her face with her shirttail.

Henry could just make out a bush-covered gully that cut into a rocky cliff behind them. He broke off a few branches so they could crawl in. Two huge boulders stood like soldiers at the entrance to the gully. Inside he found a flat rock to sit up against.

"Come sit here between my legs and lean against me," he said. She obeyed without a word, pulling her knees up to her chest. He wrapped his arms around her, hoping to give her a little warmth.

"I'm hungry and thirsty," she whispered.

"I am too," Henry answered. "But we'll be OK. It's not going to be fun, but we'll be OK."

Fannie sighed but said nothing more. They both looked through the bushes at the far-away lights of Los Angeles. The cold penetrated Henry's shirt and jeans. His toes felt numb.

After a while, Fannie's chin dropped to her chest and he could feel her deep breathing. She was asleep. He looked at the back of her head with the crooked part in her dark hair. Her body gave him a little warmth. Her hair smelled clean, despite the dust in it.

He sighed. Now he had no choice. He had to go back down. He couldn't abandon Fannie. He never should have spoken to her down there—maybe he should have gone back in the house and faced the anger of his father. He tightened his arms and felt her thin body against his. It was going to be a very long night.

• • •

As soon as the sky became light, he and Fannie inched their way back down the trail, Fannie limping, until they found a fire road. Henry saw a man in a uniform walking up towards them. He was a thin, young guy with a tired face.

"We've been searching for you all night," he said in a low voice. He put them in his jeep, gave them water and a Hershey bar to share. He drove them straight to the police station, not saying another word. As the jeep stopped in front, Henry saw two policemen come out. Fannie's frightened eyes followed them.

"It's OK," Henry said. "I've been here before. Our parents will come get us. I guess they'll be happy to know we're OK."

"They're going to be mad at us," Fannie said.

"Yes, they will. But we'll be able to go home. Your parents are nice—they can't get as mad as my father will."

"You don't know my father."

"Tell him it's my fault."

"I will not," Fannie said, turning towards Henry with serious eyes just before a policeman opened the jeep door.

The moment they walked into the police station, a policewoman and Mrs. Stafford rushed up to Fannie. Mrs. Stafford's eyes blazed at Henry for a second, before she turned away, her arm around Fannie's shoulders. Fannie turned her head to look at Henry as she was led off. "Bye," she said in a tiny voice. A policeman pushed him into a tiny room with nothing but one chair in it.

"Wait here," the policeman said, slamming the door and turning a lock—just like at home. A little window up high near the ceiling let in a beam of sunlight. He waited for what seemed hours, shaking. Where were his parents? He just wanted to go home. He wanted a shower, some food, and to go under his blanket with Jake.

Finally, the same policeman came to escort him into a long, narrow green room lined with grey filing cabinets. Two lights with cone shades hung down from the ceiling over a shiny metal table. He shielded his eyes from the light, while the policeman guided him towards a chair. He fell into it.

When he looked up, he saw hostile faces surrounding him. Next to him sat the family lawyer, Mr. Crawley, a creepy guy with a thin face and horn-rimmed glasses. Henry had seen him talking to his father at home. Inspector Brightwell, who had always been kind to Henry, sat on the other side, but now with an angry face beneath his greying crew cut.

Next to Inspector Brightwell sat his parents. His father looked at him with a screwed-up face, as if he smelled a garbage can full of rotten food. His mother tugged on a strand of her hair. Mr. Stafford, on the other side of the Inspector, looked the angriest of all, rapping his fists on the table, as if he were about to attack.

And then he knew. He was going to be sent away.

Before anyone could speak, the policewoman who had led Fannie off came in. He knew her—Angie. She sometimes talked to him while they waited for his mother or father to pick him up at the police station after one of his failed escapes. This time she didn't look at him but went off in a corner with the Inspector. Then she left.

Returning to the table and sitting down, the Inspector said, "Doctor Finley reports that there is no indication of molestation, just abrasions and a sprained ankle. Fannie's mother is taking her home." Then Henry understood. They thought he had hurt Fannie. But why would he hurt her?

"I don't believe you," Mr. Stafford shouted. "Why would he take my daughter off like that? He knew damn well what he was doing."

Inspector Brightwell stiffened. "Are you questioning, Mr. Stafford, the competency of the medical doctor? Do I have to spell out to you what she found? Your daughter is still a . . ."

Mr. Stafford's mouth fell open. "All right," he said. "I'll have Henry arrested, Dick, if it turns out the doctor was wrong. I obviously misjudged him; I thought he was a little peculiar, but not a child molester." Henry saw his father look quickly at Mr. Stafford, then back to the lawyer, his face frozen.

Mr. Crawley, rattling some papers, looked at Henry through his owl-like glasses. "Your parents and I have come to an agreement with Mr. Stafford—uh, that is, assuming the doctor's examination of Fannie indicated you had not harmed her. That seems to be the case. You are to go to a hospital for three weeks to be evaluated. You will have to stay in jail here until we get a judge to issue a court order. Tomorrow morning you will be transported to the hospital."

Henry felt his heart racing. He looked at his mother. "I didn't do anything to Fannie. I told her not to follow me. I didn't know she was behind me on the trail until it was almost dark. She'll tell you. I was trying to get to the desert—not with her—by myself. I wanted to be by myself. Please don't make me go to a hospital. I want to go home. I promise I won't ever run away again. Please don't send me to the hospital."

No one seemed to hear him. Then his mother stood up, pale and shaking. "I believe you. I don't understand what's going on here. Phil, Betty, you are our friends. Why don't you believe Henry or at least the doctor?" She pushed her chair back and started to move around the table. His father jumped up, grabbing her by the shoulders.

"Don't go near him he's dangerous. Let the professionals do their job." His mother screamed and began sobbing, struggling to get free of his father's grasp. Everyone was looking at her as a fat policeman dragged Henry out of his chair and shoved him toward a door.

"Mommy, help me!" he called out, as the door slammed shut behind him.

"Shut up," the policeman growled. "Look what you've done to her. You should be ashamed of yourself, you little bastard."

5

Henry sat in the back of a black van, squeezed against a small window by an old woman, who pressed against him with her chin on her chest, asleep, snorting. Her smell made him turn his face away. At every bend, the woman lurched into him or almost fell into the aisle, but she did not wake up. Henry stiffened his arm to keep her away. Behind him sat two old men, each talking to himself.

"Where is Dora? She said, 'I'll see you soon.' Where is she?" one said.

"God forgive me, God forgive me," the other one moaned. The driver and another man in front smoked and talked football.

Out the window he saw gas stations, cafés, billboards, and then fields and orange groves. Beyond the orange groves he saw mountains. Were they the same mountains, the ones leading to the Mojave?

"Excuse me, sir," he called out. The young man in the passenger seat in front turned his head and glared at Henry. "Is the Mojave Desert on the other side of those mountains?"

"Uh, I don't think so. But where we're goin' is pretty close. I live in San Bernadino and it just takes a few hours to get to the Mojave."

"Only a few hours?"

"Yeah, it's easy—just over some hills."

"You don't have to cross a mountain?"

"Nope."

"Thanks. I want to go to the Mojave."

"They won't let you."

"Why not?"

"They won't let you out."

"Oh."

The man turned back to talk to the driver.

Henry closed his eyes and moved in his mind to the Mojave Desert. He was enveloped in reds and oranges, pale yellows and browns. Birds were singing. He heard a distant coyote yipping. The shapes of sand dunes shifted in the wind. Behind them stood a purple mountain, its peak reaching into a pure blue sky.

He could not stay there. The sound of his heart pounding brought him back. He opened his eyes. It must be a prison he was going to, but why would his parents send him to a prison? It was bad to run away, but he had never heard of someone being sent to prison for running away. He knew all about crime from the radio, but he hadn't committed any crime. Did they still think he had kidnapped Fannie or something? She would tell them. She seemed brave, even if she cried. Girls cry. She would tell them.

Wherever he was going, it was only for three weeks. Maybe they would let him out sooner. His mother would come take him home. And she must have packed Jake in his case. He had not had a chance to look, but Jake must be there. He wouldn't be alone.

Then his eyes closed again—first the night on the mountain, then having to listen to drunks in other cells in the jail, shouting and cursing most of the night.

He woke when the van stopped. He saw out the window a huge brick building with bars on the windows. It must be a prison. The uniformed men were shouting orders to get out and take his bag from the back of the van and follow the others inside. One man led the shuffling line, another followed, yelling at one of the old men to hurry up.

He sat with the others in a small room. One of the guards stood near the door, smoking. After a while Henry's name was called and a large, tight-lipped nurse behind a desk asked him to sit down. She opened a folder, looked at it, and then at Henry. She said, "Do you know why you are here?"

"No."

"You are here for evaluation, to determine if you should stay in a mental institution or be allowed to live outside. Do you understand what I am saying?"

"I guess so. Are my parents coming to see me?"

"I don't know. That's not my business."

Whatever else she said, Henry did not hear. A tall young Negro appeared, took his bag, and led him through three heavy doors, which he unlocked with his rattling keys and then locked again behind them. Henry covered his ears with his hands; the doors squeaked just like *Inner Sanctum* on the radio, only the sound was much scarier.

He was led into a large room with a row of beds down each side. Each bed was covered with a white bedspread, tucked neat and smooth under the mattress. The floor was shiny grey.

"Can I take a shower?" he asked.

"Naw, not now, this afternoon da guys get a shower and shave. Here's ya closet," the man said. "Put ya stuff in there. Let's see. I'll get y'all ya hospital fatigues. There's your bed. Just sit there. Don't cause no trouble, OK?" He left the room. Henry sat and looked around. It had the same ugly green walls as in the police station, with two windows at the end with some kind of heavy screening and bars outside it. If it was a prison, where were the other prisoners?

The man came back with a grey top and pants and stood there, leaning against the wall, arms crossed, while Henry changed. Neither of them spoke.

"OK," the man said. "Clothes go on a hook in this closet over there, see?" Henry hung up his clothes and as he put his satchel in, he quickly opened it, but Jake was not there. There was a pair of underwear and socks. Nothing else. His father must have packed the bag—his mother would have put Jake in. But she would bring Jake to him.

Henry followed the man to a room filled with other men, a few talking to each other, most sitting alone doing nothing, some mumbling. He kept his head down, his eyes fixed on the grey linoleum floor. A television high on the wall blared but he did not look at it. Nurses in white watched them from a kind of glass box. At least he thought they looked like nurses, but why would there be nurses in a prison?

After what seemed hours, all the men were marched in a line by two more Negroes to the cafeteria. He could not eat the food that was put in front of him. It smelled burnt—some kind of stew.

He dozed in a chair in the dayroom except when they were led off to take their showers. There was another boy under the shower next to him, another blond boy. They glanced at each other.

"Hi," Henry said. The other boy opened his mouth. His lips moved as if he was trying to speak, but no sound came out. Henry looked away. They were the only kids there, but this one could not speak.

Dinner seemed to be the identical meal as lunch. He tried a few mouthfuls, but he could not swallow more—it smelled horrible. After another interminable time in the dayroom with the blaring TV showing a game show, they were allowed to go to bed. The other men glanced at him as they changed into pajamas and hung up their grey pants and shirts in their little closets, but they did not speak to him. The blond boy was in a bed way down at the other end of the room. With the lights out, he heard some of the men talking to themselves or to each other or groaning. He had always slept alone and now he was in a room filled with very strange men, crazy men. Did his father tell the police that he was crazy, too?

He tried to escape to his desert, but he could not find his way there. Everything was dark. Where was the golden desert light?

•••

The next day, the door to their room was unlocked at seven in the morning by a brown-skinned man, a Mexican. He smiled, the first smile Henry had seen in that place. "Good morning. I'm Juan," he said, looking at Henry. Henry's ward mates groaned and got out of bed. Henry had been lying awake for a long time. While the attendant leaned against a wall, whistling, the other men changed from the grey pajamas to the grey day clothes. Then they filed in groups of eight into the bathroom, where they urinated and splashed water on their faces.

They followed the attendant down the corridor, back to the cafeteria. His hunger forced him to eat the lumpy oatmeal put in front of him. The noise of clattering dishes and the patients' voices made him cover his ears, but then he couldn't eat. He lowered his hands, grabbed the spoon again, keeping his eyes down.

For what seemed like days, Henry spoke to no one except Juan. He looked at no one. If only he could stop up his ears, so he didn't have to listen to the horrible noise of shouts, curses, groans, aides yelling at the men, strange machines clanking.

Finally one morning, as the men filed from the cafeteria back to the dayroom, Juan came up to him and said, "You gonna go meet the doctor. Follow me." He led Henry down a long corridor lined with strange metal frames and leather harnesses. Were they instruments of torture like those he had heard about on *Inner Sanctum*? He saw patients strapped in chairs, mostly sagging forward, chins on their chests, moaning, drooling.

•••

Doctor Rosenblatt heard a knock on his office door and stopped writing his report, his fountain pen arrested mid-air. Juan held the door open for a blond boy—his new patient.

"Please come sit in this chair next to me. I'd get up and shake your hand properly, but as you see, I'm in a wheelchair, and it's hard for me to stand up. My name is Dr. Rosenblatt. Everyone calls me Dr. R. If you can wait a moment, I'm just finishing up this report." He saw the boy hesitate.

"Oh, I'm sorry. Just put those books and papers under the chair. Then you'll have somewhere to sit down." Out of the corner of his eye, he saw the boy stack the books carefully on the floor and gather the papers into a neat pile.

As he wrote, he glanced a few more times at the new patient, who was staring at something on the wall behind. Was he looking for a way to escape, or was he drawn to the Van Gogh reproduction of the famous sunflowers? Or the fat round red pots in the corners with the big-leafed tropical plants? The bright pink walls?

He closed his notebook with a thud and the boy jumped, eyes startled. "Sorry, I hate these reports, but I shouldn't express my anger that way." He reached for a piece of paper on his desk and looked at it. "I see you're Henry Hamblen." The boy looked down, not replying, staring at his hands.

"You are frightened. This is all very strange for you, isn't it?" The boy did not move. "I saw you looking at my walls. What did you see?" Henry looked up for an instant, then lowered his head again.

Dr. R joined the silence, watching. Minutes went by, "I really don't know what to do. I might as well be talking to myself. I think I understand how you feel. You don't know where the hell you've landed." Henry kept his eyes closed for a moment, and then raised his head. He was breathing hard. "I like this room."

"I like it, too. What do you like about it?"

"There's a black rhinoceros on the shelf over there, and is that an alligator next to him? He looks like he is made of ivory."

"Yes—they are native art from Africa. Bring them over here if you'd like." Henry jumped up and returned with the rhinoceros and alligator, placing them carefully on Dr. R's desk. He ran his hand over the smooth black wood of the rhinoceros, stroking him, before he sat down again.

"He's a beauty, isn't he?" Dr. R said. "It would be wonderful to see one in real life," Maybe not up too close. They say they are dangerous."

"Yes, and I want to see wild tigers, too."

"So you'll have to go to both Africa and India."

Henry nodded. Dr. R saw that he had hooked Henry, pulled him out of his swamp of despair, at least for an instant.

"There was something under the alligator," Henry said.

"What?"

"It's a tile with two triangles on it. Why is the alligator lying on top of it?"

Dr. R laughed. "Oh, you got me there—I'm hiding it. It's the Star of David, a symbol in Judaism. I'm Jewish. One triangle points to God and the other points to the Earth, here where we live. That's how I interpret it. There's a much more complicated explanation about the number seven—six directions on King David's shield that protected him and the whole thing is the number seven, which is the feminine influence, for some reason. I don't want people to see it, but I know it's there, and it reminds me . . ." He saw Henry's surprise when he stopped, but he could not find how to complete his thought. Strange.

"Why am I in prison?" Henry blurted out. For an instant, Dr. R imagined he had asked the same question. But why would he think that? He was the doctor; *he* wasn't in prison.

"This is a hospital, not a prison, but I know it feels like a prison. You were sent here, because you took a girl up into the mountains, and in order to avoid charges being pressed, a deal was worked out that you would come here for a three-week evaluation to decide what treatment you need."

Henry squeezed one hand with the other, staring at them. "I didn't *take* her. She followed me. It got dark and we couldn't get back down the mountain until the sun came up. No one believes me." He kept his eyes cast down.

"Well, I believe you," Dr. R said. "And the official report here says the girl only had a sprained ankle and a few scratches. No sexual assault."

Henry raised his head, eyes wide. "What's that?"

Dr. R hesitated. This boy really was innocent. "That's when you get sexually aroused with an erect penis and you force it into a woman's vagina against her will."

Henry turned his head away. "I don't know what you are talking about."

"I believe you. You don't strike me as someone who . . ." Dr. R paused. "You have been going to a special education school?"

"I can't read. I'm stupid."

"Who told you that? You don't sound stupid to me. Is it true you can't read? Let's see if you can read even a little." He pulled open a drawer, and brought out *Life on the Mississippi* by Mark Twain. He handed it to Henry.

Henry opened the book somewhere in the middle and stared at the pages. Without looking up, he muttered, "I can't read it."

"OK, give me the book. It's a favorite of mine." Dr. R took it and began to read out loud about Mark Twain's tortuous experience trying to learn every detail of the constantly shifting Mississippi so that he could navigate a steamboat without running aground on a sand bar. His teacher was the captain of the steamboat, a man who did not tolerate ineptitude.

After reading for ten minutes, Dr. R stopped. "Could you follow that? Can you tell me what this story is about?"

"Mark Twain thought it would be easy to learn how to steer the boat on the Mississippi, but he had a hard time remembering the shape of the river, which kept changing when the sand bars moved. The captain told him how bad he was and Mark Twain felt so stupid, but he worked very hard and got better."

"So you understood the story perfectly. You just don't recognize the words on the page."

"But why couldn't Mark Twain remember?" Henry was leaning forward toward Dr. R, his eyes shining.

"What do you mean?"

"He should have gone back to the picture in his mind, the picture of each part of the river. He could have strung them all together for the whole river. Then he'd have a complete map in his mind."

"Ah, so you think in pictures?"

"Doesn't everyone?"

"No, it's a special talent. I, for instance, cannot picture things very well. I'm OK with words, but I don't have much of a visual memory."

"No! No! I'm stupid!"

Dr. R placed his hand on Henry's shoulder. Henry started to draw back but stopped. "It's hard to believe, but your teachers have evidently completely missed that you may have dyslexia—what we used to call *word blindness.* Your brain isn't good at recognizing written words and figuring out how they sound. We need to give you some tests, but I think we will find that you are . . . intelligent."

Henry looked at him for a moment, then bent forward, covering his face with both hands.

"Today is Friday," Dr. R said, "but I'll see you again on Monday. In the meantime, I'll have my nurse give you those tests. You aren't the first person to sit beside me who has been labeled mentally retarded, when in fact he isn't. My wife happens to be an expert on reading problems and she sees this all the time."

"It's not true, it can't be true." Henry straightened up, his pale face shining with tears. "I'll never learn to read. I'll never finish school. I'll never go to college." Henry, still crying, blurted out, "I want to go to the desert."

"What?" Dr. R said, startled. Perhaps this boy was not quite sane after all.

"The Mojave Desert. It is so beautiful. I have a photograph."

"Is that why you ran away so often?"

"I wanted to see the desert. I wanted to live there."

"You thought you could be free in the desert?"

Henry lowered his hands from his face and stared at the doctor. "Yeah. How did you know?

Dr. R smiled. "I just guessed. We all want to be free. Maybe you can go to the desert some day."

"It's just on the other side of the mountain, but I can't get there. In the desert there are snakes and Gila monsters and cactus wrens and . . . "

"Snakes and Gila monsters—not the most beautiful animals. What would you do in the desert if you could get there?"

"I think I could work at a gas station or I could dig with a shovel on those new highways they are starting to build."

"Is that what you really want to do?"

Henry shook his head. "I don't know. I don't know what I can do. My teachers say I'm good at art stuff. Maybe I can't do anything."

"I doubt that. You've never been given a chance. We have to try all kinds of things to find out what we're good at. Maybe I can help you discover what that is.."

"Really?" A little hope came into Henry's eyes.

"I'm afraid we have to stop now," Dr. R said, "but I'll see you on Monday, OK? We'll talk more then. Today I had to squeeze you in, but on Monday we'll have an entire hour." Henry nodded.

Dr. R pushed the buzzer on his desk and in a few seconds Juan came in. "All done, Dr. R?" he said.

"Yes, thank you, Juan." Dr. R stuck out his hand and Henry shook it, looking straight at him for a second or two. Then he stood up.

"Don't forget to put these animals back on the shelf, exactly where you found them, OK? The Star of David, too." Henry nodded, picked up the alligator and rhinoceros, one in each hand, and placed them in the niche on the wall behind. He came back for the Star of David, which he placed under the alligator, and then followed Juan out the door.

Dr. R wheeled himself over to the niche, moving the alligator aside and picking up the pale blue oval tile. It felt cool in his hand. Why did he keep it? It was his father's. His father believed in God—he sang to God. And where did that get him? It didn't get him out of the grocery store. His father didn't seem to care. He sang to God, and God ignored him.

Psychoanalytic theory said that God was just an infantile view of an all-powerful father figure, and he, like all his generation, had tried to cast aside those antiquated beliefs. But his father had been a happy man.

Dr. R cupped the Star of David in his hand and brought it up against his cheek above his beard. *The Lord is Thy Shepherd, Thou shall not want.* He needed a shepherd, but where was the Lord, if He existed? Where was He when his leg was blown off? Or when his aunts, uncles, and cousins died in concentration camps? He replaced the Star of David under the alligator and returned to his desk.

6

That afternoon Henry was sitting in the dayroom, looking at pictures in a comic book. It had to do with war and Japanese pilots, but he could not read it. The other men sat around the room, some strapped up against the wall, others reading magazines, smoking, or watching TV. The blond boy was reading a thick book with a red cover. They looked at each other, but Henry did not want to try another conversation—not yet.

One of the nurses came up to him. He had seen her in the glass box. She had even smiled and waved at him once. She was the one who had red hair popping out around her white nurse's cap. He heard her laughing several times, just as the door to the glass box opened to let someone out.

"Hi, Henry," she said, holding out her hand. "I'm Ruth Richmond, Dr. Rosenblatt's nurse." Henry stood up as he had been taught and shook her hand. It felt warm and soft. A sweet fragrance came into his nostrils, like a rose he smelled once on the way to the school bus stop.

"How do you do?" he said.

She laughed. "Well, you're a nice polite one. Come with me. Dr. R wants me to give you some tests." She led him to a little room and closed the door. "Don't worry. They don't require reading. Here, sit at this table." She sat on a stool facing a metal filing cabinet, pulled open a drawer, and peered inside. Her arms, round and white, reached in, and pulled out a folder. She picked up a pen from the table and turned a page.

"Let's see," she said. "You are Henry Hamblen and it says here you were born May 1, 1935. So you are seventeen years old."

"Uh, my father thinks I'm seventeen, but my mother says I was born in 1934, so I am eighteen. And she made me promise not to tell my father. She said, 'Just pretend you are a year younger than you really are.'"

"That's strange. This information came from the Pasadena police, who probably got it from your father. We'll have to get a copy of your birth certificate. It could make a difference if you're already eighteen. Where were you born? Oh, it says on here. Los Angeles. That makes it easy. But never mind. Let's do this test."

"Do I have to take a test? I always fail."

"Don't worry—you don't have to read anything. Just answer the questions." She crossed her legs on her stool, holding the test up close to her eyes. Henry, his head down as usual, could see her white stockings way up under her skirt. He turned his head away.

"Now I'll read out these questions, and you choose whether *a, b, c,* or *d* is the best answer."

"What?" he said, confused. She laughed.

"You better start paying attention. No daydreaming, OK?"

"OK." His face felt hot—he hoped she wasn't looking.

Most of the questions seemed easy, especially the math, but toward the end, he found he was guessing. He thought probably he was too stupid to figure out the right answers. The nurse kept smiling and nodding, as if nothing were wrong.

"I'll have to check this later," she said, "but it looks like you are much smarter than anyone thought. Do you ever remember being given an IQ test before?"

"They tried. But I couldn't read it."

"And I bet it never occurred to them to do what I just did—to read it to you?"

"No—they never did."

Nurse Ruth shook her head. "And these are supposed to be special education teachers?" They stood up to leave. Henry smelled her perfume again. She was shorter than he and looked up at him, standing just inches away. She licked her red lips. "Have you ever seen a movie with James Dean?" she said. "You look like him—but you're not mean."

"I'm not allowed to go to movies."

"Oh, that's too bad. They have movies here sometimes. Maybe you'll see him. He's adorable. I wouldn't mind flying off in a silver plane with him, like in that song. Do you know it?"

"Yes, it's on the Hit Parade. But the woman is singing about her husband flying away, isn't she?"

"Well, yes, but if my husband was James Dean, I'd be sure to be on that plane with him." Clutching the test papers against her breasts, she began singing. Henry joined in: "You belong to me." Ruth gazed up at him, her eyes shining. "You have a lovely voice."

Suddenly the door opened and a grey-haired nurse came in, looking angry. "Miss Richmond, I've warned you. Everyone can hear you out in the corridor."

Ruth stepped away from Henry. "Oops, I'm sorry, Miss Gordon. Don't worry. I'll be off work in another hour. Do you want to come to a party with Patsy and me? Everyone will be singing there."

The other nurse turned to leave. "You can joke, but this is going to be one more black mark on your record. The impertinence!" She was gone.

"Some people don't know how to have fun," Ruth said. Henry stared at the closed door.

"Was she mad at me?"

Ruth shook her head. "No, of course not. It's me she's mad at. If it weren't for Dr. R, I'd just walk away from this job and go back to plain nursing. The staff here is nuts." Henry looked down. "Sorry, I shouldn't have said that. Don't tell anyone, OK? Let's go back to the day room. Dr. R is going to be very interested in this."

"That nurse is going to tell the doctor that I'm a bad person, and I'm going to get in trouble," Henry said.

Nurse Ruth patted him on the shoulder. "No, no, you didn't do anything wrong. I'm sorry if I scared you."

Henry felt his body shaking. "When is the doctor coming back? He said Monday, but I don't know what day it is now."

"Today is Friday," she said. "He'll be back in three days. He's wonderful, isn't he? All the men here love him. Do you see that blond boy over there? You should talk to him—he adores Dr. R. His name is Björn. He's older than you. He stutters a lot, but he's a nice boy, too." Henry saw the boy with his head bent over between his legs, hands holding his head, fingers splayed.

She walked in front of him as they entered the day room, humming again, her hips swinging side to side in her white skirt. Henry cast his eyes down to the grey linoleum floor. "Goodbye," she said, waving, as she opened the door to the glass box. He wanted to follow her, to listen to her sing, to smell her perfume, but the door closed behind her.

7

The next day Henry sat again in the dayroom, trying to shut out the misery around him. He looked at tattered comic books and magazines, or traveled to the desert, the golden desert, with only a whisper of wind in the Joshua trees. He spoke to no one, looked at no one. Days had gone by, and his mother still had not come.

Perhaps it was the noise that left Henry trembling at the end of dinner—the clanking dishes, the loud angry voices. As he followed a line of men being led back to their ward, he passed a tiny old man in a wheelchair, screaming and weeping, repeating over and over, "They never told me my wife is dead, they never told me—she was coming to see me today."

Another attendant, large with black hairy hands, came rushing up to him, yelling, "Shut up, you silly old man." The man screamed even louder, and the attendant began shaking him, repeating, "Shut up, shut up." When the man continued screaming, the attendant slapped him hard, not once, but three times.

Henry, breaking from the line, grabbed the attendant from behind, shouting, "Stop it, stop it," and when the man whirled around, his fist raised, Henry slugged him as hard as he could. The attendant's nose was streaming blood, and he yelled, "Help, help!" In a moment, three attendants had hold of Henry as he struggled to get free.

"You shouldn't hit that poor old man," Henry shouted. "You should be arrested."

He was hauled off, forced into a strait jacket, although he had gone limp, and then strapped onto his bed. A nurse he had never seen before appeared with a large needle. He looked at her, not speaking, as he lay there with tears streaming down his face. "You don't need this," she said. She put her needle back in a box, patted his arm and left.

"Now, you're in for it, kid," Juan said to him as he locked up the ward for the night. None of the other men spoke to Henry as he lay there. Some began snoring; others seemed to be wide awake, staring like him into the darkness.

•••

The next morning, released from his strait jacket, Henry sat by himself after breakfast in a corner of the day room, gazing at the ceiling. He gave a start when Juan poked him. "Hey, Henry, it's time to go see the doctor."

"Is it Monday?" he asked, jumping up. He followed Juan down the corridor, trying not to look at his fellow patients lined up along the wall.

As Juan opened a door, he said, "Yes—Monday." Henry entered the room and stopped. It was not the same room. This one had white walls. The doctor behind the desk was not the same doctor. He was a little man with flattened black hair. He barely glanced at Henry; he was reading something in a folder in front of him.

"Sit down," the doctor ordered. The only empty chair was the one in front of the massive desk behind which this doctor glared at him. Henry sat down, huddled over.

"You can look at me, young man," the new doctor said. "I am Dr. Wilson. I am taking over your case, because Dr. Rosenblatt has had to go away. Can you understand what I am saying?"

"Yes," Henry mumbled, still looking down.

"Let me point out right away," the doctor said in a quiet voice, "if you want to do well here, I'd advise you not to repeat your violent behavior of yesterday." Henry waited. "I want to ask you some questions. I see here that you have been going to a special education school. Do you know why?"

"Because I can't read."

"That's right. That's what it says here. Do you know why you can't read?"

"When I look at words, I can't remember what they sound like."

"Have you really tried, or weren't you able to follow your teachers' instructions?" Henry did not like this doctor. "Answer me!" The doctor's shrill voice made Henry wince.

"I want to learn to read, but I can't understand the words in books."

"The past two years you have been running away whenever you could, getting picked up by the police, and no doubt causing your father a great deal of worry. Why are you doing this?"

Henry saw a brick wall curving around Dr. Wilson, so high they could not see each other or speak to each other. And what was the use of trying to talk over that brick wall? Even if he shouted, he wouldn't be heard.

"Henry, answer my question!" Henry straightened up, staring beyond Dr. Wilson, imagining a mountain on the other side of the brick wall. "Answer me at once!" Henry's eyes looked far away, his back tight and straight.

Dr. Wilson stood up, came around the desk and yelled at him, "Answer me, answer me!" Henry clutched his head in his hands, covering his ears. Dr. Wilson suddenly stopped, returned to his side of the desk and pushed a buzzer. Two Negro aides came through the door. "Take this patient to the shock shop. He has to learn a few things."

The men dragged him out of his chair, and then each took one of his arms, bending it behind his back, shoving him out the door.

"But I didn't do anything!" Henry shouted.

The doctor was already writing, "That's not what this report is going to say."

Henry was taken to a tiny room with no windows, so when the door was closed and locked he was in total darkness, his hands handcuffed behind him. He sat down on the floor, then rolled on his side and wept, crying out, "Mom, mom, help me. Help me!"

Soon the door opened, and he was yanked to his feet again by the two aides and led into the corridor. There was the doctor he hated, his hands fluttering at his sides. "Maybe tomorrow you will feel more like talking to me," the doctor said.

Henry raised his head and looked directly into Dr. Wilson's eyes. Dr. Wilson shrank back, meeting his gaze for half a second before glancing away.

"Take him upstairs."

Henry did not resist as the aides pushed him into an elevator that slowly rose to a higher floor where Henry had never been. Two men in the room shoved him onto a metal table next to a blinking machine, then removed his handcuffs as well as his clothes. He was strapped to the cold, hard table. Wires were attached with other straps to his head and body. He struggled a moment against the strap. A searing jolt hit him and then he remembered nothing more.

•••

His first awareness came when he sensed his ribs pressing tight against something as he inhaled. Then he knew that he was tied down, his ribs meeting the taut sheets with each breath. His head was empty. He could not remember who he was or where he was. His breath spread into his limbs, into his head, his heart. His ribs expanded, then relaxed. Perhaps he was dreaming and would wake up soon—but who was dreaming? His head ached but even that pain seemed far away, belonging to someone else.

Then he felt the release of the sheets that held him. A voice was telling him to sit on the edge of the bed. Henry felt it took every ounce of strength he had to raise himself up. And he was naked.

"I'm supposed to check you for scrapes, kid. And no trouble, OK?" A man with a brown face smiled.

Henry winced as the man applied a red liquid from a bottle to painful places on his knees and elbows. He did not want to look at them. "Where am I? How did I get hurt?" he asked, his mouth moving with difficulty.

"You're in Stanyon Hospital. I'm Juan. I guess you don't remember me anymore? You had electroshock therapy. They say it's to calm you down. Yeah, right. Your body gets thrown around—what do they call it? Oh yeah, convulsions. The straps don't stop you hurting yourself. In fact, they cause these scrapes."

"I don't know. I don't remember."

"Here, put on these clothes. You've got to eat some breakfast. Then you're going to Dr. Wilson's office."

Dr. Wilson—who was he? Juan helped him into his clothes and led him to the cafeteria, where he ate the lumpy oatmeal. Juan took his arm and walked him down the corridor lined with silent men staring into space.

As he entered Dr. Wilson's office, every muscle tightened. He slumped down in a chair, guided by Juan's firm hand. He looked at the floor, his body bent toward it.

"So, Henry," Dr. Wilson began, "you seem to be quieter now." He paused. Henry said nothing. "Your father is coming to get you tomorrow. You should be strong enough to be discharged by then."

Henry looked up. "I'm going home?"

"Yes, perhaps."

"I want my mother."

Dr. Wilson hesitated. "She's ill at the moment, but you'll see her soon."

"I don't want to," Henry mumbled. "I want my mother."

"Don't worry, son. Your father knows what is best for you." Dr. Wilson smiled. He was lying.

"Where is my mother?" The doctor pursed his lips and said nothing.

Juan reappeared and helped Henry stand and led him back to the dayroom. Everthing seemed jumbled. Why was he here with these strange men? Did the doctor say he was going home? Or did he dream that? He slept in a chair in the dayroom. He followed the others to the cafeteria but could not eat. He slept again until it was time to go to bed. And once in bed, he fell instantly into oblivion.

8

As the train pulled into the San Bernadino station, Dr. R scanned the people waiting on the platform. Most held suitcases and were about to board the train. He was looking for Charlie, who always brought the wheelchair up onto the platform. He saw a woman with long dark hair pushing an empty wheelchair—perhaps for another vet, someone else with a missing limb? He looked again and realized it was Estelle. But what was she doing here and why hadn't Charlie come? Something had to be wrong. He had not recognized her at first, because her black hair, usually contained in a bun at the back of her head, was hanging down her cheeks, giving her an out-of-control look. She had a porter with her, who ran up the stairs to take his suitcase and crutches. As Dr. R. came down, using the handrails for support as he hopped from step to step, Estelle moved toward him with the wheelchair

Dr. R looked at her worried face. "What's wrong, for God's sake? Is it my mother? Max? Your mother? Charlie?"

"No, they're fine. It's that boy, Henry, you told me about."

"What about him?"

"I'll tell you when we're in the car. Please hurry," she said to the porter.

"Yes, ma'am. Where ya car parked?"

"Right in front." The long-legged porter strode off with the bag and crutches, Estelle pushing the wheelchair after him.

Dr. R transferred to the front seat of their green Oldsmobile. The porter opened the trunk, collapsed the wheelchair, added the suitcase, and slammed the lid shut. He went off whistling.

"What about his tip?"

"I gave it to him while we were waiting." Estelle shifted into first and accelerated quickly, barely stopping at the frequent stop signs.

"Thank God you're home," As she turned a corner, Dr. R had to grab the strap above the passenger door.

"Can't you slow down? I don't have two feet to brace with."

"Sorry." She tightly grasped the steering wheel as she swung around another corner.

"Are we going home?"

"No, we're going to Pasadena."

"Pasadena? Why the hell Pasadena? I've had a bad night on the sleeper train and you want to take me to Pasadena? *Oy! Bist meshugeh?*"

"No, I'm not crazy." Estelle sped up as the road straightened into the two-lane highway going west. At a red light, she brought both hands to her hair, quickly pulling it back and twisting it into a bun again, holding it while she repositioned the two tortoise-shell combs that held the bun in place.

"Forget your hair," he shouted. "Just tell me what's going on."

Estelle took hold of the steering wheel again, let out the clutch and soon shifted up to third gear. "I can't think with my hair like that. Here's the story: Ruth Richmond telephoned a few hours ago, completely hysterical. She went in early to work after being off for the weekend and saw in the log that this Henry Hamblen is being discharged today. His father is picking him up. You weren't there, and your boss was attending a meeting at that horrible place where rebellious Hollywood wives get sent by their arrogant, philandering film star husbands."

"Camarillo on Catalina Island? But go on."

"Ruth wondered why Henry was being discharged—there was a court order for a three-week evaluation, and it's only been one week. She got hold of Henry's file and saw that Dr. Wilson had noted that Henry had assaulted an attendant. So, Dr. Wilson sent him for electroshock and wrote that he would be a good candidate for a lobotomy due to his violent behavior."

"Dr. Wilson is a sniveling, two-faced S.O.B. Why would Henry be discharged—and especially if he's been violent? That never happens. And I wonder what made Henry violent? He seemed more depressed than angry."

Estelle shook her head. "Ruth heard Dr. Wilson telling another nurse he was doing a lobotomy in his Pasadena clinic today, and she put two and two together. She then called Dr. Wilson's clinic and made up some cock-and-bull story to verify it was to be Henry and the time of the appointment. We have two hours—I think we can make it."

"Dr. R looked down the long straight highway in front of them. "I smell a rat: Henry's father must have pulled strings with the authorities in Pasadena. And he's in cahoots with Dr. Wilson. They knew damn well once I got back I'd be able to stop a lobotomy at Stanyon." He turned his eyes from the passing orange groves to the face of his wife. "*Oy*, so that's why we're going to Pasadena? But what can we do?"

Estelle quickly glanced at him. "I have a plan. Ruth tried what she could. She risked her job and called the father, told him the results of the IQ test. The father told her she didn't know what she was talking about and that she'd better not interfere. Now it's up to us."

"But what can we do?"

"First, I thought we could find Henry's mother, but I found out . . ."

"What I already know. Bob McKensie called me at the Mark Hopkins."

"I gave him your room number when he tried to call you at home. I explained that your boss made you go at the last minute to that conference in San Francisco."

Dr. R pounded his fist on the dashboard in front of him. "If only Dr. Peters hadn't come down with the flu, I never would have had to go to San Francisco and this would never have happened."

Estelle reached over and patted his thigh. "Easy does it. '*Ifs*' aren't going to help us now."

"It's a weird coincidence," Dr. R said, placing his hand on top of Estelle's. "Bob is treating Henry's mother at his sanatorium in Pasadena. She had some kind of breakdown, not too serious, it seems, but her husband wants to keep her there, out of the way, for a while."

"So no mother to intervene," Estelle said, replacing her hand on the steering wheel. Dr. R rubbed his face with both hands.

"I don't see what we can do. Henry's a minor, so his father has jurisdiction. And the mother is out of the picture for the moment. "

"Ah, but Ruth found out something very interesting. When she was giving Henry that I.Q. test, she asked him to verify the birthdate she had for him. He said, 'It's the right day of the month, but the year is wrong. My mom says I'm eighteen.' He knew he had been born in L.A., so Ruth got on the phone and checked his date of birth—May 1, 1934."

"My God, that makes all the difference. Didn't the poor kid ever have birthday parties? How could the father get it wrong? Well, now I just have to convince Henry not to walk through those clinic doors. If I can do that, the father can't force him—Henry's no longer a minor."

"You'll take him back to Stanyon?"

"I don't know. Probably."

"Probably? What's the alternative? Never mind, we're near the clinic."

"As soon as you park, get out my wheelchair," Dr. R said. "May God help us. This may be hopeless, but I have to try."

•••

Early that morning, Dick Hamblen pulled into the grounds of Stanyon, fifteen minutes before the appointed time. He rolled down a window and lit a cigarette. He had tried to persuade Clive Wilson to bring Henry to the clinic, so that Dick himself wouldn't have to do it. Clive said he had to sign the consent papers. He had even asked Clive to deliver Henry to the sanatorium after the lobotomy. Clive had agreed to that at least. After that Dick hoped he would never have to look at his son again.

Dick knew he was going to have a few rough hours; he was going to have to lie to Henry, but then it would be over, and he could feel safe again. If Henry could be persuaded that they were going home, he wouldn't cause trouble, would he? He wouldn't attack his own father while they were driving, would he? When it was over, he'd have to convince Edna that the doctors had insisted on this, that Henry was extremely dangerous.

Dick looked with distaste at the stubby fingers holding the cigarette. His hand was shaking. He needed a drink but he knew he had to wait. He snubbed out his cigarette and climbed out of the car, looking up at the tall brick edifice in front of him. A face peered out from one of the windows, visible behind the bars. Was it Henry?

Entering the reception area, Dick spoke to the nurse seated behind a thick glass partition. She picked up the telephone to announce his arrival, and he sat down in one of the cold metal chairs lining the wall. There were no magazines, no water cooler, nothing. He could just see the top of the nurse's white cap back behind a high counter. He waited, shifting restlessly on the hard seat. He wanted to be ready to smile, to be calm and friendly with Henry, just as Dr. Wilson had instructed him.

•••

Henry covered his ears as Juan rattled the keys and slammed the three heavy doors leading out. But he was going home, and soon he would see his mother and Jake. And for an instant, as he glimpsed his father huddled in a chair on the opposite side of the room, he was glad to see him.

"Here's your bag," Juan said. "Good luck. I'll miss you. You're a nice kid."

Henry took the bag and tried to smile. "Goodbye."

"Hello, son. We're going home," his father said and cleared his throat. He winced, took his handkerchief out of his pocket and wiped his flushed face.

"Where's mom?" Henry's eyes shifted away from his father, looking around the room.

"Don't worry. You'll see her soon. She's been a little sick."

Henry nodded and then ducked his head.

"The car's right in front," his father said.

"OK," Henry said, but he half-turned back towards the nurse behind her glass and took a step towards her.

"No, this way, son," his father said, opening the door. Henry slowly moved past him, aware that he was a whole head taller. "Follow me," his father said. "Here, I'll put your bag in the trunk. You sit up front next to me." Henry opened the passenger door and sat down. His father came around the other side and climbed in.

"Here we go," his father said, lighting a cigarette. He started the engine and shifted into first gear. As they pulled out of the gate in the high brick wall, Henry saw low mountains not far away, but they seemed to disappear as he stared at them.

"I knew you wanted to go home and I was able to arrange it," his father said. "I hope you're grateful, after all the trouble you have caused." For once he didn't sound angry but maybe kind of sad.

Henry gazed straight forward, not wanting to look at his father, whose elbow brushed Henry's arm as he tapped his cigarette ash into the ashtray. "How long does it take to drive home? Is mom there?"

"About two hours. But we aren't going straight home. We're going to Dr. Wilson's office first."

"Who is he?"

"He's the doctor you saw at the hospital."

"That mean one?" Henry felt fear rise up to his throat with the vague memory of a little man with glasses, shaking a fist at him. "I don't want to see that doctor. I want to go home. You said I'm going home." Henry turned and clutched Dick's upper arm with both hands. The car swerved, almost crossing into the oncoming lane.

"For Christ's sake, let go!" his father yelled. He slowed for a stop sign on the edge of a little town. "Let go, dammit!" Henry released his father's arm, slid towards the window, and while his father was shifting down, suddenly opened the door. One leg was already on the asphalt as he turned to leap out.

"Henry, please. I'm taking you home. We're just stopping for a few minutes. Then we'll go home. Please get back in the car. Please." His father's voice was nice—he wasn't mad this time. Henry pulled his leg back into the car and slammed the door shut. He remained facing away, fingers on the door handle. His father let out the clutch and the car moved forward. Henry heard him blow out a breath and then swallow noisily.

"Dr. Wilson has promised to help us. He'll sign all the necessary papers so you won't have to go back to Stanyon."

Henry said nothing, still facing away.

"We'll be at Dr. Wilson's clinic for a short time, and then you can go home. He'll do a little treatment on you, sign the papers, and then everything will be fine."

"What treatment?"

Henry heard his father's exasperated sigh. "Oh, it's like a vaccination. Something that will make you feel comfortable."

"My smallpox vaccination left a big scar on my arm."

"This won't leave a scar."

Henry turned away from the window and looked down, clenching his hands together. "OK. And then I can go home to my own room?"

"Yes, you can rest."

"Will mom be there?"

"Maybe tomorrow. She's staying at a special sanatorium until she feels better."

"But she'll be there tomorrow?"

"Yes, she should be."

"Thanks, Dad. I really want to see her." Tears were running down his cheeks.

"Everything's going to be OK. Don't cry, Henry." His father sounded like he was going to cry, too.

"I'm sorry." Henry wiped his cheeks with the back of his hand.

His father cleared his throat and then reached for the knob on the radio. "Hey, let's see if we can pick up some sports news."

"OK," Henry said. He closed his eyes and tried not to listen.

After a while, Henry said, "Dad, I'm hungry. Can we stop for a hamburger?"

"No, son, we have to get to that appointment. We'll eat afterward."

"OK, but I'm really hungry."

"You'll have to wait. It won't take long." And then Henry heard his father mutter "Damn, damn, damn."

•••

As soon as they pulled into a parking lot between two buildings and turned off the engine, a voice called out, "Mr. Hamblen."

Henry looked to the left where a bearded man in a wheelchair was rolling towards them. He had seen that man somewhere before, but he wasn't sure where. His father started to open the door but stopped and rolled down the window.

"Who the hell are you?" his father yelled.

"I want to talk to you," the man in the wheelchair said.

"Get out of my way!" his father repeated. Henry's memory began to coalesce. It was the doctor with the pink room. He heard the doctor's voice, but he could not see him there below his father.

"I am Dr. Rosenblatt, the chief psychiatrist for the men's ward where your son was at Stanyon."

"Dr. Wilson is his doctor now. My son has been discharged. What are you doing here?" His father's hand was on the door handle, but he did not open the door.

"Dr. Wilson had no right to discharge your son in my absence. If you don't let me take him back, you could be in big trouble."

His father's face turned almost purple as he stared in front of him, and Henry wondered if he was going to start the car and drive away.

Then Henry turned and looked across his father out the open window toward that voice.

"I'm not going to listen to you," his father said. "Get out of my way. We're going in."

Henry squeezed his eyes shut.

"Your wife agreed? Did she sign a consent form?"

"Goddamn you, you SOB, that's none of your business!" His father opened the door, pushing his foot against the wheelchair to shove it away. It skidded backwards a few inches, so that Henry could then see the doctor. His father slammed the car door shut again.

The doctor raised both hands in front of him as if to ward off a blow, then quickly lowered them. "OK, Mr. Hamblen. You're probably planning to put him in a private institution after this lobotomy. Do you realize it will cost you a fortune to have him in a private sanatorium for the rest of his life?"

"I know what I'm doing," his father said. "And what right do you have to accost me like this? I'll call the police. They know me here."

"They certainly do. That is obvious."

"So back off, Doctor Whoever-You-Are."

"Your son is no longer a minor. I can prove he is perfectly sane. He can make his own decisions now."

"You ignorant bastard," Mr. Hamblen said. "He's only seventeen."

"You're wrong," the doctor said. "He is eighteen. It's a wise father who knows the age of his own son. He was born in 1934. We have proof."

"You're all stupid idiots. My older son was born in 1932. And Henry came two years later—oh, my God, that would be 1934. How did I get that wrong?" He gripped the steering wheel, putting his head against it. He raised it up again, staring straight ahead, not looking at the doctor below him. "My wife, the bitch, she's been telling me all along that he was seventeen his last birthday." He was silent again. "That doesn't matter. Henry will do what I tell him."

Henry began shaking. This doctor was not nice. He was going to take him back to that horrible hospital and not let him go home. "Don't let him take me," he said. His father looked at him, his face twisted into a grimace.

"He won't. We have an appointment—in there," his father said.

"Henry!" Dr. R shouted. "Your father wants to have you lobotomized. The doctor will stick needles into your eye sockets and cut away part of your brain. You won't be able to do anything after that."

"Where's my mother?" Henry cried out. He did not want to go with this doctor. He would rather die than go back to that hospital. The doctor had turned into his enemy. His father had to help him.

"I won't cause trouble if you just let me go home," Henry said. "Please, please." He saw his father squeeze his eyes shut, his jaw bulging.

"Henry," the doctor shouted again, "I'm asking you to come with me. Don't go in there. You're eighteen now. Your father can't force you to have this horrible thing done to you."

"I don't want to go in there."

"Then don't. Come with me. I know it's a big leap, but it will save your life."

"Can I see my mother soon?"

"Yes, her doctor says she's almost well."

Henry's father turned toward him. "If you go with him, I'll be sure you never see her again."

Henry stared at him. He knew his father was lying. All day he had been lying. Henry knew that tone of voice. And he did not want to go anywhere near that mean Doctor Wilson.

“Stop telling lies!” he yelled at his father, opening the door on his side. He slammed the door and found himself, to his own astonishment, walking away from his father’s car.

“Follow me,” the doctor said, wheeling toward a green car parked behind them.

“Damn you, Henry,” his father said. “You aren’t my son anymore. You’ve destroyed this family. Go. Go back to Stanyon. You’ll be locked up where you can’t do any more damage.” He rolled up the window on his side, started his car, and drove off, jerking wildly as he shifted gears.

Suddenly alone, Henry wondered if he could run from there—anywhere?

“Hurry,” the doctor said. Henry’s legs were trembling. There was no strength in them. “Take the handles of my wheelchair,” the doctor said. Henry felt he was going to fall. He grabbed the handles and the doctor pushed on the wheels. Together they reached the green car. A woman stood outside with the trunk lid up. As soon as Henry climbed into the back seat and the doctor shifted from the wheelchair to the front seat, the woman folded up the wheelchair and put it in the trunk. She jumped in, slammed her door, and started the engine.

“Let’s get out of here,” the doctor said. “Oh, my God. There’s Dr. Wilson, the bastard, coming out the door. Step on it, Estelle.” The woman backed up, then shifted and pulled out rapidly into the tree-lined street. Henry did not look back, keeping his head down.

“If he sees me, it could ruin everything,” the doctor said.

Henry collapsed against the window, his eyes closed, only aware that his body was being jarred by the turns and sudden stops. Then he heard the doctor’s voice.

“Estelle, this is Henry Hamblen. Henry, my wife, Mrs. Rosenblatt.” Henry opened his eyes. In front of him he could see black hair in a bun, some pearls around her neck, a pale blue sweater. He closed his eyes again. He did not want to listen to the doctor. He wasn’t going home.

Where was he going? "Henry," the doctor said, "you are not going back to Stanyon. We are going to take you home to our house."

"What?" his wife yelled.

"I'm sorry, Estelle. There was no time to tell you my plan. I didn't really know it myself. We'll have to discuss this later. We'll find a way. I'm sorry." The wife kept driving, saying nothing more.

Henry's eyes remained closed. Was he being kidnapped? His whole body was limp.

The doctor's voice seemed far away. "I had to take you," the doctor said. "Some day you will understand."

Henry opened his eyes. Long rows of orange trees were flowing past them, making him dizzy. He did not understand what the doctor was saying.

"One thing more, Henry," the doctor said, twisting to face the back seat. If you want to leave, you can. You can come back, too. You're free. But whatever you do, I beg you, don't go back to your father. I can't trust him right now."

Henry repeated to himself the words *free, free, free—free to go to the desert.*

At that moment, the car stopped at a red light. *Free, free, free—he could be free.* He reached for the door handle, opened the door, dashed across the highway, and ran down the crossroad, toward the mountains, toward the desert.

•••

Dr. R stared at Henry's receding figure.

"Oh, my God," Estelle yelled. "Run after him." She pulled over to the side of the road. "What am I saying? Of course you can't." She hesitated. "Shall we drive after him?"

"Yes, quickly." Estelle started to pull out onto the highway to make a left turn onto the crossroad.

"Stop," Dr. R said. "We're going to sit here. Sit here and pray. After what I just said, it would be hypocritical to drive after him. Isn't that right? Am I crazy?"

Estelle turned to face him. "Yes, you are crazy and yes, I agree, we aren't going after him." They looked down the road and saw a tiny speck moving further and further away. Dr. R reached over for Estelle's hand. "This is terrible. He can't survive on his own right now. He has nothing with him. I'll be responsible."

"We may have to go after him," Estelle said.

After a moment of silence, Dr. R. said, "I guess if there is no sign of him in about ten minutes, we'd better head down there. I don't know . . . I don't know what to do." He felt defeated. Estelle's hand trembled in his. They waited, both looking down the road.

•••

Running, running as fast as he could, Henry passed orange trees repeating themselves in endless rows. There were no cars or people. As he gasped to draw air into his lungs, his legs began to collapse under him. He had to slow to a walk, barely able to put one foot in front of another. He looked up toward the mountains, so far away.

He stopped, his feet apart, his body weaving from side to side. He looked down a row of orange trees. Their dark shadows invited him to enter. No one would find him, no one could hurt him in there. He walked into the shadows and sat at the base of a tree. He felt the cool air moving in and out of his lungs.

He closed his eyes, leaning his head against the trunk of the tree. Was he going to slip away into some unknown world? The dirt was soft under him. Almost no sun penetrated. He could go further in. No one was going to find him. He could go to sleep here. Since he wasn't strong enough to go to the desert, why not stay here forever?

He opened his eyes. Directly in front of him, a robin was looking at him as if to say, *well, what are you doing here?*

"I won't bother you," Henry said. The robin made one small hop towards him, and then cocked his head. Henry smiled. "You are cute," he told the robin. The robin hopped around, looking for a worm, and when he pulled one from the ground, he flew away.

"You could have eaten your worm here, you silly bird," Henry called after him. He stood up, his legs still shaking. What had happened? He could not remember why he was there in the orange grove. What had the doctor and his wife said to him? They wanted to take him to their house. They said he didn't have to stay. Maybe he'd better go there until he got stronger.

He looked toward the road. But probably they had driven off! He walked with unsteady steps out of the orange grove and turned back down the road. The pavement rose slightly so that he could not see as far as the highway. No one in sight. What could he do? Where could he go?

Then he heard the sound of an engine. He waited. A car came over the hump. It was . . . the green car! In a moment, it pulled alongside him, and the doctor's wife rolled down her window. "Hop in, Henry. We need to get home."

Henry opened the door behind her and climbed in. She turned the car around and they drove back to the highway.

"Thank you, Henry," the doctor said. Closing his eyes, Henry leaned back and let the blackness descend.

9

The sound of gravel crunching under the car's tires made Henry open his eyes. They were on a driveway with an immense lawn on one side. At the bottom stood a grey shingled, two-story house with a vine of deep red flowers twisted around white wooden columns in front. A man and woman came out the front door as the car stopped—the man, tall with a black moustache, the woman in a white apron. The man opened the trunk and brought the doctor his crutches. Henry did not move. He squeezed his eyes shut again.

"Henry?" he heard the doctor's voice say. And then, automatically, as if he were being pushed, he climbed out.

"Come on in," the man with the moustache said. Henry followed, and then turning back, he saw the doctor and his wife standing next to the car, talking and waving their arms. The man and woman stood there next to Henry in the hall, also looking out the open front door. Finally, the doctor and his wife came in, both breathing hard.

"Charlie and Agnes, this is Henry Hamblen," the doctor said. "He's going to live with us for a while. Henry, this is Charlie and Agnes Ortega. They look after us." Charlie nodded and Agnes smiled.

"Come upstairs," the doctor's wife said. "I'll show you your room." She led him up a broad stairway with glistening wood banisters. He felt he was dragging his body along—each stair seemed almost too high to step onto. For a moment he thought he was going to fall over backwards, back down the stairs and . . . where was he going once he got to the top? Maybe they were lying and he was going to be locked up again. Grown-ups often lied.

At the top of the stairs, he saw doors on both sides of a long corridor. The wife paused at the first door on the right, which was open. She beckoned him to follow. The afternoon sun lit the entire room through a long row of windows. In one corner stood a desk with cubbyholes covered with stacks of children's books and with two purple wooden chairs.

"This is my office," the wife said. "I tutor kids in reading here." Henry looked away. He hated children's books with their ugly pictures and words he couldn't read. Further down the room he saw an electric train set, the track laid out in a figure eight with little buildings, trees, a black locomotive, yellow cars, and a red caboose—just what he had always wanted. He took one step toward it, and then stopped.

The doctor's wife stood next to him, looking toward the train with him. "The boys keep coming back because of the train. It's a reward for struggling with learning to read. In fact, it is my husband who plays the most with the train, even though it's so hard for him to get down on the floor and back up again. When he's had a really tough day at Stanyon—well, that's pretty much every day—he comes home and runs his train."

She hesitated. "He used to do it with our son Jacob." She stopped again. "Jacob died while my husband was serving in the Navy in the South Pacific. This was Jacob's playroom. He would be fourteen if he were still alive today." Henry lowered his head, not wanting to look at her. Why was she telling him this? "You will meet Max, our adopted son, who is fourteen, too. He'll be home from school soon. But come, let me show you your room."

The doctor's wife then led him out and down the hall to a door on the left. Inside he saw a small bedroom with dark furniture—a bed with a high headboard and bedposts, covered with a green and blue patchwork quilt. Against a wall stood a dresser with a white doily on top. Above it on the wall hung an oval mirror with a dark wooden frame.

Henry went over to the windows where white lace curtains brushed his arm from an afternoon breeze. Outside he saw more lawn and beyond another orange grove, the trunks of the trees disappearing into afternoon shadows. Could he go there?

"There's a big closet you can walk into," the doctor's wife said, pointing to a closed door. "And the bathroom is here." Realizing he needed to use it, he wished this woman would go away. He walked inside. Everywhere was pale yellow tile, a huge bathtub on lion's feet and shiny chrome fixtures. Big white towels hung on chrome rods.

"It's a nice yellow, don't you think?" she asked.

He said nothing and left the bathroom. The doctor's wife followed, then walked toward the door. She stopped and turned towards him. He could not look at her. "We'll try to get your things sent to you."

My things? Will someone send me Jake?

"You can call me Mrs. R." Henry had his back to her, but he sensed she had not left yet. "You must be hungry. Do you want something to eat?" Henry shook his head. He just wanted her to leave. "We'll check on you at dinnertime, then."

She closed the door. He went straight to the bathroom to urinate and then washed his hands for a long time. He held the soft towel against his face, left the bathroom, and threw himself on the bed, not even removing his sneakers. His mind formed stretched-out thoughts with long, black spaces between each word: *She was trying to sound nice, but now she's mad at me. . . . I bet she doesn't want me here. . . . That's why they were fighting. They will send me back to the hospital. What's wrong with my legs? I can't run away with these legs.* And then he slept.

•••

Later that night, as the Rosenblatts were preparing to go to bed, Estelle sat at her dressing table on her upholstered stool, brushing her hair. Sitting on the bed in his pajamas, Dr. R watched the reflection of her face in the dressing table mirror. She brushed with quick, jabbing strokes, as if her hair had to be punished for some crime.

"You're upset, aren't you?" he asked. "And yet you were the one who talked me into this."

"He's unresponsive—not a good sign," she said, laying down the brush with a thud. "Maybe his father was right to be afraid. I never thought of him staying here, actually living with us. I thought you would keep him at Stanyon until you found a place for him to go."

"First I have to get rid of Dr. Wilson. And besides, you're just the one to see if he can actually learn to read."

"I don't know. I don't think I've heard him say a word yet." She resumed her brushing with slow strokes, as she lifted long strands off her breast. She paused. "I have to admit, when I look into that sweet face with those blue eyes and lovely blond hair, I don't see a speck of meanness or craziness. I just wish he would talk. But looks can be deceptive. We can't put Max at risk." She turned and faced Dr. R. "But I'm proud of what you did today. That took guts." She came over to the bed, her white satin bathrobe undulating. Dr. R felt his blood surge.

"Praise from my beautiful wife," he said smiling. He leaned on an elbow to look at her as she removed the dressing gown and climbed into bed, pulling the blanket up to her chin.

"I knew you could do what you did today. You weren't afraid and now I mustn't be afraid, either. There aren't many men who would take the risk you did." She turned on her side and nuzzled her face against his neck.

Dr. R covered her face with kisses, murmuring, "You gave me the courage. We may be in for all kinds of trouble. But we'll face it together. Without you, I don't know what I would do."

"And here I am," she said, snuggling closer.

A few moments later, he added, "Aren't you exhausted?"

"Yes, but never mind, this is waking me up.." She suddenly pulled back. "I have to put my diaphragm in. I almost forgot."

"I wish you would forget," Dr. R said, watching her sit up and move toward the bathroom.

"Now, don't start that again," she said crossly. Damn, the mood was broken, he thought, waiting for her. She returned, her nightgown over her arm. She laid it at the end of the bed, slid in beside him and began unbuttoning his pajama top. "Let's see. Where were we?" she murmured.

Some hours later, he found himself on the *New Jersey*. He was standing on the deck with other officers and Barney, his medical assistant and buddy. Barney was joking that the only ailments they were treating were constipation, hangovers, and gonorrhea. Everyone was laughing. Suddenly an alarm sounded. A loudspeaker blared: *KAMIKAZE—TAKE COVER*. Guns blasted, men ran, and in seconds, there was a roar, an explosion, men screaming. Barney was lying on top of him, ripped open, bleeding. Dr. R was in agonizing pain, losing consciousness.

"Wake up, Josh, wake up," Estelle's voice was shouting. She was shaking him. "You're having that dream again—you're screaming."

"Oh, God, I'm sorry, Estelle. Why did he throw himself on top of me? If he had stayed where he was with the other men, he would have lived."

"You've got to let that go. It wasn't your fault. If he could, Barney would be thanking you for adopting Max."

"If Barney hadn't died, Mary wouldn't have killed herself. Max would not have been an orphan."

"Estelle reached over and stroked the side of his head. "Do I have to say it again? She was already unstable. You yourself said that when you came back and met her." Dr. R turned toward her.

"Hold me, Estelle. I'm sorry I woke you up." Estelle slid an arm under him.

"Go to sleep, darling."

10

When he opened his eyes, Henry heard no moans or cries from tormented men. And then he remembered where he was. He was in a house with the doctor and his wife.. He turned onto his back and stared at a splash of sunlight on the while ceiling. He got up and went to the bathroom, staggering on legs that still trembled. He pulled off his shoes and clothes, and took a long bath. He had no clean clothes and he hated putting his dirty clothes back on.

Suddenly he felt very hungry, but how was he going to get anything to eat? He didn't even know where the kitchen was. He opened the door a few inches to peek out. No one in sight. He went along the hall, down the stairs, and there at the bottom the man with the moustache was trying to open a back door from outside while carrying an armload of firewood. Henry went over and opened the door.

"*Muchos gracias,*" the man said. "I have to make a fire in the living room over here. Go through the dining room and the kitchen's just behind. My wife will get you some breakfast. Everyone's going nuts getting ready for Thanksgiving."

"Thanksgiving? Today?" Henry heard his voice, raspy and choked up.

"It sure is. *Adios,* I'm going to put this wood down."

Henry went into the dining room and passed around a long, dark wood table with an enormous glass chandelier above it. Beyond was a swinging door to the kitchen.

Inside, he saw the woman who had come out the front door when he arrived. She was sewing up a turkey. "Hi," she said. "I'm Agnes and you're Henry, right? Just a minute while I finish trussing this bird. I'll cook you some scrambled eggs and bacon, if that's OK."

Henry nodded, head down.

She asked him to pick up the turkey and put it in a black roasting pan. Its skin felt bumpy and cold. His legs shook as he walked across the kitchen with it.

"That's a twenty-two pounder," she said. "That should feed us all for several days. Here, sit on this stool and I'll cook your breakfast."

She chatted away while she cooked without noticing, it seemed, that he wasn't saying anything. She talked about the Rosenblatts' mothers, who were coming for the Thanksgiving dinner, what she was cooking, what her husband, Charlie, had to do. Henry tried to listen while he looked around the kitchen with its wooden white cupboards, white tile counters, and light blue linoleum floor.

"Thank you," he said when he had finished and then headed straight out the back kitchen door.

"You're welcome," she called after him. "You're a polite boy."

Henry walked around the side of the house to the front lawn.

He looked up the driveway and saw an open wrought iron gate. He could, he knew, just keep walking through it. He started toward it, but stopped to look at some red and yellow flowers gleaming in the sun just in front of him. They had petals bunched together in the shape of an egg. He bent over to touch a yellow one. It was still wet with shining drops of water sticking to it. When he straightened up, he knew he was not going through that gate—not yet. He turned around, walking slowly to the back of the house and across the small lawn he had seen from the bedroom window. He followed a path along one side of the orange grove, which led to a white wooden cottage. He peered in the small-paned windows. No one was there. Looking back from where he had come, he saw no one watching him. He tried the doorknob and the door opened. It seemed to be a library and smelled of old books. Yes, almost all the walls were lined with books. More books and papers were scattered on a large oak desk on his right. On his left there was a smooth, dark red narrow couch with a headrest and, near it, a large black armchair. On one wall, fierce wooden faces stared at him.

Henry sat in the armchair, swiveling around, so he could look everywhere. And he suddenly remembered: this chair was identical to the one at the Staffords', the one from which he'd run away. An image of himself in that other chair filled his mind.

He stroked the smooth leather of one of the armrests of this chair. It felt almost alive. Then the door opened and the doctor came in on his crutches. Henry jumped up.

"Oh, good, Henry, you found my office," the doctor said, coming over and plopping himself down on the couch. His forehead glistened with sweat. "Damn, this pants leg has come loose again. Hand me a crutch so I can get up and then you can help me. My wife does this in the morning, but sometimes it slips out." Dr. R stood up and turned around and Henry looked down at the empty pants leg.

"Just tuck it into my belt there in back. The cuff holds it in place, more or less. At least it doesn't get in the way. Here, I've loosened my belt." Henry got the cuff above the belt and the doctor eased himself back down on the couch, as Henry returned to the chair.

"I am trying to escape the Thanksgiving hysteria," Dr. R said. "Setting the table, polishing the silver, cooking the turkey—there's not a whole lot I can do with this damned leg. Well, the lack of it, to be exact." Dr. R. sighed and leaned his head back against the wall behind the couch. "Before the War, I used to run up the stairs. Well, those days are gone."

Dr. R stopped talking and there was silence. Henry stared at Dr, R's one scuffed-up brown leather shoe. When he looked up, Dr. R was still leaning back, his head against the wall, eyes closed. His hair stuck out from the sides of his head as if he had forgotten to brush it. He had his arms crossed and his tweed coat had dark brown leather patches on the elbows. One of those patches had come unstitched and was folded back.

After another silence, Dr. R. said, "You still aren't talking. I understand how you feel. You don't know where the hell you've landed, do you?" Henry lowered his head again. "When clients come, they find the dim light in here comforting. It helps them relax. They can sink into the dark world of their unconscious. That's what we psychoanalysts do—we help people go on inner journeys—into their past, into their real desires and hopes, not what some parent or teacher has told them they should do."

"I like . . . to go . . . on journeys," Henry said. Then he closed his eyes again.

"Yes, you told me you'd like to go to the desert."

"Did I?"

"Yes—the first time I met you at the hospital."

"I don't remember.".

Dr. R shook his head. "That's the electroshock. You need time to recover. Look, if you'd rather not come to the Thanksgiving dinner tonight, my wife and I would understand. We could tell the grandmas that you aren't feeling well. And probably you aren't. Would you like that?"

Henry nodded.

"Right. And Agnes can bring turkey and all the fixings up to you later." Henry opened his eyes enough to see the doctor stretch out on the couch. "You are sitting where I, the doctor sits, and I am lying where my patients lie down and tell me what they are thinking. It strikes me as . . . well, very interesting. I don't think I would make a very good patient. Of course, I went through analysis myself. Can you see yourself as the doctor? You'd have to listen to every word I say." He laughed. Then he pushed himself out of the couch with both arms, turned to take the crutches, and began hopping towards the door. Henry got up to open it. They walked side-by-side along the path towards the house, the gravel making its crunching sound under Henry's feet. The doctor was a head taller than Henry, and swung himself quickly forward on his crutches.

Inside the back door stood Dr. R's wheelchair. He sat down in it, leaving his crutches against the wall. One crutch started to fall, and Henry moved quickly to catch it. As Dr. R turned the wheelchair to leave, a redheaded boy came bounding in from the dining room, sliding to a stop in front of them.

"Whoa, fella," Dr. R. said. "Remember? No running in the house."

"Oh, yeah, sorry, I was trying to find Henry. Would you like to play catch out on the lawn? I've got two mitts!"

"Wait a minute, Max. Don't you think you should introduce yourself first? Henry, this is Max Rosenblatt. Max, this is Henry Hamblen."

"Hi," Max said. "Wanna play catch?

Henry shook his head.

"Oh, come on, just for a little while. Please, please."

Max reached out and grabbed Henry's arm and started pulling. Henry tried to turn away. A panic rose in his throat and he shoved Max hard, knocking him backward against the wall. As he ran up the stairs, he heard Max's cry of pain, then Dr. R's voice yelling, "Don't you ever do that again."

Henry slammed his door shut and looked around wildly, wondering where he might go. And now for sure he was going to get sent back to that place where they tied him down to the bed, where he could not move. He heard a knock on the door. They were coming for him.

The door opened and Henry saw Charlie's rear end backing into the room. He was reaching down to pick up something heavy, and once inside, he turned around, carrying a large radio. Henry went over to help him. He saw the black hairs on Charlie's knuckles, which were clasped around the radio. "I better put it on this dresser here. Hey, maybe you can get underneath this thing and help me get it up?" Charlie said and smiled, showing crooked yellow teeth below his grey moustache.

The two of them hoisted it onto the dresser.

"Dr. R asked me to bring this up. He thought you would like it," Charlie said, going out the door. "Plug it in there next to the dresser, see?"

Henry sat down on the edge of the bed, not even looking at the radio. He didn't feel like listening to the radio. It wasn't his radio. It wasn't his room. Why did they bring him a radio? He'd be gone soon anyway. Yet he could not resist turning his head toward it.

It was a rich brown-red color with a yellow band around the top and bottom. There were buttons for AM and FM. His hand reached out to plug it in and then to turn the dial. A warm yellow light shone behind the station numbers. The room filled to the sound of the creaking door of *Inner Sanctum. Oh well,* he thought, *I might as well listen.* He sat down on the bed and leaned his head against the headboard, letting the familiar images from the program take over his mind.

11

Dr. R wheeled over to hug Max, who stood pale and trembling against the wall. "He didn't mean to hurt you, Max. When he calms down, I bet he'll play catch with you." Max nodded his head against Dr. R's chest.

At that moment, the front door opened and the two mothers came in. Dr. R wanted to escape to the bedroom. He hadn't changed yet for dinner and his mother-in-law would disapprove of his attire—his ratty jacket and his wrinkled khakis. Both women were talking at the same time, Carol looking down from her greater height, augmented by ridiculously high heels, to the upturned face of his mother, Miriam. Max, still upset, disappeared out the back door before they could see him.

"You went to all that trouble to make both a minced and a pumpkin pie?" Carol asked. "Why didn't you let Agnes do it?"

Miriam giggled. Her shiny brown print dress shook as it descended over her bulky shape down to the floor, almost covering brown shoes that were more like bedroom slippers.

"Oh, let me take one of those," Miriam said, turning back to Charlie, who came through the open door with a box balanced in each hand. She headed for the kitchen, Charlie following. Carol noticed Dr. R before he could wheel away, went over to him and planted a cool kiss on his cheekbone, avoiding his beard.

"How are you, dear?" She straightened up, not waiting for an answer.

"Estelle tells me you have taken on another refugee. Some people adopt dogs, but you seem to prefer humans."

Dr. R looked up at his mother-in-law's narrow face with its blue lids and bright red mouth. If he were a dog, he could snap at her. "Now, Carol, let's not judge the poor boy before you even meet him. He comes from quite a respectable family in Pasadena. Unfortunately, his father has some irrational fear of his son's eccentricities."

"Maybe he should. So where is Estelle?"

"She's in back, cutting flowers."

Carol turned quickly, opened the back door, and disappeared. His own mother emerged from the dining room, came over to him, placing her hands on either side of his face. She kissed him on both cheeks and on his nose. He grinned.

"Hello, *Mamele*," he said, taking one of her pudgy hands and bringing it to his lips. "How are you feeling?"

"Oh, you know, darling, old age is not much fun. My feet and back are sore from making those pies yesterday, but nothing serious. The cook at Happy Home has become a special friend, so she let me use the kitchen. It's horrible—the old people there have to eat pies from a commercial bakery. Can you imagine anything so awful?"

"Yes," he said, rubbing her hand between both of his. "You could be in Stanyon State Hospital with no family visiting you today or any day."

His mother looked worried. "Carol told me on the way over that you saved a teenager from having a lobotomy and he's here now. Will we meet him? Is he staying?" Dr. R released her hand.

"He didn't want to face a lot of new people today. He only arrived yesterday. After a God-awful week in Stanyon, he thought he was going home with his father, and the next thing he knew, someone he had only seen once and didn't even remember was taking him away."

Miriam wrung her hands. "Is this boy violent and crazy?"

"No. But he can't read. For that he gets thrown into Stanyon."

"How cruel, how inhumane!"

"Well, think of your parents and brother and sister, snuffed out by the Nazis." He immediately regretted saying this. Now tears ran down Miriam's face. "*Mamele,* I'm sorry. I got carried away. We're here, still alive, right?" Miriam began weeping, holding on to Dr. R's hands.

"And we came so close to losing you, too, those horrible Jap kamikazes."

He locked the wheels of his chair and stood up. He felt her comforting warm body hug him, her smell of *eau de cologne.* "Yes, but you didn't lose me."

"And your father—gone, too."

"The poor nebbish."

His mother stepped back. "Don't call him that. I know—it's my fault. Don't be like I was."

"I'm sorry. I'm under pressure—I don't know what I'm saying."

"Poor boy, poor baby." His mother closed her eyes a moment, a little smile on her face. "I just wanted you to escape the grocery store."

"OK, OK, I feel guilty for what I said. Are you happy?"

His mother turned away from him. "*Oy,* my back. I'd better go lie down in the living room." Dr. R wheeled himself to the bedroom, noting in a psychoanalytic way, as he had been trained, that he felt at the same time angry, guilty, and very unloved. Thanksgiving . . . yeah.

•••

At five in the evening, everyone except Henry gathered in the dining room. There was still some light left outside, but night was approaching. Dr. R arrived in his wheelchair but shifted to the Chippendale chair at the head of the table. He had changed into a dark grey suit, white shirt and tie. Estelle sat on his left; next to her was Miriam; and across from Miriam was Max, who stood behind his chair, trying to loosen his necktie until Estelle shot him a warning look. Dr. R stifled a smile. Max then moved up to Dr. R's right side and pulled out the chair to seat Carol. *Good boy,* Dr. R. thought. As everyone got settled, he smiled at the polished silver, the white damask tablecloth, and Estelle's arrangement of yellow and gold chrysanthemums. Surely Carol would admire all this elegance?

Dr. R put his foot on the buzzer under the carpet below him. It could be heard ringing in the kitchen. Immediately Charlie appeared, dressed in a white shirt and tie, carrying the turkey on its platter. He placed it in front of Dr. R and handed him the carving implements from the side table, as everyone made appreciative remarks. He could not stand up to carve the turkey that loomed high in front of him. Agnes appeared with a huge white terry cloth bib, which she snapped around Dr. R's neck.

"Is that a bib, Dad?" Max asked. Everyone laughed.

"All you need is a bottle to suck on," Carol said. More laughter.

"It's an East Coast thing, Max," Estelle said. "It's for eating a whole lobster with a lot of butter. I got it for your dad to save his clothes from turkey grease."

"You're even going bald like a baby," Miriam added.

"A big baby," Dr. R heard Estelle repeat quietly. His stomach tightened as he took a breath.

"OK, OK. Are we going to go on with this joke forever or shall I carve?"

As he began, Carol said, "It appears it has been a long time since you did surgery."

"You always say that. Be careful, this knife might slip." The same jokes, but he knew Carol loved it. As usual, he began carving by cutting off one leg, and then Charlie took it away to the side table to finish. A one-legged turkey, he thought. Very funny.

Agnes brought in the other dishes: gravy for the turkey and stuffing, creamed pearl onions, yams with marshmallows melted on top, green beans. Charlie piled turkey slices onto a platter. The dishes were passed and everyone soon had a heaping plate.

"Let's begin before everything gets cold," Dr. R said, picking up his knife and fork.

"Oh, Estelle, darling," Carol said. "I feel a draft. Could you see if I left my shawl in the living room?"

"Let Agnes get it," Dr. R said in a loud voice. But Estelle had already jumped up and left the room. She was back in a moment, but there was an awkward silence, no one daring to begin. Max had already managed to get a bite into his mouth and was frowning, not knowing whether it was permissible to go on chewing.

Estelle arranged the black cashmere shawl around her mother's shoulders and was about to sit down, when Carol said, "Estelle, I'm so sorry, I left my purse in your dressing room and there are pills in it which I absolutely must take before eating." Dr. R stamped on the buzzer to the kitchen with his foot.

"Sit down, Estelle."

"Agnes will never be able to find the right ones," Carol said

"No, Mother, I'll go," Estelle said. Dr. R felt his whole body tense. All right, he thought, ignore my request. At that moment Agnes appeared and Estelle sat down again, her lips tight, while Carol told Agnes where to look. Everyone began eating in silence. Agnes returned with the blue cloisonné pillbox and placed it in front of an unsmiling Carol, and left.

Dr. R breathed hard, trying to get control.

His mother, asking Max about his baseball team at school, gave him time to take a few more breaths. He reached for the cut-glass water pitcher and poured his mother-in-law some more water, a gesture she did not acknowledge. She was telling Estelle about her latest difficulties with Octavio, her cook and chauffeur, and how inconvenient it was that he wanted three full days to be with his wife and children in San Diego for Thanksgiving.

Interrupting Carol mid-sentence, Dr. R said, "Estelle, you really outdid yourself with the flowers this time."

Carol stopped and looked at the flower arrangement. Estelle smiled. At the same time, Dr. R reached his hand under the table and placed it on his wife's knee. Immediately she covered it with hers and looked at him warmly, pressing on his hand. Dr. R took another deep breath, thinking quickly. "It is a custom for us at Thanksgiving to go around the table and say what we are thankful for." Everyone stiffened.

"But this time," he continued, "I would like to ask you to say something you are thankful for in this moment, not in the past, not in the future. And not the obvious, such as parents, children, spouses. I'll start. I am thankful for these flowers that bring me joy, and of course for the hands that brought them here." Estelle squeezed his hand once more.

There was a pause. Then his mother spoke. "I am thankful for Max—he makes me feel warm inside." She and Max exchanged smiles. "I know, I know, I broke the rule. I can't help it. Grandmothers are allowed to do that, right?"

Max said, "I am thankful for this yummy turkey and I can't wait for the pies!" Everyone laughed.

Carol looked at her red fingernails. "I am thankful I have finally found a really good manicurist." Everyone was silent. Dr. R forced a weak smile.

"Well, your fingernails are definitely here in the moment, Carol."

"Can I see them?" Max asked, peering down the table. Carol raised her hands, fingernails pointing out.

"Oh," he said, "I thought maybe they would be orange for Thanksgiving." Everyone laughed again, even Carol.

"So, Estelle?" Dr. R asked.

Estelle immediately said, "I am so happy to hear everyone laughing. That's the way it should be."

They all clapped their hands and continued to eat with renewed enthusiasm, a mood that lasted through the rest of the dinner. Maybe, Dr. R thought, I've won the battle this time.

As they were eating the pies, Miriam looked at Max and said, "Max, darling, you have so much pie on your face, you look good enough to eat." Max jumped up, whipped cream on his lips, and ran around the table to Miriam, and leaned over, so his face was close to hers.

"OK, go ahead, Grandma." Miriam laughed, took her linen napkin from her lap and gently wiped Max's face. "There my *bubbala,* now you look better."

Max put his arm around her shoulders and planted a loud kiss on her cheek, which made Miriam giggle. "You are adorable," she said, kissing him back and tousling his hair.

Carol frowned, stood up quickly and said, "I am surprised that such behavior is tolerated at the dinner table. I thought you were teaching your children good manners. Well, the fruit never falls far from the tree." She walked out of the room, while Miriam and Max followed her with their eyes. Dr. R and Estelle looked at each other.

"Love is never bad manners," Dr. R said. "But we must not offend our guests."

"I'm sorry, Dad," Max said, pouting.

"It's my fault," Miriam said, and then burst out laughing. Estelle got up and followed her mother.

•••

Later that night, once their mothers had returned home, and Max had gone upstairs, Estelle was sitting at her dressing table, brushing her hair. Dr. R watched her as he rolled from the bathroom to his side of the bed. Admiring her sinuous movements, he licked his lips and then realized that Estelle had seen him in her mirror.

She laughed. "I am not your whipped cream and pumpkin pie."

"Oh yes, you are." He transferred from the wheelchair to his side of the bed. She went on brushing. "I checked on Henry. He's still not talking—at least not to me. But he ate all the food Charlie took up to him. I told him breakfast is at eight. We'll see if he comes."

"Listen," Dr. R said. "I'm sorry the dinner ended like that. Whatever got into Max and my mother? I so much wanted your mother to admire our elegance and decorum. Thanks to you, we get an *A* for elegance."

"And a *D* for decorum," Estelle said."

"I just want her to see I know how to behave despite my low beginnings."

Estelle frowned into the mirror. "When you and my mother go at each other like that, I wonder why I went to all this trouble, just to make the two of you happy."

"You mean this house?"

"Yes. This house. I know you love it but I still wish we were in a nice cozy cottage, or maybe in a row of houses with neighbors you can talk to on the front stoop. I know, we don't have stoops here in Southern California, but I remember yours."

Dr. R clasped his head in his hands. "I'm shocked. I thought you had come to love this place as much as I do. I didn't know you felt that way after all these years. I hate to think that for you it represents a sacrifice."

Estelle took off her white silk dressing gown and slid her legs under the covers, still sitting up straight. "I love *you,* not the house. And I love Max and Agnes and Charlie."

"That means a lot," Dr. R said, leaning over to kiss her cheek. "That means everything."

"When Max and Henry have gone off, maybe we won't need this huge house," Estelle said. "For now we do." Crossing her arms over her chest, she stared straight ahead, her loose hair around her face, her fierce eyes shining like a mysterious being.

"You're right about my mother," Estelle said. "She's not happy. She regrets leaving her friends in New York. She hasn't made friends here."

"I wish you wouldn't always kowtow to her." Estelle turned and glared at him.

"I'm sorry you see it that way."

"I shouldn't have said that. I owe your mother a great deal."

"Oh? You mean the money?"

"No, I mean you. She gave birth to you."

She turned to him. "Flattery, flattery."

He gently pulled down one strap of her nightgown, exposing a full breast. He began kissing the dark nipple, then sucking on it, adding little bites, a move he knew aroused her. This time she started laughing.

"What's so funny?" he said, pausing.

"You're a baby sucking on his mother's breast—just what we were joking about."

"Oh, that again? Well then, be a good mother. Lie down and give me the other one."

12

The next morning after breakfast, Estelle waited in her office, listening for footsteps. She straightened herself as she sat in the chair. Her mother had taught her good posture, insisting that she sit up straight, never slouch, and walk as if she were balancing a full glass of water on her head. It was magic, giving her a certain advantage over other girls as far as attracting the boys. She kept secret this hidden power, even from Josh. Then she heard footsteps. Henry appeared in the doorway.

"Oh, good. You came. I wasn't sure at breakfast. I'm glad you decided to come."

Now, sitting next to her, he was bent over in his chair, head down, his hands twisting in his lap.

"I want to begin with something that has nothing to do with reading," she said. "Come stand here against this wall." Henry looked up and slowly got to his feet. She pulled a ruler and pencil out of the desk drawer. "I want to measure how tall you are. It will be interesting to know how much you grow in the next few months." Henry frowned.

"Now stretch up as high as you can, right from the bottom of your feet to the top of your head, as if a rope were pulling you up. And open your eyes—you have to look straight ahead. Come on, you can stretch taller than that."

Estelle placed the ruler on top of his head and made a mark with the pencil on the wall. Henry clenched his jaw. "You can let your muscles relax a little but keep your spine stretching up. Look out the window. What is the furthest thing you can see out there?"

Henry looked. "I see a tree with purple flowers outside the gate."

"Very good. That's a Princess tree."

"A Princess tree," he repeated. "And there is a huge black bird on the top branch."

Estelle turned around to look. "Uh-oh, it's a raven. What's he doing there?" If someone called her raven-haired, she hated it. Ravens had a bad reputation. Edgar Allen Poe and all that.

"You have lots of birds in your garden," Henry said. She nodded. At least he was talking.

He dropped back into his chair, slumping again, his full lips trembling. In front of them on the desk stood a strange machine with two wheels and a thin tape wound up on one of them.

"This," Estelle said, patting it, "is a tape recorder. I bet you've never seen one of these before. I've only had this for a week, and I'm still learning how to use it." She stroked one of the reels with a finger. "I plan to use it to help my students learn to read."

"I can't read," Henry said.

"We're going to work on that. Right now I want to see how you do with the spoken word. I want to read you a passage from a book, and then I'll turn on the tape recorder and ask you some questions about what you heard. See this little microphone here? We have to take turns speaking into it. Are you willing to try that?" Henry continued to stare at the tape recorder. Mrs. R wondered if he was going to shut down again. She couldn't force him.

"OK," he finally replied. She picked up a book. "Has anyone ever read *Huckleberry Finn* to you? Mark Twain wrote it. My husband and I love Mark Twain."

"Yes, I heard it on the radio. Huckleberry Finn ran away and lived near the river. Then he was free and could do what he wanted."

Mrs. R. looked surprised. "That's right. Thank goodness for radio—and now we have TV, right?"

"I like *The Lone Ranger* better on radio than on TV," Henry said.

"You imagine him in your mind. Some people think television is going to ruin our ability to imagine things. What do you think?"

"I like nature programs on TV. I like to see animals that live in the desert or the mountains or the ocean."

"Really?" Mrs. R said. "Would you like to photograph animals? I have a Brownie camera. You could take pictures of cats and dogs—or squirrels, even birds." Estelle waited. Henry looked at her for the first time.

"Could you show me how to use it?" he asked.

"Yes, we'll do that. Tomorrow if you wish. It's really easy."

"Thank you," Henry said, straightening up for a moment and looking outside. "The raven is gone," he said.

"Thank God. They're nasty birds. OK, back to business." Estelle then read from the beginning of *Huckleberry Finn.* She could see he was listening.

He jumped a little when she turned on the machine. The wheels were turning. She asked him questions about what she had read, pointing the microphone at him when she wanted him to speak. He seemed excited about Huckleberry Finn, forgetting his silence. Finally she turned off the machine. The reels stopped.

"You can go back to your room for a little. I'm going to analyze what you said, so I know where to begin teaching you. I have a pretty good idea already. I'll call you when I need you to come back." After he left, she sighed. He understood Huck better than she did. Huck was his soul mate. She hoped reading that book wasn't going to inspire Henry to run away again. Looking at the closed book next to the tape recorder, she thought, *Thank you, Huck, you managed to get this kid to open his mouth at last.*

•••

Free, Henry thought, as he walked down the hall to his room—*free, free.* Once inside, he pulled a chair over to the window and sat, looking out at the orange trees. He saw a flash of blue amongst them and then heard the screech of a blue jay. He wished he could go outside and be with the blue jay. How long was Mrs. R going to take? There was a knock on the door. It opened and Max stuck his head in, grinning.

"Can I come in?"

"Yeah, I guess so."

Max came over to the window with two baseball mitts, a bat and softball. "Charlie can't play catch with me this morning. He's got too much gardening to do. What about coming out to the lawn with me—when you finish with Mom?"

"I've never played baseball."

Max's mouth opened in astonishment. "Why not? Everyone plays baseball, don't they? Well, maybe not girls."

"My father wouldn't let me. And they didn't play it at the special school I went to."

"What a dumb school!"

"It was for dumb kids like me."

"I have a lot of trouble learning stuff at school, but we get to play baseball."

"You're lucky."

Max put on a mitt and began whacking the center with his fist, while looking at Henry. "Would you like me to show you how to throw a ball?" Max asked.

"Well, maybe."

Max started jumping up and down with excitement, chanting: "Put on your hat, stand at the mat, pick up the bat, and that is that."

Henry stared at him.

"Oh, that's a poem," Max said. "I made it up. All those words sound like '*bat.*' It's a baseball poem. See—*bat, hat, mat.* Even *at.* The only thing different is the first letter."

"I don't get it," Henry said. Max looked puzzled.

"You know. If I sound out each letter, it sounds like *buh-aw-tuh* and when you put them together real fast it makes the word *bat.*"

"How does *buh-aw-tuh* become *bat? Ba*t is just one sound, *buh-aw-tuh*—that's three sounds."

"*Huh-ats, buh-ats, kuh-ats,*" Max chanted.

Suddenly Henry understood something. The sounds flowed together. "Just the first sound is different. Are they written the same but with a different first letter?"

"You got it," Max said, heading for the door. "See you later."

Henry continued gazing out the window while his mind repeated *bat, cat, hat, mat, sat—fat,* there was another one, and maybe . . . *pat, pat the cat who sat on a hat.* He tapped his feet on the floor, making up a song:

Pat the cat that sat on the hat
Pat the cat that sat on the mat
Bat the hat away from the cat.
The cat is fat. And that is that!

He began beating the rhythm with his knuckles on the windowsill. It seemed to dance with the leaves in the orange grove that started moving in a little breeze.

• • •

Estelle knocked on his door. She saw him seated at the window. He turned toward her with a frightened face. "You're going to be surprised," she said, smiling. She led him back to her office.

"You have the vocabulary of someone in twelfth grade, almost college level. This is what I suspected, and the tests the nurse gave you at the hospital showed that also."

"But I can't read."

"If you had had the right teachers, they would have known how to help you. And how did your father miss that?"

"I never talked much around him. And he didn't believe my mom. She said I was smart—I didn't believe her either. My dad was right."

"Your mom was right, Henry. Someday you've got to realize that. Let's begin. Do you see that chart there?" She pointed to the wall behind the desk in front of them.

"It's the alphabet," Henry said.

"That's right. Can you read the letters to me?"

"Yes. I learned that at school. Capital *A,* small *a,* capital *B,* small *b . . .*" He went through the whole alphabet.

"Very good. Now if I write on this piece of paper *B-A-T,* can you tell me what word that is?"

"B-A-T," Henry spelled out.

"Right, you know the names of the letters. But what do they sound like together?"

"*Buh-ah-tuh,*" Henry said quickly. "That's *bat,* like a baseball bat. What you wrote spells *bat.*" He stared at the paper with wonder. Estelle stared too.

"Wow! Did you already know that word?"

"Max just taught me his baseball song. He showed me that words like *bat* and *hat* and *cat* are all the same except for the first letter."

Estelle laughed. "Good for Max, the dear boy—he helped you crack the code. It's going to be tough, but now I see you can do it. The big question is . . ." She paused. "Are you willing to try?"

"I . . . I . . . don't know." Tears began to run down his face.

Estelle patted his shoulder. "It's a big shock. It goes against everything you have been told."

Henry nodded, wiping his eyes with the backs of his hands.

"We can stop now," Mrs. R said. "But we'll need to work every day. And it's important that you think about this, Henry. If you make this huge effort to learn to read, what would you want to learn? Is there something you want to know about?"

Henry was silent, his head down. Then he looked at her through the tears. "I would like to learn about all the animals and birds and plants that live in the desert."

"Great. Don't forget that. All right, we're finished for today." She jumped up. "I have another student arriving in half an hour and I want a cup of coffee." As she went downstairs, she thought *He'll slide back, he won't believe me, but at least it's a beginning. He's adorable to look at, but thank God he doesn't seem to know that yet.*

•••

Lunch was turkey sandwiches in the kitchen with Agnes, Charlie, and Max. Beside Max's stool lay a baseball and two mitts.

As they ate leftover pumpkin pie, Charlie said, "If you're looking for me to play catch with you, Max, you're out of luck. I have to start trimming hedges this afternoon. That's a three-day job. But you have Henry here. He looks big and strong." Max made a face.

"OK, let's go," Max said, jumping off the stool and picking up the mitts and ball.

"I told you, Max," Henry began, but it was too late. Max was already out the back door. Henry looked desperately at Charlie, who shook his head.

"It can't be too bad, son," Charlie said. "Max will teach you. He's got the gift for baseball." Henry sighed, got up slowly, and followed Max out the back and around to the front lawn.

"Here," Max said, handing Henry a mitt, clutching the other mitt with the ball inside it under his other arm. Henry looked at it there in his hands, unsure which hand to put it on. Max laughed.

"You put it on your left hand, see, there's a place for your thumb." Max held Henry's mitt while Henry pushed his hand into the tight pocket at the back.

"You've got big hands," Max said. "They must be as big as Charlie's. Here's the ball. See how it fits in the mitt? It's big because it's a soft ball. The professional teams use a hard ball—it's much smaller." Several times Max threw the ball into Henry's mitt from a few inches away and then left it there.

"OK," Max said. He started backing up on the lawn.

When he stopped, Henry said, "Could you come a little closer?"

"Yeah." Max advanced toward Henry. Henry threw the ball, which plopped down at Max's feet. Henry moaned. He wasn't going to be any good at this, either.

"Hey, you throw like a girl," Max said. "Start with your weight back on one leg like this. Twist your arm way back." Max demonstrated, bringing his weight forward. The ball hit the side of Henry's head.

"Ow!" he yelled, rubbing his head. He slowly turned to look for the ball and walked over to get it. He wanted to drop his mitt and go back to his room.

"Did I hurt you?" Max asked. "Sorry. I'm a pitcher. Let's try again." Henry picked up the ball, which he already hated. He tried what Max suggested and the ball went off to Max's left side. Max leapt for it and caught it, falling. He laughed, kicking his feet in the air a few times and jumped up. Then Max threw him a slow ball that curved upward and seemed to fall into Henry's raised mitt with a *thwack.* "Great, you did it."

"I didn't do anything," Henry said. "*You* did it."

"That's OK. Now throw it back, nice and easy." Max raised his mitt to a level near his head. "Just aim for this mitt, OK?"

Henry paused a moment. He imagined a curved line between his hand holding the ball and Max's mitt. He stepped back and as he threw he followed that line, releasing the ball when his arm was extended along it. The ball landed in Max's mitt.

"Wow," Max said. "That was a great throw."

"Beginner's luck," Henry said, shrugging his shoulders. They continued with Max moving back inch by inch. Henry had to concentrate as hard as he could. Their throws became rhythmical, step back, throw, *whack* in Max's mitt, Max stepped back, threw, *whack* in his mitt, except when one of them threw a wild one. The sun became stronger on the lawn. Henry was sweating. A high ball flew across a clear blue sky and then dropped through the dark green of the trees behind Max right into Max's mitt again. Henry wanted to go on forever.

Finally, Max said, "Let's take a break and get a drink. I gotta see what time it is; my friends are meeting over at the park pretty soon for a practice game. Why don't you come with me? You can watch if you don't want to play yet."

"No, I can't."

"Why not?"

"I just can't." But he wondered what the park looked like.

13

The next day Henry was listening to one of his favorite soap operas, *Life Can Be Beautiful,* when there was a knock on the door. Charlie opened it, turned around, and picked up a stack of two cardboard cartons.

"Here you go, son. Dr. R's nurse was in Pasadena with her parents for Thanksgiving. She called your father and made him pack up your clothes and all kinds of stuff. Don't just stand there; take the top one. They're heavy. Henry took the box. He recognized *Henry* scribbled in his father's handwriting on the side with red ink. He put it on the floor next to his bed. Charlie put the other one next to it.

"Two more to go—leave the door open." After Charlie left, Henry could hear voices downstairs. Did he know that nurse? He remembered the one with red hair, a nice nurse.

Charlie returned with two more boxes, Henry took the top one, and then Charlie was gone, closing the door. He no longer heard the voices. That was good. He pulled open the top of one box and recognized his clothes. He pulled open another one and found what he wanted—his stuffed animals, including Jake the Tiger. He clutched him to his chest and fell backwards on the bed.

"Jake, Jake," he whispered. "Did you miss me?" He brought Jake up to his cheek and felt his soft fur. Then he jumped up, left Jake on his pillow, and unpacked the other stuffed animals. They lay in a heap on the floor in front of him. But where was he going to put them?

"OK, Jake," he said, taking the tiger in his lap, "we'll pick out four friends to be here with you on the bed. The rest stay in their box." Henry replaced Jake on his pillow. Then he chose Talker, the brown horse with white hoofs, who only talked in Henry's dreams; Peony, the elephant with the pink mouth, named by his mother; Francis, the cocker spaniel; and the Camel with the Wrinkled Knees, whose eyes were a white button with a little black button on top, sewn on by his mother when the old eyes fell off. He tossed them onto the bed with Jake.

He shoved the others back in their box and then carried it into the closet, pushing it to the back where it was too dark to see. He felt sorry for them, sent off to prison like that, but he had no choice. And he wondered what Max would say when he saw the four he kept out. Eighteen-year-olds don't play with stuffed animals.

When he came out, he unpacked some clean clothing and went to the bathroom to fill the bathtub. He stripped off the jeans, shirt, and sweater he had worn for what seemed forever. He lay there in the deep water a long time, then dried off with the big fuzzy white towel and put on the fresh clothes.

Coming back into the room, he looked at the boxes. His feeling of joy crumbled. Not only the animals but the clothes also seemed to belong to someone else who no longer existed. And they did not belong here in this strange place; they belonged in his room in Pasadena.

He sat down on the bed, picked up Jake again, placing him on one knee with Jake's legs straddling it. He kicked one of the boxes, wishing they would all go away. What good was all this stuff going to do, anyway? He would have to leave it all behind when he ran away. There was another knock on the door. Mrs. R came in, holding a letter in her hand.

"A letter came from your mother today. Do you want me to read it to you?" she asked.

"I guess so," Henry said. "Did the nurse see my father? Was my mother there?"

"Your father was there."

"And my mother?"

"Let's read her letter." Mrs. R pulled up the chair from the desk, navigating around the boxes. She sat down and opened the letter, sitting very straight with her knees and ankles pressed together, as if she too expected bad news. She read:

November 26, 1952

Dearest Henry:

I'm sure someone in your new home will read this to you. I feel terrible that I wasn't able to help you at the police station. I knew you hadn't done anything wrong, but your father wouldn't let me speak. Please, please, don't forget that I love you very much. I may not see you for a while, but that doesn't mean I don't love you. I want to explain what has happened.

After you were taken away, I couldn't stop crying. The police doctor gave me a shot that put me to sleep. The next morning your father took me off to this sanatorium, a really lovely, peaceful place with wonderful, kind people looking after me. Dr. McKensie is my doctor, and he explained to me that I needed to rest for a while. I told him how worried I was about you going to Stanyon. "Stanyon?" he said. "My friend, Dr. Rosenblatt, works there—I'll call him. And that's what he did."

Everything happened very fast. And Dr. McKensie tells me the Rosenblatts are wonderful people. What a miracle this is. But if anything goes wrong, please, Henry, let me know. The Rosenblatts have Uncle Ed's phone number. Your father thinks you are back at Stanyon, but I won't tell him. NEVER!

Dr. McKensie contacted your Uncle Ed, and he arrived in his pickup truck late today to take me away to live with him. I want to start a new life with Uncle Ed. I'm not supposed to tell anyone where I am, but I can tell you that I have several horses I can ride, and it's wonderful, as Roy Rogers sings, to be back in the saddle again.

I will try to reach you by telephone as soon as possible, but I had to write this letter, so you would know what is happening to me.

We will see each other soon. I love you so much.

—Mom

Mrs. R folded up the letter, put it back in the envelope, and handed it to Henry.

"My mom's gone somewhere far away, and she won't tell me where," he finally said.

Mrs. R remained silent. She did not move. Henry wished she would leave him alone. Then he heard her say: "Henry, listen to me. Your mother loves you. Did you hear how often she said that? You used to run away, but your mother wanted to escape, too. This was her chance."

"I don't want to talk to her if she calls. Tell her that."

"I will not," Mrs. R said, crossing her arms and drawing back in her chair.

Henry threw himself face down on the bed and put the pillow over his head, squeezing it against his ears. He heard Mrs. R leave, closing the door behind her. He hated all these grownups—they just told lies.

14

"I think you've grown the past twenty-four hours," Mrs. R said, lowering the ruler as Henry stretched as far up the wall as he could. Henry shook his head. "What do you see out there, today?" she asked.

Henry opened his eyes. "A gate."

"A gate to a new world," Mrs. R said, so softly he could barely hear. Was she joking? She seemed serious. "OK, let's get to work. Dr. R is at the hospital today, but his mother is coming back for lunch."

They moved on to words ending in *–og: dog, fog, hog, cog, bog, frog.* "What's a *cog,* what's a *bog?*" he asked. She explained and suggested he make up a sentence using some of those words. He thought for a long time while Mrs. R tapped her pencil on the desk.

"In the fog, the dog and the hog fell on a frog in the bog," he finally said. "*Cog* is too hard."

Mrs. R laughed. "Excellent. Let's see if you can write that sentence. I can help you. I'll do the little words and you do the *–og* words. The little words are hard, right?" Together they printed out Henry's sentence. She wrote out the words that didn't rhyme for him to try to memorize. At the end of the hour, Mrs. R said. "You are making progress. As you see, you are going to have to work very hard, but I know now you can learn to read. Do you agree?"

Henry looked down at the sentences partly written by him, partly by Mrs. R. "This is kid stuff."

"It's not your fault. It's the fault of your parents and teachers not knowing how to help you. If you had a physical defect and couldn't walk properly, they wouldn't expect you to be able to run. They would have helped you to learn to use your body in the best way possible, maybe with crutches, or a brace, or a wheelchair."

"Like Dr. R," Henry said.

"Yes, like Dr. R. You are never going to be a speed-reader, but I know you will be able to read. While you are learning, we'll get people to read your lessons to you. There's nothing wrong with your memory."

"Who will read to me?"

"Maybe Max. And I have someone else in mind. We don't have much time. A new semester starts in January." Henry stared at her, panic rising in his throat.

"What? You don't mean school, do you?

"Yes, I'm talking about Redgrove High down the street."

"But I can't go to high school. I don't know anything."

"I know it's scary. You'll have to trust me on this."

"No, no, I can't."

Mrs. R patted his arm. "I have no reason to lie to you. I've seen hundreds of kids, and my predictions are almost always right. You'll see yourself soon enough."

Henry shook his head. "I don't want to go to school. I'll, I'll . . ." He jumped up, his wooden chair scraping along the floor.

"OK, we're done for today. Go find Charlie in the garden. He'll be very happy to make use of your strong arms. There's plenty of time before lunch."

She must be lying, he thought as he walked down the stairs. *But I don't have a choice—about anything.*

•••

Henry found Max in the garden shed, off behind the kitchen, sitting on an upturned bucket, talking to Charlie, who was leaning against the wall, smoking.

"*Hola,*" Charlie said. "Here's a bucket for you. Have a seat. We've got some weeds out there that are almost as tall as you. It might take both of you to pull some of them out. Mrs. R wants to grow dahlias in that spot."

Henry sat down and looked around. Rakes, hoes, and shovels hung on the walls from nails. He saw clippers and smaller tools in a wooden box on a shelf next to Max. Then he spotted in one corner some hats and jackets on hooks, and a dark green rucksack, like the one his father had in the garage at home. Charlie continued to puff on his cigarette. Henry stood up and went over to the corner and took the rucksack off its hook.

"May I borrow this?" he asked. Charlie shook his head.

"That's Dr. R's. You better ask him."

"Oh, OK," Henry said, replacing it. He wished he hadn't asked. Charlie would tell Dr. R and he'd be in trouble.

The weeds were indeed almost as tall as Max, and the ground hard with a layer of dust on top. Most of them he could pull out but he had to help Max, who wanted to quit immediately.

Henry bent over, adding his hands to the stalks of the weeds. "We can both pull on this, Max," he said.

"This is too hard," Max complained.

"You need to be strong for baseball," Henry said. "Come on, Max, you can do it." The weed came out suddenly in a cloud of dust and the boys fell backward. Max laughing. Charlie was digging up some roots that had intruded into the future flowerbed. Soon there was a huge pile of the weeds and debris, which they had to carry to the compost pile behind the shed.

"I can put the tools away," Henry said.

"*Muchas gracias,*" Charlie said. "I go help Agnes serve lunch."

"I guess we have to clean up before lunch," Max said. "See ya." Charlie and Max headed back into the house. Henry carried Charlie's shovel and hoe back to the shed, replaced them against the wall, and then walked over to the rucksack. Would anyone notice it was gone? He grabbed it, folded it as flat as he could, and stuffed it inside his shirt against his chest. He walked in the back door and shot up the stairs without encountering anyone. Then he hid it at the very back of the closet in the darkness. As he quietly closed the closet door behind him, he wondered if Charlie and Max would miss him when he went away.

As the boys came down for lunch, Henry heard a car pull up outside and Max ran out the front door.

"Grandma, grandma!" Max yelled, and Henry could see him jumping up and down as an old woman heaved herself out of the car. Max threw his arms around her to give her a hug and she bent down to plant a kiss on top of his scraggly red hair. Max hung on, still saying, "Grandma, Grandma."

"So, how's my *bubbala?*" the woman asked. Max let her go.

"I'm great, Grandma. I've got an older brother now. Did you know that?"

"Yes, darling," the grandmother said, as she moved slowly toward Henry, who was still standing in the hall. Charlie was behind her, about to open the trunk of the car. "Oh, don't bother with that now, Charlie," the grandmother said. "I have to ask Mrs. R where she thinks that box should go. Well, put it on the porch here."

"Yes, ma'am," Charlie said.

"Grandma, that's Henry." Henry held out his hand. The grandma's hand felt warm and firm.

"Glad to meet you, Henry," she said. "I am Mrs. Rosenblatt, Dr. R's mother."

"And *my* grandma," Max said. She smiled.

"Yes, dear, that's right. And you are my wonderful grandson. So where is your mother, Max?"

"She's got a girl up there in her office."

"Oh, yes, she told me. Max, I need to get off my feet. Let's go off here into the living room and you can tell me about your next game."

They moved away, and Max was already saying, "My team has won five games and lost two, but next Saturday we play Lincoln Junior High and we think they will be easy to beat."

Henry opened the front door and went outside. He sat in a chair on a corner of the porch, peering for a moment at the wooden crate that Charlie had left there. It was filled with big books, and he wanted to see if any of them had pictures in them. But he didn't dare touch them. He looked out at the lawn and the trees at the other end. Maybe he would be ready soon to disappear through that gate. He felt stronger, and now he just had to have some food in that rucksack—and some money. Then he wouldn't have to go to school.

The door opened and a dark-haired girl with pigtails in a plaid dress came out with her mother. They went past without seeing him. Henry heard Max calling his name, and he stood and entered the house. Max and the grandma were already seated in the dining room, and he saw Mrs. R coming down the stairs. She smiled at him.

"I shouldn't say this, Henry, but that poor little girl has problems that make yours look like nothing. She's not even close to reading *bat* and *hat* and *cat.* Probably brain damage at birth."

"No, no," Henry said. "I can't."

"You, Henry Hamblen, are really very stubborn. You're a hard nut to crack." She was still smiling at him.

"I'm sorry," he said.

"Never mind. Let's go in—I bet Max is starving." As they entered the dining room, Henry saw Mrs. R go around the table, lean over, and give Grandma a kiss on the cheek. It seemed everyone liked this grandma.

"Your family seems to be growing," the grandma said.

"Yes, it is," Mrs. R said. Agnes came through the swinging kitchen door with a large tureen of soup and Charlie followed with a basket of biscuits.

"This is homemade turkey-noodle soup," Agnes said proudly, placing it in front of Mrs. R and handing her a ladle. "There's honey and butter for the biscuits, and you boys only get three each, so you'll have to fill up on soup." Henry sat opposite Max, next to Mrs. R. Miriam was seated next to Max. The smell of biscuits brought an image of his mother in a red flowered apron, leaning over to pull biscuits out of the oven. Why did memories like that come back to make him sad? Henry picked up the basket of biscuits, offered them to the grandma, who took one, and then to Mrs. R, who took a small one.

"Someone has taught you good table manners," the grandma said.

"My mother," Henry said.

"Good for her. Max, you should pay attention to how Henry behaves. I bet even now you are thinking of reaching right across the table and grabbing another biscuit." She laughed as Max wrinkled his nose and returned to spooning soup into his mouth.

"Give them more soup," Miriam said. "The poor boys are starving. Just look—their bowls are empty."

"Boohoo," Max said, passing his bowl, pretending to cry. He leaned his head on his grandma's shoulder and she stroked his hair.

"Now, you two," Mrs. R said. "That's quite enough."

The grandma's warmth seemed to spread around the entire table. She acted like he, Henry, had always been there—passing him biscuits and butter, asking him for things—even with Max hanging all over her.

The meal ended with canned peaches and cookies. Then he and Max headed for the kitchen, backing through the swinging door with the dirty plates in their hands. Agnes scolded them for putting the dishes in the wrong sink. He and Max looked at each other and smiled.

After washing the dishes, they listened to *The Lone Ranger,* lying together on Henry's bed.

"The Lone Ranger always wins, doesn't he?" Max said. "Not like baseball. Sometimes you lose."

"The Lone Ranger isn't real, Max. In real life we mostly lose."

"Not always." Max said, sliding off the bed. "We're going to beat Lincoln High. They're a lousy team. Hey, see ya later."

"Yeah, Max."

15

At five in the evening Dr. R returned with Charlie from his workday at Stanyon. His mother was drinking tea in the living room. Dr. R wheeled his chair across the hall to join her. He saw her look at him with that motherly appraisal.

"You look tired," she said. Was it a rough day?"

"Very," he said, rolling up to the side of the sofa to kiss her cheek. "It's always pretty rough, but today I had to tackle this S.O.B., Dr. Wilson, the one who almost performed a lobotomy on Henry."

"Let me give you some tea and a cookie, darling." Dr. R smiled. This was his mother's solution to every problem. He held the teacup in both hands, feeling its warmth.

"So, what happened? Did you fire him?"

"It's not that simple. These lobotomies are considered God's gift, well, the wonderful Dr. Winfred Friedman's gift, to mankind. I haven't found a way to convince my colleagues otherwise. But I did tell Dr. Wilson that I have evidence in regard to Henry's discharge that could ruin him. Discharging Henry after only one week when the court order was for three weeks has to be illegal, if not unethical, and he knows it. I don't care what shenanigans Henry's father pulled with the law authorities in Pasadena. Dr. Wilson knows the sooner he moves on the better. I think he'll hand in his resignation tomorrow."

"Does he know where Henry is?"

"I told him Henry's father sent him far away and isn't telling anyone where."

"You lied?"

"Yes, I had to. And I'm guessing he isn't talking to Henry's father, after what happened in the parking lot at the clinic. I'm taking a big chance there. That's why I want Dr. Wilson gone before he finds out that Henry is with me." Miriam rolled her eyes. "Sometimes I wonder why I stay there myself. But I did discharge a man today. He's an alcoholic, but he's promised to go to Alcoholics Anonymous. That's an organization that started before the War, where alcoholics who have sobered up meet with those trying to kick the habit. This man has a family who loves him. He'll do fine, and he certainly doesn't belong at Stanyon."

"So, you are helping your fellow man. I'm proud of you."

Dr. R shook his head. "But these are just one or two people. I want to help the thousands who are facing lobotomies. They deserve a life too."

Miriam sighed. "You've done so well. Why take chances? You could lose what you've worked so hard for. You could ruin yourself with this cockamamie scheme to save the world. Why don't you stick with saving one person at a time?"

Dr. R's face burned. "Who taught me to aim high? How many times did you say, 'Don't be like your father. All he wants to do is go off to temple to sing, while we struggle with the store. Make something of yourself. Make something of yourself.' And I have."

Miriam put a hand to her forehead. "I know, I know. I wish I could take back my words. Your poor father—he was a good man." Tears ran down her face. Dr. R pulled out his handkerchief and handed it to her. She wiped her eyes and blew her nose.

"You did what you thought was best, *Mamela.* But I may lose my job for taking Henry if I don't get people behind my cause."

"You are going down the wrong path, dearest."

Dr. R felt his hot forehead begin to ache. "You are hopelessly naïve."

"And you're *meshuga* and you know it," Miriam said.

"You're saying I'm crazy? You're not going to support your own son?" Dr. R let out a loud breath.

"I'm saying be careful. You're taking too many chances."

"OK, Mother, I think I'm ready to get cleaned up for dinner."

"You're mad at me." Miriam said, patting his leg. Whenever you call me 'Mother' I know you're mad."

Dr. R turned his wheelchair to leave. "Thank you."

"You don't have to say 'thank you.' I know you don't feel it. Don't pretend with me. I'm your mother."

Dr. R wheeled out without another word. Tea and cookies—he needed more than that from her.

•••

Henry heard a new female voice down in the hall. Then Mrs. R called him and Max to dinner. In the dining room, the new lady sat where Mrs. R usually sat, on Dr. R's left, and Mrs. R sat where he, Henry, usually sat. Before he found a place further down the table, Mrs. R said, "Mother, this is Henry Hamblen. And this is my mother, Mrs. Gottlieb."

"How do you do, Mrs. Gottlieb," Henry repeated as he had been taught. The lady nodded her head once and immediately looked away. Dr. R frowned. Henry sat down, wishing he could disappear.

Agnes and Charlie came in carrying silver trays—Charlie with a champagne bottle, white napkin and two bottles of Coke, which he placed in front of Dr. R. Agnes put a tray with four wrapped presents in front of Mrs. R.

Dr. R took his wife's hand. "We have been very quiet about it today, because we have all had so much to do, but most of you know that today is Estelle's birthday."

"Happy Birthday, Mom," Max said. "Look at all those presents. Wow."

"Yes, wow," Dr. R said, smiling at Max. "Go ahead and open them, while I try to pop the cork on this champagne." However, he waited as Mrs. R opened her presents: a thin silver necklace from him, a white and blue French silk scarf from her mother, and a leather-bound diary from the other grandmother. Henry wished he had a diary like that to draw pictures in. Max had got someone to frame a picture of him in his baseball uniform, and he carried it around for everyone to look at once his mother had unwrapped it.

Mrs. R leaned toward her husband, so he could fasten the necklace around her neck. It glittered against her black sweater. Then Dr. R untwisted the wire on the champagne cork and pried it off. Henry jumped when the cork made its loud popping noise. Max laughed. Dr. R. poured the bubbling liquid into four glasses brought by Charlie from the sideboard, and then removed the caps from the Coke bottles and poured some into champagne glasses for the boys.

Everyone held up his glass, and Dr. R said, "Let us all toast my beautiful wife. Happy birthday!" They sipped their drinks and Mrs. R thanked them. Then Charlie brought in a large rib roast and handed Dr. R a silver carving knife and fork. Dr. R managed to carve it by himself. Gravy, roast potatoes, green beans followed. Henry realized how hungry he was. The grandmothers did not ask him any embarrassing questions, and he ate as much as he could. The adults discussed Senator Joe McCarthy and what they called his witch-hunt tactics for persecuting innocent people he accused of being communists.

"When I see his heavy, angry face on TV, all I can think is that he is a wicked man," Mrs. R said. Henry remembered his mother saying the same thing, but his father thought McCarthy was doing a great job. Henry wanted to tell Mrs. R, but he remained silent.

"The House Committee on Un-American Activities is just as bad as McCarthy. These movie moguls," Mrs. R said. "They are Jews like us, but they are so afraid of being blamed for the communist threat, they'll go along with HUAC's blacklisting that ruins the careers of their actors and directors. Just like they didn't protest the ban on anti-Nazi films during the war. They were afraid to be pro-Jew in an anti-Semitic society."

Henry listened. His father did not like Jews. He called them *kikes.* That word had an ugly sound.

Finally the plates were cleared, and Agnes brought in a chocolate cake with candles and placed it in front of Mrs. R. They sang the happy birthday song, and she closed her eyes to make a wish, and blew out the candles. Henry felt a knot in his stomach. The cake looked just like the chocolate cake his mother used to make for his birthday. Everything was reminding him of home and that he did not belong here.

As Mrs. R began cutting it, Dr. R said, "Do you remember when we were courting, we would go to Battle's Coffee Pot on West 125th Street and get their chocolate cake? We'd sit there for hours eating and talking."

"Side by side in a booth, hoping the waitress wouldn't bring us the bill to get rid of us."

"Didn't your friend Bob McKensie introduce you two?" the nice grandma asked.

"No, Miriam," Mrs. R said, "Bob wasn't the one who introduced us. My cousin, Rachel, who was a nurse then at Belleview, arranged for Josh and that medical student she was seeing to stay with my parents for a weekend in East Hampton. Rachel thought my parents would tolerate her boyfriend better, and besides, her own parents were way out at the end of Long Island in the summer."

"That's right," Carol said, wrinkling her nose. "You were a couple of skinny boys, who looked like they slept in their clothes. It was hard to see you as future doctors."

"Well at least I've improved since 1936," Dr. R said, smiling at her.

"Yes, it was 1936," the other grandmother, Miriam, said. That was the year my brother Jaime almost immigrated from Poland. If only he had . . ." Henry looked at Miriam, who began wiping her eyes with her linen napkin. "I . . . I remember because, Josh, you brought Estelle around to the grocery store to meet us on the very day I got a letter from Jaime saying he thought he could arrange it soon."

"Yes, you're right," Dr. R said. "We met in November 1935, and we married January 4, 1936. But it wasn't a shotgun wedding." The adults all laughed. Max looked confused.

"What's a shotgun wedding?" he asked. The laughter stopped. Henry saw Grandma Carol frown at Dr. R.

"Me and my big mouth," Dr. R said. "Max, I have explained to you how babies come into this world, right?" Max nodded, his face turning red. Henry had seen animals mate at the zoo and guessed that was what was being talked about.

"The expression *shotgun wedding* may have come out of the wild West. If a young woman got pregnant and wasn't married, her father would chase down the boyfriend, point a shotgun at him and say, 'I think you'll be hearing wedding bells tomorrow, if you take my meaning, partner.'" He tried to drawl, Henry noticed, but it didn't quite work. Still, everyone laughed, except Carol, the new grandmother.

"And it was certainly very shocking that you married so quickly," she said. "That's exactly what my family thought—a shotgun wedding and to someone . . ."

"Mother!" Estelle said sharply.

Miriam recovered quickly. "Oh, Carol, that was long ago. We weren't Waldheims, but look what we produced. The brightest student in his high school, graduating at sixteen, a doctor, a psychoanalyst . . ."

"Don't exaggerate," Dr. R said, looking pleased. "You may not know this, boys, but there is a stereotype of the Jewish mother, who constantly brings up in conversation with her friends, 'My son, the doctor . . .'"

"My son, the doctor," Miriam repeated, beaming. Everyone laughed.

"Were you married in a big church?" Max asked. No one spoke. "I'm sorry," Max said. "Was I rude?"

"No, Max, you weren't rude," Dr. R said. "It's a completely normal question. Jews go to temple, which is something like a Christian church, where we have our own religious services. Normally we would have been married in a tabernacle but . . ." He stopped and the boys looked at him. "We were married in the Bronx City Hall by a Justice of the Peace. That's called a civil ceremony, but it's a legal marriage."

"We couldn't afford a big wedding," Miriam said. "But we had wine and cake for our family upstairs in our apartment. The newlyweds didn't seem to care, they just wanted to go home and . . ."

"Miriam!" the other grandma hissed. But then all the adults started laughing, and Carol at least managed a smile. "If you hadn't been in such a hurry," she said, "I'm sure my family would have arranged a proper wedding and reception, either in our townhouse or out in East Hampton."

Dr. R frowned again at the grandma and his knife and fork clattered down onto his plate. "Well, here we are, living a good life in beautiful Southern California."

"Thanks to *my* mother," the grandma said.

"Please, both of you," Mrs. R said. "Let's go over to the living room. Boys, please help clear."

Dr. R quickly wheeled out of the dining room and the other adults followed. As Henry and Max started clearing the dishes, Max whispered, "I hate it when she's mean to my dad."

•••

Washing dishes that night took a long time, because Henry and Max had to do it without the help of Agnes and Charlie, who were preparing platters of leftover roast beef, and slices of cheese and potato salad for the family's lunch and dinner the next day. They were leaving after breakfast to spend the day with Charlie's family.

The dishes were almost finished when the kitchen telephone rang. Agnes picked it up. "Hello, Rosenblatt residence." She listened. "Henry, the operator says you have a call from Phoenix." Agnes covered the lower part of the receiver with her hand. "Why don't you pick up the extension in Mrs. R's office?"

"I don't know anyone in Phoenix."

"Well, someone knows you. Wait a minute." She spoke into the receiver. "Who's calling?" She listened again.

"Mrs. Hamblen," she said.

"My mother. I don't want to talk to her."

"Go," Agnes said, raising the receiver above her head as if she were about to throw it at Henry.

Henry turned and walked through the dining room, and as he started up the stairs, Mrs. R called to him from the living room, "Is the call for me or Dr. R?"

"No," Henry said, running up the stairs to his bedroom. He slammed his door. Then he heard a knock. Mrs. R came in, her face red.

"Henry, you can't do this to your mother. You go to my office, pick up that phone, and behave like a decent human being. Is that clear?"

"Why can't you leave me alone?"

"Because we care about you, that's why."

Henry got up slowly. "I'll do it just because you're making me do it."

"Good. Just do it." Mrs. R left so quickly that when Henry went into the hall, she was nowhere in sight.

Henry entered Mrs. R's office and stared for a moment at the black telephone on her desk. His hand reached out slowly for the receiver, paused for several seconds, and then picked it up. He heard voices and the clatter of dishes, which ceased as soon as he said, "Hello?"

"Hello, Henry. This is your mom."

"I know."

"How are you? Are you doing OK?" His mother sounded far away, her voice unfamiliar.

"I'm OK." He couldn't think of anything else to say. His head was swimming.

"I miss you so much, Henry." Silence. Henry clutched the receiver more tightly. "Are you there?"

"Yes, I'm here."

"Did you get my letter? Did someone read it to you?"

"Yeah."

"Do you understand why I had to leave?"

"No."

"Henry, listen to me. It's a miracle what has happened. Dr. R saved you from . . . your father. He wanted you sent to an institution forever."

"Forever?" Henry's head pounded. "Why would he do that?"

"He was afraid of you. Remember? I told you."

Henry collapsed onto Mrs. R's chair.

"I'm with Uncle Ed," she said.

"Aren't you in Montana? You said you would take me there."

"No, I'm not in Montana. I'm not supposed to tell you where I am."

Henry bent over, shoulders slumped, the receiver pressed painfully against his ear. "So Dad doesn't want me and you don't want me either."

"Please don't say that. We'll find a way to see each other soon. Dr. McKensie says the Rosenblatts are wonderful people. They sound nice. Are they?" Henry did not want to speak any more. Then he heard her crying. "Why won't you talk to me? Henry? Are you there?"

Henry said nothing and hung up. She was far away—she did not care what happened to him. He returned to his room and retreated under the covers with Jake.

• • •

Dr. R was in bed that night, sitting with a pillow between his back and the headboard, watching Estelle brush her hair at the dressing table. "Your hair is just like it was when we met. I don't see any grey in it yet."

She smiled, took off her dressing gown, folded it carefully over the back of her chair, and came to her side of the bed, her pink nightgown shimmering. She climbed in and Dr. R turned off the bedside light. *All signals are go,* he thought, as he moved down in the bed, slipping his arms around her warm body. She seemed relaxed, a good sign.

"Did you enjoy your birthday celebration?" he asked.

"Yes, the champagne was fun. And I love the silver necklace. But I wish you and my mother would stop needling each other."

"I agree," he said, stroking her hair. "I tried my best, but I just couldn't help myself. I am a weak man, don't you agree?"

"You need a lot of attention. But my mother needs me, too!"

She started to withdraw from their embrace, but Dr. R held on, murmuring, "Oh no, you don't. I'm going to show you just how needy I am." She giggled and began massaging his shoulders.

16

In mid-December, Hanukkah came with its eight days of lighting candles and daily presents for Henry and Max. It was the one ritual Dr. R still observed.

The brass menorah stood on the mantelpiece of the fireplace, the mirror behind doubling the number of candle flames. On the third night, after Estelle lit the third candle, they stood there, surrounded by darkness. Max began shifting from one foot to the other.

"All my friends have Christmas trees by now," he complained.

"And you're going with Henry to Charlie's parents' on Christmas Eve for a proper Catholic mass," Dr. R said. "You get a double celebration."

"And double presents?" Max asked.

"Yes, but let us continue. There's more to Hanukkah and Christmas than presents," Estelle said.

"Food," Max said.

"Light," Henry added.

"Yes, light," Dr. R. said. He saw Henry listening to the blessings he read in Hebrew, his eyes riveted on the candles.

"When I was a boy," Dr. R said, "my father always sang the Hanukkah songs. He was a cantor, not the professional kind, but he had a beautiful voice, and most of all, he loved singing in temple. His father was cantor in their *shtetl* in Poland. That's what my father should have done to earn a living instead of running a grocery store."

"He ran a grocery store?" Max asked. "Could you get all the free candy you wanted?"

Dr. R nodded. "Yes, but it wasn't worth the price. I had to spend a lot of time after school and on weekends putting cans and other goods out on the shelves. My friends were out in the streets, playing. I had to work."

"Can you remember one of the songs?" Estelle asked. "We never had the songs in my family."

"I can't remember the Hebrew, but here is one of them." Dr. R hummed, hearing his father's rather high, slightly shaky but pure voice singing the endless verses. As he hummed, he remembered a moment as a child. Staring at one candle, he had felt transported to God. The flame flickered in its bright intensity and he felt the flame was within him—that life, that promise—pulsating through his entire body. It was God within. Maybe he didn't call it *God,* but it was a sacred presence that permeated him and everything around, all the way up to some higher realm. Life lay before him in its mysterious glory.

He stopped singing. And now, what had become of that feeling?

"Can we have our money, now?" Max said.

"Yes," Estelle said, laughing. "That's your favorite part of this holiday, isn't it, Max? Your silver dollar is at your place at the table."

"Oh boy, now I have three," Max said, running off.

"Shall I carry the menorah to the sideboard?" Henry asked. "I'll be careful."

"The menorah reminds me that we have a flame inside," Estelle said, her voice quiet.

You have read my mind," Dr. R said, squeezing her hand.

"I have a flame inside, too, even if I'm not Jewish," Henry said, his back to them as he carried the menorah. Dr. R turned toward Estelle and they smiled at each other.

• • •

At dinner the last night of Hanukkah, the Rs gave Max a new, bigger baseball mitt, a tribute to his growth, which they said was not just his hands. Henry's package contained a Brownie camera.

"You've done some excellent photos with mine," Estelle said. "It's time you had your own."

"Thank you, thank you," Henry said, ducking his head. "Can I go out and take pictures right now?"

"It might not work too well in the dark," Dr. R said.

"Oh, I guess I'll have to wait until tomorrow."

"Something to look forward to," Estelle said.

"And we can play catch with my new mitt," Max said.

"I can take a picture of you with the new mitt," Henry said. Dr. R nodded. Henry had come a long way.

The boys looked suspiciously at the braised brisket and potato latkes Agnes served them. Then their teenage appetites took over.

"These potato pancakes are good, Mom," Max said. "But where is Grandma Miriam?"

"She's making the same dishes for the other Jewish residents at her rest home," Estelle said. "She's talked the cook there into ordering the ingredients and letting her use the kitchen. And Grandmother Gottlieb felt she was coming down with a cold or something. My family didn't celebrate Hanukkah, anyway."

"Why not?" Max asked.

"They do not believe in God," Dr. R said. "They are what we call *secular Jews.*"

"Do you believe in God, Dad?" Max looked worried.

"Uh . . . yes, I do."

"I'll tell Doctor Freud," Estelle said, smiling. Then she looked at Henry. "The high school is having its Christmas vacation now. I'm going to take you to meet my friend, Mr. Kellogg, who will be your homeroom teacher. He's there Wednesday for some meetings. A perfect time for you to start school is right after New Year's." Dr. R saw Henry freeze. Then, looking around, not at them, but somewhere beyond, he got up, threw his linen napkin on the table, and rushed out of the room. They heard his footsteps running up the stairs and his door slam.

"That may have been a little premature," Dr. R said.

"He'll come around," Estelle replied. "At least I hope so."

"Maybe I should try to talk to him," Dr. R said. "He's scared to death."

"Would you? You're better with these kinds of problems."

"What's the big deal?" Max asked. "School's kind of boring, but it's not *that* bad."

"Because it allows you to play baseball?" Dr. R said.

"Right, Dad!"

17

The next morning, Henry did not want to go to breakfast. He heard Mrs. R call once, then silence. He went to the top of the stairs and listened—the others were eating and talking. As softly as he could, he crept down the carpeted stairs, opened the back door slowly and slipped out. It was a sunny, mild Southern California day. He penetrated to the back of the orange grove, where a chain link fence marked the end of the Rs' property.

Close to the trunks of the trees there were no irrigation ditches. He found a friendly-looking tree, deep in shadow, where he sat down, leaning his head against its trunk. He closed his eyes. When he opened them, he caught sight of the shimmering legs of a woman in high heels moving along the path to the cottage, most of her body hidden by orange tree leaves. He jumped up, his heart racing, his face hot. Why did those legs have to go by like that? Was nowhere safe? Not even here in the orange grove? He sat down on the other side of the tree, facing away from the path. The sound of a distant car accelerating up a hill appeared, and then all he could hear was a bird singing. Then even this stopped. He closed his eyes again.

Why were they making him go to school? He would fail. He would never learn anything. The old blackness was beginning to grow in him.

He opened his eyes and looked down a row of orange tree trunks. They stood so straight, but not tall like a pine tree, because their branches began quite low. They were lined up like fat soldiers. Their job was to produce oranges that people could eat. They had a purpose, unlike him. He was useless. Well, at least he was learning to help the orange trees. Just a week ago, he and Charlie had fired up the smudge pots, because a frost was expected that night and they had to keep the oranges from freezing.

He raised his arms in the curved shape of the orange tree branches. With his arms up like that, he felt he was receiving something through his fingertips, something good. His arms began to ache and he lowered them with a sigh.

He couldn't really spend his life taking care of orange trees, could he? But what *could* he do? He was a misfit—yes, his father had called him that—a misfit. Maybe he could run away before Mrs. R made him go to that school. He closed his eyes, trying to make a plan, but his thoughts could not concentrate on anything. He waited, hoping he would figure out what to do.

"Henry." A voice broke into his desolation. He opened his eyes and Dr. R was standing in front of him, leaning on his crutches. "One patient just left and I have an hour until the next one. Come back with me and we'll have a talk." Henry got up without speaking, and followed Dr. R's slow progress across ditches back to his office. He knew he was going to be in trouble.

He had not been back in Dr. R's cottage since that first day. As he entered, he smelled again the old books and saw the oak desk and the red couch.

"You sit there on the couch," Dr. R said, "and this time I'll sit in the chair, OK? You don't have to lie down." Dr. R cleared his throat. "If you are going to run away and go to your desert, I hope you'll say good-bye."

Henry lowered his head, afraid to speak.

"I noticed that the rucksack is missing from the garden shed. I went in there to get it, because I wanted to use it to bring some books home from my office."

"I'm sorry," Henry said.

"Don't be sorry. I think it's great," Dr. R said. Henry raised his head. Was Dr. R joking? He looked at Dr. R, who looked sad—he was not joking.

"What?"

"I've told you: You are free to leave. I don't want you to go, but I won't stop you either. But you need food and money. Put some of your allowance in there and buy yourself some cans of beans and a can opener. Get ready. I won't tell my wife. And you'll need a canteen, too. Max should still have one from his Cub Scout days."

"I . . . I . . . I . . . don't want Mrs. R to see how stupid I really am. And the other kids will make fun of me." He looked at Dr. R, who had pulled off his glasses and was wiping them with his shirttail. He looked tired and bleary without his glasses on.

"Any kid who laughs at you is just ignorant. He probably has something he's ashamed of. You'll see—the mean kid will be someone with acne all over his face, or he's fat as a porker, or he's not made the baseball team, so he'll take it out on you. Grown-ups are like that, too."

"Are you talking about my father?"

"Yes, I don't know him, but he's ashamed of something."

"Does that make him mean?"

"I think so." Dr. R went silent. Henry waited. "You have more freedom than you realize. If this school doesn't work out, we'll find another one. Or you'll go off and solve your own problems. You've already made a start—planning your escape. Give yourself some credit, for God's sake." He raised both hands, fingers splayed. "OK?"

"You mean if I go to school but I can't do anything, I can just walk away?"

"That's right."

"But what will Mrs. R say?"

"I don't doubt her professional expertise, but if she's failed to accurately predict how you'll do, that's her problem. So far, she's never been wrong. Never. But of course, you could make a big effort to prove her wrong." He smiled.

"That wouldn't be fair. I wouldn't do that."

Dr. R smiled. "That was a joke."

"Oh."

"Now go into the house and eat some breakfast before the ladies get hysterical. I've got to read my notes on this next patient." Henry stood up, stopped in front of Dr. R, who was about to swivel his chair around to his desk. He wanted to say something. Instead, he reached out his hand. Dr. R looked startled, but shook it. "Feels like a deal," Dr. R said.

Henry nodded. "I'll try." On the path back to the house, he thought, *This time Mrs. R is going to be wrong. I just know it. But now I've promised.*

18

Two days later at ten in the morning, Mrs. R walked with Henry to Redgrove High School to meet Mr. Kellogg. She chatted away about how she had trained with him, how nice he was. Henry wiped sweaty hands on his corduroys as they walked. He wanted to plead with her to let him go back home, but she just kept talking.

They stopped in front of a huge, white, two-story building with walkways and lawns and palm trees in front and stairs leading up to large glass doors. Henry's feet slowed to a stop. Mrs. R turned toward him. "You'll be OK. Let's go inside."

The long halls were empty and silent, except for an occasional teacher hurrying by. Mrs. R stopped in front of a closed door and knocked.

"Come in," a deep voice said. They entered and Henry saw a very tall, large man, younger than Mrs. R, with black hair greased and combed back like a teenager. They were in a classroom with lines of wooden desks. "Sit down here, Henry," Mr. Kellogg said, pointing to a desk in the front row. "And Estelle, we'll sit in these chairs facing him."

"Oh no, I need to get back home to meet a student. You two will do fine without me. You remember how to get home, right, Henry?"

"Yes, it's easy."

"Goodbye, gentlemen," she said and disappeared through the door.

"So, Henry," Mr. Kellogg began, sitting down, "Mrs. Rosenblatt has told me about you. I've heard this story way too often." He hit Henry's desktop with a fist, which made Henry jump. "Sorry, it just makes me so angry. You were put in a special education school, which amounted to little more than babysitting, or would you say you learned something useful there?"

"I learned to paint with poster paints and do woodwork. I can make picture frames."

"Hey, that could be quite useful." Mr. Kellogg wrote something on a pad he held in his lap. "One of our new electives is a photography class where kids learn to develop and enlarge their own pictures. Some of those kids also take woodshop, and I'm sure the equipment for making frames is there. You can frame your own photos."

"You have a photography class? I was given a Brownie for Christmas. Could I develop my own films?"

"You bet," Mr. Kellogg said. "I'm writing down photography class and woodshop as your electives. Now I've got to give you some tests to see what classes would be appropriate for you."

Henry sighed. *Another test.*

"OK, this is a standardized test for English skills, math, and general knowledge. I'll read the questions and write in your answers. Can you read numbers?"

"Yes, I think so."

Mr. Kellogg looked pleased. "How did you learn to recognize numbers?"

"My mom taught me 'One, two, buckle my shoe.' She had big cards with the numbers on them and I had to point to them as we said the words together. Each number was a different color and the colors were easy to remember."

"Very impressive," Mr. Kellogg said. "So, here goes." Henry sighed again. As Mr. Kellogg began, he hunched over, staring at the scarred desktop below, his shoulders and legs tensing with each new question. He had to do math problems in his head, which began to ache. When they finished an hour later, Henry felt stiff and exhausted.

They both stood up. Mr. Kellogg raised his clasped hands above his head and stretched. As he lowered them, he said, "Go out down that corridor to the right and explore the playing fields. Run around a few times. I'll come get you when I finish scoring this. Don't worry. You did great."

Henry went outside and spotted the baseball diamond with its huge wire backstop, and further down, a football field. He walked around the football field, which seemed longer than he had imagined. He came back to sit on a bench near the baseball diamond, tapping his feet and rolling his shoulders, waiting for what seemed forever until finally Mr. Kellogg appeared in the doorway and beckoned to him. Back in the room, Henry sat down, staring at the American flag in the corner, not looking at Mr. Kellogg. "You did extremely well. Your vocabulary is at a college level, and your general knowledge is at tenth-grade level. How did you pick up so much information when you weren't even in regular classrooms?"

"Radio, I guess," Henry mumbled.

"You solve basic math problems very quickly. You wouldn't believe how bad most kids are at your age."

"I make up problems in my head."

"Really?" Mr. Kellogg asked. "Here's what I think: The best is that you go into eleventh grade. You would be bored in tenth grade."

"Eleventh? I can't."

"I won't kid you. You are going to have to work very hard. Most of the kids get their assignments done in study hall and are free to do sports or whatever after school. You won't get it done in study hall, since for now you won't be able to read by yourself, so you will have to do all that reading at home. Mrs. Rosenblatt says she has lined up people who can read to you. But everything is going to depend on your determination. I'll be here to cheer you on. Did Mrs. Rosenblatt tell you that I teach eleventh-grade English? You'll be in my class we are going to read *Moby Dick* by Melville in class for the rest of the year."

"The white whale?" Henry asked. "I've heard it on the radio. Ishmael and Captain Ahab."

Mr. Kellogg swiveled his chair around and opened a large drawer in the wall. He pulled out a dark blue book with a tiny white whale in the middle of the cover. "Here you are—an advance copy."

Henry took the book and then placed the tip of his forefinger on the whale. "He's been shrunk down. He's smaller than my finger." Mr. Kellogg laughed.

"Hey, we've got to stop. Oh, you have to choose a foreign language: French, Spanish, or Latin?"

Henry smiled. "Latin. I heard a program where a man explained the Latin roots of words. He was really good."

"Mr. Kellogg wrote again on his pad. "Who would have guessed—on the radio? Latin it is, then. It will be English with me, American history, Latin, geography, P.E, and woodshop and photography classes two times a week." They stood up and Mr. Kellogg shook Henry's hand. "See you January 2nd. That's a Friday. You'll have the weekend to recover from your first day."

"OK," Henry said. He left the room, passing a group of three young women teachers, who were laughing and talking all at once. Or were they students? They paused a moment to look at him. He passed through the heavy doors and down the stairs to a walkway leading out to the sidewalk. Was he really going to come back to this place? Mr. Kellogg was nice, but all the same . . .

He passed tidy lawns and palm trees in front of flat-roofed, low houses. Mr. Kellogg was crazy to put him in eleventh grade. Didn't he hear that he had never been to real school? Head down, he watched the squares on the sidewalk approach and pass under his feet.

Then he heard some giggling in front of him. Raising his head, he saw two girls about his age coming towards him, arms linked, dressed in dungarees and tight turtleneck sweaters.

"Hi," the one with dark hair said as they both stopped in front of him. "Do you live around here? I haven't seen you at Redgrove High, have I?"

Henry felt his face get hot. "Uh, no, I've just moved here." He considered how he might get around the two girls. Go into the street?

"What's your name?"

"Henry."

"Glad to meet you, Henry. Will you be going to Redgrove High?"

"Yes."

"What grade will you be in?" the blond one asked.

"Uh, eleventh grade."

"Great," the dark-haired one said. "We're in eleventh grade, too. We must have some of the same classes. I'm Deborah, she's Rachel."

Henry stood there, paralyzed. When the girls saw they were not going to get any more information out of him, they linked arms again and stepped onto the path to someone's front door in order to get past him. "Bye," Deborah called. "See you."

"Bye." Henry was sure they were laughing at him. Why couldn't they leave him alone?

He walked into the Rs' driveway and as he approached the house he saw Mrs. R wave to him from her office. He looked down, hoping she hadn't noticed that he had seen her. He did not want to tell her anything. But she was right about one thing: Mr. Kellogg seemed OK.

19

Five days later, after a breakfast where Henry could not manage to swallow more than two spoonfuls of cornflakes, he found himself walking to school with Max, each carrying a brown paper bag with baloney sandwiches packed by Agnes.

"Why didn't you watch the Rose Bowl game with us?" Max asked.

"I don't like the Trojans."

"Well, they won, you know. Rudy Bukich was fantastic."

"I went to the Rose Bowl a long time ago with my father and brother. First we saw the Rose Parade. I live, well, I *used* to live in Pasadena."

"You're so lucky. Last year was the first year it was on television. Before that we had to listen to it on the radio. Mom really likes college football, and Dad puts up with it, I guess."

"Didn't he play football in high school?"

"Oh, maybe. He had two legs then." A friend of Max's caught up with him and the two went ahead of Henry so they could talk baseball. Henry, his eyes on the heels of their shoes, looked neither left nor right. He did not want to tell Max that the sound of the Rose Bowl game on the television made him homesick. Now he probably would never go to that game with his father and brother again. While the Rs and Max watched, he'd stayed in his room listening to a stupid variety show on the radio. When it was over, he checked his rucksack, but so far, he only had four dollars and two cans of beans in it.

But now he had to go to school. When he looked up, he saw the other boys and girls in groups of two or three ahead of him. All the girls were dressed in skirts that went way below their knees with white blouses and sweaters. They had their hair held back by little clasps and they giggled. On their feet were two-toned or white bucks and bobby socks. The boys all wore khaki or grey slacks, plaid shirts and jackets or V-necked sweaters. At least he was dressed like everyone else. He wouldn't stick out until he opened his mouth in a classroom.

They gathered along the crisscross of pathways leading up to the stairs and big doors of Redgrove High, some stopping to greet each other before entering. Max said good-bye and loped off to his homeroom, slowing to a walk when a hall monitor yelled at him. Henry found Mr. Kellogg's classroom and entered. Many kids were already seated and some looked at him with curiosity as he sat as far back as he could. One of the girls he met on the sidewalk, the dark-haired one, waved and smiled. Henry ducked his head.

Mr. Kellogg stood up from his desk and the room quieted down. "Welcome back, eager young students," he said. Everyone groaned. "I hope you had a happy, productive vacation. Now will the proctors come up here and help me pass out your class schedules, just in case you have tried very hard to forget where you are supposed to be each hour?" The dark-haired girl was one of the kids who went forward, along with another girl and two boys. After handing some slips of paper out, one of the boys asked, "Who is Henry Hamblen?"

Henry raised his hand. "Hi," the boy said, handing him his paper. Henry looked at it. He could make out some numbers, probably the classroom numbers. He saw *H* and guessed that must be history. There was a *B,* which had to be biology. And the word *Latin* he could read.

"As you see," Mr. Kellogg said, "you come back here third period at eleven for English. Now all of you go off to your first period, but could Henry Hamblen and Joyce Nakamura come up here for just a moment?" The others left, a couple of the girls looking back at him on their way out.

Joyce came and stood beside Henry in front of Mr. Kellogg's desk. She was small and had straight black hair, longer than the other girls'. She looked very nervous. Mr. Kellogg tried to loosen his tie. His neck bulged over his white collar. "Damn," he said. "I wish I didn't have to wear this thing. OK, Henry and Joyce. You two are new to this school and I'm going to see that you both do well, OK? Maybe you can help each other. Joyce, Henry has problems reading, and Joyce, you haven't been in America very long and you are just learning to speak and read English, right?" Joyce nodded.

"I want you both to promise me something. We live in an age of conformity. Joyce, you probably don't know that word. Let's see, Henry, can you think of another way to say that?"

Henry thought. "It means everyone is supposed to do the same thing, look the same, and think the same. You're not supposed to stand out or be different."

"Very good, Henry. Do you understand, Joyce?"

"Yes," Joyce said in a quiet voice. "No different."

"That's right," Mr. Kellogg said. "The individual who thinks for himself, who strikes out bravely, is not appreciated right now."

"Lone Ranger," Joyce said. Mr. Kellogg and Henry looked at her with surprise.

"Yes, you've got it," Mr. Kellogg said. "The Lone Ranger is brave and fights the bad guys." Joyce smiled. "So, I want to ask the two of you to look after each other, OK? Henry, keep an eye open for Joyce and be sure the kids treat her with respect. Be like the Lone Ranger—charge in there and rescue Joyce if necessary." Joyce giggled, covering her mouth with her hand. "For you, Henry, the trouble will come from other boys. I think the girls may not be a problem." Joyce giggled again. Henry frowned.

"Why not?"

Mr. Kellogg smiled. "Look in the mirror sometime, Henry. Maybe you haven't noticed."

Henry's face burned. "Now off you go," Mr. Kellogg said. "Let's see, Henry, you go to Room 201 for history and Joyce, you go to Room 222 for algebra. I think you both can read numbers, right?

"Yes," they said in unison.

"Bye, see you at 11."

They went out into the corridor, crowded with students. Henry looked at the number on a door near them and said, "I think our classes are on the second floor." Joyce followed him up the stairs, where they parted.

"Good . . . bye," she said, separating the syllables.

"See you back at Mr. Kellogg's at eleven," Henry said, his throat tight.

He entered Room 201 and sat down at the back. The teacher wrote her name on the blackboard and fortunately also said it out loud. "I'm Miss Abernathy." She was short and chubby, with blond hair and bangs, little glasses on the end of her nose. She passed out textbooks, but to Henry's relief, she talked the rest of the time about research projects and reading schedules and then began introducing the subject of the industrial revolution. Some of the other kids were taking notes, but others like him just sat there, although some of them didn't appear to be listening at all. Henry sat up straight and listened as well as he could. Would he be able to remember anything?

Biology class, two doors down, was a little easier. The textbook had many pages of illustrations and diagrams. He had to tear his eyes away from looking at them in order to listen to the teacher, Mr. Benson, who seemed nervous and stuttered a little.

Back in Mr. Kellogg's room, he sat next to Joyce, who had seated herself in the back near the windows, hunching her shoulders and clasping her hands in front of her on the desk. She turned her head and smiled at him for a second, then stared at her hands again.

"Can you understand what the teachers are saying?" he asked her in a whisper.

"A little," she said in her high-pitched voice, but so quiet he could barely understand. Mr. Kellogg stood up and everyone immediately stopped talking.

"Our next book will be *Moby Dick* by Hermann Melville, an American writer at the end of the last century. It's a good story and some people feel it contains a lot of symbolism in the form of Moby Dick, a white whale. But think about this yourselves. Then we will discuss it. In the meantime, I want you to write two pages about something of interest that happened to you during the Christmas vacation. Take two pages and put your name in the top right-hand corner of each page, and number them 1 and 2. Four of you are going to have a different challenge."

He then named two other kids in addition to Henry and Joyce. "I want you four to draw a picture of something interesting that happened to you during the vacation. You can make it abstract if you want—that means not real people or places. Come up here—I've got boxes of colored pencils for you.

The other kids had begun writing and paid no attention. Henry returned to his desk and arranged the colored pencils on either side of his paper. He began drawing a picture of an orange grove with patterns of green, orange, and dark brown for shadows. He forgot everyone; he forgot where he was. He was back in the orange grove. A shrill bell brought him back. As Henry left he looked at Mr. Kellogg, who winked at him. Mr. Kellogg was a kind man. He and Joyce would have stuck out as the only two who couldn't write, but Mr. Kellogg had added two more. Their pictures were laid out on Mr. Kellogg's desk and the other two kids were obviously good at drawing. Maybe they couldn't write, either?

He and Joyce ate their sandwiches together on a picnic table under a wooden structure with a roof but no walls. They said little to each other, but sat watching the little groups of laughing kids, mostly girls with girls and boys with boys. Even Max was in the middle of his baseball buddies and only waved once to Henry.

The rest of the school day was a blur for Henry. He tried to listen, but he couldn't. When he met Max in front, he was carrying five books he couldn't read, piled on his binder, clasped against his side.

"You better bring a wheelbarrow tomorrow," Max joked.

"Very funny," Henry replied. "I feel like an idiot carrying all these books. I've been assigned a locker, but I have to take all these home. I got nothing done during the study period in the library. I just looked at pictures."

"I got nothing done either," Max said as they walked away from the school, "because my friends and I were trading baseball cards under the table, but then the librarian caught us and gave us a black mark."

"Serves you right, Max."

"Ah, don't be a sorehead. You sound like a grown-up. We're reading *Animal Farm* in English. It's about pigs who become communists—really stupid."

"How can you know it's stupid when you haven't even read it yet?"

"Oh, I can tell."

They walked a few blocks in silence until Max said, "Oops, we should have turned down that street back there to go to Grandma's place."

"I wish I didn't have to go there," Henry said. "I feel funny having her read to me like I was a little kid."

"Mom says you have to."

"I know."

They turned around and Max led him two blocks to Happy Home and then ran off. Henry wished he could follow. He wanted to be alone in his room, under the blankets with Jake.

Passing through the double glass doors, he found himself in a quiet world, very different from the school. Two old ladies on a sofa stopped their conversation to stare at him. Henry waved as he passed them. They looked like those dried up apple dolls he had made at his special school—all wrinkled and brown. The ladies' faces broke into smiles.

He went up to the receptionist behind a high counter and said, "I'm Henry Hamblen. I have come to visit Mrs. Miriam Rosenblatt."

The receptionist peered at him over her half-moon glasses. "I beg your pardon?" she said. "Would you write your name and the name of the person you wish to visit here in this register?" Henry pulled himself up to his full height, as if stretching to touch Mrs. R's ruler above his head.

"I can write my own name, but I cannot write the name of Mrs. Rosenblatt. Could you write it for me?"

"I beg your pardon?" she repeated in an even more annoyed voice. "I think I better call . . ." Before she could finish, a loud shout came from the corridor leading off the lobby.

He turned and there was the grandma shuffling towards him, arms raised, crying excitedly, "Henry, Henry, there you are! Come, come, give your grandma a hug!" Henry slapped his hand on the counter. "I *told* you so." The receptionist glared at him a second, then bent back over her papers.

Then he rushed to meet his . . . grandma, put his binder and books on the floor, and gave her a big hug. She felt soft and comforting and she smelled nice. "Let's go down here to the library," she said. "There's a little room where we can work."

He picked up his books and binder and followed her. It seemed so quiet and peaceful. No one was rushing around, no one was laughing at him. As they entered the little library with its wooden bookshelves and stuffed chairs, more old faces looked up at him. One lady with white hair said in a high croaky voice, "Miriam, where did you find such a handsome boyfriend?" The others laughed, including Miriam.

"Oh, he just wandered in, pretending to be my grandson. When I saw him, I just thought I'd keep him." More laughter.

"Good idea," the lady said. "If you get tired of him, pass him on to me!"

"Not a chance, Gertrude," Miriam said patting the lady's shoulder. "Let's go in here," Miriam said, walking into a small room next to the library. We can close the door so we don't disturb anyone."

"Oh well," Gertrude said quietly and returned to reading her book.

Henry dumped his binder and books on a small dark wooden table. Miriam tried to close the door. "This *dummkopf* door," she said. "It doesn't close. Never mind, at least no one can see us." She came over to the table and eased her large body into an armchair. Henry had placed scraps of paper in each book to indicate where he was supposed to start reading and where to stop. The passage for the Modern European History class was at the middle of the book—the industrial revolution.

"Industrial revolution," Miriam said. "This would be good for Max to read to you. He likes to hear about machines. What about this biology book?"

"Well, it's got lots of pictures. The teacher explains what they mean."

"OK, so what is this? *Moby Dick.* I know it's about a crazy captain and a white whale. How about beginning with this?" I'll read the beginning up to your marker—no, let's go further, if we can, and then we could talk about it."

"OK," said Henry. As soon as Miriam began, he entered the dirty but exciting world of whalers. He understood Ishmael, who wanted to get away and have an exciting adventure. Miriam read with a strong voice, maybe just a little slow because of her accent. She paused to put a cough drop in her mouth. "What do you think, Henry?" she asked. "Does this interest you?"

"Yes, but I wish the story moved more quickly. There are too many long descriptions of ships and whaling. This is going to take forever."

"I think authors in the last century weren't in such a hurry. And I think this author, what's his name?—Melville—is trying to teach us about whaling as well as tell a good story. We'll have to put up with those descriptions."

"Anyway, I'm required to read it."

"Well," Miriam said, closing the book. "I think you'd better get home for dinner. And we eat way too early here. In fact, in a few minutes we go to the dining room." She looked up and exclaimed, "*Mein Gott,* Henry, look out there."

Henry looked. The door was half-open. Through the opening, they could see some chair legs and some human legs as well. Miriam heaved herself up and went over to the door, opening it wider. There, just outside, was a circle of four chairs, occupied by Gertrude, a bald man, and two other old women. They all looked at Miriam with old watery eyes, smiling.

"You have been listening," Miriam said crossly. "Maybe Henry doesn't want other people listening!" Their faces sank a little.

Gertrude said, "But what you were reading was so interesting. We couldn't help but listen."

Henry hated seeing them look so sad. "It's OK with me, Grandma."

She looked at him, serious, then burst out laughing. "You're a good boy. Well, if you don't mind... Do you want to come back day after tomorrow? I think that was the plan." The old faces turned towards Henry.

"Yes," he said. "See you all then?" The group nodded their heads, and then began struggling to get out of their chairs. Henry put his binder and books on a table and hurried to help the bald man up and then Gertrude.

"Thank you, dear boy," Gertrude said, placing her cold wrinkled hand on his forearm.

"You're welcome," Henry said. He and the grandma left the library.

"It's almost five o'clock," Grandma said. "Time for our dinner. If you'd rather, we could meet next time in my room. I don't want you to feel uncomfortable with all those people listening.

"No, it's OK. They really want to hear the story."

"Yes," Miriam said. "We go back to being children and like to be read to. And those old folks can only read books with very large print, and some of them can't even do that any more."

"Bye, Grandma," Henry said. It sounded so strange to say *Grandma.*

"Good-bye, come back soon," he heard from one of the old ones. He headed out the glass doors. The light was fading, but he had only four blocks to walk home. He liked the old people. And they never asked why he couldn't read the book himself.

As he walked in the front door, he met Dr. R in his wheelchair. "So, Henry," Dr. R said, "did you survive the battle without too many wounds?"

"Yes, sir," Henry said. "At least I'm still on my feet." Dr. R looked at him, surprised.

"And how did it work with my mother?" he asked.

"We started reading *Moby Dick.* And four old people sat around the door to listen to us."

"They have their nerve!"

"No, they're really nice. They can't read very well any more. At least Grandma can."

"She probably sees better than I do, I'm so near-sighted."

"She does read kind of loud. But that's good for those four old ones outside the door. If she speaks too quietly, they're going to start to complain. We'll start hearing 'Eh, eh? What was that? What did you say?' all the time."

Dr. R laughed. "You seem to be in a very lighthearted mood, Henry. I haven't seen you like this before. What is the cause, I'm wondering, being the good psychoanalyst that I am? Any clues?"

"Uh, those old people—they don't expect anything from me. I can just relax."

"Mrs. R says I'm too driven," Dr. R said. "Maybe I project that onto you—that means you start to feel the same pressures I feel. I'm sorry if that is the case."

"Way too complicated," Henry said and moved to go upstairs.

"I'm not sure I can handle this wisecracking version of Henry Hamblen," Dr. R called up the stairs. "Where's all the gloom and doom?"

"It's just around the corner."

"Right, your old friend."

"Yours, too?" Henry shouted back. As he entered the room and closed the door, he smiled. But it was true—Dr. R seemed worried about something.

20

At lunchtime two weeks later, Max and Henry sat under a shade shelter on the edge of the playground, eating their sandwiches. Joyce, seated near him with another girl, was eating rice and cold vegetables. She and her friend had their heads together, whispering. A group of three boys stopped in front her.

"Football team," Max whispered.

One of them, broad shouldered with a flat nose, leaned over Joyce. "You eat funny food. You Chinese. Parents have Chinese laundry?" All three laughed, and then one stuck his finger in Joyce's rice, pretending to taste it and spit it out. Joyce froze. The biggest of the three pulled the sides of his eyes apart to make them slanted.

Instantly Henry was on his feet. "She's Japanese, not Chinese. Leave her alone."

"Oh yeah?" the big guy said. "A dirty Jap? They killed my uncle."

Henry pushed him in the chest. "Get away from her!" he shouted. Caught off guard, the boy fell to the pavement with a cry of surprise. The other two immediately turned and walked away while the boy scrambled to his feet. Henry began pummeling him with his fists, yelling, "Leave her alone, leave her alone!"

The boy fought back, but his size slowed him down. He tried to cover his face with his arms when Henry backed him up against a post, hitting him in the stomach and head over and over.

"Hey, lay off," the boy whimpered. The other kids started shouting and soon two male teachers ran up, grabbed Henry and pulled him away.

The boys were both marched up to the principal's office. The principal, Mr. O'Connell, a little man with a fat stomach, dressed in a black suit, stood up from his desk and snubbed out his cigarette. He was angry. Henry's eye was swollen and painful. The other boy, Oscar, was bleeding from his nose. The school nurse appeared with a first aid kit and put an ice pack on Oscar's nose and Mercurochrome on their wounds. As she left, Mr. Kellogg came in and sat down next to Henry, glancing quickly at his face.

"So Henry started this fight," Mr. O'Connell said. "He has inflicted serious wounds on this boy. We have to suspend him,"

"Have you asked him why he started this fight? Mr. Kellogg asked.

"Does it matter? You know the rules—no fighting."

"Henry," Mr. Kellogg asked, "why did you?"

Henry looked at Mr. Kellogg and took a breath. "Those three guys were teasing Joyce. They were making fun of her eyes, and what she was eating. I couldn't stand it."

"You could have called one of the lunchtime monitors," Mr. O'Connell said. "It wasn't your business."

Mr. Kellogg glared at the principal. "You know those boys would have disappeared long before Henry could have mustered help. What they did to Joyce was racial bigotry. It's those boys you should be punishing, not Henry."

Mr. O'Connell shook his finger at Mr. Kellogg, his face twisted. "We can't examine every reason someone starts a fight. We have to send a clear message that fighting is not tolerated under any circumstances."

"Let's send a clear message that racial discrimination is not tolerated."

"I knew there would be trouble if we allowed a Jap in here," Mr. O'Connell said, lighting a new cigarette.

Then Mr. Kellogg said, "Why don't you put Henry on probation for a month? If he starts another fight in that time, he's out. In the meantime, I will speak in his homeroom class about the need to respect cultural and racial differences. Someday we whites have to accept we aren't the superior race we think we are. I wish you would discuss this topic in the morning assembly also."

Mr. O'Connell sighed, leaning back in his chair. "I don't care much for your liberal views. I hope this isn't a sign of communist leanings—we can't be too careful. But all right, I'll put him on probation. So be warned, Henry. One more incident and you're out. I will have to call your parents about this—let's see." He opened a drawer and pulled out a folder. "What is your last name?"

"Hamblen," Henry said. "But I live with Dr. and Mrs. Rosenblatt." As Mr. O'Connell squinted at his list, Henry felt his eye throb with pain.

"Yes, I see that here. I will call Mrs. Rosenblatt immediately. "Oscar, I'm sorry this happened to you. Perhaps you should go home for the rest of today."

"That guy should be expelled," Oscar mumbled, lowering the ice back from his nose. He's a bully."

"Stay here while I call your mother," Mr. O'Connell said. You two can go."

In the corridor, empty because students were back in class, Mr. Kellogg put an arm around Henry's shoulders. "Good for you, Henry. I'm proud of you. You got carried away, but it was for a good cause. Where did you learn to fight?"

"I don't know. Something just took over."

Mr. Kellogg looked serious. "I see," he said.

"Dr. and Mrs. Rosenblatt will be angry with me."

"I think I know them well enough to predict they will not be upset by what you did. I, however, would be extremely upset if you did not defend Joyce. And that's that. See you later." He walked away. Henry watched Mr. Kellogg's back recede down the long corridor, not knowing what he was supposed to do next. Go home? Go to his next class? What was his next class? He could no longer remember. Then he saw two girls from his English class coming toward him. They stopped in front of him, looking serious. The one with red hair, reached up to touch his forehead above the black eye.

"You need an ice bag," she whispered. "It's all puffy." Henry backed up.

"Uh, I'll get one at home."

"She wants to be your nurse," the other girl said and laughed as they walked off.

Finally the school day ended. On the way home, other students waved at him.

"You're a hero," Max said. "Look at them."

"I bet those three guys will beat me up first chance they get," Henry said.

"Maybe we can get the Lone Ranger to come get them."

"He's not real, Max. Remember?"

21

The next night, after the boys had gone to bed and the Rs were in their bedroom, Estelle interrupted Dr. R, who was in bed reading Winston Churchill's *The Gathering Storm.*

"We received a letter today. You will be surprised."

"Who's it from?" Dr. R asked.

"Betty Stafford—does that name ring a bell?"

"Uh, no, should it?"

"Hint: from Pasadena."

"You don't mean..."

"Yes, the friends of Dick Hamblen, with the daughter, Fannie."

Dr. R pounded the bedspread with his fist. "I don't like this—she has our address!"

"Calm down. Let me read the letter." She picked up several pages of stationery from her dressing table.

March 4, 1953 Pasadena

Dear Dr. and Mrs. Rosenblatt:
Please forgive this letter from a stranger. I got your address from my friend, Edna Hamblen. Don't worry—I memorized it when Edna telephoned me last week and never wrote it down.

I know Edna told you what happened. My husband and I do not agree about this incident. I am convinced that Henry had absolutely no evil intentions toward our daughter. I believe her story that he never asked her to go with him. She's always been a tomboy with an over-developed imagination, and she thought this escapade was going to be just a few hours of adventure.

Fannie feels terrible that she got Henry in trouble and she's determined to apologize to him—in person! I am aware that you might be very nervous about such an encounter, since you may want to keep his whereabouts secret.

I have a sister in Redgrove, so I have the perfect excuse to go there with Fannie when my husband is away on business. I told Fannie I would mail a letter from her to Henry, but she knows he can't read, and she doesn't want someone else reading her letter to him. That's why I am writing. I did not want to telephone. You hear such strange things nowadays about conversations being tapped.

Doctor Rosenblatt, if you or your wife feels that such a meeting would be harmful to Henry in any way, please say so. I think Fannie would accept your decision.

Like Edna, I consider it a miracle that Henry ended up with you. Edna says he is even learning to read. I'm not surprised. I never believed he was mentally retarded. Thank you for saving him. Please write me in care of my friend, Sally. That will be the safest.

Sally Richards
210 Arroyo Seco Avenue
Pasadena, California

Sincerely,
Betty Stafford

Estelle refolded the letter, put it in its envelope and slid it into the little drawer in front of her. She turned around to face Dr. R. "But what effect would it have on Henry to see Fannie? Would he want to? It's only been two months."

"From my professional viewpoint, it might be good for him," Dr. R said. "He needs to resolve his feelings toward her."

"From *my* professional viewpoint," Estelle said, "he needs a kick in the *tokhis.*" She raised a fist in the air.

"Estelle!"

"I've tried to be patient with him, but he could be learning much faster. He's so sure he's going to fail."

"Is seeing Fannie going to help that?" Dr. R asked

"Don't you think we should ask Henry what he thinks?"

Dr. R sighed. "Only if you and I agree first.

"Have a little faith," she said. "It's going to be all right."

"The Sphinx has spoken."

"Josh, I'm warning you." She smiled at him, though, as they settled down. She was soon asleep but he lay awake, imagining the worst.

•••

The next night after dinner, the Rs asked Henry to come into the living room. Henry followed them, head down, wondering if he had done something wrong. When they were seated, Dr. R said, "We have received a letter from Betty Stafford."

"No!" Henry said. An image of her angry face flashed through his mind.

"Yes, it seems your mother told her our address, but she never wrote it down, so we hope your father doesn't have it yet. We'd like some more time for you to gain some independence before you have to face him."

"He doesn't want me," Henry began. He wanted to stop thinking about his father. His father didn't care what happened to him. "Why did Mrs. Stafford write?"

"She says her daughter Fannie wants to talk to you in person and apologize for what happened."

Henry felt bits of memory swirling around inside. "What did happen? I'm not sure I remember—I was at the police station and then I was taken to that hospital with those crazy men . . ."

"Do you remember that the girl followed you up the mountain?"

"It was cold—we were thirsty and hungry."

"She feels bad," Mrs. R said, "that she got you in trouble."

"I don't want to see her. Can't she leave me alone?"

"Of course, if that's what you want," Dr. R said.

"Henry," Mrs. R said, "Mrs. Stafford has a sister here in Redgrove, so she thought if you agreed, they would just stop by for a few minutes on the way to visit the sister."

Henry's memory coalesced into an image of the girl with pigtails sitting cross-legged on the wall. "I told her not to follow. What can I say to her?"

Mrs. R smiled. "I think you just have to listen. That's what she's asking for. When she's finished, you can say, 'Thank you' and let it go at that."

"I'm not going to say anything," Henry said, standing, and ready to leave.

"That sounds like 'yes,'" Dr. R observed. Henry was already out of the room and up the stairs, wishing he had said *no* because . . . because . . .

• • •

Ten days later on a Saturday morning, the doorbell rang. Henry was in his room, staring out the window at the orange trees. Dr. R was at Stanyon. Henry heard women's voices down in the hall and after a moment, Mrs. R called up the stairs, "Henry, your guests have arrived." He stood up, glanced at Jake on his pillow and walked over to the closed door. He stopped for a moment in front of it, not wanting to reach out for the door handle. Finally his hand moved slowly toward it. Why hadn't he said no?

Downstairs in the living room, he found the three women still standing. Mrs. Stafford came over with raised arms but stopped in front of him, dropping her arms to her side. She smiled. "Hello, Henry. Thank you for letting us come."

"Uh, that's OK," he mumbled. Mrs. Stafford looked the same—same pale green sweater he liked and tight brown skirt, same dark bangs.

Fannie came up beside her. She looked different. Could she be taller? She wore a full skirt, white with a red belt. Her hair was around her face, not braided. She wasn't a little girl anymore, but how could she have changed so quickly?

"I just wanted to say I'm sorry."

Henry looked over her head at a vase of red flowers on the mantelpiece, avoiding her sad face.

"I have asked Agnes to bring coffee for Mrs. Stafford and me," Mrs. R said. "Henry, why don't you show Fannie the garden and the art in Dr. R's office? Have you noticed the art on the walls? Every psychoanalyst I know collects strange art objects from all over the world, particularly from so-called primitive peoples."

"Oh, yes, I'd like to see that very much," Fannie said, suddenly smiling.

Henry turned and walked over to the back door. When he opened it, Fannie was right behind. He led her down the gravel path to the cottage and held the screen door open, so she could enter. He found the switch for the spotlights that lit up a black demon in a painting on the wall.

"That's a Tibetan thangka," Fannie said, going over close to it. "Isn't he scary? He's supposed to represent the evil forces within us. I have a whole book on Tibetan art."

She continued to look at the thangka as Henry stood near the door where they had come in. Her hair glistened under the spotlight, as black as the black demon. Henry felt his breath catch as a pale-yellow light gathered around her. She turned and walked over to Dr. R's desk, looking down at the photographs on it. She was no longer under the spotlight, but he noticed that the glow that had come with her, if anything, was even more intense. He wished he could say something, but no words came.

"Who is the little boy in the photo?" Fannie asked.

"That is—was—the Rosenblatts' son. He died when he was five. Max says he caught meningitis at a birthday party and was dead in two days."

"I wonder if it helps to have a photo to remind you every day that he is no longer alive?" Fannie now looked directly at Henry. The glow had faded but it was still there, close to her skin. "Do you like the Rosenblatts?" she asked.

"Yes. They treat me very well. They aren't like parents, well, it's hard to explain."

"Do you think you will stay here?"

"I don't know. They want me to finish school."

"Well, of course." Fannie turned to look at the wall next to the thangka. "Oh, that statue is African, I bet—look at his potbelly." Henry did not want to look at him—the man's penis was sticking out. Fannie went over and patted the wooden statue's head. "I want to live with a really wild tribe for a while. That's why I have to become an anthropologist. Margaret Mead got to live with all kinds of tribes in Samoa and her husband took photographs."

"He took photographs?"

"Yes, that's important for an anthropologist."

"I am learning to develop my own photos."

"Are you?" She came over to him at the door, her eyes sparkling.

Henry felt dizzy, swimming in her light. "Would you like an orange off the orange trees? There still are a few left."

"Sure," she said, and they left the cottage. When they had picked their oranges, he pulled off his sweater and spread it out so that they could sit against the trunk of an orange tree. She smiled, sat down, and they peeled their oranges. He pulled a clean handkerchief out of his pocket and handed it to her.

"Uhm, this is so good," she said, wiping her mouth with the handkerchief.

"I come here sometimes. It's cool and shady and I can hide . . . if I want to."

"But you're not running away."

"No."

"There's a robin," Fannie said, excited. "See him hopping over there?"

"Robins are good luck for me," Henry said.

"Are they?" she asked. "Does that mean you don't hate me?"

Henry straightened up, his spine firm against the tree trunk. "No, it wasn't your fault. I don't remember everything, but I know it wasn't your fault."

"You don't remember? I do."

"Dr. R says I had electroshock at the hospital. It can wipe out memory. But I think a lot is coming back."

"My friend's father had electroshock, but it didn't stop him committing suicide. They say he saw horrible things in the war."

"Dr. R had his leg blown off by a kamikaze attack on his destroyer."

"Poor man. I wish I could meet him. I'd like to ask him about his art collection, where everything came from."

Then Mrs. R called out, "Henry, Fannie—time to go."

As they stood up, Henry felt he didn't want her to go. *Take me with you, take me with you,* he kept repeating to himself as they walked back up the gravel path toward the house. And as Fannie drove off with her mother, Henry watched the car disappearing through the gate. His head felt on fire and he heard his brain repeating: *Take me with you. Take me with you.*

It made no sense, no sense at all.

22

That night, Dr. R could not sleep. Searching in the dark for his bathrobe, he hoped the sound of the wheelchair would not awaken Estelle. He returned to the living room where Charlie had built a fire earlier to warm them while they watched *I Love Lucy.* A few embers remained. He threw another log on and watched as a flicker turned to a flame.

He sighed. Yes, this fire was just like his life. Before the War, he had felt a great flame burning in him, a passion for his work, a deep love for Estelle and Jacob, whose innocent joy permeated their days. Then came the War, the death of Jacob, and the loss of his leg. Afterward, he and Estelle both worked hard. But something was gone. He glanced down where his leg used to be. He could not see the scarred end of the stump, but Estelle could. Wasn't it repulsive to her? Was she still longing for his touch or was she just pretending? Making love was not the same with one leg gone.

Even his battle to eliminate lobotomies seemed doomed. He picked up the poker and thrust it against the burning log. It sent up a protest of sparks, its glowing red underbelly exposed. He felt a wave of heat on his leg. That reminded him of his patient Björn Sorenson, the boy he still hoped to save, whose torso and legs were covered in scars from cigarette burns.

Björn's mother had committed her son at age seventeen, about six months earlier, saying he had turned violent and frequently threw ashtrays at her. The family had emigrated from Sweden ten years earlier and after only a month in America, the father had died of pneumonia. Björn stuttered so badly he could hardly get a word out. He was quickly labeled mentally retarded and manic-depressive. He sat for hours in a corner of the dayroom, head down, eyes closed, unresponsive to any humans around him.

That was the posture Björn assumed when Dr. R saw him in his office for the first time. Dr. R did not press him to speak, but sat looking at Björn's profile, his small pointed nose and his pale blond hair falling over his closed eyes. Dr. R admired his muscled biceps bulging beneath a tight blue T-shirt. The boy must have been lifting weights.

Suddenly Dr. R noticed just below the edge of Björn's shirtsleeve three small circular scars. "Björn, do you smoke?" Björn raised his head and opened angry eyes.

"N . . . ne . . . ne," he stuttered, his mouth twisting uselessly.

"So, no. Does your mother smoke?"

"Ye . . . ye . . . ye . . . ye."

Dr. R reached over and took a cigarette from a wooden box on his desk. Occasionally he offered one to a nervous patient to get him to relax enough to speak. Now he took the cigarette and pressed one end against his own upper arm. "Have you ever done this to yourself?"

Björn shook his head.

"Did your mother do this to you?" Björn nodded. "Can you show me more burns?"

"More?" he asked. Björn crossed his arms, grabbed the bottom edge of his T-shirt and pulled it quickly over his head. He stood up and turned around. His back was covered in identical scars.

"Oh, my God," Dr. R gasped. Björn calmly turned his T-shirt right side out and put it back on, then sat down, looking with questioning eyes at Dr. R. "I bet your mother said you did this to yourself, but there is no way you could do it in the middle of your back."

Björn's face registered a half-smile.

"And no one here figured this out when they gave you a physical the day you were admitted. Your report mentioned burns on your legs. The stupid S.O.B.s." Björn shook his head. "And they don't seem to have noticed that you understand English perfectly well?"

Again, Björn shook his head.

"You must have gone to school here. Can you read and write?" Björn nodded. "I'll try to get you a speech therapist. Maybe you can write things about yourself when you're in here with me. But please, stop getting in fights. Just walk away when those guys on your ward tease you. Try to stay calm. It's going to take time to get this straightened out."

Dr. R took a pad of paper and pencil he kept on top of his desk and handed it to Björn. "Can you write down why you think your mother had you committed?" Björn wrote for a minute and handed the pad back.

In perfect cursive handwriting, he had written: *I got too big for her to hold me down any more. She began shouting horrible words at me and then I threw ashtrays at her to get her to stop burning me with her cigarettes.*

" Yes, exactly what I thought. Your mother should be treated here, not you."

That first interview ended with a knock on the door, signaling that an aide had come to escort Björn back to the dayroom. Björn had stood up, shaking slightly. He nodded his head a few times with a stiff little bow, turned, and left.

Dr. R had tried, God only knew he had tried. The bureaucracy blocked the speech therapy, and Björn's mother's visits always provoked some form of violence from Björn within an hour of her leaving. Despite Dr. R's objections, Björn had been transferred to a ward for the more dangerous patients, where everyone was kept in strait jackets. The insane mother had won—for the moment. Dr. R had sent a report in to his supervisor, pleading for a meeting to discuss Björn.

Dr. R pulled the wire mesh fireplace curtain closed, and then wheeled himself toward the bedroom. The grandfather clock in the hall struck three as he passed by.

• • •

From a deep sleep, he felt Estelle shaking him. "Josh? The alarm went off fifteen minutes ago!" He groaned, sat up, and swung his leg over the side of the bed, banging a toe on the foot rest of his wheelchair, which he had left too close to the edge of the bed.

"Damn it all to hell," he muttered.

"Are you OK, dear?" Estelle asked, already at her dressing table, glancing at him in the mirror, but not turning around.

When Dr. R entered his office at Stanyon, he had barely shifted from his crutches to his desk chair when Ruth rushed in, her face pale and pinched, tears running down her cheeks.

"It's Björn, isn't it?"

"Yes, it's horrible. He had a lobotomy on Wednesday. The mother's testimony overrode yours. He's due to be discharged back to her in three days. He's still upstairs."

"Oh, God." Dr. R buried his face in his hands. Ruth reached over and patted his shoulder. "I don't want to see him—I'm afraid he'll be like the others—nothing left but a dumb animal."

"At least we saved Henry," she said.

"But Björn was just as bright," Dr. R said in a muffled voice through his hands. He raised his head. "Ruth, what am I going to do? I feel useless. Poor, poor Björn, a young life ruined by an evil, sick mother. I failed him."

A sob burst forth and he leaned his forehead on one hand, tears dropping on his desk. Ruth came around to his side, leaned over, and threw her arms around him. He swiveled his chair to embrace her shoulders. Leaning forward, their foreheads touching, they remained like that, both weeping. Then he straightened up, took one of her hands and reached for Kleenex with the other. They both wiped their faces and he blew his nose. Her small warm hand in his began to calm him.

"We mustn't give up," she said.

"Björn's mother," Dr. R said. "That insane bitch—if she were here right now, I think I would strangle her."

"I would, too—slowly."

"If only I could get into the newspapers. If only I could describe to the public cases like Björn and Henry so that people would wake up and understand." Dr. R suddenly straightened up, clasping his forehead. "My God, why did I never think of it? My wife's cousin writes about science for the *New York Times.* Maybe he can help. Yes, why didn't I think of that?" Estelle could contact him before we go to New York for the conference in May. With her encouragement, I bet he would come to my talk."

There was a knock on the door. Ruth, startled, stood up. Before she could move away, Dr. R grabbed her hand again. "Thank you, Ruth. Thank you." He held on, not wanting to let go, releasing it only when his next patient came through the door. Ruth smiled for an instant, turned and left, while the patient, tall and stooped, stared at her with open mouth.

23

After Charlie picked up Dr. R and drove him home, Dr. R wheeled himself straight to the bedroom in search of Estelle, who sat at her dressing table, staring into the mirror. He moved his wheelchair next to her, but she continued to stare into the mirror, not looking at him. He hesitated speaking although he felt he was bursting.

"I have some news you aren't going to like," she said, clearly unaware of how he was feeling.

"What?"

"My mother has booked two round-trip tickets on the Queen Mary for us to go to London and Paris from New York for the month of May. She thinks it might be her last trip. I couldn't say no . . ."

"Look at me, Estelle," he said, breathing hard. "The conference in New York is in May—I'm counting on you being there. Now it's even more important than I ever could have imagined."

Estelle remained motionless. He felt her image in the mirror was frozen in ice. Then in a tight voice, she said, "She's already bought the tickets."

Dr. R backed his wheelchair away. "I don't give a damn. She can afford to change them. Tell her to pick any other month—but not May. This paper I'm giving against lobotomies may be my last chance. Please, not May."

"I can't believe you could be so heartless, both to me and to her," Estelle said, her voice rising. "What's happened to you?"

"Estelle, please, don't do this to me. I need you with me in New York. Work it out with your mother to go a month or so later."

"My mother needs me, too. I can't go against her."

"You never go against her. And I'm begging you."

"I don't understand. You've gone before without me. Bob McKensie's already promised he'll be there to help you."

Dr. R swallowed hard, trying to control himself. "I was hoping you might consider getting in touch with your cousin, Alfie. An article by him in . . ."

"Stop!" Estelle screamed. "Don't even say his name."

Dr. R recoiled, his wheelchair sliding backwards. "How can you expect me to understand your hatred of him when you won't tell me what happened?"

Estelle shook her head. "I just can't. Please don't ask me. I'm not going to New York. I'm sorry. Can't we discuss this later? Dinner will be ready soon."

"I don't give a damn about dinner. This is about you and me, Estelle. Please listen to what I am trying to say. This may be my last chance. Can't you put me first for once instead of your mother?"

"What do you mean, 'last chance'?" Estelle gave an angry twist to the green scarf she was trying to wrap around her neck.

"Every day I expect to lose my job."

"I wish you had taken my advice and just told your supervisor about Henry straight off."

"You have no idea how the real world works," he said.

"You did what was right. That's all I care about." She looked at him with a sad smile. "Ever since you began this battle to convince the world to abolish lobotomies, I feel I've been forgotten. You used to be different. You used to ask me how I was feeling about everything. You would ask my advice. You would listen when I tried to help you."

Dr. R knew he needed to stop but he could not. He had to follow his anger. "You have your news. I came in to tell you mine. I found out this morning that my patient, Björn, was lobotomized yesterday. His new doctor ordered it. Another innocent boy destroyed by the institution."

Estelle grimaced. "That's terrible. I'm so sorry."

"Maybe you understand now why I feel so desperate."

"Let's discuss this later. It's dinnertime. They must be waiting."

Dr. R had no desire to eat. A good, strong Scotch was what he wanted, but he turned his wheelchair around and followed her. How could her mother have such power over her? And what had happened between her and her famous cousin, Alfie Gottlieb?

•••

During dinner, the boys chattered about baseball and appeared not to notice the silence between Dr. and Mrs. R. After dinner Dr. R went out to his cottage to work on his paper, the boys moved upstairs, and Estelle watched an episode of *Ozzie and Harriet* on the TV. Later, as they were preparing for bed, Dr. R wheeled over to her dressing table, took her hand, and said, "Look, we can't go on like this. Out in the office I was thinking..."

Estelle withdrew her hand. She frowned. "You put me in an impossible position. Don't you see that?"

Dr. R tried to swallow. "I'm sorry, it's just the timing."

"Josh, I don't really believe this paper is going to stop lobotomies. You know it's more complicated than that."

"It could change the tide. I know you don't want to hear his name, but Alfie might really want this story for the *New York Times.* I can be with you when you talk to him. Maybe it would just require a phone call, but if he insists on seeing you, I'll be there with you."

Estelle's face hardened. "You won't give up, will you? No matter how painful it might be for me."

"If only you could explain to me why you hate and fear this man." Estelle turned away from him and picked up her hairbrush. Dr. R slowly shook his head. "I made a sacrifice to get Henry here. This may be the end of my career. What are you sacrificing?"

"I don't like your tone of voice. Let's drop it, shall we?"

They lay side by side that night, an impenetrable wall between them.

•••

The next morning at Stanyon, Dr. R received a phone call from his supervisor, Dr. Shaw, telling him to come over to see him immediately. Dr. R looked at the black receiver after he put it down—a messenger of doom. He sighed and stood up, straightening his necktie, which suddenly felt as tight as a noose. He wheeled his chair down the long corridor, knocked on the supervisor's door, pushed it open, and rolled in.

Dr. Shaw, tall and bony, sat behind his desk, his long fingers holding a sheet of paper in his hand. He lowered it to look at Dr. R. "This is a letter from a Mr. Richard Hamblen. He claims that you forced him to turn his son over to you after he had been discharged from here, and in fact, his son is living with you. How is that possible?"

"I know it looks bad," Dr. R said. "Here's the story."

As he spoke, Dr. Shaw began drumming his fingers on the letter beneath them. "The obvious question straight off the bat," Dr. Shaw said when Dr. R finished, "is why the hell didn't you tell me about this immediately?"

"I knew that as an administrator, you would consider my actions very questionable."

"But this is worse. If this gets out into the public, as Mr. Hamblen threatens to do, we will indeed be in big trouble."

"I'm sorry. I really am. I was only thinking of one thing: to save Henry Hamblen from a lobotomy. He is already eighteen, but his father put him down as a year younger and told everyone he had parental control of a minor. The boy was minutes away from a lobotomy—now he's learning to read and performing well in high school."

"Dammit, you should have told me immediately. You know I am sympathetic to your cause. I think this wholesale lobotomizing has gone too far, for the very reasons you have mentioned: Relatives trying to get rid of a problem. If you had told me, I might have been able to find a way out. I'm glad Dr. Wilson has left; his role in this is highly suspect, too. But now, for you, it's too late."

Dr. R felt a twist of pain in his abdomen. "Meaning what?"

"I have no choice but to ask you to resign immediately. Even though the ends justify the means, in legal terms it was still kidnapping, whether or not the boy was eighteen. If this hits the newspapers, the only thing that will save my neck is to say you were asked to leave as soon as this transgression was discovered."

"*Transgression?*" Dr. R asked, his face starting to burn. "To save the life of an abused child with a genius IQ?"

"I'm sorry, Dr. Rosenblatt. You have to understand my position. If you leave today, I will write a letter of recommendation for any future job, although I would not advise you to enter the public sector ever again. Your interest in talk therapy is much better served at a private clinic, anyway."

"But it's the people here that need my help."

"You'll find a way."

"I can't abandon my patients. I've built up their trust."

"You must leave immediately. We'll take care of your patients."

As Dr. R wheeled around to leave, he shouted, "You call this taking care of patients?"

"Leave," Dr. Shaw said. As he wheeled back to his ward, Dr. R prayed he would not run into any of his patients, most of whom always looked at him with such hope in their eyes. He would first call Charlie to come pick him up, then speak to Ruth to discuss with her how she should break the news to the men that he would never see again.

24

Arriving home with Dr. R, Charlie began unloading cardboard boxes of medical books, masks, wooden animals, and wall hangings. Agnes came out to help.

"Is Mrs. R at home?" Dr. R asked.

"Yes, she's waiting for you in the bedroom," Agnes said, lifting a box from the car trunk. "The boys are off at the movies with Max's friend. His mother is bringing them home after dinner."

Shifting from crutches to wheelchair, Dr. R wheeled himself around the corner and into their bedroom. Estelle was standing near the bed. She looked tired. "So, Estelle, as I predicted, I have lost my job. I barely escaped without an official reprimand." She sat down on the bed.

"To hell with that job." She looked like she wanted some comfort herself, but Dr. R felt paralyzed with heavy grief.

"Dr. Shaw didn't even give me time to say goodbye to my patients."

"So now what?" Estelle asked, lowering her hands to her lap. She looked down, twisting her wedding band.

"Now everything depends on my paper."

"It can't be that simple."

Dr. R felt his face burning. "Why can't you understand how important this is to me? I can't just give up because I've lost my job."

Estelle's face seemed to become pinched and taut. "I don't know—I just don't think this is going to lead anywhere. The inmates are turning violent in those overcrowded wards, and the doctors are desperate. Lobotomies seem like a panacea—it's too strong a force for an individual like you to combat. I want to support you, but this time I can't."

Dr. R wheeled closer and took his wife's hands. "Something's going wrong. Maybe my mother is right," Dr. R said. "She told me yesterday she thought you and I need to talk to each other about Jacob's death, because we never could when I came home. I was injured—you took care of me. Now on this New York issue, we don't seem to be able to listen to each other."

Estelle nodded. "Yes," she said in a voice so quiet he could barely hear it. "She's told me the same thing. It's true, we haven't ever really talked about Jacob for a very long time."

"So, do you think we could put aside for the moment this impasse and give it a try? Maybe we'll get through whatever is keeping us so apart now."

"I don't know, Josh. What good does it do to go back?"

"You're always telling me that I shouldn't blame myself for Barney's death, but I still do. You still think Jacob's death was your fault, although, of course, it wasn't."

Estelle cupped both her hands around Dr. R's and brought them to her lips. "Yes, we're both wounded, aren't we?"

He moved his hands to encircle hers. "That's true. But maybe we should try what my mother suggested. Let's think about the wonderful years we had with Jacob."

She nodded. "He doesn't want us to be sad."

"Dare I ask how you know that?"

Estelle smiled. "You wouldn't believe me." Then her face became serious, intense. "You go first," she said, her voice quivering. Dr. R wanted to take her in his arms. She seemed so fragile and vulnerable. But he only held her hands more tightly.

"OK," Dr. R said. "This is what I remember about Jacob: He was born with a lot of dark hair and a very round face. He was a happy baby and we thought he was so beautiful. I was busy finishing my psychoanalytic certification, but I couldn't wait to get home to be with both of you in our apartment on Lexington Avenue. When he started walking and talking, we thought he was the smartest kid alive. He loved to cuddle and pull on my beard and glasses."

Estelle nodded, pulling a hand away from his to reach for the box of Kleenex.

"We moved here," Dr. R continued. "He was running around, excited about everything. I got the electric train, even if he was rather young. What was he then, about three? We followed him while he explored the orange grove and the garden. Charlie gave him piggyback rides."

Estelle blew her nose and took another Kleenex to wipe her eyes. "Go on."

"Then came Pearl Harbor. In '43 I was gone, and you were left alone with Jacob. You mailed me his drawings and told me everything he was doing. And then, you wrote me he had died. Gone. Our ship was engaged in the last battles of the war. I had to treat the wounded and dying, not only on my ship but even on other ships in our battalion. I couldn't come home. It was physically impossible in the midst of battle, and I guess I felt a moral duty not to desert my men, even if it had been possible."

"Then the kamikaze attack, Barney's death, my medical discharge. The Navy got me out with the other severely wounded. But you were alone for months after Jacob died. I remember you took me once to Jacob's grave when I came home. We've never gone back, have we?" Dr. R stopped.

Estelle was sobbing loudly. Dr. R slid his chair closer and put his arms around her. She leaned forward and put her forehead on his shoulder.

And then he was crying also. The tears ran onto the top of Estelle's hair. She straightened up, turned and opened a drawer in her dressing table. She pulled out a framed photograph. Her hands shaking, she placed it in his. Through his tears, he could see the three of them on the lawn in front of the house. He and Estelle were seated on a blanket and Jacob was standing between them, his hands on their shoulders, smiling.

"He was so sweet and innocent," she said, clutching the photo. Why did he have to die? If there is a God, he is a cruel God."

"We must remember his joy," Dr. R said. "Oh, we can't forget him."

"All these years I've wished I had never taken him to that birthday party. I knew there was meningitis going around, but he begged and begged. I gave in."

"You did nothing wrong," He reached out from the wheelchair to take her in his arms, but it was impossible.

"Come lie beside me on the bed," she said. "I feel weak." So he lay down with her and held her while she cried. He tried to kiss her but she turned away. "I can't, Josh," she said. "I feel completely drained. What is the point of all this?"

"Don't say that. We have our boys. We have this beautiful home. Your students need you. I need you." Estelle pulled back to look at him, her eyes glistening with tears.

"I know it's not rational, but sometimes I think Jacob wouldn't have died if we hadn't bought this huge place. I never wanted it. I thought by marrying you I would escape all this show. I thought our moving to California would get us away from my family and all that money, but then my father died, and my mother decided to move here."

"Estelle, I thought in the end you were happy here. I guess that was my projection."

"I don't know any more."

"You put your mother and me first. Maybe that wasn't right. But I don't believe there is a God who let Jacob die in order to punish you for not being poor. Please don't think that."

She shook her head against his chest. "I'm sorry—I can't help it."

"Turn around, let me rub your back." She lay still as he massaged her shoulders, and then she moaned and turned to him. The tensions were gone. They made love as they had done in the early days. He buried his face in her hair, inhaling its familiar scent. They were drunk with relief. And at last they were both satisfied and reunited.

Suddenly Estelle sat up. “I never thought about putting in my diaphragm. Is there anything I can do now? It would be terrible if. . . .”

“Go push in some spermicide,” he said, half-asleep. “Or do you have a douche?”

Estelle jumped out of bed. “I’ll do both. Oh, it’s probably OK; I’m due to get my period in a couple of days.” She disappeared into the bathroom. He heard the faucet running as she filled the douchebag. He sighed. This wasn’t the time to argue for the hundredth time that she was still young enough to have a child. She always said the same thing: She could not face the pain of losing another one.

It seemed a long time before Estelle came out, now wearing a white terrycloth bathrobe. She smiled a half-smile.

“You’ll be fine,” he said. “Sounds like you are way past ovulation, anyway.” Estelle nodded and began gathering together her clothes from inside the bed.

“The boys will be home soon. I’ve got to get dressed. But, Josh, please try to understand. I have to make this trip with my mother.”

Dr. R sighed. “I can only hope you will change your mind.”

25

On a warm spring Saturday morning a few weeks after Easter, Mrs. R brought a letter into the dining room at breakfast. "Your mother has written me, Henry."

Henry looked up from his cornflakes and saw the familiar handwriting.

"She wants to come see you in a week. She says she has been living in Arizona with your Uncle Ed, but she's moving temporarily to a ranch near Las Vegas. She's traveling with Uncle Ed and a friend of hers. She's dying to see you, and your birthday is May 1. She can get here the next day, which is a Saturday."

Both Dr. and Mrs. R were looking at him, waiting for him to say something.

"She went to the Arizona desert?"

"Evidently." Mrs. R said.

"Uncle Ed wasn't nice to her."

"That's all changed—didn't she tell you?"

"He took her away."

Dr. R nodded. "You feel abandoned. But perhaps you could give her a chance to explain her situation. She's been through a rough time, too, you know."

"Is she going to take me with her?"

"No. She can't yet. And we would like you to finish high school. Then you'll have to decide what you want."

"If I finish school."

"You will, Henry," Mrs. R said. "You will."

"So I have to see my mother?"

"You could say no," Dr. R said.

"Will she be here long?"

"No," Dr. R said. "Only one night."

"I guess that's OK." He returned to his cornflakes, which were now completely soggy and tasted like wet cardboard.

"She wants to have a birthday party for you," Mrs. R said. "To celebrate your turning nineteen."

"Well . . ."

"We'll have to celebrate it one day late."

"I don't want a party."

"It means a lot to her," Mrs. R said. "We'll do it for her. And we can practice that passage in the desert book of Grandpa Jacob's we've been working on. She'll be thrilled to see how much progress you've made."

Dr. R frowned "He might not want to read in front of an audience, especially not relatives."

Mrs. R looked at Henry with her serious expression. "Yes, of course, it's entirely up to you."

• • •

Henry was lying on his back on his bed when he heard car tires on the gravel driveway in front of the house. He waited, clutching Jake to his chest.

"Henry," Dr. R called up the stairs. Henry slipped Jake under the pillow, glanced at his worried face in the dresser mirror, and opened his door. As he came down the stairs, he saw his mother, dressed in blue jeans and a white cowboy shirt, look up at him. She smiled. Then she moved towards him and threw her arms around him. He stiffened and pulled back.

"Henry," she said, "at last."

"Hi, Mom," he muttered. She released him and turned toward the two men with her, also cowboys with cowboy hats and boots.

"Here's your Uncle Ed and Carl. Carl has the ranch next to Uncle Ed's in Montana. I grew up with him. They're taking me to Las Vegas."

Uncle Ed was broad with a round, red face; the other guy taller with grey hair and glasses. Dr. R shook their hands. The round one came over to Henry and reached out a calloused hand.

"Howdy, I'm your Uncle Ed. Edna never told me you're as handsome as that movie star—who's that guy who always has a chip on his shoulder? You know, Edna."

"James Dean?"

"Yeah. You sure look a lot like your mom. Thank God you didn't take after your father, the S.O.B."

"Ed, watch your language," Edna said, shaking her head but smiling a little.

"Please come this way," Dr. R said. "We can talk in the living room."

Henry's mother turned to him. "Give me another hug, Henry," she said, her voice trembling. Henry obeyed mechanically, his arms barely touching her. She wiped her eyes with her shirttail, just like a man. "We have to talk," she said.

All Henry wanted to do was get away, so he headed up the stairs, hearing Mrs. R say, "We've planned a birthday dinner for Henry tonight. Please spend the night. We have some cots Charlie can take out to my husband's cottage for you men. And there's a guest room upstairs for you, Mrs. Hamblen." Henry was down the hall before he could hear their response.

Entering his room, he pulled Jake out from under his pillow. Throwing himself on the bed, pillow over his head, he pressed Jake against his cheek. Was he ever going to be safe? He did not want to talk to his mother—he really did not want to. Why couldn't she just go away and leave him alone?

"Jake," he said, "you and maybe the R's—you are my friends." Then he fell asleep, dreaming of a dark shape emerging from the closet, coming towards him while he lay there, paralyzed, unable to scream.

Later, he heard a soft knock on the door. He rolled over and groaned as his mother entered the room. He swung his legs over so that he sat on the edge of the bed, running his fingers through his hair. She drew up a chair from his desk. For a long moment, they looked at each other. "It's hard to believe it's only been four months," she said, smiling a little. "In that time our lives have changed completely."

"I guess so," Henry said, looking away from his mother, toward the window, where the day was darkening.

"Everyone says your father can't take custody of you, now. Thank God, he forgot what year you were born. My little trick worked, it seems. Years ago, when I realized he had the year of your birth wrong, I somehow knew I should go ahead and let him think you were a year younger. You'd think I knew somehow that would be important at some moment. I just hope he doesn't get Dr. R arrested. He claims you were kidnapped against your will."

"Dr. R never told me that it was against the law for him to bring me here."

His mother shook her head. "The law isn't always right."

"Maybe I don't belong here or anywhere."

"I know—sometimes I feel that way too, although your Uncle Ed has been so nice to me. He wants me to be the cook for the dudes and the ranch hands this summer up in Montana. We've been living at his winter ranch near Phoenix. I'm riding a beautiful palomino down there."

"You said you would teach me to ride."

"And I will. Just as soon as you can come up there."

"What about Sam?" he asked.

Her face became sad. "I have written him at Harvard three times and never received an answer. Either he hasn't received my letters, or he chooses not to answer them. I don't know what he is thinking or feeling. I just wrote him again to tell him I'm going to Nevada to get one of those six-week divorces. I have to hang around a fake ranch with other women getting divorces. It will be very boring, but then I will be free." For an instant Henry understood something: *His mother wanted to be free, too. That's what Dr. R had told him.*

"We'll never be a family again," Henry blurted out.

His mother shook her head. "We haven't been a family since World War II began. Your father wouldn't talk about what happened when he was serving in France, but he came back a changed man. Before the war he was solid and responsible, maybe a little too serious, but someone I could count on. He was never mean or violent. I think he must have come close to being killed, and probably he had to kill Germans, because ever since the war, he's been afraid—afraid of you, afraid of a nuclear war, afraid of communist spies, afraid the stock market will crash again. I tried to get him to go to a psychiatrist, but he refused. He preferred to drink his whiskey."

"It wasn't just me?"

"No, but you scared him the most. That's because his brother, Ronnie, really was crazy."

"I never hurt Fannie."

"We know that." New tears began to overflow his mother's eyelids. "Do you have a Kleenex?" she asked. Henry stood up and went into the bathroom and brought one back. "Thank you," she said, daubing at her eyes. "You have a family here who loves you, Henry," she said. "And I hope you and Sam and I will be a family again some day. We may live in different places, but we can always come together."

There was a knock on the door. "Dinner in twenty minutes," Mrs. R called out.

His mother jumped up. "I'm going to change—I brought some dresses with me." She hesitated, then walked toward Henry, leaned over, taking his head in her hands and kissing his nose. Henry tried to turn away. "Henry," his mother said in a hurt voice, then straightened up and left the room.

"Oh, hell," Henry said to Jake.

He glanced over at his desk and saw on it the large desert book that had belonged to Grandma Miriam's husband. He remembered he had promised Mrs. R to read something at his birthday party, but he hadn't even looked at it for days. He would never remember those words. Maybe Mrs. R had forgotten. At that very moment, he heard steps in the hall, and Mrs. R called through the door, "Don't forget to bring your book, Henry." He wanted to yell back: "But you said it was up to me!" This did not feel like that at all.

26

When Henry walked into the dining room, he saw the two grandmas, his mother, the Rs and Max, and the two men, all their faces glowing in the light of many candles. He sat down, staring at gifts piled in front of him. Everyone was looking at him.

"Go ahead—open them," Mrs. R said. "Then we'll have dinner. Agnes needs a few minutes to fry up some extra chicken for us." Henry wanted to go back upstairs. This all felt so strange. He slowly picked up one package and unwrapped it. It was a leather belt from Grandma Miriam. His mother had brought him a genuine black cowboy hat. There were some new baseball cards from Max, cookies from Agnes, and a white dress shirt and tie from Grandmother Gottlieb. Then Dr. R handed him one more. Inside was a new camera, a Finetta IV with an extra lens. Henry felt his heart beat with excitement.

"Oh, thank you! My teacher has one of these and he takes great pictures with it."

"Henry develops his own films at the high school darkroom," Mrs R said. "They teach photography there now. Maybe he'll show you some of his photos."

"I'd like to see them," Carl, the man in the glasses, said. "I am an amateur photographer, too. I try to get shots of the wild animals up in Montana. And I have my own darkroom at my winter home in San Diego."

Henry looked at him. "Wild animals?"

"Yes, bears—well, Yellowstone Park bears, begging along the road—and elk, hawks, and even a mountain lion."

"Yes, Carl has some fantastic cameras," Edna said, giving the man a big smile. Henry looked down at his gifts, away from his mother smiling at that man.

"Wow," said Max, as fried chicken and mashed potatoes were served.

"Henry," Uncle Ed said, "your mother is a great cook. I never knew that. When she's done her six weeks in Las Vegas, she's going to join me in Montana and cook for all the dudes and cowhands. We've been hiding out at my other ranch near Phoenix. I figured we were far enough away from that S.O.B. so he couldn't come after her. And she's already started cooking for the dudes at the Phoenix ranch. We have 'em in both places, so there's lots of cooking to be done—and plenty of horses for her to ride. That's what she loves most, to put her rear end on a horse and gallop off."

Grandmother Gottlieb, on Henry's left, stiffened, frowning at Uncle Ed. Henry looked more closely at him. He wore a red plaid shirt and suspenders. He had sandy hair like Henry's mother and himself, but with a thick neck and fat cheeks.

"This room is sure fancy," he said. "But we've got a long table up in Montana, too, only it's made of pine planks and people sit on a bench along both sides." He turned toward Max. "Someone told me you like baseball. After high school, I played in a minor league out of Bozeman—that's the closest real city to us up there in Montana."

"You did?" Max said, eyes wide.

"Yes, and I'm a big fan of the Chicago Cubs, who do their spring training in Phoenix now. Too late to see them this year, right? The season's about to begin."

"April 13. I can't wait," Max said. "I root for the New York Giants, but Henry likes the Boston Red Sox."

"Let me tell you about the Chicago Cubs," Uncle Ed said. The two launched into baseball talk, their heads close together. Henry wished he could cover his ears and not listen any more.

Cake and candles and the "happy birthday" song followed. Maybe Mrs. R wouldn't ask him to read. They would leave the table, and he could dash to his room.

Then Mrs. R said, "Henry has a surprise for you. You'll have to turn on all the lights. Everyone looked at him. Seeing there was no way to escape, he lowered his head, then slowly reached under his chair for the desert book.

"Jacob's book," Miriam said. "I mean my departed husband, of course, not the other Jacob." Dr. R reached over and patted his mother's shoulder.

Henry felt his hands shaking and perspiration on the tips of his fingers. Why did he ever agree to this crazy idea? Read in front of all these people, his mother? Yet his hands opened the book at the marker. He felt sure he would not recognize a single word. Then, slowly, he began to read, as if someone else in him knew how to read. The passage he had chosen and practiced with Mrs. R described desert animals, whose names he had no trouble recognizing: bighorn sheep, kit fox, desert tortoise (not pronounced *tor-toys* as it looks), California leaf-nosed bat, kangaroo rat, rattlesnake, leopard lizard, a bird called a thrasher, cactus wren (don't pronounce the *w*), roadrunner, Panamint chipmunk, ladder-backed woodpecker, pinyon jay. All of these lived in the Mojave Desert, and just the sound of their names thrilled him. There were many pauses, but he read about his animals for five minutes, not daring to let his eyes leave the page. When he finished, he raised his head and managed a small smile. There was a brief silence.

"Wow," said Max. "You can read." Miriam, soon joined by the others, broke into cheers and applause. Henry pulled out his handkerchief to wipe his moist eyes.

"Four months," Mrs. R said. "That's what I call progress."

"But I've got to get better," Henry said.

"And you will," Mrs. R replied. "You will."

Henry's mother jumped up and came over, pressing her face against his. "I'm so proud of you, Henry. This is incredible."

Henry turned his face away from her, looking down at the carpet. His mother returned to her seat. He could bear it no longer. He stood up, grabbed his camera and ran upstairs, as he heard Dr. R say to the others, "This is a lot for him to assimilate."

Henry splashed water on his face, muttering, "I'll be OK, I'll be OK." When Max came in after dishes, Henry was examining the camera, holding it and turning it, as if it were the most precious, fragile object on Earth.

Max frowned. "What's so special about a camera? They could have given you your own baseball mitt."

"Well, Max, maybe with this camera, I can take pictures of you batting the ball without it blurring."

"Oh, great. That will be supercool." As Max left, Henry went over and very slowly and quietly pushed the doorknob in and turned it to lock the door. It was the first time he had done that at the Rs', but he did not want to face another human being that night, and especially not his mother.

•••

After dinner, Estelle took Edna off to her dressing room to have a talk. Charlie drove Miriam home. Ed and Carl ended up in the kitchen, helping Agnes with the dishes and laughing loudly. Dr. R found himself alone in the living room with Carol. He served her a demitasse of coffee that Agnes had placed on a table next to his wheelchair. He watched Carol for a moment as she stirred in a cube of sugar.

"So I hear you lost your job," she said, looking up.

"You might say I was strongly encouraged to resign," Dr. R said.

"So what are you going to do now?" Carol wrinkled her nose, as if, Dr. R thought, he had acquired a bad odor.

"I'll try to find work in a private sanitarium. Talk therapy is practiced and appreciated there. The only problem is, the down-and-out people who need it the most can't afford those private places."

"Haven't you done your duty to the riffraff of society?"

"You mean the riffraff who lost their minds defending us from the Nazis and Japanese war mongers?" He swallowed, hoping to beat down the rising anger.

"Oh well," Carol said. "We've had this conversation too many times, haven't we?"

Dr. R saw his chance—he could not resist. "Perhaps you have heard that I am placing great hopes in this paper I am delivering at the Psychiatric Conference in New York in May?"

"Yes, and I'm sorry I have to take Estelle away for my trip. I think she told you."

"There is one thing you could do to help me," he said after a moment's silence. He had not forgotten that Estelle did not want any mention of Alfie. He knew he should stop, but he could not. In the end, wouldn't Estelle understand? And she wouldn't be there in New York. She did not have to see Alfie or have anything to do with him. It was out of her hands. There were other Henrys and Bjorns out there and he could not abandon them.

"What is that, Josh? I can't imagine how I could help you." She smiled, a sign Dr. R took as justification to go on.

"You have a nephew, Alfie Gottlieb, at the *New York Times.*"

"Yes, he's done well. The family is proud of him."

"He's a respected columnist and he covers science and medicine. My paper advocating the abolishment of lobotomies might be of interest to him. If he covered it, my campaign might be successful. The whole country would be alerted to the horror of this practice."

"Why, of course. I'll write him a letter tomorrow. I'm surprised Estelle didn't think about this sooner. I'm sure he would be glad to help you."

Even now, Dr. R knew he could withdraw his request, but he hesitated. Then he heard women's voices down the hall.

"Uh, Carol, Estelle has something against Alfie. Would you mind not mentioning this to her?" Carol straightened up, lowering her chin, and frowned at him.

"That is something I can't promise," she said in a flat voice.

•••

The next morning after breakfast Edna asked Henry if she could come up to his room to say goodbye. Henry nodded once and started up the stairs. Edna followed. They sat in chairs next to the window, facing each other. "I'm glad you've met Carl and Uncle Ed," she said, smiling. Henry clenched his fists.

"Is Carl some kind of boyfriend? Already?"

His mother's smile disappeared. "He's a friend."

"I don't care if he likes photography."

"Oh my God, you're jealous."

"You've not even divorced yet."

She shook her head. "I didn't realize . . . yes, I'll ask him not to come when I get back to visit you."

"I don't care." He gazed up at the ceiling. He heard her sigh.

"You can't forgive me for not protecting you from your father's insanity."

"Don't talk about him," Henry shouted.

"I tried to protect you. I know I didn't do a very good job. We were afraid. But now we have both escaped."

Henry's head dropped. He heard his heavy breathing. He didn't raise his head but he heard her footsteps coming toward him. She lightly stroked his hair—he could barely feel it. "You always had such beautiful hair," she said.

Henry raised his head and she withdrew her hand. He looked at her standing there in front of him, a half-smile forming around her trembling lips. "Mom! What a dumb thing to say."

"Henry, listen to me. I love you and Sam. You were worth all the agony with your father. Now I want to live again. You are finding your way in the world, and that's what I want to do, too. Carl and I always were good friends. I think he wants more than that, but I've told him I need time. I want to go to college and study English literature, maybe write some short stories. All those years while you and Sam were at school and your father at work, I read novels. Maybe I'll write a novel about ranch life."

"Just keep that guy away."

"I will . . . if that's what you want." She hesitated. "I have to go straight from Las Vegas to Montana, because the dudes start coming in June. But we'll be back by October. It starts snowing up there and the tourist season is over. We can see each other then. I'll come with Uncle Ed. Not Carl."

"Sure, Mom."

"We can talk on the phone."

"OK."

His mother stood up, started to walk toward the door, and then came over to him at the window. He looked up, afraid she was going to make him kiss her. Instead she reached into her purse and pulled out something. "Here's a photo of me on that palomino. Maybe you'd like to have it."

Henry took the photo and looked at it. "You're holding a gun. Is that a real gun?"

"Yes, that's a pistol my father gave me a long time ago. Uncle Ed kept it—maybe he hoped I'd come back some day. I'm just pretending to shoot it, of course."

"Gosh, mom. A gun."

"So, good night. See you in the morning." She moved quickly to the door, blew him a kiss, and was gone.

"Jeez, Jake, she really has changed," Henry told his tiger on the pillow. "She's turned into a Wild West cowgirl—with a gun."

27

Edna, Ed, and Carl left immediately after breakfast to drive to Las Vegas. Four days later, Estelle began to pack for her trip. Dr. R spent hours in the cottage working on the references for his paper. The morning before her departure, Estelle came in the cottage door, something she rarely did. He looked up, startled. Her face was grim as she came up to his desk.

"I was just talking to my mother on the telephone about our trip. She was complaining how much she had to do and then she said—I couldn't believe it—she said she had to write my cousin Alfie about your coming to New York. When I said, 'What?' she said, 'Oh, Josh thought a letter from me might encourage Alfie to write an article in the *New York Times* about his paper.' Estelle advanced. "Please explain how that possibly could have happened."

Dr. R drew back in his chair. He lowered his head a moment, closing his eyes, then raised it and looked into her flashing eyes. "I know you told me not to, but I felt compelled to. Ever since Björn's lobotomy, I've felt everything I've been working for depends on getting written up in the *New York Times.* You won't have to have anything to do with him. Can't you let go of this, and just let me talk to him?" He felt his palms sweating. His forehead pounded.

Estelle came up to his desk, placed her hands on it and leaned towards him. "I was clear, wasn't I? I told you not to try to contact Alfie. You betrayed me. As my husband, you should have respected my wishes."

"If you won't tell me the reason for this hatred, how can you expect me to understand? Can't you sit down so we can talk?"

Estelle turned and headed for the door. "This is such a breach of trust. My mother has promised not to write Alfie. And don't you dare try to contact him. When I get back, we'll talk about this. Don't write me, either. Let's make a complete break for this month I'm gone. I can't stand what you've become." Then she slammed the door behind her.

He sat there, stunned. Could this be happening? He would promise her that he would have nothing to do with Alfie. Why had he spoken to Carol. Yes, Estelle had been more than clear he was not to. Maybe it wasn't too late to convince her that he would honor her wishes. He could not lose her. No, that would destroy all he had left.

But when he returned to the house, he learned from Agnes that Charlie had driven Estelle to her mother's, and Carol's chauffeur would be driving them the next morning to the San Bernadino station to catch the Super Chief for Chicago, and then on to New York. He tried to telephone, but no one answered. He knew it would be useless to have Charlie drive him over there. He had to wait, not knowing for a month if she would forgive him.

28

One week later, Dr. R in his turn was driven by Charlie to catch the Chief at the San Bernadino train station. No Super Chief for him—the Chief was less expensive, less luxurious. It had been paid for by Stanyon before he was fired. At least Dr. Shaw had the decency not to cancel the ticket. He would not see any celebrities or movie stars in the dining car. They all took the Super Chief.

Each day while he was at breakfast, the Negro porter converted his bed back to a seat in his Pullman compartment. He then spent most of his time there, making small corrections in the manuscript for his talk. He went upstairs to the observation car to view the Rocky Mountains, ate in the elegant dining car, and swore at the difficulty of maneuvering the aisles with his crutches. Three days later, he arrived in New York.

When he checked into the Plaza Hotel, he was handed a note from Bob McKensie.

Dear Josh:
I should have called you before I left for New York a week ago. It turns out I did not travel alone. I am engaged to be married to the most wonderful woman in the world. Her name is Diana. You'll meet her soon. We are in Room 432. So, of course, I can't share a room with you after

all. I got you a single room one floor below us. Give me a ring when you get in.

—Bob

"I'll be damned." Dr. R frowned at the clerk who had handed him the note.

The young man in his dark suit and bow tie straightened up and said, "Sir?"

"Tell the bellboy to take up my bags. And I believe a wheelchair will be provided for my use in the hotel and for the conference downstairs?"

"That's right, sir. It's already in your room."

Dr. R watched as the red-uniformed bellboy with his perky red cap unpacked his clothes and laid out his dark suit for dinner. He tipped the boy, who saluted and left. Then he asked the hotel operator to connect him to Bob's room. A woman's voice answered.

"Uh, hello, may I speak to Bob?"

"Of course. Darling, it's for you."

"Hello?"

"Bob, what's this? I had no idea."

"I'll tell you all about her over dinner, tonight. You won't mind, will you, darling?" Dr. R could tell Bob was covering the receiver so he could talk to his darling. "Yes, Diana's worn herself out, what with visiting her relatives and my relatives, and shopping for her trousseau. She wants to get room service and turn in early. Why don't I make a reservation in the Oak Room for 8 p.m.?"

"Fine. I'll come on my crutches—the wheelchair might be awkward."

"Right. Bye." Dr. R heard laughter in the background before he hung up.

Dining in the Oak Room of the Plaza Hotel was hardly in the budget of Dr. R in his student days. As he entered the huge room with its oak paneling, gigantic chandeliers, and myriad lights on the walls, he caught his breath. All that light—and waiters in tuxes, wearing white gloves.

He saw Bob waving to him from a corner near the entrance. He tried to ignore the glances of people who heard the creaking of his crutches. A waiter appeared immediately to help him into a rattan chair and take his crutches away. Bob reached across the table to shake Dr. R's hand. His blond crew cut and pink cheeks made him look like a teenager, despite his brown suit and blue-striped tie.

"Love has made you look twenty-five, not forty-five, Bob. So you've ditched me for a pretty lady."

"Sorry about that. She's a nurse at my sanitarium. She's never married—well, she's thirty-two—and she wants children, as I do—as soon as possible."

"It sounds like you're working on it already."

"Yes, she's very uninhibited. But we're being careful. The wedding's in a few weeks. We're going to the City Hall in L.A. I hope you'll be a witness—Estelle, too, of course. One of Diana's four sisters is coming from here to be a witness on her side—an excuse to show her boys the sights. We'll have a few days with them, and then we're off to the Caribbean for a honeymoon. Late in the summer we'll have a big reception back here in Queens for all our relatives." Bob grinned. "Getting married is complicated."

Scotch on the rocks arrived. Dr. R lifted his glass. "Here's to your happiness," he said, his voice heavy. Then he sighed.

"Uh-oh," Bob said. "I don't like the sound of that."

"Estelle and I, suddenly we're having troubles." He related the recent events.

Bob shook his head as their second round of Scotches appeared. "It seems if a woman feels betrayed—and it doesn't have to be sexual betrayal, although that's the worst—it's hard to win back her trust."

"My mother convinced us we needed to talk about Jacob."

"Good for her," Bob said. "She's a good psychologist."

"I think she was right that our silence about Jacob was hurting our relationship. Sharing our memories of him was painful but cathartic, but we did it and we felt very close afterward. I don't understand how it all turned so wrong. If only she could understand how crucial it is for me to get publicity for this paper."

"So what did this Alfie do that so offended Estelle years ago?"

"I don't know—she won't tell me."

Bob's grin disappeared. "Are you blind? I bet he raped her or something like that. It was something so shameful, she can't bear to talk about it. Why else would she be so determined not to tell you, or her mother?"

Dr. R's stomach tightened. "The way she talked about him, I never would have suspected that. Maybe you're right—I was blind. She used to say he was an obnoxious kid, a few years younger than her, and he always followed her around like a puppy dog. She made it clear that she didn't like him and was glad he lived so far away. But she often complained about her relatives, not just Alfie. I guess I missed something there. If it's true and she's kept something hidden all these years, no wonder she couldn't bear to hear his name. I wish she had been willing to be analyzed. I've tried for years to convince her to do that."

"Josh, listen. Estelle is a treasure."

Dr. R frowned. "You don't need to tell me how wonderful she is, Bob. I sometimes think she can't stand going to bed with a one-legged husband. This ugly stump—what woman would want that in her bed? I thought at least she'd be proud of me if I got some publicity for exposing the cruelty of lobotomies. I'd be a hero in her eyes."

Bob took a gulp of his Scotch and set the glass down carefully. "That's really crazy thinking. Estelle values character. You were her ideal, so different from her family."

Dr. R grimaced. "I guess I've disabused her of that illusion."

Bob smiled. "Why don't you write her and beg forgiveness?"

"That's exactly what I want to do, but she wouldn't even give me the names of their hotels in London and Paris."

"She told someone. Don't give up."

"Oh, hell," Dr. R said.

"OK, let's drop it. Let me tell you more about Diana. I can't wait for you to meet her." Bob then launched into a description of how they'd met, their little crises, and his proposal. His eyes sparkled while Dr. R felt worse and worse.

Finally, he interrupted Bob. "Here comes the waiter with our steaks."

•••

Three hundred psychiatrists gathered the next afternoon in a large meeting room on the bottom floor of the hotel. Only a handful were psychoanalysts. The keynote speaker, a Dr. Covington from Chicago, read his speech in a dull, ponderous voice on the subject of overcrowding in state mental institutions, a fact no one could fail to be aware of. But more promising topics were on the printed program. Dr. R skipped the next talk, since he was to lead off the second morning. He had room service for dinner that night and spent hours making sure that his notes fit on two index cards. He would speak from the heart, not read from some damned printed page, like that boring Dr. Covington.

The next morning, Bob accompanied him as he slowly hopped with his crutches up the five steps onto the stage. His wheelchair had been placed there and the microphone lowered to the right height. Pulling the index cards out of his pocket, he laid them on his lap, took a breath and began.

"Lobotomies have become the preferred treatment for violent mental patients. Some hospitals line up twenty patients at a time, an assembly line of lobotomies. As you know, the results vary from a calming of violence while retaining some ability to function in life to turning the patient into a passive, vegetative invalid. What I want to talk about are those people who get sent to a mental hospital because of a misdiagnosis or because a relative wants to get rid of a difficult, perhaps rebellious, family member. That includes adolescents, who fight back against cruel treatment, or wives who try to have some independence from their domineering husbands, and are *ipso facto* considered crazy. And if such people then dare to challenge the inhumane treatment they receive in the hospital, they could end up with a lobotomy, when what they really need is a strong advocate at home, or some compassionate conversations with us, the doctors who are there to heal them."

Looking out over his audience, Dr. R saw some of his colleagues glancing at their programs. Some were looking at him with hard eyes. Someone in back was slipping out of the hall. He went on, fear rising up into his throat, so that his voice came out slightly hoarse. "Let me tell you about two boys I have treated. Their histories are tragic and avoidable."

He related the story of Björn and then Henry's misdiagnosis, simply saying that Henry had barely escaped being lobotomized. When Dr. R next scanned the audience, he saw some doctors looking at him with interest. He paused.

"Although I know there are strong opinions about this, I feel it is my duty to say that I consider one-on-one talk therapy as a highly effective alternative to lobotomies for at least 70 percent of patients, even ones diagnosed as psychotic. All humans need someone to listen to them. They need to describe their suffering. I often find even one session of intense, sincere listening is enough to calm violent behavior."

Dr. R heard some programs being rattled noisily. Should he stop? No, he had one more point, even though it would be the most unpopular. "I question the use of group therapy, which is so common now. So often one patient gets put in the hotspot and humiliated in front of others. It can turn into a means to subdue a rebellious patient, to rob him of his humanity. We must always remember that the patients are suffering human beings who deserve compassion and understanding. We can even learn from them."

He now saw openly hostile looks coming from some in the audience. "I only bring this up to demonstrate that there is another way to think about mental illness, other more compassionate ways of treating patients.

"I would like to see not only lobotomies eliminated, but also electroshock treatment and submersion in cold baths. Keep restraints, of course. The staff must not be endangered."

Many were now shifting restlessly in their seats. Dr. R knew he had lost. "I have prepared references to many studies that prove my points. I can provide those of you who are interested with my complete paper. I'll stop and let you ask your questions." He tried to smile but it was more of a grimace.

There was the dispiriting sound of polite applause. It seemed louder from the nurses' section.

Then a psychiatrist stood up, a heavy, balding man. "I have been the chief psychiatrist at several state hospitals here in New York. In my experience, psychotic patients cannot relate to words well enough to engage in talk therapy. Psychoanalysts like you persist in your hopeless mission to convert the rest of us. Only fear of punishment keeps psychotics under control. Lobotomies have reduced the violence and chaos perpetrated by these disturbed individuals. Perhaps, Dr. Rosenblatt, you need to face the facts." More applause than Dr. R had received greeted this short speech. The psychiatrist turned towards the audience, bowed slightly and sat down.

Dr. Cohen, a Freudian psychoanalyst Dr. R had trained under, stood up next. His pointed white beard and thick glasses made him resemble Freud himself. He spoke in a high, quivering voice. "As you well know, Dr. Rosenblatt, psychoanalytic theory and practice do not support the analysis of psychotics. You misrepresent our profession by claiming it does." He sat down with a thud.

Dr. R rebutted with Freud's famous case of Eve, who clearly had psychotic symptoms. This was received in silence. No one came to his defense. No one else spoke. And then the moderator suggested that everyone adjourn for coffee. Bob helped him down the stairs and a technician handed down the wheelchair.

"It bombed, didn't it?" he whispered to Bob.

•••

The conference continued with three more talks that day. Dr. R knew that his talk had provoked little interest. No reporter came up to him; no one really important spoke to him. He wished he could go home. He wished Estelle would come home. He wished Bob had time to talk to him, but Bob was in a daze of love and had only given Dr. R a few minutes of sympathy.

The next morning, he was finishing breakfast alone in a smaller restaurant of the hotel, when a rotund, greasy-haired man in a tweed sports jacket stopped at his table, a cigarette hanging out of thick lips. "Doctor Rosenblatt?"

"Yes?"

"My name is Alfie Waldheim. You may have heard of me. Your mother-in-law is my aunt. I've rather lost touch with her and Estelle. May I join you?"

Dr. R felt an immediate revulsion toward the man. But he could not get up, and he could not reach his crutches. His body seemed paralyzed. "Uh, yes, I just have a few minutes."

Alfie lowered himself onto a chair. "So how are Aunt Carol and Estelle?"

Dr. R winced, hesitated, and then said, "They're fine as far as I know. They are off in London and Paris right now."

A long ash dropped from Alfie's cigarette onto the table, which he flicked off onto the floor. "I haven't seen Aunt Carol since she moved out to California with you after Uncle Ruben died. When was that, about twelve years ago? And Estelle I haven't seen since we were college students at NYU. I'd like to get out there to see them some day."

"Well . . ." Dr. R began, but he could not bring himself to offer the expected invitation.

Alfie frowned and snubbed out his cigarette. "I saw your name on the program, so I came to your talk."

"Oh, it's an unpopular cause." Dr. R saw he was close to groveling.

"No, it's a great cause—and you must know about Joe Kennedy's poor daughter? She ended up a vegetable after her lobotomy. The Kennedys try to keep it a secret."

"I won't give up," Dr. R said. *But I will not ask him for help,* Dr. R thought. *This is going to be hard enough to explain to Estelle.*

Alfie pulled a cigarette out of the breast pocket of his jacket and lit it with matches on the table. He took a long drag. "But have you heard the rumors about that new drug, chlorpromazine? They're testing it in Paris now. A friend of mine, a correspondent for *Le Monde,* has been telling me about it."

"I just heard something yesterday. What is it?"

"It's a drug that calms down violent patients. I'm planning to write an article on it soon. I'd hoped to get more information at this conference, but no one here seems to know about it yet. But people in Europe are saying it well might make lobotomies completely unnecessary. Some poor nut might be forced to take drugs, but he won't have his brain cut up."

"That could change everything," Dr. R said softly. "My battle would be won by a drug. So be it. The sooner the better."

"You bet." Alfie said, standing up. "I would have reported on your article, but this other thing is really hot news. Hey, I'll send my aunt a birthday card—it's next month, right?"

"Uh, don't feel you have to. I'll pass your greetings on to her."

Alfie glared at him. "You're telling me not to send a birthday card to my aunt? Good-bye, Dr. Rosenblatt." He walked away, leaving Dr. R to stare at his receding figure.

"God, I hope he forgets about it," Dr. R muttered to himself. "I've got to get a letter to Estelle and explain."

29

Charlie met Dr. R at the San Bernadino station four days later. As they drove toward Redgrove, he saw Stanyon in the distance. Who was doing his job? Was he missed? He knew Ruth had left for a nursing job in a hospital in Los Angeles while she waited for her husband to get home from Korea. And his former patients? Was Björn still there or home with his crazy mother?

"How are the boys?" he asked Charlie.

"They're OK," Charlie said. "Henry's studying a lot and has been over at your mother's almost every day. Max has a book report due in a couple of days, but it's hard to get him away from baseball practice. Even after dinner he wants to go to the park with his friends."

"And my mother?"

Charlie winced. "Ah, I think her doctor wants to talk to you."

"Is something wrong?"

"He'll have to tell you. Henry says she's coughing a lot."

"I've only been gone ten days. Her lungs have been bad recently, but she always bounces back."

"Do you want to go straight there? The boys don't get home from school for a couple of hours."

"Yes, let's do that." His mother's unconditional love was exactly what Dr. R needed at that moment.

He found her in bed. He forced himself to smile as he walked over to give her a one-armed hug, holding onto the railing of her hospital bed with his other hand.

"Hello, my darling," she said stroking his head. "How are you? I've been waiting for you."

"Your lungs are giving you trouble again?"

"Yes," she said and sighed, ending in a deep cough. "I feel tired."

"What do the doctors say?"

"Not much. They don't want to tell me the truth. I'm getting weaker. Thank God you're here."

Dr. R held her hand, which felt cold. "You'll get better in a few days."

"Maybe. How was your trip?"

Dr. R sighed as he sat down next to her bed. "No one seemed interested in my paper. Most of these doctors still think lobotomies are the only solution—God, I almost said 'the final solution.'"

"I'm so sorry, darling. But you tried your best." She closed her eyes, smiling slightly. "You are a good boy."

"I wish more people felt as you do."

Miriam's eyes remained closed. "Oh, I know, you and Estelle are having trouble."

"Has she told you that?"

"She doesn't need to. You're both a couple of open books, dear children that you are. But I'm not worried."

"Well, I am."

"You'll both be all right—after you learn a few lessons," she said, opening her eyes.

"That sounds very prophetic."

"Yes—this is a dark time for you."

"I see," Dr. R said.

"You are sweet. You always say 'I see' when you don't want to accept some unpleasant truth." Her laugh finished with coughing. Dr. R reached for the glass of water on her bed stand and held it to her lips. She drank a few sips. Her head sank back into the pillow, her eyes closing again.

Dr. R felt like putting his head on his mother's bosom and weeping. A few tears welled up. He took out his handkerchief to wipe them.

"I think I'll take a little nap now," she said. "Tell the boys and Estelle I love them very much. And most of all, I love you, my dearest son."

"I love you, *Mamela.*" His voice quivered. Was she saying goodbye? She began to breathe slowly, laboriously. Misery overcame him. He lowered his head, wishing he could pray. He withdrew his hand from hers and left, hoping the creak of his crutches would not wake her up.

Charlie was waiting for him outside in the car. He helped Dr. R into the front seat and laid the crutches across the backseat.

"The nurse says she has pneumonia," Dr. R said as they drove off. "And the antibiotics don't seem to be working."

"I wish Mrs. R was here," Charlie said, shaking his head. "She would know what to do."

Dr. R did not reply. What was Charlie trying to say? That he was incompetent?

At home out in the cottage, he sat in his chair, staring at the evil spirit in the Tibetan thangka, transformed at that moment into a messenger of Death. One patient was coming that afternoon—the only one he still had. In the space of one month, all the others had left, finishing their analysis, or moving away, or perhaps switching to another analyst. It was uncanny how they all vanished at the same time, like rats deserting a sinking ship.

An image of his mother lying there, struggling to breathe, flashed through his mind. "What am I doing here?" he said to the black telephone in front of him. He picked up the receiver and rescheduled his patient. He took his crutches, hopped down the path, got into his wheelchair inside the back door, and wheeled into the kitchen where Agnes leaned over and hugged him, tears in her eyes.

"You look tired, Dr. R. I've got some sandwiches for you."

"I'm not hungry, Agnes. Maybe later. My mother isn't doing well. She lost a lot of ground while I was gone."

Agnes put her hands on her wide hips. "If I were you, Dr. R, I'd go straight back to the hospital."

Dr. R took a breath. "You're right, Agnes, as usual. Yes, I should go back."

Agnes headed out the back door. "I'll tell Charlie to bring the car down."

Dr. R entered his mother's room. She appeared to be asleep, breathing heavily. He took her hand in his. It felt warm, a good sign. He stared at her round, barely wrinkled face. He rubbed her hand with his thumb. She opened her eyes, tried to say something, looked at him, then closed her eyes again. A nurse came in—Linda, his mother's favorite. She asked him to step out into the corridor.

"Dr. Rosenblatt, I probably don't need to tell you. Your mother may not make it."

Dr. R shook his head. "Maybe she'll come out of it. Where's Dr. Mathews, for God's sake?"

"He was just here. He tried to call you, but he's gone now."

"Call him and tell him to get right back here. He must have put her on the wrong antibiotic. Pneumonia is curable now."

Linda gave him a certain look, one Dr. R knew all too well. "You can call Dr. Mathews at his office." And then she marched away.

Back at his mother's side, he leaned over and whispered to her, "I love you." Miriam's breathing became more labored. He listened. "*Mamela,* can you hear me?" He pressed her hand but there was no response.

As he sat there, he felt she was sending him love. It filled the room, enveloping him. His own breathing seemed to be following his mother's, as if he, too, were breathing his last.

Her hand in his felt warm and alive, but the pause between breaths became longer and longer. Her body struggled to produce each gasp. Then she opened her eyes. She seemed to be looking past him, her eyes shining, her mouth trying to form a smile at its edges. Then her eyes shifted to look at him. "I love . . ."

He squeezed her hand. "*Mamela,*" he said.

Then she closed her eyes, and took one more breath, a kind of audible sigh. He waited, but she was silent. He put his ear on her chest. Her heart was no longer beating.

"Good-bye, *Mamela.* Good-bye. Oh God, why do you have to go?"

He closed her eyes, which had opened but no longer saw. He held one of her hands in both of his and felt it begin to grow cold. Yet he half-expected her to open her eyes again. He placed his palm on her chest below her collarbone. It was still warm. He began to weep. Linda came in and patted his shoulder. "We all loved her. She told me what to do when my son, Bobbie, got in trouble. She helped everybody." Dr. R straightened up, wiping his eyes.

"Call my home. Tell Charlie to come for me. I must wire my wife and tell my sons."

Charlie, silent for once, drove him the few blocks home. As they approached the front door, Dr. R felt for a moment he did not know where he was. Everything had utterly changed.

He went to the kitchen to tell Agnes and left her sobbing in Charlie's arms.

"Tell me when the boys come home," Dr. R said. "I'm going out to my office to look at my mail. There must be something from Mrs. Rosenblatt. I must wire her immediately."

"The boys got postcards," Charlie said, looking over his wife's head buried against his chest.

Dr. R had to struggle alone to get through the backdoor with his crutches, muttering to himself, "That means in Charlie language that she didn't write me. How the hell am I going to wire her, if I don't know where she is staying?"

The stack of mail on his desk confirmed his suspicion—nothing from Estelle. He hopped back on his crutches to the house, and sat down next to the telephone in the living room. He dialed the number at Carol's, hoping her housekeeper was there. No one answered.

A few moments later, Max and Henry came in the front door.

"I'm in here, boys," Dr. R called out. They both came running in, full of smiles and youthful energy, leaning over to hug him at the same time, even Henry.

"How was your trip?" Max shouted, making Dr. R wince. "Did you bring me anything from New York?"

"Sit down, boys—I have some bad news." The two suddenly looked frightened and sat down. "I think you knew your Grandma Miriam has been sick?"

"Yes," Henry said. "I was there yesterday and she said she's better. She was excited that you were getting home today. She wouldn't let us call you to tell you she was sick, because she didn't want to spoil your trip."

"Sometimes old people wait for a loved one to arrive so they can die . . ."

"No!" Max shouted, jumping up.

"Yes, I'm afraid it's true. She just died about an hour ago—very peacefully—no pain. Her last words were that she loved you both very much."

Max started crying. "I don't want her to be dead," he sobbed. He came over to Dr. R on the sofa, and Dr. R put his arms around him. "I want my Mommy," Max wailed. Henry got up without a word and disappeared out the backdoor.

Half an hour later, after consoling Max, Dr. R walked into the orange grove, knowing exactly which tree Henry would be under. He appeared to be asleep, leaning against the trunk, head down.

Dr. R stopped fifteen feet away. "Henry, I'm going over to the old folks' home. I want to sit with my mother's body for a while before she is taken to the funeral home. Do you want to come with me? Max isn't coming—he's up in his room kicking the wall, as far as I can tell. Best to let him deal with this in his own way."

Henry stood up. "Yes, I want to come."

Charlie drove them there. They navigated through the personnel coming to say something. One young aide hugged Dr. R, her face wet with tears. The door of Miriam's room was closed. Henry opened it slowly and held it for Dr. R. Miriam was exactly as Dr. R had left her, eyes closed, hands folded on top of the white blanket.

Two chairs had been provided. He sat in one, leaned forward and laid his head on the edge of her bed, as if praying. He was not praying. He felt like Max—he didn't want her to be dead. After a while, he straightened up and looked at Henry next to him, sitting straight, not moving. His face was stern, the face of a mature man.

"This is just her body," Henry said. "She's not in it any more, is she?"

"I don't know. I thought a lot about this during the war. Especially when Barney was killed. He was such a happy-go-lucky guy, a lot like Max. I couldn't believe he was really gone."

"Dr. R," Henry said in a low voice. "I hope I'm not dreaming, but I think she is still here in this room—not in her body, but here in the room. She hasn't gone yet."

Dr. R shook his head. "If she's here, she's here for you. I can't feel it."

Henry slowly nodded his head. "She was the best grandma I could ever have. I just wish she could have seen me graduate."

"Who knows? Maybe she will." And despite the shock and grief, he felt a moment of happiness that Henry had let slip that he expected to graduate.

•••

Carol's housekeeper had agreed to send his wire to the Paris hotel as that allowed her to keep her promise not to divulge its name to Dr. R. Estelle responded with a telegram, saying: *I loved your mother STOP She has contacted me and says she is well STOP Hope you are OK STOP Can't telephone from here STOP Estelle.*

She had these psychic tendencies, but was it true she could not telephone? Another telegram came addressed to Max and Henry. She was thinking about all of them—a good sign.

The funeral was two days later, and Miriam was buried in the Jewish cemetery on the west end of town. For some reason unknown to Dr. R, she had requested the previous year that the family not sit *shiva* for her. Dr. R was relieved, because where was his Jewish family to sit *shiva?* All of them were dead, except Estelle and Carol, of course, who were not there.

Estelle was due back two weeks later, just about the time the boys would finish school. At least she had asked in her telegram if he were OK. Maybe she had decided on her trip that she was going to forgive him? Wouldn't she feel a little sympathy, knowing he would be grieving for his mother? But he was worried. The housekeeper had also agreed to mail his letter to Estelle in Paris, in which he tried to explain what had happened in New York and to warn her about a possible letter to Carol from Alfie. It seemed unlikely the letter would get there in time, even by airmail.

He, with the help of Charlie and Agnes, emptied Miriam's room. How few possessions she had kept—a photo of her with him and his father, another of her with her parents and siblings, all dead, murdered by the Nazis, a few clothes, and to his surprise, pushed to the back of the drawer of her bedside table, a Christian Bible, in which she had underlined the words of Christ that spoke about forgiveness. Could she forgive the Nazis? Impossible. But she had changed so much over the years. Was the Bible a clue?

Tired and listless, his limbs heavy with grief, he spent hours at his desk in the cottage, planning to write letters to inquire about jobs, but in reality, not writing them. He stared at the photos on his desk of Estelle and Jacob, wishing he could go backward to that life before war and death changed everything. Meals with Henry and Max were almost silent—no one wanted to talk. He knew he should do something for them, but what?

God, if he believed in Him, answered his question. A few days later he received a letter from Uncle Ed, saying that he and Carl were heading up to Montana, where Edna would join them at the end of June. Could they stop by and see his nephew and that "cute little feller," Max—he had some baseball paraphernalia he thought Max might like. He was driving up from Phoenix, meeting Carl in San Diego, and the two of them could be there in a week if he got the go-ahead.

Dr. R struggled up the stairs to Henry's room and knocked on the door. Henry was pointing his camera out the window. He turned and looked at Dr. R with a half-smile. "Henry, I've had a letter from your Uncle Ed. He wants to stop by here with Carl. How does that sound to you?"

"That's OK," Henry said. "Carl wrote me while you were gone. He wants to give me a tripod he isn't using anymore. He's not a bad guy."

"No, he seems really interested in your photography."

"My mom wants me to like him."

"Well, I hope that's not a reason to *dislike* him."

Henry smiled. "Very funny, but, yeah, I guess I do. My mom says they are getting married soon."

"I'm not surprised," Dr. R said. "How do you feel about that?"

"She's not going back to Pasadena. He's a nice guy."

Dr. R turned to leave. "I think, in fact, he's the *right* guy."

He wrote back and asked Uncle Ed and Carl to stay as long as they would like. Maybe those cowboys would cheer them up.

30

The cowboys arrived a week later. Henry was struggling to keep up with his classwork with neither Grandma Miriam nor Mrs. R there. Max could help him with words he couldn't read and he showed his written assignments to Dr. R, but Dr. R seemed tired and sad and hard to talk to. Maybe it wouldn't be so bad to have Uncle Ed and Carl there. Carl had written twice about how to keep the camera shutter open for night photography, and Max had read the letters to him. Henry had questions he needed to ask Carl, especially since he couldn't decipher the technical terms in the instruction manual that came with the new camera.

Uncle Ed arrived in his battered white pickup and Carl in a newer black one. Uncle Ed with his stocky figure in blue jeans, a matching denim vest, and white cowboy shirt, filled the dining room with jokes and laughter. "Hey, you're still eating fancy, even without the little woman here," he said, wiping his mouth with a big white linen napkin. "I'll go out after dinner and tell Agnes what a great job she's doing."

"She'll appreciate that," Dr. R said. "My wife has trained her well."

"Oh, well," Uncle Ed said, "it's a talent certain women have, such as my lovely sister. Can't wait to get her up to the ranch and she can't wait, either. The Phoenix spread has horses, but it's not the beautiful Northwest, right, Carl?

Carl smiled. "Did you know that the three of us grew up together? We went to the same school, we rode together, we did chores together."

"Such as lifting those damned bales of hay onto the flatbed trailer," Uncle Ed said.

"And clearing rocks from the pastures," Carl added.

"And we got into trouble together, too," Uncle Ed said, "like the time we put pine pitch on the outhouse seats."

"Didn't you have toilets?" Max asked.

"We sure didn't! We only got them a couple of years ago. It was cold going to the outhouse in winter—of course, we had chamber pots for the night."

"What are they?" Max asked.

"Oh, you know, something you can piss in and then empty in the privy in the morning."

Dr. R smiled. "Perhaps it's just as well Estelle isn't here . . . and especially not her mother."

"Oh, sorry," Uncle Ed said, stretching out his legs under the table. "Hey, Max, did you unpack those pennants I brought you? I think you'll have most of the teams in both major leagues."

"You bet," Max said. "I'm going to put them up all over my room. My friends will be real jealous . . ."

"Well, I spoke to your father and he said it was OK to ask you if you wanted to go to a minor league game up in L.A. tomorrow. The Stars versus the Angels—you know, the big rivalry. I'm rooting for the Angels, of course. They're affiliated with *my* team, the Chicago Cubs."

Max bounced up and down in his chair. "Really? Can I go, Dad?"

"Of course—just don't tell me about it when you get back."

"Dad!"

Everyone laughed, except Henry, who had his head down. Uncle Ed said, "You can come, too, Henry."

"I have to study," Henry said in a low voice.

"On the weekend? I think Carl has another proposition for you." Henry turned to look at Carl.

"Uh, yes," Carl said, clearing his throat. "I was wondering if you might like to go with me back to my home territory in San Diego and go to the Balboa Park zoo? It'll only take us a couple of hours. I'd like to show you how my Leica camera and telephoto lenses work. I even have a roll of that Kodachrome film you could try out."

"Color?" Henry said.

"Yes, you need a slide projector to look at them. The prints tend to be really poor quality color. And you have to send the film off to Kodak to develop."

"I wonder if you can take pictures of tigers?" Henry muttered to himself, looking down again.

"In full color," Carl said.

"Tomorrow's Saturday," Dr. R said. Sunday you'll have time to work on that *David Copperfield* paper. Maybe I can help you, even if Mrs. R would have been much better."

"I guess so," Henry said, nodding his head.

"Good," Carl said. "Let's make an early start."

• • •

Everyone was back in time for a late dinner. Max couldn't stop talking about how the Angels creamed the Stars. Dr. R yawned.

"What animals did you photograph, Henry?" he asked, when Max finally paused to eat his chicken.

"I took pictures of three different tigers."

"Is that all?"

"Well, a lion and an orange orangutan. And a zebra. With that telephoto lens, they look so close."

"How much do those lenses cost?" Dr. R asked.

"Plenty," Carl said. "About $200, and you have to have the right camera to go with it, probably another $300.

"That's a lot of money," Henry said. "I get $1.00 a week allowance."

Carl looked at him with a serious expression. "This photography hobby is expensive. Forget about color for now. Figure out how to get a better camera and lens. Sometime in the Fall you might like to come see my darkroom, and we could develop and print photos together. Maybe you'll have more time to take pictures once school is out? How much school is left?"

"Just one week, but then I have summer school—two sessions—to catch up. And I'm going to do gardening work for Mrs. Davidson down the street. I'll start saving."

"Atta boy," Uncle Ed said, and he and Max immediately launched into more baseball talk.

Dr. R finally interrupted. "OK, boys, it's ten o'clock. You better get off to bed. You don't have to do dishes tonight."

Henry stood up. "Uh, thanks, Carl."

Carl took off his glasses and wiped them with his napkin. "I've got your film in my pocket. I'll send you the slides as soon as I can get them developed. Maybe your teacher at school has a projector or else you can get a little hand one."

"I hope I didn't move the camera too much."

"You'll find the tripod will really help. You can practice here in your garden."

"Oh, OK, I'll try. Thanks."

He and Max left the dining room and climbed the stairs together.

"Uncle Ed knows a lot about baseball," Max said.

"And Carl knows a lot about photography. You should go see that San Diego zoo, Max. It even has koala bears from Australia."

"They don't play baseball in Australia. They play cricket."

"I don't care, Max. And Carl's even offered to take me to the Mojave Desert and Death Valley next winter."

They came to Henry's room. "Anyway," Henry said. "Uncle Ed and Carl are kind of nice guys, aren't they?"

"You bet," Max said. "I wish Dad liked baseball."

"He's rooting for you, Max. You're lucky. My father never liked anything I did."

"That's so mean," Max said. "Well, I'm going to bed. See ya."

31

Estelle arrived home ten days later. Early in the morning, Charlie met her and her mother at the San Bernadino station, where they disembarked from the Super Chief. Charlie and Agnes, not Dr. R, had received the telegram with the details of their arrival. In his cottage, he heard the sound of the Green Monster coming down the driveway. He hastened on his crutches to the back door and through the house to the front door, but when the car stopped, he saw only Charlie get out and walk around to the trunk.

"Where is she?" he asked.

"She's helping Mrs. Gottlieb unpack and open all the mail that's come the past month. She'll call when she's finished."

"Did she mention getting a letter from me in Paris?"

"No, she said nothin' about that."

"Damn, I should have left her a note at Mrs. Gottlieb's. I thought she'd come straight here."

He turned back to the house. Charlie took Estelle's bags to their room. Dr. R transferred to the wheelchair and followed him. From the doorway, he stared at the four pieces of pale white leather luggage. They left him no room to enter.

He and the boys were just finishing lunch when the telephone rang. Dr. R felt he had been waiting all day. Charlie picked up the phone in the kitchen and came through the swinging door to say that Mrs. R wanted to be picked up at Mrs. Gottlieb's home.

"I wish Mommy would get home," Max said, his lower lip trembling.

"We all do, Max," Dr. R said. He sighed, wiped his mouth with the linen napkin, threw it down and wheeled away from the table, determined to push the luggage away so that he could greet Estelle in the privacy of their bedroom.

He had shifted from the wheelchair to the bed, his back against the bedstead when he heard her heels clicking on the hall floor. Estelle, in a brown tweed traveling suit, stopped in the open doorway and stared at him without smiling. Her face was obscured in shadow, backlit from the hall windows. She looked tired.

"Estelle!" He held out both hands but she did not take them. She moved around the luggage and sat down on her dressing table stool. "Tell me what's going on," he said, hearing his pleading voice.

She looked up with an angry face. "Get out. Leave. I don't want you here anymore. You're not the man I married. That one had ideals and wouldn't lie or do things behind my back. While I was looking over my mother's mail, I saw a letter to her from Alfie. I asked her to open it. I couldn't believe it. He said he met you in New York."

"I wrote you in Paris. Didn't you get my letter? Your mother's housekeeper wouldn't give me the phone number of the hotel in Paris, but she finally agreed to mail my letter to you. What I explained in the letter is that Alfie came up to me at breakfast one morning. I couldn't avoid him. He had no interest in my paper and I did not ask him to do anything."

"I don't believe your story, but even if it were true, you could have made up an excuse and left when he came up to you. You knew I did not want you to speak to him."

"Estelle, listen to me. I couldn't get up that quickly, not with this damned leg, and the waiter had put my crutches off in a corner where people wouldn't trip on them. I couldn't move, but it was a short, meaningless conversation."

"I don't believe you. I won't ever believe you again."

"Don't, Estelle. Can't we talk about this? I made a terrible mistake going behind your back to ask your mother to write Alfie. I'm sorry, I really am."

"I don't want to talk about it. This is my house, and I want you to leave."

Dr. R felt he was going to lose consciousness. Or go blind. A black curtain had come down over him, heavy and suffocating. "What are you talking about?" he said with a rasp in his throat. "You're saying you want me to move out? You won't even listen to my side of the story? Please, Estelle, don't do this. I've made mistakes, but you know I love you."

"I can't believe that any more. I made up my mind on the trip that if you met with that man, I couldn't bear to have you near me."

"This is so unfair, Estelle. What about Henry and Max? Are you thinking about them?"

"They will survive without you."

"That's absurd—you know they need both of us."

"Maybe not if I told them the truth."

"The truth," Dr. R said with a groan. "You call this the truth?"

Estelle picked up her perfume atomizer from the dressing table and threw it at Dr. R. It missed him and smashed on the wall behind the bed, flooding the room with the scent of Arpege, his gift to her. "Just get out. Now."

Dr. R felt his chest heaving in short breaths. "I can't believe you are condemning me without hearing my side of the story." She turned away from him, covering her face with her hands. "I'll go to the cottage. Maybe in the morning you'll give me a chance to explain."

"Never," she said in a muffled voice.

Dr. R looked around the bedroom. He closed his eyes and immediately had a half-dream of being poised in his wheelchair at the top of wooden stairs. He was about to roll down those stairs and ahead of him slid a dark shadow, like a pool of blood, the harbinger of death. He shuddered, opened his eyes, and seeing Estelle bent over, her back to him, he wheeled out.

At seven in the morning, Dr. R was awakened by a knock on the cottage door. He had only fallen into a restless sleep an hour before, when the sky was already a pale blue. All night he had agonized over what had happened. Had Carol finally convinced her that he was no good? Was she just exhausted? Or maybe she had met someone on the ship. Was he really being kicked out?

Charlie came in, grim-faced, and handed him a note, turned abruptly, and left. In the note Estelle said she was leaving the house at six-thirty to go to her mother's. He could have breakfast with the boys, tell them whatever he felt he needed to tell them. He should pack and be out by noon. Charlie could drive him wherever he wanted to go.

"How can she be so cruel?" Dr. R said out loud.

At breakfast an hour later, Dr. R looked at Henry and Max, eating their cornflakes, silent and tense. "Boys, you may have already guessed. Mrs. R and I have been having troubles. She's angry at me." Henry and Max stared at him. "She has asked me to move out—for a while. I hope it won't be too long, but right now she is very upset."

Max started crying. He wiped his eyes with a hand. "Did I do something wrong, Daddy? Is it because I haven't been doing my homework?"

"No, of course not. This is strictly between your mother and me. Maybe it won't be for too long."

Henry stood up. Clenching his fists at his side, he shouted, "Why can't grown-ups stay married? They don't care about us—they just don't care." Then he rushed out of the room. Dr. R heard the back door slam. Henry was right. The world of safety he had tried so hard to create for Henry had been destroyed.

• • •

At five o'clock that evening, Charlie pulled up in front of Bob McKensie's house in Sierra Madre. He walked around to the trunk and pulled out Dr. R's two suitcases and walked slowly with him through a white wooden gate to the front door.

Bob opened the door, his freckled face smiling as usual. "Hi, Josh, Charlie. Come in. Let me take those bags."

"I'm goin' back for the wheelchair," Charlie said. Dr. R stayed in the doorway, watching Charlie, who pushed the folded wheelchair in front of him, lifting it over the doorstep. Charlie left it in Bob's hall and then turned around, facing Dr. R. His eyes were glistening.

"It can't be for long," Dr. R said. Charlie shook his head.

"This is *loco.*"

"Tell the boys I'll arrange for them to come see me as soon as I find a place to live. You can bring them or they can take the train."

Charlie placed a hand on Dr. R's shoulder and patted it a few times, and without smiling, turned and left, slamming the door behind him.

"Down here," Bob called from the other end of the house. Dr. R found the corridor leading there and swung his way down on his crutches. He entered a rather bare room—a single bed with a white chenille bedspread, a dresser, a closet, and a bedside table with a little lamp. Bob placed Dr. R's suitcase on the wood floor.

"I wish we could offer you something better," Bob said. "Bad timing, as I explained on the phone. One of my nephews will be in this room the day after the wedding. Diana's sister, Meagan, came out early to visit a friend in San Diego. We'll meet her at Union Station just before we go to City Hall. Her husband and two boys arrive the next day. They want to go to Knott's Berry Farm, La Brea Tar Pits, Universal Studios, the beaches. They'll miss the wedding by one day, but they couldn't all squeeze into the Justice of the Peace's office anyway. Settle in and come out for a drink. You look like you could use one."

Fifteen minutes later, Dr. R was seated in an armchair in the living room. The familiar clink of ice in his glass, followed by a deep gulp of

Scotch, brought a rush of warmth to his stomach.

Bob lit a cigarette, frowning. "So she kicked you out."

"Yes. Estelle saw a letter her cousin Alfie wrote her mother and she went insane. She wouldn't believe me when I said the jerk just happened to walk over to my table at the Plaza. But maybe she had already made up her mind while she was off on her trip with her mother."

"What's got into her?" Bob asked. "It doesn't sound like her to act like this."

"I can't bear losing her, Bob."

"I would like to talk to her. Is that OK with you? Maybe she'll tell me what's going on."

"Sure, she likes you. Maybe you'll find out something. In the meantime, I've got to find some temporary place to live. What am I going to do? I have no money, because Estelle has always managed our finances, even my paycheck. I suspect she's so angry, she won't give me a penny. I've lost my job, my clients, my mother, my home, my boys and my wife. I seem to have made a mess of everything."

"I've got friends who are psychiatrists at some of these private sanatoriums." Bob said. "I can ask about openings."

"Thanks. I appreciate that. And I'm going to write everyone who might be able to help me. I'm going to apply to the VA hospital. That's where I should have gone after the war. Stanyon offered me more money."

Bob stood up, taking Dr. R's empty glass and his own for a refill. "It seems so unfair," he called back as he went into the kitchen. "You save Henry and this is your reward."

Dr. R caught himself staring at a painting on the wall, a reproduction of a man screaming on a wooden bridge, both hands on the sides of his head, the sky behind streaked with blood. He couldn't take his eyes off it. Bob returned and placed the new drink on the table next to Dr. R's chair.

"Why do you have that painting there? It's ugly as hell."

Bob smiled for a second. "It's a reminder for me that deep inside we are all screaming with pain."

"Come on, Bob, even after years of psychoanalysis?"

"I no longer believe that psychoanalysis ever removes all the pain. We're still asleep. Something else is needed to wake us up."

"What kind of crap is that?" Dr. R asked, taking a sip of his whiskey.

"Never mind. I'm exploring some new ideas. Psychoanalysis brings us very close to something—an unknown capacity in us, another intelligence. But something is missing. Don't you feel that sometimes? Maybe something that religion used to bring—a connection to a higher intelligence. Remember how we used to talk about these things?"

Dr. R shook his head slowly. "I don't have the luxury of such thoughts now. I've lost everything, everything I worked so hard for since the war. I have to start over from scratch and it's very frightening."

"No wonder you don't like that painting!"

"It's just ugly, that's all."

"You've had your very expensive Oriental rug pulled right out from under you," Bob said, raising his glass. "Let's drink to the wisdom of insecurity." They drank.

"And on top of everything else, I'm worried about the boys, especially Henry. Max somehow always lands on his feet."

"Estelle won't abandon them."

"I hope not."

"Let's take one step at a time," Bob said. "For example, where are you going to live? I have to boot you out in three days, the day of the wedding."

"I have no idea. I don't really have enough spare money to pay for an apartment, even for a few months.

"Well," said Bob, "I know of something through a friend of mine. I called her after you telephoned this morning. You probably won't like it, though. It's working for room and board."

"What kind of work?"

"I'm not sure. She has a fancy women's clothing shop in L.A. She's French—her name's Pauline de Beaufort. She's a widow with no kids—the Nazis killed her husband while he was fighting in the Resistance. She's ended up in L.A. because she has a sister living here who married a G.I. after the war. She lives in an apartment above the store and she always has somone living with her who works for her doing odd jobs. She has to spend most of her time running the store. The woman who had the job has just left to get married. I could ask."

"I can't do much with this disability."

Bob stubbed out his cigarette in an ashtray and frowned at Dr. R. "Your disability is that you don't want to do menial tasks, right?"

Dr. R felt his face grow hot with anger. Then he sighed. "Yes, it's true. I remember my mother ordering me around in the store: 'Put these cans over there, no, not like that. Stack them in a pyramid. Don't you see that can is dented?' Even before losing my leg, I was very happy Estelle and I could afford live-in help to deal with all those tasks."

"So I won't ask her. It's your choice." Bob slapped the side table next to him, making his drink slide off its coaster. He retrieved it and replaced it slowly, not looking at Dr. R.

"No, I'd better meet her. I don't have many options. With luck, it will only be for a short time. Maybe she won't really make me do much. After all, I'm your friend."

Bob smiled. "Don't count on it. She's a very practical lady."

"Whatever that means," Dr. R said.

"You'll find that means a great deal."

A car door slammed. Bob jumped up. "Oh, there's Diana. I'm going out to help her bring in the groceries." He rushed out the front door.

"*He* doesn't mind carrying groceries," Dr. R said, addressing the screaming man on the wall. "It's love, I guess."

• • •

Estelle had not seen the boys that day. The day before, after telling Josh to leave, she had tried to compose herself before they came home from school. She hugged them, gave them souvenirs from London and Paris, and sat down to dinner with them. But she could not eat and explained to them that she was exhausted from the long train journey and needed to go to bed. She would speak to them the next day. They looked at her with anxious faces and remained silent. The following day she had fled early to her mother's so as not to be there when Josh drove off with Charlie. The boys were in school by the time she came back from talking to her mother, who, to her surprise, seemed very upset about Estelle's decision. She wanted to say, "But you kept telling me I could have done better and now I have a chance to..." To do what? She did not know. The rest of the morning she spent consulting the family lawyer at his office in San Bernadino. She had left a note for the boys. on the breakfast table saying she had to be out doing errands all day but would be there for dinner.

As she walked into the dining room that evening, the boys stared at her. She sat in her usual place, the boys opposite her. All too obvious was the emptiness of Dr. R's place at the head of the table. "I'm sorry. This must be terribly confusing for you both."

"But why did Daddy go away?" Max said. "Is he coming back soon?"

Estelle shook her head. "I wish I could explain. I told him not to do something and he went ahead and did it. I'm so angry I can't stand having him here anymore."

"When can we see him again?" Max asked in his high-pitched voice.

"Once he finds a place to live..."

"Is he here in Redgrove?" Henry asked.

"I don't know, but I would guess he's gone to Dr. McKensie's. I don't think he'll go far away. But I won't let him come back—not for a long time. Please don't get your hopes up."

Max turned his head away, arms crossed, shoulders hunched. Henry continued to stare at Estelle, his eyes half-shut with a frown. He looked down at his uneaten meatloaf and pushed the plate away.

"May I be excused?" he said, emphasizing *cused,* and for an instant Estelle heard "*I accuse.*"

32

For most of the next two days Dr. R remained in his room. He had letters to write—painful letters. He wrote to Max and Henry, telling them he would write often. Would Estelle block those letters? And if she didn't, would Max read Henry's letter to him?

He stayed out of the happy pre-wedding commotion, not wanting to inflict his black despair on them. Diana grated on his nerves. She laughed often and loudly and cooked hearty, tasteless meals. Macaroni and cheese. Tuna casserole. Bob soaked up this feminine onslaught in a dazed, happy oblivion and hardly noticed Dr. R. Or maybe Bob had the good sense to avoid the cloud of doom surrounding him.

On Friday morning, the wedding day, they left to meet Diana's sister at Union Station. The Justice of the Peace in the Los Angeles City Hall was not far from Mme. de Beaufort's shop. The plan was that Bob would drop Dr. R there with his luggage for an interview immediately after the wedding lunch. If Dr. R decided not to take the position, or if Mme. de Beaufort decided not to offer it to him, he would have to go to a nearby hotel until he found some other solution. Bob had wanted to lend him some money, but Dr. R had hastily refused—and then regretted it.

He and Bob, in dark suits and uncomfortable white shirts especially starched and ironed by Diana, waited next to the car in the driveway like a military guard as Diana came out the front door to join them. She was dressed in a white wool suit and a matching hat with blue ribbons dangling over the brim. As Bob opened the door for her, they smiled at each other. Dr. R got into the back seat with his crutches.

Diana sat close to Bob as he drove. They giggled, joked, and touched each other as much as the act of driving allowed. At one point, stopped in traffic on the Pasadena freeway, Bob managed to have one arm around Diana and his left arm hanging out the window with a cigarette between his fingers.

As they started up again, Dr. R said, "Bob, put your damned hands on the steering wheel. You're behaving like a teenager."

Bob laughed and dropped his cigarette out the window.

Diana's sister, Meagan, was waiting outside Union Station. She had dark hair and wore a red dress with a full skirt that took up most of the back seat so that Dr. R. had to squeeze himself into a corner, cradling the crutches on his and Meagan's laps. The others joked and laughed as they proceeded to City Hall, their excitement mounting.

Meagan leaned over to whisper to Dr. R. "We thought Diana was going to be an old maid for sure—she's 32, you know."

Within half an hour, the couple was married. They walked to a fancy restaurant nearby and all indulged in fresh lobster shipped from Boston and between them they drank two bottles of champagne, all happy and laughing. Dr. R wished he were somewhere else, anywhere else. Bob had a secure job, now he had a wife, he was in love and hopeful about the future, while Dr. R's life was in ruins.

He remembered his own wedding—his and Estelle's joy and hope as they drank cheap champagne in his parents' cramped apartment above their grocery store. The fact that Estelle's family, on the insistence of her mother, boycotted the entire event, not only did not depress Estelle but added to her obvious joy. He himself was submerged under the spell of her dark magic and the promise of intense hours under the sheets soon to come.

Now on a warm, hazy Los Angeles afternoon, the wedding party drove to Mme. de Beaufort's shop, Paris à la Mode.

"How did you meet this Mme. de Beaufort?" Dr. R asked, pushing Meagan's red tulle skirt off his lap. "Was she one of your private patients?"

"No, it's more the other way around," Bob said, turning his head back when they stopped at a red light.

"What the hell does that mean?" Dr. R asked.

"Never mind; it's a joke. Diana knew her first—you met her through your friend, Sally, didn't you, sweetie?"

"Yes, Sally loves fashion. She worked part-time in Mme. de Beaufort's shop a few years ago while she studied fashion design somewhere in Hollywood. Now she works for Edith Head doing the actual sewing. She got me this suit—it's actually an old Chanel."

"Do you get to keep it?" Meagan asked.

"Well, no," Diana said. "That's all right—I'm not a fashion freak like she is."

"I would die for that suit," Meagan said.

"Wait till you see the dresses at Paris à la Mode," Diana said, laughing. "But they're so . . . expensive."

Bob found a parking spot one block from the store. The women rushed ahead, while Bob pushed Dr. R in his wheelchair toward the shop, his crutches and suitcase piled across the armrests of the wheelchair. They passed other elegant shops, mostly women's paraphernalia—perfume, cosmetics, handbags, wedding dresses, hats, more dresses, even one for swimsuits. The pedestrians passing him were all women, mostly in pairs, chattering and carrying shopping bags. Some glanced down at him with surprise as they stopped in front of Paris à la Mode. Diana and Meagan had disappeared into another shop. In the display window Dr. R spotted two very thin mannequins, both dressed in something long, narrow, and black. Looking up, he saw small wrought iron balconies on the second floor with pots of flowers on them. Although fancier, something about it was the same as his parents' store with the living space above—just what he had wanted at all costs to escape. And here he was.

The door of Paris à la Mode was open. Inside he saw a middle-aged blond woman behind the counter, chatting in a French accent with a customer, who was as thin as the mannequins, although dressed in a pale beige suit.

"*Merci beaucoup, Madame. Au revoir,*" the woman said, as the customer turned, stopping for a moment in front of Dr. R's wheelchair, then walking around him, rattling her white shopping bag that had Paris à la Mode and an Eiffel Tower printed on it.

The woman smiled, coming around the counter. "Ah, *Docteur* Rosenblatt, *Bonjour,* welcome. I am Mme. de Beaufort. Hello, *Docteur* McKensie." Bob smiled and took the suitcase and crutches off of Dr. R's lap.

"How do you do?" Dr. R said, leaning forward in his chair with a slight bow before they shook hands.

"European formality, it's nice to see," Mme. de Beaufort said, still smiling. "Just a minute. Let me speak to my assistant in back. Then we go upstairs." She soon reappeared, followed by a young girl with black hair and bangs and bright red lips. "This is my niece, Caroline. Caroline, this is Dr. Rosenblatt. You know *Docteur* McKensie."

Caroline nodded without smiling.

"She is working for me this summer. She's completely Americanized, but she looks French, don't you think?"

"I've never been to France," Dr. R said. "I came out here to start my career and then there was the War. I went in the other direction."

"But you must go. There is nothing like Paris. All these clothes are made in Paris and the Americans love them. Well, let's go—come get me, Caroline, if Mrs. Meyer comes in. She will require my particular attention, *c'est à dire,* she's very rich." Caroline laughed in a rather obligatory way. "We'll deal with your bag and wheelchair later. You have your . . .

béquilles . . . what do you call them?"

"Crutches," Bob said.

"Ah, *oui,* crutches—a funny-sounding word."

"I don't care much for it myself," Dr. R said.

"Oh, *pardonnez-moi*—I did not mean to be rude." Mme. de Beaufort looked very distressed for an instant, and then recovered her polite smile.

"I have to go," Bob said. "Remember, I just got married today."

"And you do not bring Diana in to see me?" Madame. asked.

"We'll be back soon. Don't worry," Bob said, turning to leave.

"Wait a minute," Dr. R said. "What if I need to, you know . . . what if Mme. de Beaufort doesn't . . ."

"*Pas de problème*" Mme. de Beaufort said. "We'll manage quite well, I'm sure."

"*Au revoir,*" Bob said, patting Dr. R on the back before rushing out. Somehow Dr. R knew this had all been planned out ahead of time. He was being committed, just like his patients at Stanyon—against his will.

"Let's go upstairs," Madame said. "We will talk." She watched with attention as he locked the brakes on the wheelchair, braced himself on the arms in order to stand up and reach over to where Bob had leaned his crutches against a wall.

At the back of the store, they moved along a narrow aisle between racks of dresses. Dr. R's hands on the crutches brushed against the soft fabrics. She then led the way up a narrow wooden staircase. There was no railing and the stairs were steep. Slowly he hopped up one step at a time. Mme. waited at the top of the stairs, watching him.

"Will I have to go back down these stairs?" he asked, at the top, out of breath.

"The front steps have a railing. You enter them at the door to the left of the shop. You will find them more *commode,* what do you say, more convenient?"

"There's no elevator, then?"

"No, we don't need it." She looked at him with a stern face, indicating with a gesture of her hand that he should follow her into the apartment, where she invited him to sit in a brocade-upholstered armchair in the living room.

In the modern style, the kitchen, dining room and living room had no walls separating them—one flowed into another to form a large space. She pulled up a straight-backed chair and sat just a few feet away, facing him. Dr. R looked at her, waiting for her to speak, but she said nothing, although her face had softened. She was dressed in a brown tweed skirt, a pale green blouse, and a dark brown cardigan, with a beige scarf around her neck Her blonde hair, probably dyed, was short and wavy, a style he remembered from the '30s. She was elegant but not beautiful. He fixed his eyes on her hands, folded in her lap, her fingernails manicured with pink nail polish—no rings.

As one minute and then another passed, he began to feel confused. Was he supposed to speak? This was strange. "Uh, Doctor McKensie said you might have a room I could rent for a short period until I can find something more permanent."

"Not to rent," she said, smiling. "I need someone to help me. But let me show you the room—then we can talk." She jumped up and walked quickly toward the front door of the apartment. They entered a hall and another stairwell, this time with a railing on both sides. Dr. R groaned.

"Oh, yes, I see," Madame said. "*C'est impossible.*"

"Yes, it's impossible," Dr. R said firmly, determined to call a taxi as soon as he could. The taxi driver would know the nearest hotel, and he might have enough money for one or two nights.

"You will stay on this floor, behind the kitchen. It is not so nice, but it will have to do." They passed through the kitchen and she opened a door. The room had creaky floorboards, white lace curtains on a narrow window, a single bed with a grey army blanket, a dresser, and an old-fashioned wardrobe in the corner—clearly once a servant's room. "And here," she said, "is a sink. You see it is low—useful for men if the bathroom is *occupée* but please run water while you are . . . doing it."

Dr. R laughed. "'Doing it' could have several interpretations . . ."

She nodded. "Oh yes, well, do what you wish." As she left the room, she said over her shoulder, "*Pas très chic* but you can add your own decorations." Dr. R said nothing. She acted like it was a done deal. "I will make us some coffee," she said and left the room.

When he followed her, she invited him to sit at the kitchen table while she boiled water in a little saucepan, poured it on ground coffee that she spooned into a ceramic pitcher, and then strained it through a sieve into demitasse cups. She offered him sugar cubes but no milk. The coffee was strong and delicious.

"So," she said, putting her cup down, "I want to explain the jobs I require. In exchange you have your room and your meals, although most of the time you must do your own cooking."

"But I don't know how to cook."

She shook her head, expressing how hopeless he was, perhaps how hopeless all men were. "I have some simple cookbooks here—in English. Look there on the shelf—*The Joy of Cooking.* Very American, but it explains everything. I have had some girls who didn't know a thing about cooking. Shocking—what were their mothers thinking? This book became their teacher."

"I could go to the delicatessen . . ."

"No, I don't have an account at the delicatessen—all those horrid meats they sell. But there are some very good stores around here—a butcher I like, a bakery, a grocery store. Almost like Paris. And the very best produce is at Le Grand Jardin, yes, it's owned by a Frenchman, Monsieur Lepoutre from Lyons. You'll see he has real vegetables, not these horrid cans you Americans seem to think are better than fresh vegetables.

"So you need to shop every day and prepare my lunch, because I eat it in the back of the store, in case an important customer comes in. I will need you to chop some vegetables or fruits for the evening meal for both of us. I will cook the meal and then you can take your portion to your room, unless I request you to eat with me. I have guests come, so then you will have to shop for more. If you want alcohol or cigarettes, you have to buy them yourself."

Dr. R shifted his weight in the chair. "I don't think I can carry a plate of food downstairs to you."

"I don't see why not," she said in an unsympathetic voice. "There is always a way. You will have to be . . . *astucieux.* Oh, what's that word in English?" She paused. "Ah, yes—*clever.* Well, maybe most of the time someone can do it for you. Ah, I just remembered--we have a dumbwaiter. What a strange name. You ring a bell and then we pull the rope. It's so slow, I never use it. If I am with a customer, please do not ring the bell. You can come downstairs and pull down the dumbwaiter yourself."

Dr. R stared at her, his lips pressed together. "And the shopping? Don't these stores deliver? In New York, we just call in our order and it's delivered." He did not mention that for years he was the boy delivering the groceries.

"This is not New York. I have a shopping cart. Maybe we can fasten it to your wheelchair and you can put your crutches in it."

Dr. R shook his head. "You must realize, I am totally unqualified for this job. My disability makes it difficult to get around and I know nothing about shopping or cooking."

"*Non, non, non, au contraire,* you are just the type of person I want. It will be good for you to learn these things. I will help you. My housekeeper, Rosaria, can teach you many things." She paused. "Oh, yes, you must sweep the sidewalk in front of the store every morning before we open. And once a week wash the windows. We must be *impeccable.*" She looked at her watch. "Oh, I must return to the store. Caroline has to leave. Good. It's settled then" She stood up. Dr. R struggled to stand up. She held out her hand and he automatically took it.

"I, I . . ." he mumbled.

"Maybe Caroline can bring your *valise* up before you go shopping.

Oh yes, *voilà,* right there on the counter is a key. I will cook you some dinner later, OK? *Au revoir, Monsieur Le Docteur.*" Without waiting for an answer, she turned and disappeared with a clatter down the back stairs.

"I think I've just been snookered," Dr. R said as he picked up the key, staring at it as if it could explain what had just happened. Caroline arrived immediately with his suitcase, which she put in his room without a word before running back down the stairs.

He unpacked his clothing into the dresser and hung his jacket in the wardrobe. There was a hook near the sink for the towel and washcloth Agnes had provided him. He took off his glasses and washed the lenses, using his handkerchief to dry them. He saw the handkerchief needed washing . . . was there a laundry nearby? He replaced his glasses and looked at his face in the little mirror above the sink—a tired, anxious face, his beard in need of a trim. Hell, he couldn't even afford to go to a barber.

He sat on the edge of the bed, thinking he really needed a nap. Just as he lay down he heard the quick footsteps of Mme. du Beaufort coming up the back stairs. He had not closed the door and she appeared in the entrance.

"Oh, *pardonnez-moi,*" she said. "Here is your shopping list. Just go out to the right—you'll find the grocery store two blocks down, and someone there can direct you to the other stores. You see, I have written them all down. And I have accounts with all these *très gentiles proprietaires.*"

She came over with the list and handed it to Dr. R, who had sat up and swung his leg around so his one foot was on the floor. He felt like saying, "Can't I just rest a little?" Instead, he tried to decipher her handwriting.

"The shopping cart is in the store—I'll show you. I have left you a piece of rope to tie it to your *chaise roulante*—what do you call it?"

"Wheelchair," Dr. R said, spitting out the word.

"Wheelchair. Yes. That's going to be a challenge. When you get back, I come up with you and show you how I like things arranged in the *frigidaire.* I will show you how to prepare the vegetables and fruit. I have a guest tonight, so you will have to eat in your room." She turned to leave. "There is a washing machine in the basement and a clothes line, but you don't want to go down there too often, do you?" She disappeared.

He looked again at her list. "Hell, is this English or French? And what *is* 200 g butter? Doesn't she know we're not on the metric system?"

It turned out the storekeepers were used to her lists and knew exactly what she wanted. Some of them looked at him with concern, seeing how awkwardly he maneuvered the shopping cart using one crutch, leaving the wheelchair outside on the sidewalk. As he wheeled back to Paris à la Mode, with the cart tied around the back of the wheelchair and the crutches sticking up inside it, he thought he saw alarm in the eyes of the women who passed him.

"I am a foreigner here," he muttered and then opened the door to enter the shop. He glanced at his watch and saw he had been gone an hour and a half. Was he going to have to do this every day? No customers were in the shop. Mme. de Beaufort came out from the back.

"Good, you are back. We must hurry to get things prepared for tonight. Caroline is here and will mind the store—I like that expression—*to mind the store.* I think it is English-English? Here, let me take one of those bags so it will not be so heavy." She peered in the cart. "Ah, yes, here are the vegetables. I will go ahead and get them washed. And *voilà,* here is the dumbwaiter." She pulled open two brown doors in the wall and Dr. R peered into a dark shaft where a large wooden box was suspended on ropes.

Dr. R smiled. "We have one of these in our home, but we never use it," he said.

"Why not?" Madame. asked, smiling. "*C'est très utile.*"

"Well, the help carries everything."

"*Exactement,*" Madame. said. She picked up the bag with the vegetables and ran up the back stairs. Dr. R's head began to burn with anger. He loaded the other bags into the dumbwaiter, closed the door, wheeled to the corner at the back of the store where he was told to leave the wheelchair, switched back to the crutches, and slowly made his way up the stairs.

After a lesson on where to put everything in the refrigerator and little pantry, Madame. said, "So sit down here at the table." She brought a cutting board, a knife, a peeler, and a colander full of wet potatoes, carrots, and green beans.

"So this is how to prepare each vegetable . . ." and she demonstrated how to use the peeler, how to string the green beans, and what size to cut them. Then she left the kitchen to set the table for two in the dining area, returning to arrange the flowers he had purchased for her.

"Don't peel toward you—peel away from you. It's much faster." Dr. R paused, peeler midair.

Madame. laughed. "You'll get used to it. *C'est pas difficile.*"

"That is a matter of opinion," Dr. R said, frowning at the peeler.

"I go down to the shop to get something. *Bon courage.*" She left. Dr. R wished he could get up and leave for good, but he continued peeling. When Madame. came back, he had three bowls filled with each vegetable.

"*Très bien, pas mal pour un débutant.* Not so bad for a beginner. Now stay here and I will show you how I prepare this meal." She smiled at him as she carried the bowls over to the stove. "Can I offer you a glass of white wine? I know you Americans prefer bourbon, but I don't have any. Will wine do?"

"Yes, of course. Thank you." She opened the refrigerator, took out a bottle and poured the wine into two ordinary tumblers. She handed him one, clinked glasses as he raised his, and said, "*À vôtre santé.*" They drank. "*Ça fait du bien, n'est-ce pas?* Oh, excuse me. I forget to speak English." She put down her glass and turned away to pull out some pots and fill them with water.

Dr. R smiled. "I think I can surmise what you were saying, because the very thought I had was, 'This hits the spot.'"

Madame turned her head around. "'Hits the spot'? That is a very odd thing to say." They both laughed. She began to cook, her attention very concentrated, as if he were not there at all. Then the doorbell rang. "There's my guest."

Dr. R braced his hands on the table to get up and leave.

Madame went over to the front door to press the button to open the door down on the street. "Oh, wait *un petit moment,*" she said. "I want to introduce my guest." A young woman appeared, dressed in blue jeans and a plaid western shirt, dark-skinned, her black hair pulled back in a ponytail. She looked . . . maybe Mexican.

"Alice, I would like to present Dr. Rosenblatt. Dr. Rosenblatt, Alice Starfoot." Alice smiled when she heard his name, nodding her head slowly, more like a formal bow. Perhaps she was part Japanese?

"He is my new assistant," Madame explained. There was a silence as Dr. R and Alice looked at each other. "So," Madame said, "Alice and I need to talk. Then we will have dinner. I will let you know when you can come out for your plate."

The women seemed to be listening to the creaking of his crutches as he moved toward his room. Why did Madame speak as if he were a dog waiting for his dish to be put down on the floor? He didn't even have time to drink his wine. He reached for his flask of Scotch in the bottom drawer of the dresser. He needed it. How long would he have to endure this? Why hadn't he heard from Dr. Gilbert at the VA hospital?

There was a knock on the door. Alice entered with his dinner, the vegetables now cooked with the addition of two lamb chops. "Don't get up," she said. "I think there is silverware over here in this drawer, oh yes, here's a linen napkin, too." She handed these to him, gave him a shooting glance with very dark eyes and turned immediately to leave. "Bye," she said. The door closed.

Dr. R was hungry and the food was delicious. Was a dessert coming? As he waited, he pulled a little notebook and fountain pen out of his breast pocket. *How to Afford My Own Place?* he wrote at the top.

Underneath in parentheses he wrote (*and get the hell out of here*).

1. *Telephone Dr. Gilbert to see if he has received my letter re VA hospital.*
2. *Find some private patients and a place to treat them.*

He paused. Perhaps he could ask Mme. de Beaufort if any of her wealthy customers would be interested in psychoanalysis? She must have a wide circle of friends.

Exhaustion descended. He hung his clothes over a chair, used the sink as Madame had indicated, and fell naked into bed.

33

The next few days brought no relief—more shopping, more struggling up the stairs, unpacking groceries, and maneuvering with one crutch in order to have a hand free to put them away on shelves in the refrigerator—and more peeling. Madame showed him how to scramble eggs, put bread in the toaster, and make his own coffee. She taught him to make grilled cheese sandwiches under the broiler for his lunch. He did the sweeping early in the morning, when no one could see him trying to handle a broom from a wheelchair.

Rosaria, a short, squat, ever-smiling Mexican lady, old enough to be Dr. R's mother, came on Thursday mornings to clean Madame's apartment. She showed Dr. R how to wash his sheets and clothes in the noisy machine in the basement, put them through the wringer, and hang them on the line strung along the basement ceiling. She taught him how to sprinkle clothes and roll them up before ironing them.

"Here is a man's shirt I wear when working," she said. "I show you how to iron so you can do your own shirts."

Dr. R looked with distaste at the iron and ironing board. "Don't shirts go out to the laundry?" he asked.

Rosaria laughed. "You have money?"

"Oh," Dr. R said. So he blundered his way through her instructions, until he smelled a burning odor. "Oh my God, I burned it, damn it all."

Rosaria laughed again. It seemed he was providing her enormous entertainment. "Oh, no problem. I got others. Keep the iron moving. Then it won't burn."

Back upstairs, she showed him how to tuck in the bottom sheet as they did in hospitals so it wouldn't end up in a crumpled ball in the morning.

"Thank you," he said, as they looked together at his perfectly made bed.

"You will learn, Doctor," she said, patting his shoulder. "Practice, practice, practice. *Adios,* I go clean the kitchen now."

"Hell," he muttered after she left. "Rosaria could be Charlie's mother teaching me. And laughing at me while she does it."

That evening Mme. de Beaufort invited him to stay for dinner. They ate swordfish steaks with mashed potatoes. She had set one end of the dining room table for the meal. In front of them was a silver candelabrum with three long white candles burning. As soon as she had served him, she switched off the fluorescent lights in the kitchen and turned on a table lamp off in the living room.

When she sat down, Dr. R looked at the candles and smiled. "When I was a boy, I thought the Hanukkah candles were sent by God."

"So what happened?"

"What do you mean, what happened?"

"Did you forget God?"

Dr. R felt a muscle in his cheek twitch. "Of course I did. That was a childish dream."

"Or . . ." Madame's lips formed her little half-smile, "perhaps that is the one real thing in you. It's been buried, but it is still there."

Dr. R shook his head. "I no longer have time for mystical daydreams."

"No? What a pity. But never mind. Perhaps you put your hope in psychoanalysis?"

"Yes, I discovered many things in my own analysis."

"So you are searching, that is the important thing. Now let's finish our dinner before it gets cold." They ate in silence. He had noticed Madame never engaged in small talk unless she was flattering a potential customer.

Then she personified a sophisticated, refined French woman of exquisite taste, who, with reluctance, would share a few of her hard-won secrets about glamor and attracting men. But now her silence made him want to chatter about something—anything. But she sat there relaxed and quiet, as if she were giving all of herself to the act of eating. He remained silent also.

As they finished, Madame suddenly asked, "Is psychoanalysis like hypnosis? I hear hypnosis helps people recall painful childhood experiences, and that helps them heal psychic wounds. Is that what psychoanalysis does?" She looked at him with warm eyes.

"No, it is not hypnosis. We use free association—allowing a person in a relaxed state with eyes closed to speak about whatever images or memories come up in their minds, trying to go deeper into the unconscious."

Madame smiled. "Ah, but what is the unconscious? I would say it is the real Self, hidden behind the rational personality that thinks it controls one's life. One's essence is what is hidden and therefore we are seldom conscious of it. The personality develops as we grow up, but it not what we really are. Sometimes it is called a mask—on rare occasions the mask comes off. That can be shocking."

"Dr. R thought for a moment. "Well, that's pretty close actually, maybe just different words." There was a pause. Was this his golden opportunity? "Uh, speaking of psychoanalysis, you know I can't stay in this situation. I must pursue my profession."

"No," she said, "although you just begin . . ."

Dr. R put a hand flat on the table. "I am a medical doctor, a psychoanalyst. I must return to the profession for which I spent years training."

"*C'est vrai,*" she said quietly. "Very true."

"Have any of your customers or acquaintances expressed an interest in being analyzed? Perhaps I could find a few clients to begin to form a practice again?" Dr. R pressed his lips together. Did he sound like he was begging? Probably.

She shook her head. "*Non, non, hors de question.* No, I don't think so. Yes, some of my customers complain about their analysts, but I would not consider it proper to make any suggestion. What if they came to you and then were *malcontentes*—dissatisfied? And these women are always *malcontentes,* always blaming their unhappy state on others. But that keeps them buying clothes—for a moment they are happy. If they thought you were no good, they would stop coming to my shop. Even worse, if you succeed to help them, they might realize they don't need all those clothes to be happy." She wrinkled her forehead. "That would be *horrible, n'est ce pas?* I have to be practical, don't I? Business is business, as you Americans like to say."

Dr. R felt his face burn. "I'm sorry I asked."

"*Du courage, mon cher,*" she said, placing a manicured hand over his. "*Bien sûr, Docteur,*" she said, smiling, "you must find a new life. But I have an idea! Come to dinner tomorrow night. I have invited four of my friends who do very interesting work. They might be able to help you. The guests come at seven. There will be shopping and food preparation. So much to do." She touched the tips of her thumb and index finger to her tongue before pinching each candlewick in turn. They spluttered in protest.

Dr. R. wanted to ask what kind of people were coming, and what kind of work they did, but he sensed that would be a rude question. "Thank you," he said, standing up to clear the table, one plate at a time, with one crutch under the other arm. He sat on a high stool to wash the dishes as she had taught him, stacking them carefully in the rack and drying the wine glasses with a clean towel. Meanwhile, Mme. de Beaufort prepared the shopping list for the following day. How many stores was he going to have to drag himself to this time?

34

The next morning, Dr. R did his rounds, cursing that he had to go both to the fish store and the butcher, and a wine shop that imported some French white wine called Viognier. He got the groceries into the dumbwaiter and then himself up the stairs and unpacked all the food into the fridge or onto the kitchen counter. Back in his room, he glanced in the mirror; while out shopping, he had gone to the barber to have his fringe of hair and his beard trimmed, despite the cost. The night before, he had ironed a white shirt himself without burning it. He had to look professional at the dinner that night.

• • •

"You're very quiet today," Madame remarked. Dr. R was chopping onions at the kitchen table and his eyes were streaming under his glasses. "Perhaps you are *un peu fatigué?* You aren't accustomed to so much exercise?" She smiled, half-closing her eyes.

"I hate exercise," Dr. R said, hearing his voice hiss the words.

"Do you? But you are a doctor—you know your body needs exercise to be healthy."

"I treat the mind and the emotions, but not the body."

"We need all three, of course," she said, looking up from the fish she was deboning. "If one of these is undeveloped, you aren't really a man." Dr. R stopped chopping and stared at her. "Or a woman, *bien sûr,*" she added with a laugh.

Dr. R was beginning to realize that Madame was trying to tell him something, something he could not understand. Not wanting to continue the conversation, he began peeling and chopping his third onion and then turned to the carrots she had peeled for him. Finally, she said he had done enough. The clock in the living room struck six.

"I need to clean up and change," Dr. R said.

"But of course," Mme. du Beaufort said, with a formal, quick nod. "I will call you when all the *invitées* are here."

Back in his room, looking at his image in the mirror, he asked the face in front of him, "Are you a doctor or a kitchen boy?" The face frowned, but remained silent.

He was ready long before he heard the doorbell ring. Then ten minutes later, he heard it ring a second time. He listened, but could not hear any voices at all. Probably they were talking about him. At last he heard the familiar, "*Monsieur le Docteur.*" As he reached for the door handle, the two crutches under one arm, he thought, "Well, at least there will be no doubt about my profession."

Three women were placing silverware and napkins on the long dining table, and one was arranging flowers in a vase at the kitchen sink. It seemed Madame didn't mind putting all her guests to work. They finished in a moment and stood smiling at him. Madame made the introductions. One was a Negro woman, rather large in a voluminous long flowered skirt and black hair piled on the top of her head. Her name was Margaret Edwards. Another was clearly Mexican—short with a round face, Consuela Sanclamente. The third was the woman, Alice Starfoot, whom he had met his first night there.

"Please sit here, Dr. Rosenblatt," Madame said, pointing to the end of the table. "Alice, take his crutches." Alice then served the puréed carrot soup that Madame dished up. As they ate it, Madame, on Dr. R's right, began speaking.

"These women and I are involved in a most interesting project in the Watts District. Perhaps you have heard about the Watts District?"

"I know it was a respectable working-class district before the War, and then there was a huge influx of Negroes from the South, who came here to work in the war factories. They hoped to find a new life here, but there hasn't been enough work since the War."

"Yes, and that's led to poverty and crime," Consuelo said. "There are Mexicans there, too—some are here illegally. They try to make a living by selling tourist stuff, but they have a very hard time also."

"And what about the Whites who stayed?" Alice asked. "They feel resentment toward these people, who they say bring down the neighborhood—the gangs and drugs and prostitution."

"So," Madame continued, "we have formed a private foundation with our own money and with help from some business friends to start a recreation center for kids from about age ten through high school. We have a basketball court and some boxing equipment, and volleyball and baseball outside. We try to get the parents to come evenings for some educational classes where we give them advice on how to help their kids succeed at school. *C'est difficile* . . . and we don't have enough money, really." She shook her head, eyes closed.

"I bet those kids have health issues and psychological problems, too?" Dr. R asked.

"*Bien sûr,*" Madame said. "They live in terrible conditions—rats, dirt, not enough to eat, or bad food. And here we are," she continued, "living in luxury. Dr. Rosenblatt, can I offer you some wine?" With a smile, she passed him a carafe of white wine. Dr. R took it and offered to fill everyone's glass.

"So," Madame said, lifting her glass, "let us toast our sports center.

May it flourish." They all took a sip of wine. Then Alice and Madame got up and served halibut with a cream sauce on warm plates. The fresh peas Dr. R had spent half an hour extracting from their pods were passed in a blue ceramic bowl with a silver spoon. Seeing the spoon, he was, for an instant, back in his own dining room with silver and candles. But this was not his home.

"What kind of doctor are you, Dr. Rosenblatt?" Margaret asked.

"I am a psychoanalyst," he said.

Margaret frowned. "I know nothin' about that."

"Psychoanalysts help people to talk about hidden memories that interfere with how they live their lives."

"That's interesting," Alice said. "How many lifetimes do you go back?"

"I beg your pardon?" Dr. R said.

"How many lifetimes do your patients have to remember to understand their problems?" Alice spoke as if she were explaining something very elementary to a child.

"Uh, we just look at this lifetime. I am not a Jungian psychoanalyst. He would agree with you."

"But sometimes the problem is much further back, maybe hundreds of years." Alice smiled.

"Freud was very scientific," Dr. R said. The women all laughed. Dr. R tried to smile and then took a big gulp of wine, which made him choke, causing the women to laugh even more. When he stopped coughing, he wiped his mouth with his yellow linen napkin and closed his eyes. Why did Madame invite him? He was not going to get any patients from these women.

"Perhaps," Alice said in a low voice, leaning toward him, her black hair glistening around her temples, "you might know some doctors who like to work with kids? We need someone who is good with adolescents, who knows how to talk to them, and maybe help them stay out of trouble."

"I don't, I'm afraid. Psychiatrists and psychoanalysts are only just beginning to work with kids. Even at the state mental hospital where I worked, I seemed to be the only one who really related to the young ones who ended up there—some as young as sixteen."

There was a silence as the four women looked at him with all-knowing smiles.

"Oh, no, I'm here for only a short time."

"We all are," Margaret said, looking upward.

Dr. R shook his head. "I was not referring to our mortality. I need to find new patients who want psychoanalysis. That is my profession."

"We really do need a doctor," Alice said. "but we don't have the money to pay one. I am a nurse—I do what I can for the kids when I am here in Southern California. My husband works as a bus driver down here during the school year, and I work full time at Good Samaritan Hospital. And then in the summer we go home to Idaho."

"Where do you live in Idaho?" Dr. R asked, ready to change the subject.

"I live on the Fort Hall Shoshone Indian Reservation near Pocatello. In the summer, I work with my own people—many suffer from alcoholism and diabetes. Our medical care is below the level you have here in a large city like Los Angeles. I was lucky—I got my nurse's training here."

"I am a nurse, too," Margaret said. "My husband is a businessman. He's been able to provide support for the sports center, and both Alice and I spend as much time as we can there—all volunteer, of course."

"Do you live in the Watts District?"

"No," Margaret said. "It's much too dangerous. We live in Sugar Hill, a nice neighborhood. Middle-class Negroes can get around the restrictions and buy houses there."

"In any case, ladies," Dr. R said, placing both hands on the table in front of him, "you have your ethnicity on your side in working with these kids. What you don't need is a one-legged, middle-aged Jew, who, unfortunately has had almost no contact with other races—except white Anglo-Saxons, of course, and then our hired help in Redgrove."

The four women fell silent. Then Alice jumped up to clear the main course and to serve a chocolate cake one of them had brought. The joy had left the gathering. After coffee in demitasse cups, Madame stood up and said in her formal voice, "We must excuse ourselves, Dr. Rosenblatt. We have serious matters to discuss now. Thank you for joining us." Alice handed him his crutches, a clear dismissal. The others moved toward the living room.

Dr. R entered his room, sat down in the one chair, and took one of his crutches to push the door shut. *Madame engineered this gathering in hopes of getting me involved in their sports center. She knew perfectly well these ladies weren't going to refer patients to me for psychoanalysis.* His face began to burn. He loosened his necktie, then pulled it off and flung it on the floor.

He had to get out of there. Bob or someone would lend him some money. One of his letters inquiring about a job would get a positive response. Dealing with a bunch of adolescent criminals and drug addicts who came from backgrounds he detested, like the rotten neighborhood he grew up in—that was the last thing he wanted to do. It was the kind of stupid thing Barney had wanted to do, with no consideration that he had a wife and child to support.

In fact, he remembered Barney talking about something that sounded similar. Barney hadn't thought about all the Negroes flooding California to get jobs in war factories to escape the appalling discrimination in the South. No, Barney had been worried about kids in Harlem. Well, these were Negro kids, too. Drugs, poverty, crime—it wasn't much different, but were any of these kids ever going to overcome the odds?

Dr. R shook his head. "Poor Barney," he whispered. "You were such an idealist. You even talked about training those kids to box, to build their self-confidence as well as their bodies. How strange. Here I am being asked to help these kids. Are you behind this, Barney?"

Dr. R wanted a drink. He had to stop talking to Barney. He didn't like where his thoughts were going. In the bottom drawer of the dresser, he had his flask of Scotch. He wheeled himself over to the dresser, poured a shot into the silver cap of the flask and downed it neat. It burned his throat before its warmth spread throughout his body. He replaced the flask, sighed, feeling some hidden tension in his solar plexus relax. He could not avoid the obvious truth: some Higher Power had played a trick on him, putting this harebrained sports center right in his face, as if daring him to do what Barney dreamed of doing.

Hell, what did he have to lose? If a decent job came through, he could always quit and finally get his own place. He even liked Madame. She was up to something, and he wanted to find out what it was. What strange confederacy brought these women together?

He took his crutches and went over to the closed door and listened. He could hear nothing. He turned the doorknob, slowly backing up to make a crack in the door. Through it he could see all the way into the living room, where the four women sat silently in a circle of chairs. Were they praying? He couldn't interrupt them, could he? He closed his own eyes and felt his heart beating faster than usual, his nostrils drawing in air. When he opened his eyes, the women were standing up, preparing to leave. He backed up further until he could open the door fully and moved out into the kitchen. They heard his crutches and turned to look at him, clearly surprised.

"Uh, well, perhaps I could visit your recreation center? It sounds interesting."

"Oh, would you?" Margaret said, raising her arms with a wide smile, her skirt rippling and twisting. "That would be wonderful!" The others showered him with a chorus of warm good nights and *bon soir, cher Docteur,* as he returned to his room. When he was inside with the door closed, he heard some laughter on the other side. What chance did he have with those women? He might as well submit.

35

Lying on his back on Max's bed the first day of summer vacation, the shades pulled down to keep the June heat from penetrating, Henry turned on his side to look at Max, who sat cross-legged on the floor, silently sorting baseball cards. "Do you think your mom is mad at me?" Henry asked. "She didn't say a word to me at breakfast this morning. She just rattled her stupid newspaper. She doesn't smile. And she didn't even answer when you asked her again if your dad would be coming back soon."

Max stared at the baseball cards still in his hand, then slowly let them spill out onto the floor. "Maybe I should have studied harder. Then he wouldn't have gone away."

"No, Max. It's my fault. I got Dr. R in trouble. He lost his job and then your mom wouldn't go to New York with him. Remember? We heard them fighting. If I hadn't come here, that wouldn't have happened. My dad said I ruined his life and now look what I've done to your mom and dad."

"Mom said *he* did something bad."

Henry looked down at the mess of cards in front of Max. "What did he do?"

"I don't know. I wish I could talk to him more. He's only called twice."

"He writes us letters a lot."

Max started to gather up the scattered cards. "I thought we would be doing fun stuff this summer. I guess I'll be playing baseball with my friends. That's it."

"And I'm going to work in Mrs. Davidson's garden. I'll earn some money."

"Maybe we could go to the movies sometime?"

"Yeah, let's do that."

"I'm glad you came here," Max said. "We can do stuff together."

"Yeah, Max. We can."

•••

The next afternoon, when Henry returned tired and dirty from his first day gardening for Mrs. Davidson, Mrs. R called to him from the living room as he came in the front door. "There's a letter for you on the hall table." He picked it up, and seeing immediately it was from Fannie—that much he could read—he headed upstairs.

He ripped open the envelope. There were three pale lavender pages, with large writing on both sides and all the letters joined to other letters. He could not recognize anything other than "Dear Henry," which he knew had to be there. He could not read anything. He was going to be forced to ask Max to read the letter to him, and that was going to be horrible. In his exhausted stupor, he began tracing the letters with his fingers, as if somehow he would understand the words through touch. And then, suddenly he did. It seemed like magic. His finger stopped moving but the sound of the words resonated in his brain.

June 13, 1953

Dear Henry:

I hope you don't mind getting a letter from me. I hope you can read it.

I am sitting in one of my secret places under a tall pine tree, which I get to by walking along a pathway below our house. No one ever comes here.

I can hear a squirrel scolding me, but I can't see him up there above me. Two lizards have darted past me, going from one rock to another. One stopped and stared at me as if to say, "What are you doing here?" I'm sure that Indians used to walk along this path, hunting deer.

I brought a book by Margaret Mead (my idol!) with me and I'm going to put this letter in it to hide it and I'll mail it at the post office when I next run errands for my mom—I just got my driver's license two weeks ago, right after my sixteenth birthday.

If we want to write each other, we need to find some place where you could send letters to me without my father knowing about it. I asked my mother and she had a good idea. She knows Dr. McKensie—and he's the one who took care of your mother. Isn't that amazing? My mom met him a long time ago, because they both visit an Indian woman in L.A. My mom goes nuts about Indian stuff, too. She's the one who got me interested. She has lots of funny ideas from the Indian woman. She says Dr. McKensie, you, me, the Indian woman, we're all in some kind of spider web together. I don't know who the spider is—and are we just food for her? Spiders in stories always seem to be female and in real life they often eat their husbands.

My mom likes you and doesn't agree with my dad that you did anything wrong. She's mad at your dad. She won't let him come over here anymore. My dad still plays golf with him.

Dr. McKensie lives in Sierra Madre just two blocks from my piano teacher, where I go every Friday. My mom talked to him and he agreed to let us use his address. Here it is:

Robert McKensie, M.D.
24 Sycamore Drive
Sierra Madre, California

I will stop by his house in about ten days to see if you have written back to me. I hope you can read my handwriting. I've tried to make it as neat as possible, but I have to balance this pad on my lap.

Sincerely,
Fannie

Henry folded up the letter and replaced it in its envelope. He raised it to his lips, hoping it might have a trace of some perfume she used—his mother always smelled like flowers—but he could not smell anything. Yet every word he could read was somehow special. He put it under his pillow, after pushing Jake deeper into the bed. He had to write her back. She would see how bad his handwriting was, but he couldn't ask Max or Mrs. R to correct his spelling. But he had to write her something. He could send her a drawing. Then maybe she wouldn't think he was completely stupid.

June 20, 1953

Dear Fannie:
Thank you for yor letter— I cud read most of it. I'm sorry I can't spell beter.

I am sitting in the orange grov behind the Rs hause. Just like you I hav my secret plase where I can be alone. These trees are my frends. It is peesful here. And the shade makes it kul. All the oranges have bin picked now. I'll draw you a piktur of a orange grove.

I havent seen lizards in her, but there are blue jays. Thay make a lot of noyz. I have seen robins, to. They lik the earthwurms under the trees.

Here are two more drawings—a robin and a blue jay.

I hope you will rite me again.

Sincerely,
Henry

For two weeks he heard nothing. Probably she hated his letter. She had beautiful handwriting, and he was sure she never misspelled a word.

Then one day at the end of a lesson, Mrs. R said, "Mrs. Stafford is coming to see her sister soon. And she's bringing Fannie. Fannie would like to come and see you again."

Henry ducked his head, blushing. "Uh, sure—I guess that's OK."

•••

On Saturday morning they arrived. Fannie wore blue jeans and a white shirt tied at the waist, revealing some skin. Her hair was pulled back in a ponytail. Mrs. Stafford, plump and bustling, came in with big smiles and some homemade jam.

"It's not too hot today," Mrs. R said. "You young ones might want to go outside—Betty and I are going to have a coffee in the living room."

Fannie led the way, as if she knew exactly where she wanted to go—back to the middle of the orange grove.

"Wait a sec, Fannie. I'll get something we can sit on." He ran off to the garden shed and returned with a dark brown blanket he often kneeled on while weeding. They found the same tree where they had been before. Sitting again with their backs against the trunk, close together, Henry looked down at Fannie's blouse covering the curve of her small breasts. They rose and fell as she inhaled and exhaled. He would have been happy just to sit there, absorbing her presence into every cell of his body. But he had to say something.

"Mrs. Rosenblatt and my English teacher, Mr. Kellogg, think I'll be able to get into Cal Berkeley if I work as hard as I can my senior year. I'll never be a great reader or speller, but my teacher, Mr. Kellogg, says that a special program is starting at Cal to help people like me. I really want to go there."

Fannie looked up, smiling. "I bet you didn't know that I have my heart set on going to Cal too? My father went there, so he's all for it. But I have a special reason: Professor Kroeber is still there, even though he's retired.

He's a famous anthropologist. That makes it the best place for me."

"Well, maybe we'll be there at the same time."

"That would be nice," she said. "But what is your aim?"

"Aim? You mean what do I want to do for a living?"

"No, not just that. What will you give your life to? What is your purpose?"

Henry could hardly breathe. "I don't know. I don't even know if I'll be able to finish high school. Everyone says I will, but I have so much to catch up on. I can't think about anything else."

Fannie frowned. "Something must inspire you, something more than what society expects you to do. I'm expected to get married, have children, keep house—things I don't want to do."

Henry could not tell her what he had been thinking: That was just what he wanted—with her. "Well, I have one idea," he said. "I want to help wild animals. My mother's friend, Carl, says I could be a park ranger, like in Yellowstone. I could even photograph animals as part of that job. And when I talked to my counselor at school, he said there is a new major at Cal called Wildlife Preservation. Well, it's part of the Forestry major. That's perfect for becoming a ranger."

At that moment, they heard the angry chattering of a squirrel above them in the branches. They both looked up. In fact, there were two grey squirrels looking at them, tails twitching. Fannie and Henry laughed.

"They follow me everywhere," she said. "I wonder if these guys are going to start throwing things at us. I've seen them do that."

The squirrels chased each other off into the next tree. "They're just having fun," Henry said.

"Do you love animals more than people?" Fannie asked. "I love animals, but I want to study people who haven't been ruined by our civilization."

"I don't trust people," he said. "They lie and try to make me do what they want, not what's good for me. Animals don't do that. But some people—someone like you—you're different."

"So are you. You're more interesting than the boys at my school. They would never even notice a squirrel right above their heads. They wouldn't notice if the squirrel were *on top* of their heads." They both laughed.

"I remember," Fannie continued, "that day when we met on the wall. You liked my story about the Indians. You tried to keep me warm on the mountain. I felt safe. Sometimes I feel lonely. It's like I'm on a completely different path than all my girlfriends, who just want to get married and have kids. My mom says I follow the beat of a different drummer."

"I feel safe with you, too." Henry reached out for her hand, but Fannie jumped to her feet, looking down at him, her lips tight.

"No, no, I don't want a boyfriend. I don't really want to be safe. I want adventure. I want to take risks. I have to carry out my plan."

"Fannie, don't go." But Fannie marched off toward the house. He remained leaning against the tree, sure that he had lost everything. Five minutes later, he heard a car drive away. She was gone. Forever.

•••

At dinner that night, Henry felt Mrs. R watching him. "You must have had a spat—that can happen."

"She'll never speak to me again."

"Why don't you write her a letter and apologize?"

"She'll never answer."

"Don't be too sure. I'll see Mrs. Stafford in a couple of weeks. She has talked me into meeting an Indian shaman—that's like a medicine man, except this one's a woman. Mrs. Stafford's crazy about Indian culture and for some reason, she thinks I'd like this woman. She's determined that I meet this shaman before she goes back to her tribe in Idaho for the rest of the summer."

"Mrs. Stafford won't know *anything.*"

•••

A few weeks later, he wrote Fannie.

July 14, 1953

Dear Fannie:
I'm sory I made you mad. I promiz never to do that again.

—Henry

He put Dr. McKensie's address on the envelope. Would Dr. McKensie tell Fannie there was a letter there for her? How would he do that? Then he waited.

A week later, coming into his room after summer school, he saw an envelope had been slipped under his door.

Dear Henry:
I am very busy now with my advanced classes at Pasadena Community College. I have met a nice boy there. But maybe we'll run into each other at Cal someday.

Sincerely,
Fannie

Henry wished that he had never learned to read.

36

A few hot weeks passed before Estelle was to have her lunch date with Betty Stafford and meet the Indian woman. She dragged her body through her obligations, hoping the heat would break and she would feel better. Then in mid-July, she drove for her rendezvous, meeting Betty at Tommy's Hamburgers on Beverly Boulevard, which lay between Pasadena and the Watts District.

"Why the Watts District?" Estelle asked Betty as they ate their hamburgers and fries. "Isn't it dangerous? Couldn't I have met this..."

"Alice Starfoot," Betty said.

"This Alice Starfoot—couldn't I have met her somewhere a little more respectable? And a sports center for delinquent Negro kids?"

"I know, I know," Betty said. "I'm putting you through a lot. But I have a feeling you'll like her. You'll get along just fine." Betty smiled, popping another French fry into her mouth. "I'll lead you there, if you want, but then I have to get back home for my Junior League meeting."

Estelle sighed. "Yes, we Jewish women only have our Councils."

"That's going to change," Betty said. "We'll have Jews in the Junior League some day..."

"Not some day soon."

Betty jumped up. "Well, let's get going. Do you think you can follow me?" They arrived half an hour later in front of a plain one-story beige building with a fenced-in baseball diamond on one side.

"Just go in that little door on the left," Betty said. "On your right you'll see a little office. She should be there." Estelle said good-bye and went in, wishing she could turn around and drive home. This was crazy.

When she opened the door to the office, Estelle saw a woman with long loose black hair in a black dress, turning toward her from the window, obviously having watched her come in. Her features were partially covered by an almost transparent black shawl, yet she seemed young. She smiled slightly as Estelle walked toward her. "I've been waiting," Alice said.

"I'm Estelle Rosenblatt. How do you do?"

"Yes, I know who you are. Let's not waste time. I've been told you have some psychic powers. Would you like to tell me about them?"

Estelle hesitated. This was a strange beginning. Why didn't this woman at least ask her to sit down? "I sometimes see omens in nature," she said. "A raven in a tree is a bad one for me. And I was in Europe when my mother-in-law died and before anyone told me, I had a dream in which she said she was all right and not to worry."

"But perhaps you have lost that power?"

Estelle felt her body stiffen. "What do you mean?"

"I've met your husband..."

"No, that's impossible."

"Not at all. We're all connected. You are going to have three big shocks very soon. They will show you just how connected we are. One will be delightful. I'm not so sure you will be so happy about the other two. One will be very soon."

"Are you trying to frighten me?" Estelle asked, trying to smile as her heart began to pound.

"Oh, no. Don't be afraid. It will be very good. Your husband, poor man, is suffering terribly. He is a difficult case." Estelle tightened her jaw. "Oh, I'm not blaming you," Alice said. "You did a very good thing. Now he's learning many things from Mme. de Beaufort. Oh, but you don't know Mme. de Beaufort. Maybe he will find his Spirit again—but he misses those boys. And you."

Estelle felt a lurch in her stomach. A weakness descended, her legs shaking. "I must sit down," she said. Alice pointed to a chair near the window.

"I think," Alice continued slowly, "that the baby is going to ask that you and your husband begin a new life together."

"What baby?" Estelle said. Did Alice have some vision of Jacob?

Alice laughed. "Don't tell me you don't know you are pregnant?"

"Of course, I'm not."

"Oh, yes, you are. If you were a seventeen-year-old girl, I would ask you when you'd had your last period. But you are a mature woman. Surely you must know. Your baby is already ten weeks along."

Estelle's hands instantly clasped her abdomen. Alice watched her. "I always miss periods when I'm upset. And when I'm upset, my stomach always goes funny." She glanced down at her abdomen, unbelieving. "This can't be," Estelle said. "I'm always so careful . . . well . . ." She wished she had never got mixed up with this weird woman and her clairvoyance. "If it's true, I won't tell him. No one must tell him. I don't need him, I'll . . ."

"Yes," Alice said. "He's just the father." She covered her mouth with her hand to hide a smile.

Estelle stood up. She had had enough. "I don't believe you—you're playing some trick on me."

"You will have an easy pregnancy, and the baby will be born in January, a very good time for a new life."

"I remember now," Estelle said, almost whispering. "In that dream when my mother-in-law appeared, she also told me that I was going to have a baby girl and she asked me to name her Miriam. I don't understand how I could have forgotten that. Now what am I going to do?"

"Sometimes we need to forget."

"Not something important like that."

"Maybe someone wanted you to forget."

Estelle shook her head. "I can't follow that . . ." She paused, then nodded. "Well, actually I agree. It's the baby who wanted me to forget, isn't it?"

"Yes, of course. Perhaps the old Miriam, too." Alice smiled.

"It's too late, isn't it? Even if it isn't, I can't go through . . . an abortion."

"Good. Here's something that might help. Come over into the next room. I want to show you something. This is another surprise for you."

Estelle raised both hands as if to ward off a blow. "I've had enough surprises for today."

"I think you will be able to handle this."

In the little room next to the office, there was a large window with four metal chairs in front of it. Through it she could see boys, black and brown boys of different heights, practicing their basket throws. She could hear the thud of the balls and the rattle of the backboard.

"Come sit down," Alice said. "This is a one-way window. On the other side is a mirror so they can't see that we are watching. The kids have been told that people who are interested in what we do here might come and watch, but once they start playing basketball or lifting weights, they don't care."

Off to the left in the bleachers, more kids, including some girls with badminton rackets, sat in a tight bunch. One of the boys was standing, wobbling from side to side as he tried to balance a crutch on his head. Everyone started clapping and shouting. The boy finally caught the crutch as it fell and sat down with the others. In their midst was a man they seemed focused on, a white man with a beard. And then Estelle saw it was Josh.

She gasped and then turned towards Alice, sitting next to her, her insides turning. "You have no right doing this to me. You and Betty Stafford tricked me into coming here. I should have been warned he would be here."

Alice's face seemed unperturbed. "You are angry. I understand. We wanted you to see what he is doing now. He doesn't know you are here and you don't have to speak to him. Before you go away mad, just look a little at what he is doing with these kids."

Estelle looked back, breathing hard. Josh was talking to them, gesturing with his hands and arms, as he always did. The kids had stopped moving as Josh began to speak about something. The kids listened and then one of them spoke. Josh pulled out his little notebook and his fountain pen and quickly drew something, which then was passed around. The one-way mirror muffled what they were saying. But Estelle could see that Josh was happy and relaxed, yes, happier than she had seen him since the War.

"He has a medical bag and patches up the kids sometimes," Alice said. "They get in fights out on the streets, even the girls. Some of them are in gangs. We've lost a few. So tragic. I've helped him sew up some knife wounds. But the ones who come here regularly often stop fighting."

"But he's a psychoanalyst," Estelle said. "He hasn't practiced regular medicine since his student days."

"I am a nurse. I've helped him with some basic first-aid. We send the ones with really bad wounds to Emergency. A group of women meet with Mme. de Beaufort, where he lives. We asked him to come here. We thought he could help these kids."

"Not with basketball. He never was athletic."

"No, but he likes kids. And these are not easy kids. Maybe he's like a father to them and many of them have no father."

"Yes, he had two boys at home he called his sons. Our adopted son, Max, and our Henry."

"He's told me about them."

Estelle felt her anger rise again. "You people are interfering with my life. Do what you want with my husband, but let me make my own decisions."

"Of course. You are free."

Estelle turned and rushed out. Not knowing exactly where she was going, she was relieved to see her car where she left it in front. No broken windows, no slashed tires. She gripped the steering wheel tightly on the entire drive back to Redgrove, which seemed to last twice as long as the trip to L.A. just hours before.

37

Henry felt nothing was right in the Rosenblatt home without Dr. R there. The heat penetrated everywhere despite the drawn curtains. The house was dark and too quiet. He missed the familiar squeak of Dr. R's crutches. At breakfast Mrs. R looked at the newspaper and hardly spoke at all. She picked at her food at dinner and often left the two boys to finish alone. Sometimes she asked him and Max about their summer activities, but she did not seem to pay attention. Only in her office during his lessons did she seem to wake up, at least enough to keep him working. Henry did his gardening for Mrs. Davidson every morning and went to a remedial geometry class at summer school in the afternoon. He and Max watched television some evenings or lay on Max's bed looking at comic books.

Weeks had gone by and Fannie had not written. She did not want anything to do with him; that was clear. Once at the end of his lesson, he stood up and started to leave but turned around in the doorway. "Uh, Mrs. R, my spelling is so bad. What can I do if I need to write a letter or something? I don't want other people reading my letters—aren't letters supposed to be . . ."

Mrs. R smiled. "Private?"

"Yes, private."

"Of course. But here's what you can do. You don't have to show the letter to anyone. Just write down the words as a list, maybe mixing them up. You could even start at the bottom of the list and ask me, or maybe

Max. He's not too bad a speller. If you're pretty sure you know how to spell a word, don't put it on the list. If it's a word you really don't want anyone else to see, you'll have to find it in a dictionary by a process of elimination. You'll miss a few words, but your correspondent, the one you are writing to, must know you have this problem and won't mind. People love to get letters. Writing letters used to be a great art. The telephone has made that rarer. Letters you can save and go back and read again and again many years later."

"Some letters," Henry said grimly.

"Yes, some letters are too painful to reread."

Henry raised his head. "Has that happened to you?"

"Yes—I tore them up."

"I've torn up letters, too."

"Burning them is even better," Mrs. R said.

"Really?"

"Forget I said that, Henry, we don't want you setting this house on fire."

• • •

One night after dinner, the phone rang. Mrs. R never answered the phone any more, but Agnes called up the stairs. "It's for you, Henry."

"Hello, Henry." It was Dr. R. Henry wanted to scream, *Can't you come home?* But he knew he could not do that. Maybe Mrs. R was listening from downstairs. "I miss you," Dr. R said.

"I miss you, too. Max and I got your letter."

"How are things going?"

"OK, I guess. I'm earning two dollars every morning doing gardening for Mrs. Davidson. She makes me move dirt and big stones to make a new vegetable garden at the back of her house. I'm getting strong."

"That sounds good. How is summer school?"

Henry smiled at the receiver in his hand. "You won't believe this. I find geometry easy. It's all pictures. I'm even helping some of the other kids who flunked geometry last year. I'm the only one who has never taken it before."

"I'm not surprised you do well at geometry. I was terrible at it, and I didn't like it."

"Really?"

"That's right. How is Max?"

"He's off playing baseball all the time. We go to the movies once a week in the afternoon. They have air conditioning in the movie theater."

"It's not as hot here in L.A. because we're near the ocean."

"Oh."

"Have Fannie and her mother come to Redgrove again? I have met a woman here who knows her mother. It's strange."

"An Indian woman?"

"Yes, how did you know?"

"Fannie wrote me about her and said how weird it was that Dr. McKensie knows that woman and so does my mom."

"Yes, it's very weird. So you're still in touch with Fannie?"

"No, she's mad at me."

"What did you do?"

"Uh, nothing. Well, I tried to hold her hand, but she didn't like it."

"Did you apologize?"

"I tried, but she wrote back that she's busy and I should get lost. That's not quite what she said."

"Henry, don't give up. Write her again. She went to all that trouble to come see you and apologize. She obviously likes you. Don't give up."

"She says she's met another boy."

"So, how long is that going to last? Don't give up."

Henry wanted to ask Dr. R if he had given up or maybe he was happy living somewhere else. He wanted to tell him that Mrs. R wasn't happy, but he did not dare.

"Is Max there?" Dr. R asked.

"Yes, he's in his room. I'll go get him."

"We'll talk soon. And I'll write you both again."

"OK. Well, good-bye." He opened Max's door and Max ran down the hall to the phone. Henry threw himself on his back on the bed and squeezed Jake against his chest.

"I wish Dr. R would come home. I hate this."

38

For the next week Henry kept remembering Dr. R's words: "*Don't give up.*" Finally he decided to make a drawing for Fannie of his favorite tree in a nearby park, a white, pockmarked skeleton of a tree trunk, squat, with a large hole at the bottom. It appeared balanced on three short legs, the remnants of its trunk that still touched the ground. But this tree was not dead—a few scraggly branches with clusters of small green leaves disappeared into the foliage of the trees behind. Somehow it kept living. He had drawn that dead thing and photographed it many times before he had seen its few defiant leaves. He liked it best on those early mornings when fog transformed it into a tree-ghost and he could imagine it slithering on its stubby legs to terrify anyone passing by. Off to one side was a wooden bench where romancing couples sometimes sat, unaware of the sinister thing so near them.

On a corner of the drawing Henry wrote: *This tree looks dead but it isn't. It is in a park near here. Henry*

He checked every word with Max to be sure that it was spelled correctly. He folded the drawing like a letter, mailed it in the box down the street, and waited without hope.

August 20, 1953

Dear Henry:
I haven't been taking my piano lessons during the summer, but I went by Dr. McKensie's to say hello and there was your drawing. I have tried to draw trees, but they don't look real like yours. I still want to be friends. I like talking to you and you are the only one who writes me letters.

Maybe I could come with my mom again to visit Aunt Marianne? I would like to see that tree.

Sincerely,
Fannie

PS – I lied about meeting a nice boy. I was mad at you. I don't want a boyfriend, but I want us to be friends.

He was able to read her handwriting—his dyslexia seemed to disappear. Henry folded up the letter and struggled with trembling hands to put it back in its envelope.

"You see, Jake," he said, whacking the tiger with the wrinkled envelope. "I guess she still likes me. Maybe Dr. R was right."

•••

Two days later in the late afternoon, Mrs. R shouted up the stairs to say there was a call for Henry. He picked up the receiver in Mrs. R's office—fortunately, she had no student then and was downstairs.

"Hello?"

"Hi, Henry. This is Fannie." Henry felt his hand on the receiver shaking.

"Uh, hi."

"I'm at Dr. McKensie's. He's letting me use his telephone in his office, and he closed the door so no one can hear."

"Uh, that's nice."

"I'm coming to Redgrove with my mom this Saturday. My dad's off in Nevada, looking at some mine. We'll spend the night with Aunt Marianne, but I think my mom wants to talk to Mrs. Rosenblatt. They've become great friends. They all seem to be going crazy over that Indian woman, but my mom won't let me meet her yet. That's so unfair. She says it's her *project* and I'd better concentrate on my classes." She paused. "I like talking to Dr. McKensie and his wife. They talk about things my parents never talk about."

Like what?"

"Oh, it's too hard to explain. They talk about waking up, as if we go around half-asleep or something—stuff like that."

"Dr. R has started talking like that, too. He writes me letters and Max reads them to me. Sometimes he telephones. He says he's learning he has a body and feelings as well as a mind."

"Well, duh, of course he does."

"I wish he would come home. He never used to talk like that."

"Adults are strange. My mom and Mrs. Rosenblatt talk to each other about Indian stuff and visions and tapping into some special force. But she won't tell me anything."

"It must be a contagious disease, like the measles or something."

Fannie laughed. "Could you show me that tree on Saturday?"

"Sure. That would be great."

• • •

Fannie was behind the wheel when she and her mother drove up. She wore a pink-flowered dress with no sleeves, her black hair shining. As soon as her mother joined Mrs. R in the living room, Henry and Fannie looked at each other, nodded, and rushed out the front door, heading for the park.

Henry pointed. "It's right down there. See it? We can sit on the bench."

The tree itself no longer seemed strange or evil. Fannie walked straight up to it, laid a hand on it, and then sat down.

"Yes, it's just as you drew it. It's a beautiful old thing, isn't it? But you have to look up to see that it really has leaves. They seem to be hiding up there. The trunk looks like it's been dead a long time. Do you think birds live up there?"

"No, just squirrels." They laughed.

"Do you have a favorite tree?" Henry asked.

"I like that deodar outside our living room window. Do you remember it?"

"Yes."

"I can climb way up it. The branches are almost like a ladder, going straight out from the trunk. But I want to go to jungles and see trees dripping with vines and maybe with monkeys in them. I want to study the people that live there, maybe in New Guinea."

"The cannibals? I don't want you to go there."

Fannie's face tensed. "But I'm going. That's why I want to be an anthropologist."

"I can't believe your parents would let you go."

Fannie smiled. "By the time I have my PhD, I'll be making my own decisions." She paused. "And where are you going?" she asked

"To the desert—I want to go there and see the light."

"The light?"

"Yes, the light at all different times of day. With no people to spoil it—no buildings, no automobiles, no asphalt."

"I thought you wanted to be a park ranger. Do they have parks in the desert?"

"Yes. I read in *Arizona Highways* that Death Valley is a national monument, but it has rangers."

"The Indians were smart. Even if they hunted in the desert in the winter, in the summer they moved up to the mountains to escape the heat. The desert is no place for humans. I want a jungle, one full of people and animals."

Henry pulled himself up to his tallest posture, as Mrs. R had taught him. "We're young—we can go all kinds of places. We could go to the Antarctica and see the emperor penguins."

Fannie looked at him wide-eyed, and then smiled. "There are some primitive people on Tierra del Fuego. It's near the Antarctic, but it's so cold there. Still, it's so exciting to think about." Her eyes shone with their special light.

"A photographer can have an exciting life, too," Henry said. "But I want to photograph animals and teach people about them."

"Well, maybe we'll see each other at Cal, before I go off to the jungles and you to the desert."

"Don't say that."

"You don't want to see me at Cal?"

"That's not what I meant, Fannie, and you know it." He started to stand up.

"Well don't look so sad." She reached out her hand and he grasped it tightly. "Ouch, don't squeeze so hard," she said.

"I'm sorry." He loosened his grip, his heart beating loudly. They sat there, silently gazing at the tree. Henry thought it was watching them. He leaned toward Fannie and kissed her cheek.

She frowned but did not pull back. The frown changed to a half-smile. "That's nice, Henry. But remember what I told you."

The tree suddenly looked old and ugly. "Let's go back," Henry said. "I bet your mom wants to get over to your aunt's."

"Don't get mad." And Fannie jumped up and almost danced down the path leading out of the park, her hair swinging from side to side. How could black shine with so much light?

39

Estelle waited, unsure, for guidance from some unknown source. At last she agreed to go to Bob McKensie's to meet Josh on the last day of August. Lying in bed early that morning, she wondered if it was too late to cancel. She breathed in and out. A sigh, almost a moan, escaped her lips. She sighed again and sat up in bed. She looked over for a moment at Josh's side. She had never been able to move into that space. She got out of bed and let her body perform its morning rituals, as if it were someone else who had decided she was going through with the meeting. She showered, dressed in a light grey gabardine suit that was businesslike. Wasn't this going to be a business meeting?

This time she drove herself. She planned the trip at a moment when she knew Charlie and Agnes were going to visit his family for a barbecue. She had not even told them where she was going.

She arrived in front of Bob's house. As she got out of the Green Monster, she pulled the jacket of her suit down over her abdomen, hoping that no changes showed yet. The heat of the day made the gabardine cling to her body—exactly what she did not want. She marched up the concrete pathway and rang the doorbell. A full-figured blond woman opened the door.

"Hi, I'm Diana," she said, extending her hand to shake. "Please come in. Your husband just arrived ten minutes ago. As she walked into the living room, she saw Josh was standing near a sofa. He smiled weakly as Estelle approached. He looked tired. She did not smile in return.

"Hello, Josh," she said and sat down quickly in an armchair. He sat on the sofa. Diana instantly disappeared.

"How are you?" Dr. R asked.

Diana slipped back in with a tea tray, deposited it on the table and was gone again, turning at the kitchen door. "Did Bob tell you we are expecting a baby in seven months?"

"That's wonderful," Josh said without a trace of joy.

"Congratulations," Estelle added, wondering for a moment whose baby was being spoken about. "I'm OK," she said. A silence followed.

"You wrote me that you wanted to talk," Dr. R said. She saw he was looking down at his missing leg. And his face was drawn and sad.

"Yes, it's time we talked about . . . arrangements . . . for the future. I want to file for divorce. My mother is moving back to New York, and I want to begin a new life."

"Without me."

Estelle took a deep breath. "Yes, without you."

Dr. R nodded and raised his head to look at her. "I betrayed your trust."

"Yes, you did."

"I wish to God I had not spoken to your mother. Do you realize, though, how desperate I was? I wanted to prove my worth by winning the lobotomy battle, not only for the memory of Barney, but much more to win approval from you and your mother. And I wanted to be a knight in shining armor for the poor bastards stuck in these hellholes of mental hospitals."

Estelle crossed her arms. "You didn't mind destroying our marriage in the process."

"I was selfish beyond belief. I kept thinking you would understand somehow. I should have respected your wish to stay away from any contact with—that man. I don't expect you to forgive me, but I am sorry. You knew all my weaknesses, but I guess this one was too much."

"It broke something in me."

"I understand that now."

Estelle turned away from her husband, her chin held high. She did not want to look at him. His crestfallen face was eating into her.

"You don't need to worry about me," he said. "Things are looking up a little. Bob introduced me to a child psychoanalyst in Sierra Madre, who is in his eighties now, and not in good health. He has been looking for someone to take over his practice. I met with him three times. He liked me and is giving me his practice. It's kind of a miracle."

"I'm glad. It sounds like you will be OK financially."

Josh nodded. "We'll have to think about Max. It seems Henry is in good hands with Carl and Edna. You must know what Max told me, that he's going to live with Uncle Ed and go to a high school there that feeds a lot of kids into the minor leagues. Ed said you were in favor of that. It fits into your new plans, right?"

Estelle nodded. "I told Max he had to have your approval."

"But he'll want to be with you or me during the vacations, won't he?"

"Of course," Estelle said.

"I'm renting a little house near Bob's in Sierra Madre. I'll commute twice a week by bus to L.A. I'm working part-time pro bono at a sports center in the Watts District."

"Yes." She paused. "I've heard that. Sierra Madre . . . is your house like Bob's?"

"It's tiny—only three little bedrooms. But one has a separate entrance from the garden that can become my office for psychoanalysis."

There's a garden, too?"

"Yes, just a backyard, really."

Estelle felt swept into a wave of grief and bewilderment and began sobbing. She covered her eyes with her hands, leaning forward in pain.

"Here," Josh said, pressing his handkerchief between her fingers. She took it and dabbed at her eyes until the sobs subsided. "What's wrong,

Estelle?" She heard his voice trembling. "Have I offended you again? I didn't mean to."

"I . . . I . . . I've always wanted to live in one of those little houses in Sierra Madre. I never told you, but I thought Bob's house was just perfect. This is bizarre. You're going to have what I've always wanted."

"Your mother and I talked you out of your dream of a little house, didn't we? That's another reason to hate me."

"I don't hate you."

"No?"

A silence fell. Estelle struggled to regain some composure. Now at last she was clear. She had two things to tell him. "I know I am not blameless in our breakup," she began. "I never told you what happened between Alfie and me. I was afraid if you knew, especially if you knew after Jacob's death, you would be horrified."

"Try, Estelle—please try."

"Now it doesn't matter. I better tell you. I have nothing to lose, do I?

"When I went off to NYU, my mother was pushing me to be nice to Alfie, who was at NYU, too, a year behind me. I was so relieved to have finally escaped home, I'm afraid I went wild. I was sleeping around, as they say. I was convinced for some idiotic reason that I was sterile and didn't have to worry about contraceptives—the arrogance of youth. I had always had a kind of love/hate relationship with Alfie. He seemed to idolize me, and followed me around like a puppy dog at family gatherings, which really annoyed me. But he was very handsome, too, so I was attracted to him, even though he was my cousin. So, I finally told my mother I'd go out to dinner with him." She paused. "I know, we agreed when we met that we wouldn't talk about previous love affairs, but I have to tell you this. Alfie and I went out to some fancy restaurant, where we drank too much wine. He took me back to his apartment, where we drank some more. We started kissing and I said to myself, *why not?* I didn't care about him at all. It was the wine. I could have stopped him, but I didn't.

Really, I seduced him. I think it was the first time for him. Afterward, he said, 'Oh my God, we're cousins.' I said, 'If you tell anyone in the family, I'll get a gun and shoot you.' He looked scared and said he wouldn't. And I told him never to speak to me again. I was so cruel."

"It was a foolish fling, that's all."

"But this time I got pregnant. I had to have an abortion and it was terrifying. But I was OK. No infection, nothing. But I hated it and I felt I was killing a baby." Tears rolled down her cheeks again and she wiped them with Josh's handkerchief.

"Do you think I would have loved you less if you had told me?"

"I was sure of it. I felt a little less guilty when Jacob came along, but then . . ."

"The meningitis virus killed Jacob." Josh said. "You did not kill him. You must accept that. But now I understand why you feel that way about Alfie. You saw the abortion as murder, and then Jacob. This is terrible. If I had known, I might have been able to comfort you. Analysis would have helped, too, but that's not your path. You have no idea how many times I have heard women clients relate the same story of an abortion and the guilt they've experienced. But if you'd had the baby and it was known Alfie was the father, it would have torn your family apart. You did the right thing. I'm just glad you survived it—physically at least."

Estelle suddenly felt a quiet relief in the middle of her body. "I should have known you would say that. I stopped fooling around after that. There was no one until I met you. I thought if I told you about Alfie, you couldn't possibly love me. And I wanted you so much."

Josh shook his head. "In the end, though, I didn't give you the life you hoped for, did I?"

"No, but it was my fault, too. I couldn't go against my mother when she insisted on buying that house."

"But now your mother is leaving, isn't she? She came to see me and told me she wants to be back with her friends in Manhattan. That was kind of her to come and tell me in person."

"Yes, and now I'll have to go back East to see her at least several times a year."

"You are a good daughter. I know I've complained about her, and I'm sorry."

"She loves me in her own limited way."

"Yes, she does. But now you can have the life you have dreamed of. No one to tie you down."

"Well . . ." Estelle felt her body sag. It seemed they would soon go their separate ways. Josh looked so defeated, so tired. "There's something else I have to tell you."

Josh's eyes opened wide with surprise, his bushy eyebrows arched up.

"Do you remember that time, about four months ago, when we talked about Jacob and then ended up making love, but I forgot to put in my diaphragm?"

"Yes, and I've asked myself a million times why things could have gone so badly after that magical moment."

"Well, I'm pregnant."

"No!"

"Yes."

Josh's face went pale. "You aren't thinking about an abortion, are you?"

"No, of course not. I would never do that again. At first, I was horrified, but now for some reason, it feels fine. The baby will be part of my new life."

"And what about me, the father?" Josh clenched one fist in his other hand and glared at her.

"I don't know. I haven't been able to picture it."

"I can," he said. He grabbed a crutch and pushed himself up to his full height, his eyes looking down at her. "I will tell you, and then you can laugh at me. Let's decide for the sake of the baby to try again. You move in with me."

"To that little house in Sierra Madre?"

"Yes, but I'm paying the rent."

Estelle felt herself melting. "You still want me after what I told you?"

"Of course. You are more important than anything in my life."

"Not just because of the baby?"

"The baby . . . yes, the baby. I won't lie, Estelle. The baby is a sign that we should be together. But I will love you no matter what, with or without the baby."

"Well, let me think about it."

"Come over here, Estelle." Soon she was in his familiar embrace. She felt his wet cheeks next to hers. "Give me back my handkerchief," he said. She pulled back and stared at the crumpled handkerchief she still clutched in her hand. "I washed and ironed it myself," he said.

"A great accomplishment," Estelle said through her tears. "But you can't have it back."

Dr. R looked at her, serious and silent. "That is the most beautiful thing you have ever said to me."

"I mean it, Josh, you can't have it back." She opened her handbag and put the handkerchief in, closing it with a decisive snap. Head down, she stared at her hands.

"I've discovered that I can do almost everything, even with one leg," Josh said. "And we had a guy come to the sports center to talk to some kids who have lost limbs, a guy who is both an engineer and a doctor, and he's helping me get the latest prosthetic leg, which he says works quite well, even with a stump as short as mine. I could get rid of these damn crutches . . ."

"You could walk a fussy baby up and down."

"Like I did with Jacob? Oh, damn, give me that handkerchief back."

Estelle opened her handbag, took out the handkerchief and wiped his eyes. And then it seemed everything was settled.

40

The next morning Dr. R asked Madame if he could speak to her before she went downstairs to the shop. When he sat down at the kitchen table, she offered him a café au lait in a small bowl. She gave him her little smile as he lifted the steaming bowl to his lips.

"Uh, I need to tell you . . ." He paused. "My wife and I have reconciled. She wants me back—it seems we are expecting a baby."

"*Mais, oui,*" Madame said. "That explains something Alice said—*très mysterieuse*—about life renewing itself in your family. I never had children, but I have seen that it is a very special time."

"My wife seems to have been greatly helped by Alice. At first she hated her, but now she loves her. Alice may have brought us back together."

"She is quite special. She has gathered together a group of women."

"Yes, Estelle told me she is joining that group."

"And, as you have seen, that group meets with me . . ."

"You mean Consuela and Margaret as well as Alice?"

"Yes, plus others. You have only met those who work with me at the sports center. There are others who are trying to wake up, but those women are also passionate about social justice. There is Betty Stafford, for instance."

Dr. R shook his head. "You seem connected to almost everyone I know, at least the women. Don't tell me you've met my wife?"

"Not yet. Alice has only just convinced her to meet with the other women."

"It seems Estelle and Betty know more than I do. I have seen that meetings take place here, and I've suspected that more is going on than organizing the sports center. You obviously don't think I'd be interested."

Madame smiled. "I did not want to force anything."

Dr. R laughed. "Not force anything? I'm afraid that's not the way I would describe the past few weeks. But it's true—you've never asked me to a meeting. I saw a book on your coffee table with the title *The Seekers of Truth*. I confess I opened it up one day when you were downstairs in the shop. I found it interesting—what it says about the possibility of people working with others in a special way under the direction of a teacher. I've always felt that something in us could be developed that is more sensitive, more intelligent." Dr. R pointed a finger at her. "I think you are one of those teachers. You have been a hard taskmaster. I have had to face things about myself that even psychoanalysis never revealed and I want to learn more."

Madame waved a hand. "Oh, I would not claim to be such a teacher. That would be 'orrible. But I was fortunate to study with a real teacher in Paris, before and during the War. He is dead now. Life has brought me here, so in order to continue working on myself, I have tried to gather a few people around me who also wish to study these ideas and practice them in their lives. What is essential is to live them. "

"Did your teacher write that book?"

"No, that was a Russian student of his. Many of them had to escape Russia during the Bolshevik Revolution. My teacher was from the Caucasus, but he started groups in St. Petersburg and Moscow. Most of his students were White Russians, even aristocrats. They escaped just in time. Those who stayed behind did not survive. He and his followers finally ended up in a chateau near Paris."

"I'm surprised at myself," Dr. R said, "but I feel drawn to whatever this is. I never really knew I had a body until you pushed me to my limits.

And working with those kids who have everything stacked against them makes me happy. People always told me I was good with kids, but I never listened. I always liked being around them, but now I want to help them. They need attention and love."

Madame nodded. "*Bien sûr.* We all do. Perhaps attention *is* love."

"I'm almost never attentive and quiet like you, except in the psychoanalytic setting. There we are trained to listen, both to the client and to ourselves. I wouldn't have got in so much trouble if I had listened to Estelle—I know that now. Your meetings are so quiet. I can sense, even from my room, that a special kind of listening is going on."

Madame smiled. "You have tasted something..."

"Do you have a beginning group where I could explore this a little more? Not a women's group, of course."

"What I do with the women is a little different, maybe because of Alice. We try to understand what is common in different religions and cultures. It's *très passionante.*

"But, yes, there is a beginning group, whose leader you happen to know—Bob McKensie. They meet downstairs in the back room of the shop. I visit sometimes."

"What? Why didn't he ever tell me?"

"Oh, well, he said he tried a few times. You...were not so interested. But then when you became... how do we say... *désespéré*... desperate, he had this idea to send you to me."

"So I was bamboozled..."

Madame laughed. "I don't know what *bamboozled* means, but I can guess from your tone of voice."

"A set-up job—I was led into a trap." Dr. R shook his head.

"Well, yes, *c'est vrai,* but you know, you could have refused. You could have borrowed money from someone, if you had been able to swallow your pride."

"Which of course I could not, but you took care of that."

"And now I am going to lose you," Madame said, "but don't worry. A young woman has been waiting. I told her it would not be too long before she could move in."

"But, wait a minute, Madame. I don't want to abandon the kids at the sports center. And how can I join Bob's group? Redgrove is an hour and a half or two hours away and we won't be living full time in Sierra Madre until after the baby is born. Our live-in couple will stay for a little to help us. What am I going to do?" Maybe I can coordinate the days I'm in Sierra Madre for my practice with the sports center and Bob's group?"

"The new woman will go in your room—she prefers that. You can always use one of those little rooms upstairs—of course, it will be *très difficile* for you to get up there . . ."

"I beg your pardon, but that is not what you have been teaching me."

"Then be my guest, *cher Docteur.* You are most welcome."

"So how soon can I move out without inconveniencing you?" Dr. R asked. "My wife needs me."

"You can go tomorrow. Pack up now. I'll fix us a little dinner to celebrate this new phase of your life. You go and pack."

"I don't need all day to pack. Isn't there any shopping?"

"No shopping today. You will have to live with yourself all day. Maybe it will be the last time you can be quiet and just be."

"Be what?"

"Be yourself."

"But who am I? I don't know anymore. Maybe I will know when I get back to Redgrove. Or when we settle permanently in Sierra Madre. Yet I'm not sure I want to go back to the old life."

"It won't be the same. There's the baby."

"Yes," Dr. R said, "the baby."

"*Très bien.* So today, abandon yourself to yourself."

"I'll read the newspaper . . ."

"*Bon.* I see you are going to be stubborn. The newspaper is not going to tell you who you are. Now I must go downstairs."

"Thank you, Madame." He stood up, took up his crutches, and moved off to his room.

• • •

Dr. R packed his belongings, read the newspaper, made a ham sandwich, and finally went back to the coffee table in the living room to read some more in *The Seekers of Truth.* Madame came upstairs to fix their dinner, refusing any help from Dr. R. He continued reading, pausing a few times to smell the odor of *coq au vin* coming from the kitchen. Finally Madame joined him in the living room. She arranged two straight-backed chairs facing each other next to the coffee table.

"Let's sit here a little before we eat," she said. "Perhaps we could try a little experiment, since it is your last night. You spoke about wanting to learn to listen. Let me show you something." Dr. R sat down, laying his crutches on the carpet beside him.

"Do you know you have a spine?" she said.

"What?"

"Look how you are sitting. You're slouched over like a depressed person. How can you have an intelligent thought in that posture?"

"What does my posture have to do with how I think?"

"You will have the same old thoughts if you stay in that posture. And they are going to be sad or anxious thoughts, because that's what your body is telling you." Dr. R's jaw clenched. He straightened up, crossing his arms. "That's not much better. Now you have completely closed off your chest area."

"Madame, my body hurts and it hurts even more when I sit up like this."

"Good. You are sensing your body. If you can also be aware of your feelings, we'll start to get somewhere."

"They are not very pleasant at this moment."

"Yes, but at least you aren't dreaming—you're more awake. It's what you are at this moment. And this is just the beginning. Close your eyes and just sit here, very still, for ten minutes and see what happens—that is, if you are willing."

Dr. R sighed. "All right." He saw her hands were folded in her lap, so he folded his as well.

"I will sit also," she said, "and I'll tell you when the ten minutes are up."

Dr. R heard a clock ticking, some cars and voices down on the street, and then his own breathing. He opened his eyes and peeked at Madame. Her eyes were closed, her face relaxed. A muscle in his lower back began to hurt, but he did not dare move. His thoughts drifted off to Estelle, the baby, what it would be like to go back home.

"Come back," Madame. said softly. "Sense your body, feel your weight on the chair." For only a moment, Dr. R felt the tensions relax. "The time is up."

"My thoughts took me away," Dr. R said, opening his eyes. "Just at the end, my body felt something. I can't explain it."

"No, fortunately, you can't."

"It's so hard to be quiet inside."

"You could try this every morning as soon as you get dressed, before you drink coffee or eat, before the talking machine starts up. You can speak about your discoveries in the group. But that's enough. Let me get the champagne and we'll drink to the happiness of you and your wife."

"I have more questions for you," Dr. R said as they clinked their champagne glasses.

"First," she said, "let us enjoy this meal. My teacher was an extraordinary cook, but above all, watching him eat was a teaching in itself. He gave it all his attention, as if it were—what could we say?—a kind of sacrament, something sacred."

Dr. R and Madame ate silently for some minutes. She cleared the main course and brought a wooden bowl with a plain lettuce salad. "Let us eat our salad and then we can speak."

Dr. R had no desire to eat the salad, so he ate it quickly with a few jabs of his fork and then had to wait while Madame. ate hers with a studied slowness.

"I've been reading that book today," he said. "It has diagrams and charts, but it's not really science as we know it, is it? And it doesn't follow a specific religion. What is it?"

"My teacher brought a new teaching based on ancient knowledge but adapted for contemporary people. Its aims are close to religion but without the dogma of religion. It is scientific because it insists that a person verify for himself everything it says, even an idea as profound as the cosmology of interpenetrating worlds, worlds of finer and coarser levels of materiality. What is called higher consciousness or enlightenment is a moment of accessing these finer substances. We don't need to live in our heavy, dark world of negativity and narrow opinions. Perhaps you have had such a moment of experiencing this possibility of a different life?"

"I don't know about finer substances, but on Friday evenings at the beginning of Shabbat, my mother always lit the two Shabbat candles. Flames have always fascinated me, even the tiny flame of a candle. My parents used to argue a lot, but at that moment, everything was peaceful, and the room was filled with that special glow of the candles. My father would sing the candle-lighting prayer in Hebrew, and I remember feeling bathed in God's love. It's hard to explain."

"Yes," Madame said, nodding. "There are great truths in these religions. It is a mistake to reject them when we react to all the abuses. I had the same experience growing up in the Catholic Church. I loved going with my mother to light a candle for my deceased grandmother in one of the little chapels in our church. Many other candles were already lit, and I sat next to *Maman* while she prayed. Just in front of me was Christ on the cross, glowing in the candlelight. It felt so mysterious. The Catholic religion calls that *Spirit.* When I met my teacher, I knew I was looking for that sense of the sacred in my life."

"I hated all the rules of Orthodox Judaism," Dr. R said. "I saw hypocrisy and intolerance. Yet I loved the lighting of the Shabbat candles."

"This teaching is not a religion. It doesn't rely on faith in some distant God. Yet it seems we all want to return to the Source, to search for something in us that can relate to a much bigger world, that quiet space inside where I experience the richness of life, not just while meditating but right in the midst of our daily life."

"I don't understand much of what you are saying, but I want to learn more. At worst, it will be just another illusion."

Madame. smiled. "Yes, only you can decide that. And now we must stop. Oh, I will miss the sound of your crutches squeaking out all your complaints and self-pity."

"Madame!" And then they both laughed.

41

The next day Charlie arrived to take Dr. R home. Hearing Charlie's footsteps coming up the back stairs, Dr. R felt a stir of excitement. He was really going home.

"*Hola,* Dr. R," Charlie said, shaking his hand. Charlie's lined face beamed.

"I have to go down the front stairs," Dr. R said. "You go ahead down the back with my suitcase. The wheelchair is in the shop."

Dr. R emerged onto the sidewalk, glanced at the Green Monster waiting in front, and then entered the shop, where Mme. du Beaufort was seated at a little antique desk doing paperwork. "Here are my keys," he said, placing them on the desk. Madame looked up.

"Oh, yes. You must be 'appy to be rid of them. On to your new life. What will it be? Who knows?" And then she returned to her work. Dr. R regarded her bent head. Then he turned and left. He could not even say good-bye after such a clear dismissal. She was strange.

As they left the city and began driving past the fields and orange groves, Charlie said, "The boys start school soon. Henry is excited about it, but Max is complaining that he won't be able to play as much baseball, and why does he need to go to school anyway, if all he's ever going to do is play baseball? I heard Mrs. R tell him, 'It will be wonderful if you get on a minor or major league team, but maybe you'll be a P.E. teacher, and for that you'd better have a high school diploma and a teaching degree.' Henry had something to say too: 'Max, don't a lot of minor leagues recruit straight from college baseball teams? You aren't going to go to college if you don't finish high school.' 'Really?' Max said. 'They recruit from college teams?'"

"Good for Henry. He's become a good older brother." Dr. R paused. "My wife must have told them that I'm coming back?"

"Yes, they had a long talk in the living room last night. And she's told us . . . uh, you know, she's going to have a *bebé.*"

"It's a lot for the boys to absorb . . ."

"Have you heard my news, Doctor?"

"No, don't tell me Agnes is expecting a baby?"

Charlie laughed. "No, no way, Doctor. Agnes can't have *niños.* My news? Mrs. R didn't tell you? An uncle of mine is retiring and he's sold me his nursery. It's out in the San Fernando Valley. Agnes and I are leaving. It was going to be before Christmas, but now Agnes is saying she can't leave your wife before the baby is born, and not for the first few months, either."

"But you can't leave, Charlie. What will we do?"

Charlie frowned. "But Mrs. R says you're moving when the baby is old enough."

Dr. R blew out his breath. "I'm sorry. Of course, it's working out well. But it's such a shock. I've missed you and Agnes as much as the others—you are such a part of our lives."

"I've always wanted a nursery business. And Agnes will help me. And she can spend time with her sister's five kids—kind of makes up for not having any herself."

"I may have to show off my new cooking skills," Dr. R said gloomily. "Although they don't go much beyond chopping and slicing and grating."

"Well, that's something."

"I can't imagine anyone else working for us."

"You'll find someone," Charlie said, pulling into the driveway. And there was everything, just as it had always been—the red trumpet vine over the portico, the sound of gravel under the tires, the grey shingles, and white-trimmed windows.

Both Agnes and Estelle came out the front door as they arrived. As soon as Dr. R was out of the car, Agnes threw her arms around him, her eyes shining. He almost lost his balance. Estelle also hugged him and he felt her body against his, its welcome softness.

They wasted no time. The boys were due back from baseball and gardening around four. They disappeared into the bedroom. Had they been apart only three months? It seemed more like a year. Their bodies found each other again and knew what the other needed.

"And we don't need to worry about birth control," Estelle said, as they began to make love again.

"Not for a while," Dr. R said, pushing back her long hair to kiss her ear.

They were dressed by the time the boys arrived home, drinking tea in the living room.

"Hi, Dad," Max said, leaning over to give him a hug. Henry raised a hand in greeting, his face lit with a smile. Dr. R half-expected some anger and withdrawal from them, but Estelle must have worked her magic on them.

"I know it's idiotic to say, but you've both grown . . ."

•••

The next morning, Henry and Max were already seated when Mrs. R pushed Dr. R's wheelchair in to breakfast, then gave him a kiss on the cheek before sitting down. Henry saw Max make a face. Grown-ups were completely impossible to understand. What had happened to make everything OK again? As Agnes and Charlie brought in the hot coffee and scrambled eggs and bacon, Henry saw Dr. R breathe in deeply. "Ah," he said, and everyone smiled.

As they ate, Dr. R said, "I have some news that none of you know about. When Uncle Ed was last here, he gave me a bad time about not driving, especially once he heard that, of course, I drove before the War. He told me I was an idiot not to know that some cars have automatic transmissions now. So no clutch, and luckily I have my right foot for the brake. His friend who's a Chevrolet dealer in L.A. brought a Custom Imperial around for me to try out in an abandoned parking lot near the sports center, and believe it or not, I had no problem driving it. And it even has air-conditioning. As soon as I save up enough money, I'm getting one. "

"Oh, Josh . . ." Mrs. R began.

"No, Estelle, don't say it, I'm going to buy this car. I'll manage with the damned public transportation until I've saved the money."

Mrs. R smiled. "Well, all right."

"Wow," Max said, "you'll be driving soon."

"It's been so long, I'll have to get a new driver's license. And it's time you were driving, Henry. Charlie and I can give you lessons. Maybe you can drive the Green Monster."

Henry looked shocked. "I . . . I . . . I don't know how I can pass the written test."

Dr. R nodded. "We'll memorize the whole damn handbook. Or we'll make them dictate the test to you." Henry looked at Mrs. R who only nodded.

Breakfast became a celebration. As they finished, Dr. R cleared his throat. "Uh, I want to say something. I want you to know that I love you all very much." He put his hand over his eyes for a moment.

Mrs. R raised her empty orange juice glass. "Here's to new beginnings."

42

On January 15, 1954, Miriam Carol Rosenblatt was born at the Redgrove Community Hospital after a short three-hour labor. Dr. R stayed with Estelle during all the visiting hours. Miriam seemed completely healthy, and Estelle insisted on breastfeeding her, despite the nurses' efforts to automatically give her bottles. Dr. R bathed in the joy on Estelle's face, brought her flowers every day, and cautiously held the tiny bundle, his daughter.

After ten days in the hospital, Mrs. R moved to a bed in the big room between her office and the baby's space on the other side. She nursed her in a rocking chair, with a diaper over her shoulder. Dr. R managed the stairs with difficulty on his new prosthetic leg, and then stayed as long as he could with Estelle, rocking the baby to sleep so that Estelle could take a nap. The electric train had been put away to make room for Miriam's nursery, and Dr. R wondered if she might like trains when she was older, even if she was a girl. He felt completely happy rocking the baby, and looking at Estelle napping on her bed. Everyone said Miriam was a good baby—quiet and happy. Dr. R thought she was beautiful, even if Henry and Max joked that she looked like a frog.

After a few weeks, Dr. R began the trip to Sierra Madre twice a week. He only had to be away one night in the beginning, staying in the rented house there and seeing young clients Friday afternoons and Saturdays.

Carol had been preparing for a long time, and once she had a chance to hold her granddaughter, she was ready to leave for New York. Everyone was on the platform as she mounted the Super Chief. She turned, waved like royalty before her subjects, happy and smiling, and disappeared.

•••

Fannie and her mother came to visit in early March. While the women engaged in baby worship, Henry and Fannie rushed off to their tree in the park. Seated on the bench, they looked up at its new leaves appearing in the tangle of overhead foliage. The park was rich in springtime blooms. Fannie was wearing her sleeveless pink-flowered dress with its billowing skirt.

"That's a pretty dress. You look like spring."

Fannie smoothed her skirt. "My mom got this for me. She thinks I'm getting too old for blue jeans. She thinks girls should wear dresses and that's what Aunt Marianne expects, too, she says."

"I like it."

"Well, I like blue jeans. Katharine Hepburn wears pants and so can I."

"My mother wears blue jeans now, too. She's gone back to being a cowgirl."

"Good for her. But I don't need cows." They laughed.

"I have some good news," Henry said. "I've been accepted at Cal."

"That's wonderful," Fannie said, throwing her arms around him and hugging him, but when he tried to keep her encircled in his arms, his breath hot against her cheek, she withdrew.

"Remember," she said. "Let's not spoil it." She smiled and Henry did not know what to do. "So here's my news: I think I'll be going to Cal just one semester after you." I've already completed the required courses and now I'm taking college level classes at Pasadena Junior College."

"You'll be there when I am?" Henry said, wishing they could hug again. “Let’s go get a Coke to celebrate. We’re both going to Cal. Isn’t that perfect?”

Fannie nodded, with a serious expression on her face.

In the booth at the drugstore, Fannie, on the other side of the table, stopped sipping her Coke and pushed the glass away. “I’m worried about my father. So is my mother. He’s beginning to wonder about our coming so often to see Aunt Marianne. One time when he was off inspecting a mine, he tried to call home several times to get a phone number he needed, and my mom wasn’t there to answer. When he asked her where she had been, she said we had come to Redgrove to visit Aunt Marianne. But he’s not dumb. He knows you are here. He hasn’t asked me yet, but I’m afraid he will soon, and he’ll be furious if I tell him the truth. And my mom is getting uncomfortable about this. As she says, she’s living a lie. My dad’s noticed that I don’t seem to be dating any of the local boys. My mom just says, ‘Oh, she’s such a brain. Don’t worry, she’ll get interested in boys once she’s in college.’”

What is your dad going to do if he does find out about us? We aren’t doing anything wrong, are we?”

“That’s not what he would say. He won’t change his mind. He’s sure you made me go up the mountain. Your father thinks that too, and they’re still friends. I sometimes hear my mom and dad arguing about him. She won’t let your dad come to our house anymore.”

“I wish my dad would stop saying bad things about me. Does your dad know that I’ve done OK in high school?”

“Would your dad have told him?”

Henry sighed. “I don’t think he even knows. He’s never written me, and I don’t think my mom has any contact with him. Dr. R says some day I should talk to him. I’m not sure I want to.”

Fannie took hold of the glass of Coke and pulled it back toward her, clutching it with both hands. “My dad worries about me. He says the reason girls go to college is to find a good husband, settle down, and have children. He says women shouldn't do a man's job. I think he hopes once I find a husband, I'll give up my dream of being an anthropologist. He can think that if he wants, as long as he lets me go to Cal."

"Can he stop you?"

"He could refuse to pay for it."

"So? You can get a job."

Fannie shook her head. "I don't want a job. I want to study. And what can I do? Babysit or something stupid?"

"You worry too much about your dad. You're almost grown-up."

"I know, but I don't want to do anything that will make him think I'm a bad daughter. So I've decided I shouldn't come to Redgrove for a while. I'll go on some dates with some of those guys. They're always asking me. Then my father won't be suspicious any more."

"Don't do that," Henry blurted out. "Don't date those guys."

Fannie straightened up, her chin pulled back. "Don't tell me what to do."

"You do what your father says to do, don't you?" Henry said. "Why is it always your father? Don't I count at all?"

Fannie stood up, biting her lips. "Don't shout. People are looking at us. It will be less than a year before I get to Cal. I hope my father forgets about you by then."

"He won't forget me. He'll always hate me."

On the way back home, they walked side by side, not speaking. Just outside the gate, they turned to each other. Fannie looked up at him.

"Kiss me good-bye," she said. Henry instantly put his arms around her and found her lips. Then she pulled back. "Well, good-bye," she said, turned and walked ahead of him down the driveway. Ten minutes later she drove off with her mother.

No, no, Henry kept repeating to himself. *Don't say good-bye.*

43

Henry continued with a full load of classes for his final semester of high school. His acceptance at Cal was provisional on completing the required subjects. Mrs. R gave him extra time when she wasn't with Miriam and he worked hard, hoping that somehow Fannie had not really said good-bye. Finally two months later he wrote her, searching for almost every word in the dictionary.

May 2, 1954

Dear Fannie:
I hope Dr. McKensie will tell you about this letter, so that you will get it. I miss you very much. Do you think we could write each other again? Do we have to wait until we are both at Cal? Please write me. Yesterday was my 20th birthday.

—Henry

A month went by with no letter from Fannie. Maybe he was never going to see her again—unless he got into Cal. He made himself work even harder. Finally, just before graduation, a letter came. He stared at her handwriting on the envelope. He expected bad news.

Dear Henry:

Dr. McKensie has been away visiting his family in New York. He finally got back and gave my mom your letter. I haven't written, because I didn't know what to do. My mom and I had a talk yesterday and we have decided I must tell my dad that I saw you several times in Redgrove. I'll even tell him we wrote each other sometimes. And I'll tell him you are going to Cal. No more secrets. No more lies. My mom thinks he will be mad at both of us, but we're hoping he won't stay mad. Wish us luck. Maybe he'll let me come see you again soon. I hope he does.

—Fannie

Henry held the letter as he walked over to the window of his room and looked out over the orange grove. A breeze stirred the leaves of the trees below, as if nodding approval.

Thank you, trees. Thank you.

•••

Henry graduated from high school in June. His mother, Uncle Ed, and Carl were there. Fannie and her mother were not. At the celebration dinner, that night, Henry received just two presents on behalf of everyone—his own Leica camera and a telephoto lens.

"This is fantastic," he said, staring at the heavy apparatus in his hands. "Will I ever be able to learn everything this camera can do?"

The others clapped. Miriam, in her high chair, startled, began to cry. Dr. R reached over, pulled her out, and clasped her to his chest. "That's all right, sweetheart." Miriam laid her head against his shoulder and stopped crying.

"What a good dad," Edna said. An image came into Henry's mind of his own father pushing him into his room and locking the door. He glowered at his mother on the other side of the table as she raised her glass of water. "I am so proud of you, Henry." Then she turned to the R's. "And we owe so much to these wonderful people."

Dr. R patted Miriam on the back and smiled at Henry. "We're proud of you, too," he said.

"And he's getting to be a damn good photographer," Carl added.

"He'd be perfect if only he could play baseball better, right, Max?" Uncle Ed added.

"He's good at other stuff," Max said.

All the smiling faces turned toward him, everyone full of praise, began to press on him. It felt like they were talking about someone else—someone who really was intelligent, talented. Finally, everyone began complaining about Senator Joe McCarthy's latest outrageous behavior, accusing some Army guy of espionage on the televised hearings of his Senate subcommittee, and Henry was able to slip away unnoticed, as he had done on that day at the Staffords, up the stairs to his room. He was staring at the diagrams in the printed instructions for the Leica when he heard Mrs. R call up the stairs. "Telephone, Henry."

He dropped the instructions on the floor and rushed down the hall to Mrs. R's office. It was Fannie. "I'm over at a friend's house up the street," she said, barely able to speak between sobs. "I had to sneak out of the house. Something terrible has happened."

"What?"

"When I told my father about you, he blew up. I've never seen him so angry. I thought he was going to hit me, and my mom was yelling at him to let go of my arm. Now he says he won't give me a penny towards Cal because I'm a liar and a cheat. He says he knows a dean there so he can block me ever getting accepted."

"Can he do that?"

"I'll never meet Professor Kroeber. Maybe I'll never go to a decent college. I'll never be an anthropologist."

"Yes, you can. We'll find a way."

"I better hang up and go home before I get in even more trouble."

"Fannie, don't go."

"No, no, no. I never should have kept seeing you. I didn't know what I was doing. This is going to ruin my life. I'm going to promise him that I will never, ever see you again. And Henry—I mean it. Maybe he'll change his mind and let me go to Cal."

"Don't Fannie. Listen, we can . . ." Before he could finish, she hung up. Henry stared at the receiver, hoping she might still be there. But the phone was dead. As he replaced the receiver, his heart turned cold.

44

"What do you mean Henry has disappeared?" Edna said in a trembling voice as they all stood in the hall.

"Yes, I'm afraid so," Dr. R said. "I just knocked on his door. No answer. I went in and he wasn't there. I sent Charlie out to the garden shed and the rucksack was gone. He used to keep it in his room in case he wanted to run away, but he returned it a month ago."

"And Jake is gone, too," Estelle said, holding the squirming Miriam.

"Did he take the camera?" Carl asked.

"I think so," Dr. R said. I didn't see it."

"Thank God. That means a lot."

"What do you mean?" Edna said, beginning to weep.

"He wouldn't take the camera if he was planning to kill himself."

"Carl," Edna cried. "How can you say such a thing?"

"He's right, Edna," Dr. R said. "That's very encouraging."

"I bet you something happened between Henry and Fannie," Estelle said. "Betty told me the last time they were here that she couldn't go on hiding their meetings from her husband."

"Does he have money?" Carl asked.

"He's been earning money gardening for Mrs. Davidson," Estelle said.

"This is terrible, terrible," Edna said. Carl put his arms around her. "And we were so happy last night."

Carl, Edna and Uncle Ed had to leave that day for Montana. Three days passed with no news from Henry. Estelle tried to speak to Betty Stafford, who, in a quiet tense voice said that she could not talk on the phone.

On the fourth day, the Rs had a phone call from Carl. "I've got some good news. Henry sent me a letter. Fortunately I gave him my address up here in Montana. It's postmarked Boulder, Colorado. Here, let me read it to you:

Dear Carl:
Will you let my mom and the Rs no I am OK? I want to be alone. I don't want anyone to try and find me. I have a job washing dishes in a hotel. Don't try to find me.

—Henry

Dr. R felt a stab of jealousy. "I wonder why he wrote you and not me?"

"Yes, I don't understand it."

"Well at least we know he's OK. I bet he's nowhere near Boulder. He's not going to mail a letter postmarked from where he actually is. If he's working in a hotel, it's not hard to get someone to mail a letter when they return home. I'm afraid I used that technique myself to hide my whereabouts from my parents."

"So even you sowed some wild oats, huh?" Carl said. "But I agree. Edna feels a little better; she's gone to bed. I don't think she slept since we got the news. She was starting to act crazy again from lack of sleep. I was getting worried."

"A mother's heart," Dr. R said. "And sleep deprivation can make you temporarily psychotic. I don't think you need to worry. Just help her get some rest. Estelle's angry with him. Now she'll probably be mad that we aren't sending out a search party or calling the police or something."

"He's in touch. It's not a big black unknown any longer."

"Let's hope that satisfies the women for a little while," Dr. R said. "You know, Carl, I bet he's gone to the desert."

45

It is so hot here. Summer in Death Valley is hell. Only the swimming pool cools me off. But at night, that's when life begins. The burning sun goes down, taking its reds and oranges with it. Then the heat pours out of the sand and rock. How do rocks absorb heat? They look like nothing could enter them, yet they are sponges for the sun. All day they collect that warmth and then they give it back at night so the next day they can take it back in again.

I am walking in this narrow canyon, early in the morning. Here it is cool. I see lizards and even a desert rat. Insects crawl and fly around me. I am looking back down into the valley. Already the sun has hit the sand down there, driving all life underground. Only up here a few brave, scraggly trees grow out of cracks in the boulders, way up there at the top of the cliffs.

Here I am in a black shadow. The cool night is making its last stand, knowing that soon the sun will eat it up. I like this dry creek bed. They say when it rains, water pours down here. It has carved out this dark place that protects me. Here is a soft world. In an hour the sun will rise above the crest of the hills and even here, life will run for cover.

To take pictures in this darkness is hard. I have to guess what f-stop and shutter speed I need. I won't know if these photos will come out until they are developed. So I try to photograph with my mind, too, in case this beautiful darkness does not appear on the film. I have to stand very still and not let my mind wander. That is so hard to do. Why did I never notice that? I think I did have a moment once somewhere else when my mind stopped, when I felt my breath going in and out. That was all—in and out. When was that? I don't remember.

No one knows I am in this valley. I could let its darkness swallow me. Disappear into this soft warm black world. Someday they would find my white bones. I want to photograph the blackness of these cliffs, how they rise up above me, making me a tiny little creature, hardly visible.

I wanted to be in the desert, and here I am. I imagined a blue stream running through it. Here there is no blue stream.

Two hawks are circling up above, crossing and crossing again the narrow slit of pale blue sky. Are they hoping I might be their next meal? They want some poor desert rat, whose eyes are watching for that dark shadow to swoop down on him.

I am so tired—I will lie down here and listen to the hawks crying. I got no sleep last night. I wrote that letter to Mr. Stafford after I found a dictionary in the hotel lobby. He's got to let Fannie go to Cal. Will those people from Minnesota remember to mail it when they get home? People believe me when I say the person I'm writing is collecting postmarks. I hate lying, but I have to do it.

I can hear my breath as I lie here. It sounds like sighing.

•••

July 15, 1954

Dear Mr. Stafford:

You think I am bad and you don't want me to talk to Fannie. You and my father are friends and my father does not like me, so he may tell you bad things about me.

But Fannie has not done anything wrong. She likes to talk to me, but she does not want me to be her boyfriend. She wants to be an anthropologist more than anything else.

Mrs. Stafford got to know Mrs. Rosenblatt, so they came here several times. Fannie and I started talking and then we wrote letters, too. She wanted me to practice writing, and my spelling is much better now. I just graduated from high school. Everyone says I will do OK.

I am writing you to ask you to let Fannie to go to Cal. I promise not to ever try to see her again. I no longer live in Redgrove and no one knows where I am. If I go to college someday, I promise not to go to Cal, so she won't meet me there or anywhere. Please let her go.

Sincerely,
Henry Hamblen

• • •

On an October morning before daybreak, Henry left the Furnace Creek Inn on foot and returned to the same canyon, this time going to the very end where he followed a steep trail up to the rim. His Leica camera case hung from a strap around his neck. On top, the valley appeared as different shades of grey and black below him, as the sun had not yet risen above the mountains.

Suddenly a ray burst upon him from behind. He turned around to see the top of the sun rising over the mountain behind the valley. He felt dizzy and raised a hand to shield his eyes. He must have fainted, because he was falling, sliding on his back down toward the rim of the black abyss below. There seemed nothing to grab hold of—nothing to stop him. Then he was caught up in the branches of one the stunted trees that rimmed the cliffs, his head hitting a boulder with the impact.

For an instant, he was flooded with an unbearably bright white light and then all was black. When consciousness returned, he felt intense pain in his rib cage as he tried to draw in air. The sun beat down mercilessly. How long had he been there? He did not know. He tried to drop a foot toward solid ground, but he was too weak to move. Through half-open eyes, he could see all the way down to the canyon floor, now lit by the sun.

Still he could not move. He could not even lift an arm. His face and neck were burning. He was going to die.

He closed his eyes, on the verge of losing consciousness again, when he heard some voices below. Someone was down there. But they would never see him. He tried to shout but no sound came out of his mouth. He opened his eyes with huge effort and saw two figures walking along the canyon floor. One of his hands hung down and his fingertips were touching a rock. He stretched his arm with all the strength he could muster and pushed that rock toward the edge. He pushed it harder. And then he heard it roll down the cliff with a loud cracking noise as it bounced off ledges.

"Watch out!" he heard a man shout. "Louisa! There's a man hanging in that tree." Then there was silence. He no longer heard anything. He had lost consciousness again.

• • •

His body shuddered as water hit his head and neck.

"He's still breathing," a woman's voice said.

"Pour some on his back," a man's voice said. Hands moved along his arms and legs.

"Nothing broken here. We'll have to hope his back isn't," the woman said. "Can we get him back up on the path?"

"We're too old," the man said. "We've got to get help before he dies of dehydration." And then his consciousness slipped away again, until he heard someone calling him, wiping his face with a wet cloth. He opened his eyes. He saw the green shirt of a park ranger in front of him. He was on the ground, and someone was shading his body with a heavy cloth.

"We have to get some water in you," the ranger said. "Here—we're going to sit you up." Henry groaned with pain.

"I think it's his ribs," the woman said. A metal cup was brought to his lips and water tipped into his mouth. He swallowed and felt the water's coolness on his swollen, dry tongue.

"We're gonna walk you down to the canyon floor," the ranger said. "We have a pickup down there with a cot in back to take you back to Furnace Creek. This lady here is a nurse, and she says she can treat you there. It's a long way to a hospital."

Henry was only aware of his ribs hurting as the two rangers walked on either side of him, his arms hanging over their shoulders. First it was up the slope he had slid down, then the more tortuous descent down stone steps and a twisting trail to the canyon floor. Most of the time Henry kept his eyes closed, wincing with the pain. Only as all four of his rescuers worked together to get him into the back of the pickup and onto the cot, to which he was strapped, did he notice that the man and woman were really old, both with white hair. They sat in back with him as the truck bounced down the sandy canyon road.

"I've got your camera," the man said. "It was still around your neck. Looks like a fancy one."

"Thank you," Henry whispered, groaning with every bump until they hit the paved road. The man got out at the little parking lot to drive his own car back.

"I'm Louisa," the woman said. "My husband is Guy. We come here every October; we love this place. It's really hot today—must be around 100 degrees. Usually it cools down in October, but not this year. You could have died of dehydration."

"I know." Henry turned his face away from her.

Martha, the plump redheaded lady in charge of the dishwashers, came out, drying her hands on a towel, as the rangers took Henry through the employees' entrance. "Oh my God," she said. "What have you done to yourself?" She pointed up the stairs and told them where his room was.

The rangers got him onto his bed, where Louisa with her first-aid kit went to work. She was thin and moved quickly. She removed his clothes and washed his abrasions with warm water from the sink, and then used cotton balls to apply Mercurochrome, followed by gauze bandages. Henry clenched his jaw and tried not to groan.

"Hold still, I know this stuff stings. What else hurts?"

"My ribs . . ."

"Probably cracked a few—does it hurt to breathe?"

"Yes—a lot."

"I hear you work here. Where are your parents?"

"They—don't know where I am."

"That must be terrible for them. They must worry about you all the time."

"Oh, I don't know . . ."

"We'll talk about that later. I'll check on you in a while. Drink as much water as you can. See, Martha brought a pitcher and a glass. You'll have to sit up to drink—wish we had a hospital bed." She helped him, and he gasped with the pain. Once he drank, she gently lowered him back down and then left.

Henry lay on his bed, cradling Jake on his chest, groaning every time he moved. He sighed—even that hurt. If he lay completely still and took little breaths, the pain almost disappeared.

Quietness pervaded his mind. He lay there, not thinking about anything. Even the pain did not seem to frighten him. He could sense his limbs right to his fingertips and the ends of his toes. He had never thought before that it might be possible to die. It was a strange feeling. He could not imagine being dead like a squashed rabbit on the road, vultures eating his rotting flesh. Had the vultures been waiting in nearby trees as he lay there in the murderous sun?

Then he fell asleep.

• • •

The next morning, Louisa brought him breakfast on a tray—bacon, eggs, and pancakes. He groaned again as he sat up to eat. Once he finished, she changed the bandages on his arms, applying more stinging

Mercurochrome. "Martha says your name is Tom Bradley." She raised her eyebrows.

"Yes . . ."

"I bet you a dime to a dozen that's not your real name."

Henry looked at her. "What makes you say that?"

"Woman's intuition. You're running away from something or someone. Martha thinks so, too."

Henry lowered his head. "I wish people would leave me alone."

"So you don't have to tell me your name."

"It's Henry Hamblen. But don't tell Martha."

Louisa smiled. "You don't look like a criminal, unlike some of those dishwashers down there. Probably someone broke your heart, or you're running away from horrible parents."

Henry nodded. "Both. Well, I had to get away from my father, but I was living with . . . kind of foster parents, and my mom is . . . quite nice, actually."

Louisa made a face. "Oh, quite nice, is she? I bet she adores you."

Henry felt sadness descend. "Yes, she does. She's married to someone else now, so I have a stepfather. I write him once a month to say I'm OK. But no one knows where I am."

Louisa pulled her chair up close to Henry's face. "So tell me how this all happened. Here—let me arrange your pillows so you're more comfortable. "

Slowly at first, Henry spoke about his dyslexia and Dr. R having "kidnapped" him to save him from a lobotomy. He spoke of his life with the Rosenblatts, his parents' divorce, his moments with Fannie and their breakup, how Carl had helped him with photography. Finally he paused. Louisa shook her head.

"Except for your misguided father, it sounds like these people love you. Even Fannie—maybe. Not your father. He sounds like a real ass."

"Yes, except for him, I guess they do love me."

Louisa wrinkled her nose as if something smelled bad. "You guess they do. But if you are hiding and they don't know where you are, you are causing them a lot of pain and grief."

"I'll never be good at anything. I've let them down. They should be happy to be rid of me. Maybe it would have been better if I had died."

Louisa stared at him. "That's a lot of baloney. You've just told me how much they care about you. And why should they suffer just because some girl ditched you?"

"Maybe she would be sorry, if I had died."

"Maybe she wouldn't. Do you think the world revolves around you? When are you going to pay back these people who love you?"

"I... I guess I didn't think about that."

"Henry, you have that doctor and his wife, and you have your mother. And you said your stepfather goes to all that trouble to help you with your photography. How lucky can you get? Maybe it's time you think about them. At least let them know where you are."

"Then they'll try to make me come back."

"That's up to you, isn't it?"

"I miss them."

"So think about the Golden Rule. Have you ever heard of Christ's Golden Rule?"

"No, my father wouldn't let my mom or me go to church. She wanted to take me."

"Never mind. You don't have to be Christian. Most so-called Christians aren't really Christians. Christ said, 'Do unto others as you would have them do unto you.' Those people love you and miss you. Do them the kindness of letting them know where you are."

Henry had had enough. He did not want her wrinkled old face so close to him, talking to him. He turned his head away and closed his eyes.

"Think about it," she said. He heard her footsteps leaving the room. He lay there, trying not to move. What did an old woman like Louisa know about being in love? She should mind her own business. But maybe she was right about the others. He wished he hadn't told her so much, because now he did not know what to do.

Henry waited and waited and finally Louisa returned the next day and sat down in a chair next to his bed. "How's the patient doing?" she asked, peering at him.

"I've been thinking," he said. "Maybe I lost Fannie because I wanted her to be part of my dream, but it wasn't her dream. She kept trying to tell me that. But I think she really liked me. She came to see me and she wrote me letters, even though she had to do it secretly."

"It's hard for women nowadays," Louisa said. "She's attracted to you, but she sounds terrified of getting caught in the housewife, mother role. She has other ideas about her life. Some women want to be independent, and she sounds like one of those. I became a nurse, because I had to earn a living and there was a shortage of nurses. It was hard work, but it was rewarding. I wanted to work even after I got married to Guy, and he was fine with that. He likes to cook more than I do, anyway." She laughed. "I think I would have made a good doctor, but I had no one to guide me, to tell me that even women can be doctors. Your Fannie sounds determined to get what she wants."

"Even my mom wants to go to college now," Henry said. "She took care of my dad and my brother and me, but my dad wasn't nice to her."

"It's time you started thinking about women in a different way. They aren't there just to make your life a piece of cake."

"I don't even know why Fannie liked me. She can marry some really smart guy, another anthropologist or some brilliant scientist, someone who can help her in her career."

"Did she ever say *why* she liked you? It must be more than your looks, although at her age that would have done it for me." She laughed, noticing, Henry felt sure, that his face was turning red.

"She said I was more serious than all the guys she knew. And she liked my drawings and photos. We both like animals."

"In fact, you have more obvious talents than she does. She's a good student. That's about it, right?"

"No, no. She has all the talent. I'm just . . . a dishwasher."

"Just a dishwasher. Hmm, am I supposed to believe that?" Louisa held up both hands and began to count, touching each finger of one hand with the index of her other hand. "Let's see. One: You are learning to read despite that dyslexia. Major accomplishment. Two: You have picked up the basics of gardening. Three: You can draw. No, you didn't tell me that one, but I see damn good drawings of Death Valley scenes pinned up there on the wall. Four: You know how to take photographs and develop them. And Five: You graduated from high school in what? A couple of years—even though you had almost no schooling before then? You're not a failure, that's for sure."

Henry shook his head. "I had tons of people helping me. Most kids do it on their own. But now everyone expects me to be some great success. Maybe I won't be. It was Carl, my stepfather, who said I could be a park ranger. I thought that sounded like something I would like to do. But I never thought of it myself. I just follow what people tell me. I wish I could decide things myself."

Louisa smiled and patted his arm lying on the blanket with her wrinkled, blue-veined hand. "How do you think any of us learn anything? Someone has to tell us, encourage us. Then we have to see what works for us. I wasn't born knowing I'd be good at nursing and would even enjoy it. You will find out what you can do and want to do."

"If I ever get the chance."

"You will, dopey. But yes, I see now. Maybe that's why you ran away. You needed to escape all those well-meaning people helping you. You are trying to find out who you are by yourself. That's normal for someone your age, but you've had a rollercoaster ride so far. Your father and those damn special education teachers told you directly or indirectly that you were stupid, your mother defended you, then the doctor and his wife gave you the guts to try to succeed in school, and then Fannie said you're ruining my life, and blah, blah, blah. No wonder you're confused. But it's good. And no one ever told you to love the desert, did they?

"That's one thing that's your very own." She patted his arm again, smiling.

"I guess so."

"But what are you going to do now?"

"I'll think about what you said."

"That's a good boy. Maybe you won't stay here forever."

"I have nowhere else to go."

"Do we have to start this conversation all over again?" she said, wrinkling her nose.

"Well . . ."

"At least let those people know where you are."

"Well . . ."

Louisa stood up, leaned over and kissed Henry on the forehead. "Guy wants to head home. I'll give Martha my address. I want you to write me someday and tell me what you've done with your life."

"I'm not very good at writing."

"No excuses—you're good enough." Louisa waved goodbye and disappeared before Henry could say another word. She and Guy had saved his life. And he hadn't even said thank you. Maybe that was what she was talking about. He wondered if one of his photos of Death Valley might be something he could send her? Except then he had to get the photos developed. Carl could do that. And he would know if any of them were good.

What would happen if he sent them to Carl? Everyone would know where he was. Even if he had someone mail them from another state, the photos would give him away. Did it matter? Maybe Louisa was right. He could refuse to go back, but ever since he told her about his family and the Rs, he couldn't stop thinking about them. And not once had he ever stopped thinking about Fannie.

Louisa said he didn't know who he was. How was he going to find out? He couldn't stay in Death Valley washing dishes the rest of his life. It was too lonely. Girls came and talked to him at the pool, sometimes suggesting late-night dates, but he had resisted. No one compared to Fannie.

After a week he could move without too much pain, so he resumed work. For a month, the rolls of film sat on the table in his room. Once he threw them in the wastepaper basket but pulled them out again the next day. Finally, he asked Martha for some brown paper and string, wrapped them up, and mailed them to Carl at the little post office next to the ranger station.

46

Just after Christmas, when Henry reported for work at noon, Martha spoke to him as he entered the kitchen. "Tom, you aren't by any chance using an alias, are you? A tall guy in a cowboy hat came in this morning, looking for his stepson. He had a photo and it sure looks like you. If it's the police or something I'll put him off. I'm not a squealer."

"That's OK," Henry said. "I knew he was going to show up. Yes, Tom is not my real name. My real name is . . . Henry Hamblen. That man is my stepfather."

"Uh-oh, I bet I'm going to lose you. Such a sweet boy." Martha chucked him under the chin.

Henry craned his head away. "Yes, I think my time is up. But I promise to come back and see you. OK, wish me luck. He may be real mad at me."

"I don't think so. I can tell he's a nice man."

Henry left the kitchen and headed for the reception desk. And there was Carl, talking to Steve, the nervous little man behind the desk.

"Carl," Henry called out, suddenly excited.

Carl turned. "Henry."

Steve muttered, "I thought he's called Tom."

Carl smiled. "I made some prints of your photos. I thought you might like to see them."

Henry approached Carl, not knowing what to do. Then he held out his hand. They shook hands, rather formally.

"Come up to my room," Carl said. "I'll show you."

Carl's room looked out over the slope of the rocky terrain leading down to the valley floor's expanse of white sand with its dry patterns of winding lines left from rain runoff. He and Henry stood for a moment at the window regarding the view.

"Maybe you could take me down there and show me some of the places you photographed," Carl said. "I haven't been here for years. I've got some color film, if you want to try that."

"Sure, well, I guess so." Henry said. He waited for the lecture that must be coming, how he had caused so much worry and trouble.

Carl went over to the old-fashioned wooden desk next to the bed, one of those that had a lid that opened to reveal a flat surface and behind were lots of little drawers for writing materials. In fact, it looked just like Mrs. R's, where Henry had spent so many hours struggling to read. Carl picked up a stack of black and white photos that had been enlarged. He handed them to Henry.

"Go ahead. Have a look. I'm going to unpack my things. I arrived late last night and went straight to bed." Carl went off to the other end of the large room where his suitcase sat on a luggage stand near a four-poster bed.

Henry slowly looked through the stack of photos, moving the top one to the back when he was finished examining it. Many looked dramatic, dark, and mysterious. He had made some lucky guesses about how to set the camera. There were only about twenty photos, so he knew Carl had only brought the best ones. He pulled out one and stood it up against the desk's cubbyholes. Carl noticed and came back, standing next to Henry. The photo was one taken early in the morning. Black cliffs filled most of it, with a tree against a slit of sky at the top, perhaps the very tree that had saved his life. A narrow shaft of light, which was the sunlit valley below, seemed to cut the photo in half.

“That’s exactly the one I have chosen. Now don’t get mad at me,” Carl said. “I sent it in to a photo contest I heard about.”

“What?”

“Yes, I read in one of my photo magazines about a contest for black-and-white photos of landscapes. I just submitted it on a whim.”

“OK—I’ll never win.”

“We’ll see,” Carl said, smiling. “I really like this one. It’s like an abstract painting, a metaphor for the darkness and light in life.”

“Oh, come on, Carl.” Yet Henry felt pleased.

Carl suddenly looked serious. “Henry, I’ve got to give you some news. Maybe we should sit down.” Fear immediately cut through Henry, down his spine and into his stomach.

They sat in the huge soft and grey armchairs near the window. “There’s no nice way to say this. I wouldn’t have come here just to show you your photos or to try to get you to come home. Your brother Sam has had a serious brain injury.”

“Did he fall?” Henry asked. Instantly he saw Sam on a ladder, falling backwards.

“No. He was in an automobile accident. Your father was driving.”

Henry felt the familiar sick feeling in his stomach. “Was he drinking?

“Yes, that’s what everyone says. They were on the freeway returning from some Christmas party.”

“Is Sam conscious?”

“No, he’s in a coma, but there is some hope he might come out of it. He may be permanently incapacitated though. You know, not able to function normally.”

“I wish I could kill him . . . my father, I mean.” Henry jumped up and stood, staring out the window.

“Damn it all, Henry, never mind your father. Knowing he’s responsible for this is his punishment. But your mother needs you. Think a little how she must feel. One son has disappeared, and one may be mentally retarded.”

"What I was supposed to be," Henry said.

"Yes, and thank God you are not."

Henry lowered his head. "I'm ready. "

"I'm glad."

"OK. And I want to see the Rs."

"Dr. R told me he loves you as a son. And I do, too."

Henry sat down again, bent his head, hiding his face with one hand on his forehead. He felt Carl's presence, silent and accepting.

Finally, Carl said, "Let's spend today exploring. Show me the places you love. I've got some Kodachrome film, if you want to give it a try. Then tomorrow, if you are willing, we'll drive to L.A. I'll telephone your mom. She'll be so happy you're coming back."

"Don't you think we should leave right away?"

Carl rubbed his grey hair. "Yep, I guess you're right. But let's come back here together some day, OK?"

"Yes, let's come back."

•••

By evening, Henry and Carl entered Sam's room at the Good Samaritan Hospital in downtown Los Angeles. Sam lay on the bed, his round face relaxed with eyes closed, as if he were sleeping. Edna jumped up as they came in, rushed over to Henry as he approached the bed, and threw her arms around him. He embraced her, feeling her thin body against his.

"I'm sorry, Mom. And now this . . ."

Releasing him, she looked at him as if he had been gone for years, absorbing him back into her soul. "Maybe Sam will wake up now that that you are here."

"He's forgotten me. I can't make him wake up."

"Come talk to him," she said. "Who knows?" Henry looked back at Carl, hoping he might explain to his mother how silly her hope was.

What could he do? Carl made a quick gesture with his hand. He wasn't going to help. Carl brought up a chair and Henry sat down next to her. They both stared at Sam. He had not changed since Henry last saw him, so long ago it seemed, but it wasn't really—just the summer before last. Sam's breathing seemed more like short gasps, as if there were some great physical effort going on within him.

"He's fighting," Edna said. "Speak to him."

"Sam, it's Henry. Can you hear me?" Henry thought he saw a flicker of Sam's eyelids, but they did not open. "We're here. We want you to get better."

His mother took Sam's hand, lying outside the white blanket. A nurse entered the room, asked them to move, and took his blood pressure. When she left, they returned to their seats. Henry glanced at his mother. She looked tired and tense. Her fingers were laced on her lap and she kept squeezing and releasing them.

"Did you go back to the hotel last night, Edna?" Carl asked from further back in the room.

"Uh, I can't remember. No, I guess I didn't."

"You've got to get some rest. Come back to the hotel with me. You can't go so many days without sleep."

"I'll be fine. Don't worry. I'll come back with Henry. Reserve him a room, OK?"

Carl came over and kissed her cheek and then left, looking back once with a worried expression.

Once he had left, Edna turned to Henry. Her unruly hair was now sticking out in all directions, as if a strong wind had blown it. Her face looked old. "I'm so angry at your father. Look what he did to Sam. First you, now Sam."

"Sam was an accident."

"It wouldn't have happened if he had been sober. And what he tried to do to you was no accident."

“He won’t come here, will he?” Henry asked. “I don’t think he even knows where I am and I bet he doesn’t care.”

“He kept Sam from getting letters from me. I wrote him many times at Harvard. Sam and I finally talked just before the accident. He thought all this time I didn’t want to contact him. That’s what your father told him. Betty Stafford heard Phil talking on the phone to your father to set up a golf date. She heard him say, ‘Oh, I forgot—Sam’s home from college.’ She knew how heartbroken I was, so when the men were off playing golf, she went over to our house—well, our old house—and she talked to Sam and told him where I was, that I was remarried, what happened to you, and that you were off working, but we didn’t know where. I only got to talk to Sam on the phone, but we were planning to meet. Sam was going to tell your father he must not stop him from seeing me. And now this.”

“I don’t think Dad will come here, will he? Henry looked toward the closed door. “He must know you’re here.”

“I’m sure he thinks I ended up in Montana. I don’t know.” Edna pressed her fingertips against her forehead, squeezing her eyes shut.

“Mom,” Henry said. “There’s a big chair back there in the corner where Carl was sitting. There’s one of those things you can put your feet up on.”

“That’s called a hassock.”

“OK, a hassock. Go put your feet on the hassock. I’ll sit here with Sam and then we’ll go to the hotel.”

“Well, all right. I do need to close my eyes for a few minutes. Wake me up if Sam does anything.”

“I will.”

His mother went into the corner, disappearing at once out of the bright lights around Sam’s bed.

Henry remained next to Sam, watching his chest rise up and down under the white blanket. He himself felt his eyelids begin to close. Were they all falling asleep, joining Sam in some dark, unconscious world?

Henry jumped at the sound of the door opening. One of the nurses came in, followed by a man. "There's your son," the nurse said in a flat voice and immediately went out again.

Henry stood up, not knowing if he was going to run out or stay. There was his father standing near the foot of the bed, staring at Sam, not even noticing Henry. Every muscle tightened in Henry's body. He waited. And then his father saw him.

"Henry," he said, almost in a whisper.

"Dad."

"What are you doing here?"

"I came to see Sam."

"It wasn't my fault. I had to swerve to avoid hitting a stupid old woman who was barely moving on the freeway. Sam was thrown out of the car when we hit the overpass." His father looked small, his hands trembling. He continued to stare at Sam's motionless face.

Suddenly Henry realized that his mother, his father, Sam, and he were all in the same room together again.

"Dick!" Henry heard his mother say. He and his father both turned around to face the dim corner of the room. His mother had stood up and was pointing something at his father. It was her pistol.

"Mom!" Henry yelled. His father seemed frozen, and then after what seemed a long space of time he slowly backed toward the door.

In an instant, Henry leapt towards his mother, knocking her down. As she fell, the gun slid away from her hand. Henry picked it up. The barrel felt cold. He looked down at it, and then raised his head to look at his father, who had stopped near the door.

"Henry, put that thing down," his father said. Henry heard his mother moaning on the floor behind him.

Henry moved toward his father.

"Don't come any further," his father said. "Put that gun down."

Henry took one more step toward his father.

"I'll have her arrested—you, too, if you don't put that gun down."

"Just get out of here," Henry yelled. "Everyone says you were drunk. We'll get the police report on you."

His father's hand was on the door handle.

Suddenly his mother spoke, her voice flat and cold. "The gun isn't loaded."

Henry remembered Mrs. R's injunction and pulled himself up to his full height. His father was only four feet away but seemed tiny, as if some alien force had shrunk him down. His eyes flickered, as he reached behind him to open the door. Then he turned quickly and disappeared.

"Quick, Mom, hide the gun." She came over to him with her purse, took the gun from his hand, threw it in and snapped the purse shut. "Mom!" Her face was white.

"I just wanted to scare him. I half-expected him to show up here. He has no conscience."

The door opened and one of the older nurses, with a grey chignon and glasses hanging from a thin chain on her bosom, came in. "What's going on in here? I heard some yelling. This is a hospital, not a place for family fights. Have some respect for the patient."

Henry, feeling strong, his blood coursing through his veins, smiled at her. "We're real sorry, Nurse. We'll leave now and let you do your job." As the nurse stared at him, he took his mother's arm and marched her out of the room. Alone in the elevator going down to the street level, his mother remained silent, her eyes on the elevator door.

"Mom, this isn't the Wild West."

"I know, Henry." She took out a handkerchief from her purse and wiped her eyes. "Carl was right. I need some sleep. I wasn't thinking. At least I had enough sense to take the bullets out back at the hotel. I was afraid I would kill your father if he showed up. I wanted to kill him, but I guess I knew that wasn't going to bring Sam back from his coma."

"No. I just hope Dad doesn't get us in trouble."

"He won't. He knows what's in that report. He's probably got his cronies at the police department to hush up the accident. He won't say a word about this." The elevator came to a stop and they walked out onto the street, passing a security guard at the door, who gave them a suspicious look.

On the street, walking towards the hotel, his mother took his hand and squeezed it. "You were brave, Henry."

"I wanted to shoot him, too, Mom."

"You didn't know the gun wasn't loaded, but you didn't pull the trigger."

"No. He looked so small—and scared."

"I don't feel sorry for him."

"Mom, forget about him. I'm back, and you have Carl. And maybe Sam will wake up."

His mother squeezed his hand again. "Yes, you've come back. And you're so grown-up. You even charmed that angry nurse with your good looks and smile."

"Mom, I had to. And promise me you'll give that gun to Carl."

47

Charlie met Henry at the San Bernadino train station, tears in his eyes as they hugged. "*Buenos Dias,*" Charlie said, taking Henry's satchel. "You're gonna see how happy the Doctor and the Missus are to have you back—my wife, too. She's baking you an apple pie right now."

"They aren't mad at me?" Henry asked as they walked to the car.

"No, not now, but the Missus sure was. Now you'll be lucky if they pay any attention to you, they're so *loco* about that little girl. She's walking now. You'd think she's the first kid to ever figure out how to walk. So, there's one of those wooden gates at the top of the stairs. They'll tell you a million times not to leave it open."

Charlie pulled the car into the garage at the top of the driveway and they walked down together.

"The magnolia tree is blooming," Henry said. They both stopped to look at its pink blossoms.

"And the oranges are almost ready to pick," Charlie said as they neared the front door. At that moment, Dr. R came out, holding Miriam, who stared solemnly at Henry, her thumb in her mouth. Mrs. R and Agnes followed.

"Wave to Henry, darling," Dr. R said, taking Miriam's pudgy arm. Mrs. R and Agnes rushed down the steps to embrace Henry. Then he went up and put an arm around Dr. R, trying to avoid Miriam.

"Welcome, home, Henry," Dr. R said. "Look how she's grown. Say hi to your brother, Miriam." She shrieked and began crying. "She's not used to you," Dr. R said. "Can't you smile for Henry, sweetie?"

"Dr. R, I need to talk to you. Something happened yesterday."

Dr. R immediately handed Miriam to Agnes. Miriam stopped crying as she gave Henry an angry look. "Yes, we have many things to talk about," Dr. R said. "Let's go straight out to the office. We have time before lunch."

Seated once more in his chair facing Dr. R, Henry sighed. Dr. R was frowning at him. "You have a lot to account for, Henry. I always said you had the right to run away, but why did you keep secret where you were? We, your mother, Carl, we all worried about you."

"I'm sorry. I didn't want anyone to find me. But when Carl told me about Sam—well, I knew I needed to come back."

"All right. You chose to go away and you chose to come back. I respect that. Don't be surprised, though, if you encounter some anger from those of us who were wondering all this time where the hell you were."

"But I wrote Carl once a month to say I was OK."

"That was just barely better than nothing. But I've said it now. Let's move on. So what happened yesterday?"

Henry described what he remembered. "I can't believe my mom actually planned to pull out her gun and scare my father. Does it mean she is actually nuts? And maybe I'm nuts, too?"

Dr. R appeared as a dark silhouette in the shuttered cottage, even though he was only a few feet away. "I can't speak for your mother, but *you* are not nuts. We all go insane at times, anyway. And what is *insane?* We all do things we later regret. I bet your mother hadn't slept for days—just that can produce temporary psychosis."

"What's worrying me now is—I almost raised that gun. I wanted to shoot him."

"What stopped you?"

"I don't know. It was almost like a voice inside said *don't do it.* But I could already feel my finger tightening on the trigger."

"Sometimes the unconscious speaks to us and saves us in a moment of crisis."

Henry looked past Dr. R, seeing the black demon in the thangka on the wall behind him. Was the demon in the painter's unconscious, waiting to attack someone? "Ever since yesterday, I keep seeing the same thing over and over, as if in slow motion: My mother pulling out the gun, me throwing myself at her, my father looking so scared. Then the whole scene replays again—and again. It's a horrible nightmare that won't go away."

Dr. R nodded. "I still have images repeating the kamikaze attack and Barney lying dead on top of me."

"Oh, God, am I going to have this go on until I'm old like you? Uh, sorry, you're not old."

"Don't worry, Henry. I'm not insulted. Yes, it's been ten years and I'm not free of it yet. I had to go back on the psychoanalytic couch for a year when I got back, and I rarely relive that moment now—maybe once a year. I'm trying to tell you it's normal. It's the unconscious processing pain. During the war and after, we called it *shell shock*. Talking about it can really help."

"I don't want psychoanalysis—lying around on that couch, talking about myself."

Dr. R smiled. "I'm not asking you to be analyzed. If you continue to suffer, you might change your mind, but for now, I hope you'll take whatever time you need to figure out what you want to do next."

Henry shook his head. "I just don't know. I really don't know. I want to help my mom if I can, but then . . . ?"

"What about college?"

"I don't know if I can face going to college. Maybe I've forgotten everything I learned. Maybe I should be a gardener, or maybe I could work for a photographer developing his pictures."

"Take your time. Let your wounds heal."

Henry frowned. "Did someone tell you what happened to me in Death Valley? I haven't told anyone."

"No. What happened?"

"I fell while hiking and broke some of my ribs. I couldn't move, I was stuck in a tree, but some people found me and got help. I almost died of dehydration."

Dr. R reached out and put an arm around Henry's shoulder. "Another trauma. You've had your share. I'm glad you told me, but you know, Henry, I wouldn't tell Mrs. R or your mother. Especially not your mother—she's in too much pain herself right now." Dr. R dropped his arm from Henry's shoulder after patting it gently. "You will grow from all these experiences. Carl Jung would say none of this is accidental."

"I guess I'm not grown-up yet. Is that what you mean?"

"I mean inner growth—spiritual growth."

Henry felt his head swim. "How is that different from just growing up? I want to have a normal life and do something good for animals. I want to be normal. I don't care about some kind of spiritual growth. I'm not religious."

"You're too young—that's good."

"Too young for what?"

"For being fed up with what life has to offer."

"No, I'm not fed up. I thought I would never have a life at all. Now I don't know what I want or even what I can do. I know I've always wanted a family, but maybe I'm never going to have one."

"Yes, you are old-fashioned in your values. You wanted a happy family, but that's not what you got."

Henry shook his head. "But I did—with you and Mrs. R."

"Right. And every day you were plotting how to escape."

Henry grinned. "You were the one who told me that the desert was calling me."

"Wise guy. Well, you're back and I'm very touched that you consider us family. You see, though, it hasn't been easy for Mrs. R and me. Sometimes I think it is just luck that we are back together. We've always loved each other, but sometimes even that isn't enough. My dream to stop lobotomies overpowered me, and I wouldn't listen to her or anyone warning me that I was headed for trouble."

Henry felt his jaw clench. "Fannie didn't really love me. She wanted to be independent and have a career, but in the end, she did what her father told her. I didn't matter."

"She panicked. Have you tried to contact her, or has she tried to write you?"

"I don't care . . . I don't care." Henry lowered his head. "I have you and Mrs. R and my mom—and Carl. And Max. I don't need her."

"Come on. You don't expect me to believe you don't care, do you?"

Henry raised his head and looked at a smiling Dr. R. "No, I guess not."

"Which one of you will be the first to break the silence this time, I wonder?" Dr. R said. He reached out and gently touched Henry's arm. "What's unusual here is somehow Fannie keeps popping into the conversation. How do you explain that?"

"I had to run away."

"The desert was calling you—I really believe that. Something in us is more intelligent than all these momentary emotional explosions. I believe that, too. Mostly we're ruled by accident, but sometimes another force operates."

"Are you talking about God? You don't believe in God, do you?"

"I hear mockery in your voice. Yes, I believe there is an intelligence in every person that can appear in certain emergencies. Look what happened to you—that voice that stopped you wanting to shoot your father."

"Fannie's not going my way. She turned her back on me."

"Poor things," Dr. R said, shaking his head. "You poor young things."

Henry felt his anger rise. He stood up, fists clenched.

"You see?" Dr. R said. "You see?"

"I hate this," Henry said.

"So, don't worry. You'll find someone else who really wants to go down the same path with you."

Henry moved toward the door. "I don't want someone else. I want Fannie."

"That's what I thought," Dr. R said. Hearing Dr. R laugh behind him, Henry slammed the door as hard as he could. He wished he had never come back. Dr. R didn't know anything.

Henry went into the orange grove and sat under a tree. He had just come home and here he was getting angry with Dr. R—for telling him the truth.

He looked at the trees near him. They were silent, the leaves not moving. They had nothing to say on the subject. They just stood there. He felt his breath quiet down. The entire grove seemed to be listening. As he gazed up through the leaves, he saw a bird fly across a patch of sky. It seemed a good sign.

48

The next morning, Charlie put Henry on the train to Los Angeles. From Union Station, he could walk to the Good Samaritan Hospital. He found his mother sitting next to the bed, while Carl sat near the window, looking at a photography magazine. Henry went over and leaned down to kiss the top of his mother's head. She looked up at him with her tired face.

"His eyes have been flickering, and the doctor says that's a good sign," she said in a tiny voice. "I just keep staring at him. Here, take my place. I need to move a little. Carl, let's go get a sandwich." The two left the room, Carl tossing him the magazine.

"You can see the photograph in there that won the contest. Have a look."

Henry sat down and without another glance at Sam, flipped through the magazine. And there, filling an entire page, was his photo at daybreak of the canyon in Death Valley, and at the bottom, his name.

"Oh, my God," he exclaimed, clutching the magazine to his chest.

"He . . . He . . . Hen . . ." a voice croaked from the bed. Sam's eyes were open, looking at him.

"Sam," Henry shouted, dropping the magazine on the floor. "Sam, it's me, Henry." Sam's mouth moved but no further sound came out, but his eyes watched Henry. Jumping up, Henry ran out into the corridor and began shouting, "Mom, Mom, Carl!"

Immediately two nurses appeared and without speaking to Henry, rushed past him. Henry followed and they all stood around the bed, looking at Sam, whose eyes were open and alert.

"He's come to," the younger nurse said.

"But is he really conscious?" the older, solid-looking one, asked, leaning over to peer at Sam's face.

"Why don't you ask him?" Henry said.

The younger nurse took Sam's hand and pressed it. "Sam, how are you feeling?" she asked. Sam's lips moved but no sound came out.

"He's trying to speak," Henry said.

"Let's get the doctor," the older nurse said. They left the room.

"Maybe you should close your eyes and sleep," Henry said. Sam's eyelids immediately fell. Henry continued to watch his face.

After what seemed hours, Edna and Carl returned with a short, stocky doctor with a bald head.

"He looked at me and tried to say my name," Henry said.

"That's a good sign," Dr. King said. "Mrs. Hamblen, speak to him."

"Sam? Sam?"

"Let's go down to the cafeteria," Carl said. "Too many people in here staring at him." Henry scooped up the photo magazine from the floor and followed him. In the cafeteria, Carl bought him a ham sandwich and Coke and coffee for himself. As they sat down at a little table, Henry handed the magazine back to Carl.

"Did you find anything of interest?" Carl asked, smiling. "Hope you're not sore at me. It is a damn good photo. You can put this in your portfolio."

"What's a portfolio?" Henry asked. "What artists have?"

"That's right," Carl said.

"But I'm going to be a ranger. I don't need a portfolio."

"You never know. A check for $400 came with the letter. I'll mail it to you."

"The $400 will help if I ever go to college," Henry said.

"I hope you do. It's not too late."

"Yes, I could start late January for the next semester at Cal. I didn't even remember taking the acceptance letter with me to Death Valley, but there it was—still in the rucksack. I got my boss, Martha, to help me write the registrar. They even wrote back before you came. I'm . . . what do you call it? Reinstated."

Carl stood up, his coffee untouched. "That's great news. Aren't you going, then?"

Henry shook his head. "I don't know. I just don't know."

Carl started to say something, but stopped. "I think we ought to get back upstairs."

• • •

As they entered Sam's room, they found his mother weeping, her forehead on the hospital bed next to Sam's chest. Sam's eyes were closed.

Henry knelt down next to her and threw his arms around her. Carl stood, patting her head. Edna turned toward Henry, put her head on his shoulder and continued sobbing.

After a while, she stopped. Henry glanced over her to look at Sam, whose eyes were still closed. Standing up, Henry rubbed his sore knees.

"The doctor says he is coming out of the coma," his mother said, "but he warned me not to expect miracles. When he's well enough to go into a wheelchair, he can come home to us. Carl, you'll still want him, won't you?"

"Of course. That's what I said."

"We don't know," she said, "if he'll be a complete invalid, or if he'll recover some of his mental functions."

"That's terrible, mom."

"No, Henry, it's not terrible. That's not why I was crying. I was crying with relief, because now I know he's going to live."

49

One foggy morning a week later, Henry found himself walking to the park to see the old tree, a place he had avoided since his return. Sam was making slow progress—speaking a few words and feeding himself, although it was far from clear if he would ever be the same. They thought he could be discharged in another week. Henry spoke to his mother on the phone every night and made one more trip back to Los Angeles on the train to spend the day with her and Sam at the hospital. Sam smiled at him but struggled to say anything more than "Hi."

Now Henry felt he had to go back to the tree. Maybe it would inspire him to face what was ahead for him. He had promised Fannie's father not to go to Cal. He could not tell anyone that. Maybe Mrs. Stafford knew, but he had run out of the hospital when he had heard she was coming to visit. He couldn't face her. And he was afraid to contact Fannie. If she wasn't going to Cal, did that mean he could go? He was unable to think clearly. The past few days he had sat amongst the orange trees, helped Charlie in the garden, and wandered around the neighborhood, distracted, lost.

As he entered the park, the green lawns and oak trees were dim and subdued in the mist, the dark figures of a few high school students barely visible as they rushed along the asphalt paths, their voices muffled.

Coming up to the white skeleton tree trunk, he noticed a woman sitting on the bench. That seemed strange. Why would anyone sit there on a cold foggy morning? Her face was hidden from his view by the hood of a dark brown raincoat that enveloped all of her. Long ago he had looked at a children's book with pictures of monks in long brown robes hoeing a vegetable garden, their heads covered like that. The woman was hunched over, both arms bent as if holding her stomach. Was she in pain? He moved over onto the lawn at the side of the asphalt, being careful to stay out of her line of vision, in case she looked up.

For an instant, he saw the face of the Madonna. He had seen paintings of the Madonna, that sad yet joyful face. And here she was. With her arms crossed that way in front, he even saw her, just for a long second, holding a tiny baby.

Then he recognized her.

"Fannie!" The face looked up. Yes, it was Fannie. Henry felt panic inside. She did not recognize him. "Fannie," he repeated, going up to her.

"Henry," she said in a flat voice.

"Why are you here?"

"Yesterday was my aunt's birthday. I came with my mother."

"I can't believe this," Henry said. "Why are you sitting here in the cold?"

Fannie shook her head. "Oh, I don't know. I must have been thinking about something..."

"May I sit down?" Henry asked.

"Sure, I guess so." Fannie moved to the edge of the bench. Henry sat down. Her face was turned away. Her hands, clenched together on her lap, were the only visible signs of the Fannie he once knew.

"I have wanted to tell you for a long time," Henry said, "that I think I know now why you had to break off with me. It wasn't just your father, was it?"

"No," the hooded figure said in a low voice.

Henry's heart was racing. "You aren't sick, are you?"

"No, I'm just tired. I've been working very hard."

Henry felt the air going in and out of his lungs, as if he had just learned to breathe. She could tell him to get lost forever, but he felt strangely happy.

"Didn't I always make it clear that more than anything I want to be an anthropologist? I never lied about that, did I?"

"No, you didn't."

"You were my best friend."

"I was?"

"Yes."

He could not see Fannie's face and her voice, muffled by the hood of her raincoat, was almost inaudible.

Their conversation ended. Henry's heart continued to pound. Finally, he said, "Did your mom tell you what happened to Sam?"

"Yes, she did." Fannie frowned. "That must have been horrible. Now my father won't have anything to do with your father. He says the accident was the last straw. And he knows now that everything your father said about you was wrong."

"Really?"

Then Fannie looked at her watch. "Oh, my mom is going to wonder where I am. I walked all the way from Aunt Marianne's house. I've got to get going." But she did not move.

The fog had lifted. A weak sun had taken its place.

"I think I'd better walk back by myself," she said.

Henry wanted to stop her, stop her from walking away. "Wait a minute, Fannie. Did your father get my letter?"

"Yes. That really helped. I'm starting Cal in February." Fannie smiled at last.

For a moment Henry felt joy course through him, and then a cold thud. "That means I can't go. I promised him I would disappear from your life. I promised."

Fannie sighed. "I can't believe it. You are willing to sacrifice your own education for me? Even after I ditched you?"

"I can go somewhere else, like UCLA. I'll be OK."

"But that special program for students with disabilities—isn't it just beginning at Cal, and nowhere else?"

"Yes, but I'll manage somehow."

Fannie suddenly pulled her hood off her head and looked directly at Henry. "My dad liked your letter. He believed you. Once he got over being so mad, he told me he was proud of me for telling him the truth. He now agrees with everyone else that your father is sick and needs to go somewhere to stop drinking."

"He may have stopped after what happened to Sam. He gave a nurse a note saying that to give to my mom. He doesn't dare come in Sam's room again."

"My dad says your dad even lost his job."

"He did? That's terrible. He loved his job. He kept hoping he would work up to a vice president or something."

"You feel sorry for him after what he did to you? And to Sam?"

"I saw at the hospital that he really is afraid of me. And now he's lost everything he worked for."

Fannie's eyes flashed. "I don't feel sorry for him."

"That's what my mother says too. But you're OK now, Fannie. You're going to Cal."

"Except I'm female. I've already had one school counselor say, 'Why don't you become a high school teacher? Women shouldn't be professors.'"

"That's not going to stop you."

"No, I don't think so."

"You knew a long time ago where you were going. In Death Valley, I learned something about myself: I don't know who I am. One day I think I'm one thing and the next day, or even the next hour, I seem to be somebody else. I was kind of a happy kid before the War. Then as I got older, I believed everyone who said I was crazy and stupid. Then the Rs convinced me that I could go to normal school and even to college. Then you broke up with me, and I was alone in Death Valley. I was just a dishwasher."

"You're not just a dishwasher."

"The thing is, Fannie, I'm always starting over. Now I don't know what I'm going to do. What can I do? I'm not like this tree. I don't have roots. I'm not solid. And I won't go against my promise to your father. I won't go to Cal."

"No, Henry. Don't say that. My dad has changed. He told me he's had to face how much he wants to protect me, but he's trying to let me go my own way. It's painful for him, but he's going to try. And I tell him all the time how thrilled I am that he wants to support me at Cal, that I need him. And I do. He's my father."

"You're lucky. Your father loves you. But I promised him."

"Henry, I would have written you, if I had known where you were. I only just heard from my mom that you were back. My father told me he plans to write you and tell you he wants you to go to Cal. I think he wants to apologize."

"Really?"

"Really. I came here because I thought the tree might give me the courage to write you myself. I wasn't sure you would want anything to do with me after what happened."

Henry looked at the tree. "That's exactly why I came here. I thought the tree might tell me what to do next."

"My mom would say this tree is our guardian angel," Fannie said. "It's kind of surprising we both came here today," she said, her voice quiet. She turned toward Henry, reaching out a hand towards him. When he did not take it, she quickly withdrew it. "Aren't we still friends?" Her voice sounded more like a child's.

"Fannie, don't you see? I have to grow some roots. I wanted you to be my girlfriend, not just a friend, but now I have to do some work first."

"Work?"

"That's what Dr. R calls it."

"I see," she said softly. She continued to look at him, her eyes glistening, until a tear spilled over and ran down her cheek. She did not move.

"I see," she repeated. Then a tiny smile appeared, but Henry saw she was trembling.

"Can't we go on talking sometimes at Cal?" she said.

"Yes, of course, if I go."

"I'm not as solid as you think," she said. "I want my father to love me, but he may never be able to accept that I want a very different life than his—or my mother's."

"At least he apologized. I've given up expecting anything like that from my dad. Dr. R and Carl are fathers to me now, but they let me be. And my mom thinks whatever I do is wonderful. Well, not the part about running away and not telling anyone where I was. But everything else."

"My mom's like that, too. And you were right. It's not that hard to get a job. Before he found out about us, my dad took me up to Berkeley to show me around Cal, and I insisted we go to the Lowie Museum of Anthropology right there on campus, because I knew there were wonderful Indian artifacts there, and I had this fantasy that I'd run into Professor Kroeber. When I talked to the curator, he seemed to think I would make a good docent, because I already knew so much, and he offered me a part-time job without my even asking. It's so exciting." Her eyes shone with their special light once again.

"Maybe if your dad is OK with us both being there, I could go to Cal after all?" he said.

"You bet," Fannie said, jumping up. "I'll see you there. We can talk."

"I'll tell you about Death Valley, if you would like."

"Yes. And I want to see your desert photos. I saw the one that won the contest. It's beautiful."

Henry wanted to say *not as beautiful as you* but he stopped himself. He had to be strong. Someday he could tell her.

"I'll be working at the Lowie Thursday, Friday, and Saturday afternoons," she said. "I can show you around, if you want to come by sometime. It's a wonderful place." And then Fannie stood up and strode away, her black hair swinging.

"Can I phone you after I get your father's letter?" he called out.

"Yes!" She did not stop, but she raised both arms above her head in a victory V.

Henry did not move until she disappeared from sight. And then he turned back toward the tree, glistening white in the late morning sun, full of life once again. He went over to it and laid a hand on its rough, pockmarked trunk.

"Thank you," he said. "You arranged this, didn't you? I'll come back some day and tell you if I've grown some roots of my own." He turned and walked away—back to the Rs, Max, Agnes, and Charlie—his family and his home.

Fredrica Parlett grew up in Pasadena, California, in the 1950s, the place and time of this novel. She graduated from Stanford University in 1961, magna cum laude, with a B.A. in Psychology. She married Beresford Parlett in 1960 and both her children were born in Manhattan in the early 1960s. She was a student and cherished leader in the Gurdjieff Foundation of California from 1965 until her death in 2020.

•••

The title of the book, *Seekers of Truth,* that Dr. R finds in Mme. de Beaufort's apartment is a fictionalized name for *In Search of the Miraculous,* an account by P.D. Ouspensky of his time with the teacher G.I. Gurdjieff. For more information, email info@gurdjieff-foundation-california.org.

CPSIA information can be obtained
at www.ICGtesting.com
Printed in the USA
LVHW090655130621
689976LV00011B/178

9 781954 744011